MW01620890

Published works up to May 2022:

Escape Through Time Series:
Timeless Knights
Her Place in Time
Time For Magic
Winsome Regency Romances:
The Black Duke
That Wicked Earl
The Melancholy Marquess
Untamed
The Villager's Conspiracy
Christmas Cracker Romances (Time Travel Romances):
The Christmas Cracker
A Viking Christmas
Stand-alone books:
An Angel for Julian
(A contemporary angel romance.)
Back Beyond Series:
Dance With Me
Watch Your Step
Remember to Breathe
Pride & Prejudice Novels:
Pemberley Haunted
(Continuation)
A Witch For Mr. Darcy
(Variation)
Lizzy's Curious Talent
(Variation)
Searching For Darcy
(Variation)
Compilation Volumes:
Summer Starter Set
(Includes the first book of my three series)
Christmas Cracker Chaos
(Contains both of my Christmas Cracker Romances)

A compilation of short stories written as Jessica Lund:

Waiting for the Master

Charming Mr. Darcy

Jessica L. Jackson

Published by Bru E-books

Word Count: 110,397

ISBN: 978-1-926467-29-0

Cover Art by Trifle Ink Design
trifleinkdesign@gmail.com

In Gratitude

I have a number of people to thank for their assistance with this book. First off, as always, I want to thank my sister, Marina, for all her advice and counsel. Secondly, I am thankful for the members of my critique group for their reviews. Even when we disagreed, I knew that my story was the better for their comments.

There are often people who help me with my research. I write to them and they send me information without charge and out of the goodness of their hearts. Without naming names, I am grateful for them.

Chapter One

Monday, February 17th, 1812…

Lizzy Bennet knocked on her father's book room door and entered as soon as he responded. She paused as she crossed the threshold to smile fondly at him. He looked very well.

Papa is only fifty and has many years left. Yes, he has sloping shoulders—no doubt caused by decades of hunching over books—but Mama should not be so worried that he will pass on before all five of their daughters are married.

He sat behind his wide maple desk, a book on his lap as usual, with the window at his side so the golden morning light shone on the pages. She reveled in the aroma of old books and pipe tobacco. To her, this was her dear father's scent.

"Good morning, Papa."

"Good morning, my dear," he said, closing the book so his finger marked the page. Mr. Bennet nodded at her hand. "What do you have there?"

Lizzy held up the unfolded piece of cream-colored paper and her bracelet of iron charms jingled pleasantly. "It is the letter I expected from Charlotte."

"Oh? Is it interesting enough for me to read it?" he asked, his gray eyebrows rising, then falling dramatically. "Or not?"

She chuckled. "You may read it if you wish, Papa, but it merely contains her invitation for me to visit her at the Hunsford parsonage."

"Ah, yes. Just as we expected. Does she mention how you will go? Am I to hire an escort for you?"

Shaking her head, Lizzy moved across the room to lean against the front of the desk. "Sir William is to go, as is Maria. I am to travel with them."

"And when were you proposing to go?"

"At the end of the week, Papa. Friday. That is when Sir William is going."

He took off his spectacles and pointed them at her. "I remember hearing that you meant to go in March. That is still two weeks away."

Lizzy looked down at the letter. Puzzled, she said, "Though Charlotte does not say so, I sense there is some sort of urgency in her request for us to come earlier."

Mr. Bennet snorted in a genteel fashion and raised an eyebrow. "If I had been her, I would not have married that milksop. She has her own home now, and I must suppose that she is pleased with that, but she is obliged to endure my nephew. I am heartily sorry for her."

Privately agreeing with him, Lizzy folded her arms and tilted her head to one side. "Do you have an objection to my going earlier?"

Mr. Bennet pressed his lips together and sighed through his nose. He replaced his spectacles and stared over them into the middle distance for a moment before finally responding, fixing his gaze on her. "Both your mother and Lydia have recently become particularly loud and…disconcertingly…annoying. I cannot concentrate. They encourage each other in their gaiety."

"I have noticed," Lizzy said, frowning. She knew why her mother acted so gay, even though her father did not. Lydia, however, merely copied her mother's behavior. She had more energy than all four of her sisters.

"If you insist on going, depriving me of the only person in this house capable of rational thought and behavior, then I must insist you carry Lydia off with you."

Lizzy straightened, alarmed. "Lydia? Papa, you cannot mean it."

"Oh, can I not?" he asked. "Your sister Jane is away still in London. She would keep your mother company and soothe her nerves if she were here. If you do not take Lydia, you must remain home until Jane returns. *Then*, you may go without Lydia."

"But Charlotte will not expect me to bring one of my sisters. And it may not be convenient for her to have an extra guest."

"Charlotte will be delighted," her papa asserted. "You shall write her today and inform her that you will be bringing a companion." He appeared pensive. "You had best not tell her that it is Lydia."

"You may be sure that I will write to her. However, I do not believe Lydia will come," Lizzy warned, playing her only real trump card. "She will throw a tantrum."

"Nonsense. She will keep Maria company. They are great friends."

"And Kitty? She will not want to be separated from her sister."

Mr. Bennet swiped his hand over his high forehead, and then shrugged before he opened his book again. "She will remain and be a companion for your mother instead of chasing around behind Lydia. And your sister Mary, as you know, will not enter into any of her mother's chief concerns. She proses on and on, which is no comfort to her mother."

Lizzy inwardly cringed. If only their mother and father would enter into some of *Mary's* chief concerns, perhaps her morose sister's humors would settle into a more cheerful habit.

"Do you disagree with me, Lizzy?"

Brushing a stray lock of dark hair back behind her ear, Lizzy sighed. "I cannot. Mary is incapable of diverting Mama in any positive way. Perhaps she should come with me in Lydia's place."

"But that will not save *my* sanity," Mr. Bennet said, shaking his head. "Some time away from the militia officers would not go amiss, either. For Lydia, I mean. If there was room enough on the Lucas' carriage, I would send Mary with you as well."

His attention returned to the pages of his book and Lizzy left, knowing there would be no useful purpose in her pursuing the matter further. She gently bit her lower lip. Lydia's reaction to the treat in store for her was not the only one to be feared.

Lizzy sought out her mother in the morning room they used to break their fast. She still sat at the table, drinking a second cup of coffee. Dismayed, Lizzy discovered that both Kitty and Lydia remained, lingering over the last of the meal. She had hoped to talk to her mother alone.

Lydia sat on the edge of her chair, her eyes shining with excited anticipation. "Mama, Lieutenant Denny has asked to walk with me—"

Kitty interrupted her sister. "With *us*, you mean."

Lydia flapped a hand at her. "Yes, yes, with us. Mama, may we walk out with Mr. Denny this afternoon?"

"Of course you may," their proud mama replied, beaming. "Will that nice Mr. Wickham be with him? Now that is *my* idea of an officer.

So attractive. Just the right bearing. A gentleman, through and through."

Lizzy had begun to doubt that measure of Mr. Wickham's character. He enjoyed walking with girls who were too young for his twenty-six years. Lydia had only fifteen years and Kitty barely two more. If he was honorably looking about for a wife, he should be searching for women properly out.

Lizzy automatically glanced swiftly around the morning room, turning to close the door behind her, without focusing on anyone, or any *thing*, in particular.

Oh, dear.

Her family was not alone in the room.

The room *appeared* to be empty except for them, but it was not.

Keeping her head down and her eyes focused on her mother's countenance, Lizzy approached the table. Mrs. Bennet's wide expression told her that she also had noticed their guest. But there would be no discussion of the guest that the two youngest could not see.

No acknowledgment.

No salutations.

"Lizzy?" Mrs. Bennet asked. "What did your father say? Are you to go to Hunsford?"

"I am," Lizzy said, and watched her mother's shoulders sag a little. "I will not be gone much beyond a month, Mama. And, when I return, I shall bring Jane back with me from London."

When she replied, it was with such a cry of gaiety that anyone might think that Lizzy was off to see the king, instead of an old and dear friend.

"You shall have such a wonderful visit, my darling," her mother exclaimed. "Will she not, girls?"

"*I* should not like to be going into Kent to visit Charlotte," Lydia said, grinning. "Not when there are officers aplenty here." She giggled.

Lizzy switched her gaze from her mother's almost maniacal one, and fixed them on Lydia. "That *is* unfortunate, for you are to accompany me."

Lydia abruptly stood. "What? Not I. You are jesting, Lizzy. You must be."

"What about me?" Kitty demanded, also jumping to her feet.

"Papa says that you are to remain here with Mama and Mary."

"Nooo," Kitty wailed, tears starting.

"I will not go," Lydia stated, and punctuated her words with a stamp of her foot.

From the extreme corner of Lizzy's eye, she noticed their guest glide closer, fascinated by the emotions swirling about the room. She grabbed Lydia's arm.

"Mama, you bring Kitty," she said, beginning to drag her youngest sister toward the tall French doors.

"Lizzy!" Lydia shouted, struggling against their forward momentum. "Where are we going? Let me go!"

"We are going beyond the ears of the servants," Lizzy said firmly, throwing open the doors. "Come. *Now*."

"I am *not* going outside!" Lydia claimed. "It is freezing outside." She grabbed onto the door jamb with her free hand.

Before she could get a firm hold, Lizzy swung her own arm up and broke Lydia's grip. Her sister gasped, and in that moment of reaction, Lizzy had her outside on the paved terrace. Their mother and Kitty followed.

"If you are going to make a fuss, you can do it in the iron garden," Lizzy told her.

"Mama!" Lydia yelled.

"Here," Mrs. Bennet said, shoving a wool shawl at her daughter while herding Kitty along with her.

Kitty hugged her own shawl tightly around herself and hurried past Lydia and Lizzy. She knew where they were headed. The wild iron garden had been their place to express their emotions well outside of the strictures of polite drawing rooms. They had always been permitted to say whatsoever they wished there, though more than one slap had been issued to Lydia and Kitty in the past because of their unguarded tongues, even there. They had since learned to make others stand well back when they spoke their most heated opinions while holding onto an iron staff driven into the ground in the middle of the garden.

The moment all four had entered the space, Lizzy closed the iron gates. Black-painted iron pikes also decorated the top of the six-foot stone walls.

"Now," Lizzy said, tugging her own navy-blue wool shawl tightly around her, "we shall stand in the middle of the garden and state our minds."

As the topic under discussion primarily concerned her, Lydia raced ahead and clamped a hand around the staff. The others took their places on individual flagstones ranged in a circle about the youngest Bennet sister.

"I am *not* going to Kent," she stated, glaring at her mother and then at Lizzy.

"Why?" Lizzy demanded. "Maria is coming and she is your good friend."

Lydia stamped her foot. "Mr. Denny will not be there. Is that not reason enough?"

"No, it is not," her mother said unexpectedly. Her countenance, now that they were all out of the occupied morning room, had calmed and she appeared reasonable and assured. "I wish you to find a husband, but not when you are only five-and-ten. And Mr. Denny is only nine-and-ten. You are both too young to marry."

"But I *like* him!" Lydia shouted, obviously dismayed by her mother's seeming betrayal. "If I go, Kitty will take him!"

Kitty gasped and looked like she would attack her younger sister. "I am prettier than you," she growled instead, remaining at the very edge of her flagstone. "If Mr. Denny likes me, then I shall have him. *I* am old enough to marry."

"Mama!" Lydia cried. She pointed at Kitty. "You see!"

Lizzy spoke up. "Mr. Denny has no intention of marrying for several more years. I overheard him saying so to Lady Lucas. It is useless for you to fight with Kitty over him."

Lydia sneered. "You lost your chance at a husband when you left Mr. Bingley to Jane and let Charlotte marry our cousin, Mr. Collins. You even let Mr. Darcy—who no one wants—escape. You do not wish *any* of us to be happy!"

In a cold voice, Lizzy said, "If you are going to be offensive to me, then yield the staff. I shall take hold of it as I will be the center of our discussion."

"I will not," Lydia said in a more subdued voice, making no move to relinquish her position. "I am not done. You cannot make me go to Kent."

"*I* am not making you go to Kent. It is our father's wish. I warned him you would be like this," Lizzy admitted. "He thought you would jump at the treat. He thought you would keep Maria company."

Lydia dropped her hand from the staff. "I will not go."

She turned and marched out of the garden, slamming the iron gate behind her. Kitty looked hesitantly between her mother and older sister before hastening after Lydia. Once they were alone, Lizzy approached her mother.

"I am sorry for the scene, Mama."

Mrs. Bennet heaved a sigh and walked toward the stone bench beneath three tall rowan trees that shaded the garden in the summer. She brushed dried orange rowan berries off the seat before sitting. Patting the surface, she invited her daughter to join her.

"You gave away your shawl," Lizzy said, sitting and taking off the one around her own shoulders to wrap around her mother's. "I should have fetched one for you as soon as I knew Papa's will. But I did not know until I entered the morning room that—"

"Yes, yes," her mother hastily said. "You know I do not wish to talk about…them."

"I know," Lizzy said softly. She slipped her arm through her mother's. "Will you be all right while we are away?"

Mrs. Bennet's brows furrowed. "The house may be safe again soon—when Lydia takes her anger away with her. I am so tired of being gay. I need a rest from it. And, you know, this garden needs some tending. I will supervise the gardeners."

It was a wild garden, needing almost no tending, but Lizzy understood. It was the iron. "Perhaps you could have the gardeners add some lily-of-the-valley beneath the rowans. And some butterwort in the damp northwest corner. They have lovely deep-purple flowers."

"I like the smell of lily-of-the-valley," her mother said, nodding. She patted Lizzy's arm. "You will not like to have Lydia with you for so long."

"I cannot deny that she can be tiresome. Charlotte knows her ways, though, so she will not be shocked. Our cousin may not be so happy, but I admit to caring little about that. Unless it inconveniences Charlotte, of course. Still, the village of Rosings is quiet so Lydia and Maria might run about as they please."

"And Hunsford? Is it also a quiet town?"

"So Charlotte says."

"Why does she wish you to come early?"

Shivering in spite of the sunshine, Lizzy shook her head. "I do not know. She did not say. I think she is troubled by something, but she has not stated what it is in the letter."

"You go ahead into the house," her mother said. "You shall catch your death out here."

"I will wait with you a little while longer. The smell of the damp ground is pleasing. The promise of spring is in the air." Lizzy pointed across the garden. "And see there? Crocuses."

"Thank you, Lizzy dear. You are a great comfort to me."

Lizzy leaned her head against her mother's shoulder, and they sat quietly for a while in the garden surrounded by iron.

ꟹ

Darcy climbed down from his carriage in front of the Bingley townhouse in London. The black door with brass hardware swung open in welcome, framing Hodges, the Bingley's London butler. He had a tall, imperious mien, with a shock of white hair and piercing blue eyes.

"Hodges," Darcy said, crossing the flagstones and the three stair steps that took him to the threshold. "Is your master at home to visitors?"

The butler bowed and moved aside, permitting Darcy to enter.

"He is, sir. May I take your hat and coat?"

"Yes, thank you." Darcy waited until Hodges had passed his clothing to a footman and then asked, "Is Bingley in his study?"

"He is, sir."

"There is no need to announce me."

"Of course, sir," Hodges said.

Even so, he walked briskly ahead of Darcy so he could reach the doorknob first. He opened the door, bowed, and stepped out of the way.

"Thank you," Darcy murmured, passing him.

Bingley did not sit at his desk. Instead, he stood in front of a cheerful fire, his hand on the dark marble mantelpiece, staring down at the flames. The morose expression on his face disappeared as if by magic when he glanced up and saw his friend.

"Darcy!" he cried, crossing the carpet with quick, lively steps in order to clasp his visitor's hand. "I did not expect you back until this evening. Wait, what time has it gotten to be?"

"It is early still. Three-of-the-clock," Darcy said, frowning a little at him. "What is the matter, my friend? You looked to be in a brown study."

Bingley forced a laugh. "It is the weather, only."

Darcy did not think it had anything to do with the weather, but he let the explanation lie. Jane Bennet was the reason. Bingley missed her. Darcy had seen her on the street yesterday, escorting a group of children to the park. She had glanced his way and he had given her a civil nod, but nothing more. Flushing, she had averted her gaze. He had no intention of telling Bingley that the woman he thought he loved had come to London. The less his friend saw of Miss Bennet the better in his estimation.

"I have come to tell you that I cannot be one of your theater party this evening."

"What is this?" Bingley asked, his eyes wide and questioning.

"My cousin, Colonel Fitzwilliam, has begged me to come with him to Rosings Park, our aunt's home in Kent. We were to go next month, but Fitzwilliam has been ordered to Upper Canada. There seems to be some trouble brewing with our former colonies south of the border, and he is being sent to make a report. He is to leave in three weeks so we must make our visit to Aunt Catherine sooner than expected."

Bingley grinned. "I know how much you love to visit your formidable relation and her daughter. Do you mean to tell your lovely cousin, at last, that you will not marry her?"

Darcy grimaced. "The time has come, I believe. She needs to know that she is free to seek a husband elsewhere. At twenty-and five, she must be wondering if she will ever marry, since I have not come up to scratch."

Bingley nodded absently. "Will you come back to London after your visit? Or return to Pemberley until the Season begins?"

"I am uncertain as to whether I will come to London for the Season at all this year, so I shall return to Pemberley. You should come for a visit."

"Caroline would kill me," Bingley said, one side of his mouth lifting in a half-smile. "My sister demands my escort nearly every night."

"You must marry her off this year," Darcy advised, turning toward the door.

His friend chuckled. "I could, if you would have her."

"Not I," Darcy said, opening the door. "She needs a gentleman who enjoys living in London most of the year."

"True," Bingley said, sighing dramatically.

Darcy laughed and left him.

ꟾ

Sir William's carriage drove through the front gates promptly at seven in the morning on Friday, just as the sun was rising. Lizzy stood on the front porch, waiting beside two trunks and two portmanteaux. She wore a fur-lined green pelisse and held a matching muff. A stiff breeze teased the hair at her temples and she was thankful for her bonnet.

Her father must have been on the look-out, for he joined her in the entryway and stood beside her, wearing an overcoat and waiting for Sir William and Maria.

"You were right, Lizzy," he said, shaking his head and adjusting his spectacles.

"About what, Papa?"

He waved at the house behind them. "About Lydia."

Lizzy tried not to roll her eyes. She really, really tried. But it was no good. Her eyes seemed to roll of their own accord.

"I do not envy you or Sir William. Lydia's company when she is in a snit is beyond anyone's ability to enjoy. I am afraid, my dear that you are in for an uncomfortable drive. I am sorry, as well, that your mother is prostrate today."

Lizzy replied in a calm voice. "I suspected she would not be able to come down and say her goodbyes. Has she the headache?"

Her father nodded and clasped his hands behind his back.

"I am heartily sorry for her," Lizzy said.

"Her gaiety has subsided, thank the good Lord," he mentioned, frowning deeply. "I suppose, with her favorite going away, she believes she has little to be gay about."

That was not the reason, but Lizzy did not refute his hypothesis. "She will enjoy having Kitty to herself. And Kitty will be the better for not having Lydia around for a while."

Perhaps Mary will have her share of the attention when only two daughters are at Longbourn.

The carriage drew to a halt in front of them. Mr. Bennet looked over his shoulder at the entrance to their home. "It seems none of your other sisters have risen in time to say their goodbyes."

"I did not expect them," Lizzy assured him. "Where is Lydia? Will we have to drag her from her room?"

At that moment, she exited the house, wearing all black, a bonnet with a heavy black veil covering her face. She lifted her head and looked away from her father and sister, marching to the carriage. Sir

William, a slightly stout and generously-humored man, stepped down to greet their father. Lydia climbed immediately into the carriage without saying a word of greeting. Shocked, Lizzy curtsied, suspecting she looked as mortified as she felt.

"Well, well," Sir William said, smiling at Mr. Bennet and Lizzy. "She is anxious to be off, is she not?"

Lizzy managed to utter only two words. "Yes, sir."

The footman and the Lucas' groom attended to the trunks and portmanteaux, giving Mr. Bennet time to shake Sir William's hand.

"How are you today, sir? Are you ready for a long journey?"

"We are," Sir William promised, grinning with *bonhomie.* "We have games to play, books to read aloud if we are so inclined, and treats to eat along the way. Hot bricks for our feet, too."

"Do you expect to reach the Hunsford parsonage before dark?"

"I do. There are sixty miles to travel and even reasonably good horses should get us there in nine hours. We shall stop for lunch, and to occasionally stretch our legs, naturally, but I am reasonably certain we shall arrive in good time."

"Excellent," her father said, nodding and smiling. "Be careful on the road, now."

"I have the very best driver. Highly skilled," Sir William promised, turning and walking toward the carriage. He held the door open for Lizzy. "Have no fears for your daughters' safety, sir. I shall treat them like my own."

"Thank you." Mr. Bennet leaned his cheek down for Lizzy's farewell kiss. He whispered to her after the kiss. "I suppose I must have fallen beneath my youngest daughter's regard for I have been rated as unworthy of a parting kiss from her."

"Oh, Papa, pray wish that God will grant me patience with Lydia," she begged softly.

"That is not a wise request," he parried. "If we ask the Lord for that gift, He will surely send you trials to test your patience."

Lizzy sighed. "Because only through trials are we strengthened."

"As a testament to the truthfulness of my assurances, I shall tell you that I pleaded for this gift when I first married Mrs. Bennet."

Covering her mouth with her hand, Lizzy stared at him, tears of laughter filling her eyes.

"More fool me," Mr. Bennet added. "Now, get on with you. The sooner you go, the sooner you will return."

"Yes, Papa," Lizzy choked out, turning away and approaching the carriage door where Sir William waited, smiling at their fond farewell, she assumed.

Once inside the carriage, she sat on the seat facing forward, since Lydia had taken her place beside Maria, who faced backward.

"Hello, Lizzy," Maria said, grinning widely. "I am so excited to be going to visit Charlotte. She is quite my favorite sibling. Are you excited?"

"I am."

The carriage swayed when Sir William climbed in. He sat beside Lizzy. The groom closed the door, climbed onto his horse, and the carriage lurched forward.

"And we are off," he said, smiling at all three girls. "I am the happiest man to have the company of such beautiful young ladies."

Lydia sniffed in her corner and turned her head to look out the window. Lizzy wondered how she could see anything through that heavy veil.

Two hours later, they stopped for a chance to walk a little in the brisk air. This was Lizzy's first opportunity to speak privately to her sister.

"Lydia, are you going to keep that on for the entire journey?" Lizzy demanded, pulling her to one side. They stood on a stone bridge that spanned a babbling creek, connecting some farms to the village. Maria and their host ambled along the path that led them past the few shops the village possessed. "This affected behavior does not suit a gentlewoman. Is this how you repay Sir Williams' kindnesses to us?"

Her sister, facing away from Lizzy, stiffened. She lifted her veil, tucked it into the band of her bonnet, and slowly turned around.

Lizzy gasped in surprised, stepping backward.

In a harsh whisper, she demanded, "What have you done?"

Chapter Two

"They made me do it," Mary wailed softly, glancing this way and that as though worried someone would notice her.

Lizzy narrowed her gaze. "Who? What am I saying? It must have been Lydia and Kitty."

Mary nodded miserably. The black garb did not improve her pale skin. Two blazing spots of embarrassment marked her smooth cheeks.

"Where are your spectacles?" Lizzy demanded. She did not let Mary answer before she started in on her again. "You are next in age to me. Nineteen years and obviously still capable of letting our two youngest sisters force you into this debacle. What am I to say to Sir William? What will Charlotte say when she sees you? And do not expect me to shield you from the sanctimonious lecture our cousin is likely to give you."

"I must confess I wished to come with you," Mary said scrupulously, digging her spectacles out of her reticule and fitting them to her face. "So, you see, Lydia and Kitty did nothing more than produce a plan where I might take Lydia's place."

Lizzy blinked at her, surprised. "You *wished* to come with me? But you hate to travel."

"As you say, I do dislike traveling," Mary said, sighing. "However, it is an evil that must be borne if I am to see anything other than our own back garden. St. Augustine said, *'The world is a book, and those who don't travel read only one page.'*"

Lizzy turned away, well used to her sister's habit of quoting anyone she thought supported her point of view, and walked back and forth for a few steps each way. Every time she returned to Mary she muttered something.

"We cannot ask Sir William to take you back."

Pace.

"We cannot leave Lydia at home with Mama."

Pace.

"Why not?" Mary asked before her sister could deliver her next statement.

"I beg your pardon?"

"Why can Lydia not remain at home with Mama?" Mary restated. "They are the best of friends."

"Because Papa wished her to go so that he would not be bothered by her nonsense," Lizzy stated more truthfully than she might have if she had taken a moment to think. "I have come to believe that Mama needs a rest, too, and you must admit that Lydia is not restful. The more excited Lydia gets, the worse is Mama's exhausting gaiety."

Mary slowly nodded. "Very true. I have noticed this. But surely Mama can cope for a few weeks."

Lizzy ignored Mary's comment and wrung her glove-encased hands, making her charm bracelet jangle. "I shall write to Papa when we get to Charlotte's. Perhaps he will bring Lydia and take you home."

Folding her arms, Mary glared at her. "Am I so unwanted?"

"No, no, that is not it. Mama—"

"Is it not? Surely, even *I* am a better companion than Lydia," Mary said in a hurt, but clearly angry tone. "Or am I not lively enough? I am too dull. Is that it?"

"Yes." Lizzy gulped at her own answer and immediately said, "No."

"I understand," Mary stated in a monotone. "Mama is simply an excuse."

Lizzy took hold of her sister's shoulders and shook her a little. "No, you do not understand. Mama's health is not an excuse. You are more restful. I wanted Mama to have a rest and she cannot rest with Lydia at home. With the militia in town, Lydia has become wild to a fault."

"Mama is gayness itself," Mary pointed out, frowning heavily. "She likes officers in uniform as much as Lydia. You are merely making excuses to send me back."

"Truly, I am not," Lizzy swore. She released her sister and took a deep breath. "I do not know if Charlotte has enough room for all three of us if Papa brings Lydia."

"That concern does not answer. Lydia could sleep with Maria and I could sleep with you," Mary said practically. "You know that Papa dislikes traveling as much as I. There is a good chance he will not bestir himself to bring Lydia. He knows that if he does, she will make the journey miserable for him. Lydia told me of her intent if he insisted she go to Kent after he discovered her trick."

Lizzy bit her lip. Mary was right. Even so, she felt sure she could convince her father of the exigency of bringing Lydia to Hunsford.

In a weak voice, Lizzy murmured, "You do not understand."

"I do not understand because you do not take the trouble to explain it to me."

Wincing at her sister's biting words, Lizzy hesitated.

"I am not a stupid woman," Mary added, in something close to a hiss.

Taken aback, Lizzy blinked rapidly at her. "I do *not* think you stupid, Mary."

Her hands on her hips, Mary asked, "Then why can you not explain to me the great secret between our mother and yourself? *That* is what I do not understand. Jane knows the whole of it, but none of the rest of us do. I am not even certain our father does."

Swallowing, Lizzy tried to find words of explanation. So many years of secrets weighed down her tongue and made it difficult for her to speak of them. Even she and her mother did not speak openly about their troubles. They only alluded to them in the slightest way.

"Does it have to do with your skill at dowsing?" Mary ventured.

Lizzy's breathing paused and then began again with a deep, shuddering breath. "What? Dowsing? What makes you ask that? Anyone can dowse with a little patience and practice. There is nothing remarkable about my skill."

Mary's demanding expression transformed into one of scornful incredulity. "*I* cannot dowse." She turned on her heel and stalked back to the carriage where Sir William and Maria waited next to the open door.

Maria, recognizing her, screeched softly. "Mary? Has it been you all along?"

It was a foolish question, but typical of Maria, who had more hair than wit in the opinion of her family and all her neighbors.

Her father's bushy eyebrows shot up.

"It has," Mary said. She curtsied, focusing on their host. "I must beg your pardon for deceiving you, Sir William. Pray forgive me."

Sir William chuckled. "I know you did not instigate the jest, Miss Mary." He shook a playful finger at her. "You have deprived us of two hours of entertainment, though. I thought you in a snit and so disinclined to play. However, now I shall expect you to participate fully. Is that agreed?"

"Yes, sir," Mary said. "I enjoy games." She disappeared into the carriage.

Maria scrambled in after her. Lizzy approached Sir William.

"I must add my apology to Mary's. Pray forgive my sisters' ruse."

Sir William chuckled. "I have seven children, my dear. I am accustomed to the bobbery of young people. I expect Lydia thought she would be better entertained among all the jollifications that the neighborhood is planning on behalf of the officers."

"No doubt," Lizzy replied dryly.

"After you, my dear."

Lizzy returned to her usual seat, opposite Mary, and settled in for another few hours of travel before they would stop for a meal. Everyone jerked in their seats as they began the next leg of their journey. Maria opened a book of travel games and perused them for a moment while Mary looked over her shoulder.

"Ah, let us play the picnic game," Maria said. She closed the book and looked across at her father. "Dear sir, you start."

Sir William beamed. "A bear, a rabbit, and a pig go on a picnic. The bear brings…honey."

"That's a good one," Maria praised. "I am next. A bear, a rabbit, and a pig go on a picnic. The bear brings honey…and a blanket." She turned to Mary. "Now you."

Lizzy listened to her sister's recitation and then took her turn. Mary would win. She usually did in memory games. All that memorization of quotations and poems and musical pieces stood her in good stead.

ꕥ

As Sir William had predicted, they arrived in Hunsford before dark. The sun was setting, and long shadows spread across the early spring landscape. The passengers peered out of the carriage windows at the village, which seemed to consist of several dozen houses, a row or two of cottages, and several larger homes. The high street held the usual number and combination of shops, similar to those of Longbourn village. Brick walls predominated, along with rendered ones dotted through-out.

"It is a clean village," Lizzy remarked.

"Indeed," Sir William said. "I believe Lady Catherine dispenses her practical advice liberally to the village counsel."

"Does she?" Lizzy asked, her eyebrows arching. "Charlotte mentioned the same to me in regard to the parsonage."

He nodded in agreement. "Mr. Collins and my daughter are fortunate to have a patroness who has so much care for their comfort."

Meddlesome, is what I would call it. Still, Charlotte has seemed happy with her new lot whenever she writes. Rather, in all the letters except the last one. What is wrong?

"I am certain they are kept cognizant of their good fortune," Lizzy said wryly and immediately regretted her words. Sir William, however, did not appear to notice the tone of her comment. Lizzy glanced at Mary and her sister raised an eyebrow.

"As John Donne said, *'O Lord, never suffer us to think that we can stand by ourselves, and not need thee.'*" Mary folded her hands and appeared to be waiting for their comments on her quote.

Frowning, Lizzy asked for elucidation, having learned that to ignore a quote was to invite another. "Are you saying that Charlotte and our cousin should be thankful to the Lord for the blessing of Lady Catherine?"

"I thought the middle more apropos," Mary explained. "Each of us needs others. And to help others is a blessing to ourselves and to those we help."

"Ahh," Sir William said, beaming at the sisters. "I may not have attended Oxford or Cambridge, but I do know that Donne also said *'No man is an island, entire of itself;'.*"

"That part of the quote applies," Mary admitted.

"We are here!" Maria squealed.

Lizzy's heart leapt. She was heartily tired of being in the carriage and anticipated a warm welcome from her dear friend.

Their conveyance drew to a halt in front of a two-storey golden-brick house. Everyone gathered up their belongings while they waited for the groom to open the door and let down the step. Sir William exited first, followed by Lizzy, Mary, and Maria. Both Charlotte and her husband awaited them beside their open garden gate formed of decorative iron swirls. A half wall of brick, topped by narrow iron balusters, painted black, surrounded the property. Mr. Collins hurried forward, his hand outstretched, to greet his father-in-law.

"My dear Sir William," he said, grasping hold of his hand with both of his. "How welcome you all are."

"Mr. Collins," Sir William said, grinning. "Thank you for your warm invitation." He tugged his hand free of his son-in-law's grip and addressed his coachman. "Thomas, take the equipage to the Silver Fox coaching inn. They are expecting you. Call on me here tomorrow morning for your orders."

The coachman nodded and drove away after leaving their luggage on the front porch where Mr. Collins' houseman took them away. Their groom followed behind the carriage.

Sir William faced his daughter. He opened his arms. "Well, Charlotte?"

"Father," she said, smiling and embracing him. "How well you look."

"Me? I look the same as ever." He held her away from him. "You, however, look very well, indeed. Marriage suits you."

Lizzy had to admit that she did look well. Her worry about becoming a spinster had disappeared, leaving her brow smooth.

"Cousin Lizzy," Mr. Collins said, approaching her, "were you also admiring how well my Charlotte appears?"

Smiling a little, she nodded. "I was, indeed. And yourself? You also seem well. Does being married agree with you?"

"I have never been happier in my life," he said in a gushing way that sounded shallow to Lizzy's sensitive ear. "Lady Catherine said to me just yesterday that I look younger than my twenty-and-five years. 'Mr. Collins,' said she, 'your choice of a wife has done you credit. Mrs. Collins is a fine, sensible woman. You should be happy with her.' And, I am, Miss Elizabeth. I am."

Lizzy could not tell if he was happy merely because Lady Catherine told him he should be, or because he truly cared about Charlotte. Then, she decided, it did not matter. As long as he respected her friend and treated her with courtesy, Lizzy would manage to be pleased for her friend's good fortune in finding a husband two years her junior—one that could be so easily led, as well.

"You are very good," Lizzy said in response to his assurances.

Since her friend appeared occupied in exclaiming over Mary's appearance on her doorstep instead of Lydia, Lizzy ventured to ask Mr. Collins a question. "Will we have the pleasure of meeting your illustrious patroness soon?"

He flushed and excitement shone in his small gray eyes. "We are to bring you all to Rosings Park tomorrow afternoon. She has promised us tea of the utmost deliciousness, freshly arrived from China."

"I like a good cup of tea," Lizzy acknowledged. "In the afternoon? How original. And how kind of Lady Catherine to share her precious supply with us."

Mr. Collins' eager countenance evolved into gravity. "She *is* kind. The kindest of patronesses. But do not mistake her generosity for extravagance. Oh, no. After we have our tea, the servants will be permitted to use the leaves for themselves."

"She treats her servants well," Lizzy observed, hoping her words did not sound as wry as her thoughts. She wondered how Lady Catherine could stop her servants from re-using the tea leaves. *She could throw them in the drawing room fire, I suppose. In not doing that I must acknowledge her generosity.*

"That she does," her cousin said in gratified pride.

"Husband," Charlotte said, extricating herself from her family to come and greet her other guest.

"Yes, my dear heart?"

"My father is anxious to be shown about the house. Also, Mary has come instead of Lydia. Pray show her the room we have prepared for Maria and Lydia." She took her favorite friend's hand, squeezed it, and added, "Lizzy and I will take a turn about the garden so we might greet each other without Maria interrupting our discourse."

"Of course, my dear," he said, beaming at her. "I shall show them the improvements Lady Catherine suggested we make. Our guests shall enjoy seeing how we have implemented them."

"I am certain they shall," Charlotte said, smiling. "Off you go now."

"Yes, dear," he said, hastening away. After shepherding their other guests through the door, he paused at the front entrance and looked over his shoulder at them. "Full darkness will fall soon, my dear. Do not catch a chill."

"We will not be long," Charlotte promised.

He entered the house and closed the door behind him.

"You have him well-trained already," Lizzy whispered.

They both covered their chuckles behind their hands.

Charlotte embraced her. "Oh, Lizzy, how I have missed you."

Lizzy hugged her back. "I have missed you too, dearest Charlotte."

They linked arms and strolled into the garden where early-blooming pansies could just be seen in the twilight, dotting the beds beneath rose and camellia bushes.

"This is a pretty garden," Lizzy observed.

"Thank you. Mr. Collins often works out here," Charlotte said. "It provides him with exercise and fresh air. Being close to growing things is exceedingly beneficial to one's humors."

Lizzy folded her lips between her teeth to contain her smile. When she could sound solemn, she said, "I have also heard that. Possibly from Mary."

Charlotte laughed. "You always apply any extraordinary knowledge to your sister."

"She is very helpful in that regard."

Dabbing at the corner of her eyes with a crooked finger, Charlotte struggled to speak over her laughter.

"Your drollery is something I have missed the most," she confessed. Heaving a sigh, she indicated a stone bench. They both sat and turned toward each other. "How came Mary to be here in Lydia's place?"

Lizzy glanced up at the darkening sky, searching for the patience she had hoped she would have with Lydia. She took a deep breath through her nose before she spoke.

"Kitty and Lydia came up with the idea for the subterfuge." Lizzy made a frustrated gesture with one arm. "Mary came out of Longbourn wearing a heavy veil and said nothing, so we could not tell it was Mary. None of us had any suspicion of her true identity since my sisters did not come down to say their farewells."

"Surely, you did not expect them to rise so early?"

"I did not expect Lydia," Lizzy admitted ruefully. "But I had thought Mary would have taken the trouble. I believe Lydia and Kitty were awake, however, for they must have assisted Mary to dress. I imagine they hid in Kitty's room, giggling behind their hands and whispering to each other to shush."

Charlotte chuckled. "I can see it. I am surprised they could make Mary take part in this trickery."

"She told me she wished to come, if you can believe that," Lizzy said, shaking her head. "I mean to write to my father to have him bring Lydia and take dear Mary away." She looked significantly at Charlotte, the only other person who knew their secrets. "Mama needs a rest. Lydia's volatility draws *them*, and she has been particularly volatile since the militia arrived in Meryton."

"Ohh, I see," Charlotte murmured with suddenly in-drawn brows. "Write to your father, if you wish, but if he brings Lydia, he need not take Mary away. Since she is pleased to visit, then she is welcome."

Smiling, Lizzy impulsively gave her a quick embrace. "I thought you would say so. What a wretch I am to foist my two troublesome sisters on your household."

Laughing, Charlotte drew her to her feet. "Let us go in before Mr. Collins, in his anxiety, comes searching for us. We kept back dinner and it must be ready to serve by now."

"You are assuming that my cousin has finished displaying the advantages of the vicarage." Lizzy linked her arm with her friend's. "Perhaps we shall need to chivy him along."

Once they reached the front porch, Lizzy stopped her from opening the door.

"What is it?" Charlotte asked.

Lizzy tilted her head to one side and tried to look behind her without turning her head. An impossible task, of course.

"It is busy here, my friend," she whispered. "Extraordinarily busy."

Charlotte blinked rapidly and only just stopped herself from turning around. "Is it?" she asked with a squeak. She cleared her throat and tried again. "Is it?"

Lizzy nodded. "Shall we go in?"

Her friend threw open the door and dragged her through it, shutting the barrier with a decided smack.

ꟹ

Darcy sighed and unnecessarily made the comment, "We have arrived."

The liveried groom opened the door the moment the carriage came to a halt and let the step down.

"You *must* be tired," Colonel Fitzwilliam said, a smile in his voice.

"You sound remarkably pleased to be at Rosings."

Chuckling, Darcy climbed out of the chaise. The lamps had been lit at the bottom of the sweeping steps and beside the entrance. Billings, their aunt's butler, a tall, stately fellow with a pronounced abdomen, unhurriedly walked the eight steps down to the fine gravel drive.

"Welcome to Rosings," Billings said, executing a three-quarter bow. "Mr. Darcy, Colonel Fitzwilliam, her ladyship is waiting in the copper saloon for you. Have you eaten, sirs?"

"Yes," Darcy said. "Do not bestir yourself on our behalf."

"No doubt you will wish to have tea?" Billings asked. He moved ahead of them up the steps. "Cook has made a Canterbury apple tart, sirs. And a Kent Lent pie. It is early for the pie, being only February, but when Cook heard you were coming early, she insisted on making it—even though it is not her ladyship's favorite."

"They both sound delicious," Colonel Fitzwilliam said, grinning, patting his flat stomach. "I love Kent puddings. I was hoping for a ginger cobnut cake."

"Cook is serving that with breakfast, sir," Billings assured him.

"Will there be custard with our tea?" Fitzwilliam asked hopefully.

"Undeniably, sir. Cook prides herself on her custard."

"I must say, Billings, that your wife is the best cook I know," Darcy's cousin praised.

Darcy raised an eyebrow, but said nothing, even though Fitzwilliam had once claimed that the Pemberley cook was the best in the entire world.

"Thank you, sir," Billings said. "With your permission, I shall tell her so."

"Please do."

"Be warned, Fitzwilliam," Darcy said, his mouth crooked upwards on one side. "Cook will expect to fatten you up during the fortnight you are here. She will not believe that any colonial cook will manage to keep you alive on bannock and dried moose meat."

The colonel shuddered. "Bite your tongue."

"The last time you returned from Upper Canada you had lost two stone," Darcy reminded him.

"I choose not to remember that horrifying situation," his cousin said. "Oh, the woes of being a younger son."

Once in the white and gray marble-floored entrance hall, Darcy and Colonel Fitzwilliam removed their traveling coats and handed them off to their valet and batman, who stood waiting to receive them. They had been sent ahead earlier in the morning and would have arrived a few hours since.

Darcy and Fitzwilliam murmured their thanks, and then simultaneously turned to the great, gilded mirror hanging on one wall to check on the state of their cravats—Darcy's pristine white and the Colonel's pitch-black, since he wore his uniform. Once satisfied, they followed Billings to the saloon.

"Mr. Darcy and Colonel Fitzwilliam, my lady," Billings said upon opening the double doors in a grand fashion.

Their aunt, a fine, haughty woman of middle years, lifted her gold lorgnette and peered at them with annoyance showing in her sharp gray eyes. "Your servants arrived two hours ago. Where have you been?"

Darcy inwardly winced and tamped down on his irritation. His cousin came to his rescue. He presented an elegant leg dressed in regimental white, bowed low over it with inimitable grace, and straightened.

"My dearest, Aunt. How well you look," he praised, grinning widely. "We left London three hours after we sent Thomas and Guildford. So, you see, we have made excellent time."

"Exhausted your horses, no doubt," Aunt Catherine said peevishly.

One of Darcy's eyebrows lifted. "Not at all."

She harrumphed and gestured to two chairs opposite her. "Anne has gone to her own sitting room. Mrs. Jenkinson is keeping her company. They will not come down again tonight."

"How is Cousin Anne?" Fitzwilliam asked, lifting the tails of his red coat out of the way so he could sit comfortably.

"Fair, fair," Aunt Catherine said with an airy wave of her be-ringed hand.

Darcy had often privately observed his aunt's inability to admit that nothing could be done about her daughter's ill health. Rather, she preferred to claim that Anne had a delicate constitution, as though that leant her some kind of remarkable distinction separate and above that of sickly. His cousin did not have the backbone of a gnat, and, as far as he knew, had never once stood up to her mother's forceful personality. His aunt would admit to no one, not even herself, that a daughter of hers could not be made well if only she found the correct cure. To

Anne's credit, she succumbed patiently to all of her mother's efforts.

He sat, and said, "That is good to hear."

His aunt fixed him with a gimlet eye but only uttered a sound and a word. "Hmm. Indeed."

"I am off to Upper Canada, Aunt," Fitzwilliam said, drawing her attention.

"You already told me that in your letter," she said testily. "What you did not disclose was the reason for such a *demned* fool thing to do. You have already been to Upper Canada."

Colonel Fitzwilliam coughed slightly behind his hand. "True, Aunt. But those *demned* Americans are getting restless. I am to go and write a report for Lord Liverpool."

"I see. How long will you be gone?" she demanded.

Frowning, he sighed. "Four months at least, I think. Longer if things progress poorly."

She flicked her closed fan in a gesture of annoyance and turned her focus back to Darcy. He steeled himself for her next words of censure. He fully expected her to order him to "come up to scratch" in regard to his cousin Anne. In her mind, they were already betrothed. In her mind only.

Unless Anne wishes the marriage, too?

He could not marry his cousin. She would not suit him. Besides, he had another in mind for the post. Fortunately, before his aunt began in on him, the door opened and Billings entered, leading two footmen who carried heavy silver trays loaded down with various treats and the tea set.

"Tea, Billings?" Lady Catherine demanded, clasping both arms of her French chair. "At this hour? I have only just finished eating."

"Yes, my lady," Billings said, pointing to the appropriate tables where the footmen set down their burdens before leaving. "Colonel Fitzwilliam and Mr. Darcy expressed the wish for some tea."

"Very well," she muttered peevishly. "Let them fill their plates. I shall only drink some sweet tea. No milk tonight."

"Yes, my lady."

Darcy and his cousin stood and moved to the viands. Darcy took a small slice of Canterbury apple tart, poured custard on it, took a cup of ready-made tea from the butler, and returned to his seat.

"I am to have guests for tea tomorrow," his aunt stated.

"Are you?" Darcy asked, putting down his cup on the small table at his elbow.

"You may have met them."

"Oh?"

Fitzwilliam excused himself and walked between them to his chair. His plate had both tart and pie smothered in sumptuous custard, even though the Kent Lent pie was already made with *baked* custard. His aunt gave him a ferocious stare but he did not see it for he was busy with his teacup and saucer.

"Who is coming for tea tomorrow, madam?" Darcy asked.

"Mrs. Collins has visitors," she explained to him, tearing her gaze away from his cousin. "Her father, her sister, and her good friend, Miss Elizabeth Bennet. Oh, and one of Miss Bennet's sisters, too."

Darcy almost dropped his plate. He steadied it with his other hand and raised his eyebrows. "Indeed?"

Miss Elizabeth…here?

"Yes."

His aunt poured some of her tea into her saucer and supped it, which gave him time to recover his thoughts and smooth the emotions from his face.

"Do you know them?" his aunt asked, raising her eyebrows.

"I do. Their father's estate is near to Netherfield, Bingley's home."

"I hope she is a genteel woman," Aunt Catherine commented before taking another sip of her tea.

"She is," Darcy assured, and then took a big gulp of his own tea, almost burning his tongue and throat.

"You should pour it out like I do," his aunt advised. "Hot tea curdles your innards."

He made no reply, which did not matter because she had more to say.

"Mrs. Collins' father, Sir William," she said, frowning. "Is he a gentlemanly man?"

"Yes," Darcy said. "He is full of goodwill."

Lady Catherine's lip curled a little. "One of those, hmm? A toady, is he?"

Darcy gave a half-shrug and half-nod.

"I thought as much."

She sounded annoyed, but her nephew knew that she loved toadies more than any other member of the class below her own.

"He has numerous children," his aunt mentioned. "I shall give him a great deal of advice on how to marry them off."

"I do not believe they are all of an age to marry," Darcy pointed out.

"That does not matter," she said airily. "They will all marry eventually and my advice will last through to the final child."

Darcy shoved a forkful of pie into his mouth to prevent himself from making a comment that she would make him regret.

"You are always so helpful to your neighbors, Aunt," Fitzwilliam said, smiling widely.

Toady.

The door banged open and Darcy jumped, hastily swallowing his mouthful. Both he and Fitzwilliam rose to their feet.

"M'lady, m'lady," cried Mrs. Durling, the middle-aged housekeeper. She stopped in front of his aunt's chair, wringing her hands. "It's Miss Anne, mum. I went to her room an' told her that Mr. Darcy had come safely an'...an' Mum...she fainted plumb away."

Chapter Three

Darcy and his cousin held back while their aunt marched out of the room, followed by the butler. He looked at his cousin, who frowned quizzically at him.

"Our Anne does not seem pleased to hear you have come. Your frowns have finally frightened her nigh unto death," Fitzwilliam said, shaking his head in mock-solemnity. He returned to his seat and his tea. "Are you going after our aunt?"

Darcy frowned. "No. I would be very much in the way. I have no place in the sick room. Aunt Catherine is more than capable of assessing her daughter's concerns. If she needs us, Aunt will send for us, or send us for the doctor."

"Precisely my evaluation," his cousin said. "You may as well seat yourself, Darcy. You are hovering like a gargoyle."

Obediently, Darcy returned to his chair and picked up his cup. He took a sip of tea, set the cup down, and reached for his half-empty plate.

"You should marry," he said calmly. "You are too old to still be a bachelor."

Colonel Fitzwilliam snorted. "Who would marry me? I need to marry a woman of means, as you know. And there are not so many of those waiting in their drawing rooms for an officer of thirty-and-one to propose to them, as you must know. A younger son, too."

"You look very fine dressed in your regimentals. Ladies like officers. However, I think you should look amongst the colonial daughters while you are away."

"Oh, you do, do you?"

An unexpected thought came to Darcy. "How much of a fortune do you require? Would twenty-thousand do?"

Fitzwilliam frowned heavily at him. "Do you know a colonial lady with that sort of dowry?"

Darcy shook his head. "No. I was thinking of Charles Bingley's sister, Caroline."

"But you just said…"

Shrugging, Darcy smiled. "I have rethought that idea. If you married a colonial woman, you might have to move there to keep her happy."

"Not I. I would bring her home to England." His cousin stared at him intently. "What is all this talk of marriage? You have never concerned yourself with my marital prospects before. Are you contemplating that blissful state for yourself?"

Darcy stiffened. "I am only twenty-and-six. There is time."

"Hmm," his cousin hummed skeptically. "At least you do not require an heiress. You may choose whom you wish."

"I have my name to consider," Darcy reminded him. "And one does not simply marry the woman, one marries her family too."

"Are you looking for an orphan, then?"

Darcy clicked his tongue. "She need not be an orphan. Merely, her family needs not disgust."

"You have a narrow view of what is due your name, cousin."

"Perhaps. Would you like me to marry a milkmaid?" Darcy demanded.

"There is a significant gulf between a milkmaid and a woman of high rank and breeding." Fitzwilliam shook his head. After consuming the remainder of his portion of Kent Lent pie, he casually said, "I seem to recall how you once told me that Miss Bingley did not have the sort of character you wished to find in a wife."

"Did I?"

Fitzwilliam pointed his fork at him. "You know you did. Is her character one *I* would find pleasing?"

Darcy's lips hardened into a grim line.

"I see. The answer is no. Why did you suggest her name to me? Did you think I cared only for the dowry of a prospective bride?"

Folding his arms, Darcy glared at his cousin. "I did not think that. Otherwise, you could have married a social-climbing Cit's daughter years ago." He squirmed uncomfortably in his chair, remembering Charles' comment to him only yesterday. "Caroline Bingley is a handsome woman with an elegant figure. Her education comes from an exclusive London seminary. It is true that the family is not well-connected, but she is accomplished and would not disgrace you."

Fitzwilliam rose and strolled across to the refreshments. He poured himself some more tea and turned back to look at Darcy. "I think she must be after you, old fellow. My miserable portion of less than one thousand per annum would not tempt her. And, I expect she likes to waste the ready. Wealthy merchant's daughters always do. I thought you liked me, Darcy."

Darcy chuckled and shrugged. "Most of the time. Beneath your gentle coaxing, Miss Bingley's disposition could undergo a transformation, you know."

"This gets worse and worse," his cousin suggested. "How old is she? Twenty, is she not? I am almost old enough to be her father. I want a lady of quality in charge of her own fortune and who is sufficiently old enough and sensible enough to cope when I am away on government business for months and months at a time. I should search in Bath."

Deliberately trying to sound pensive, Darcy asked, "Must she be handsome?"

His cousin laughed. "You dolt. Of course, *I* must think her so. She could be a widow, even."

"With children?"

Fitzwilliam sobered. "What is this? Do you have someone else in mind? Are you offering to be my intermediary while I am away?"

Darcy held up his hands, palms forward. "Not I. You should permit your mother to find someone for you."

Fitzwilliam smiled softly. "My dear mother is too busy with her grandchildren to focus on my poor lot. Besides, I am past old enough to find my own wife, thank you."

Darcy chuckled.

The door opened and he stood, expecting his aunt. It was only Billings.

"How is Cousin Anne?" Darcy asked.

Billings bowed his head solemnly. "Miss Anne has awoken. However, her ladyship has requested me to send word to the doctor. I have done so. She also wished me to inform you both that she will not be back downstairs tonight. There is a fire in the billiard room and I shall bring you some brandy, if you desire it."

"Thank you." Darcy looked at his cousin. "Do you wish to play a game?"

"I shall trounce you this time," Fitzwilliam claimed, heading toward the door.

"You may try."

ꟿ

"Why did you drag me inside?" Lizzy asked, leaning back with Charlotte against the slammed door.

Charlotte turned her head and frowned at her friend. "But…you said…I mean…I thought you meant that…" she waggled her head, bounced her eyebrows, and whispered, "…you know…that…*they* were out there."

Lizzy's puzzlement disappeared. "Oh. I beg your pardon. Forgive me, dear Charlotte, for frightening you. That is not what I meant."

Straightening, Charlotte swept her palms down the front of her skirts. "Well? What did you mean?"

Mr. Collins and Charlotte's other guests chose that moment to clamber down the wide oak stairs that faced the modest entrance hall.

"Dear heart, there you are," Mr. Collins said, frowning a little. He reached the bottom of the stairs and stepped aside so his in-laws and Mary could join them, crowding the foyer.

Charlotte smiled at him. "Are you finished the tour?"

"I am," he said, negotiating his way through the others until he reached her side and deposited a buss on her cheek. Color climbed up Charlotte's neck. "You see, Cousin Lizzy? Before you stand a most happily married couple."

"I do see," Lizzy said, smiling at them both for her friend's sake.

"Dearest," Charlotte said in a gentle, reasonable voice. "Kindly take Lizzy's outer things so she might be comfortable. We shall go into the dining room."

Mr. Collins obediently took Lizzy's muff and waited for her to remove her pelisse, gloves, and hat. "I shall place these on your bed."

"You are very good," Lizzy murmured.

"It is a shame you missed our tour," her cousin said over his shoulder as he mounted the stairs.

"I shall show her around tomorrow morning," Charlotte promised, taking Lizzy's arm. "Come, everyone, follow me. Cook has made us a joint of beef." They entered the dining room and she said, pointing to the table, "Father, you shall sit to the right of my husband. Lizzy, you and Maria shall sit on each side of me. Mary, please sit opposite my father."

Everyone moved around the table until they stood behind their chairs. Once there, they examined the unfamiliar room, smiles of pleasure on their countenances.

The dining room in the parsonage, though not commodious, easily provided enough room for a table and eight chairs, a Welsh dresser holding Charlotte's good china, a wedding gift from the Bennet family, and a dark sideboard with cupboards and drawers for table linens. The plaster walls had been painted the identical blue of mistle thrush eggs. The shutters, currently being closed by the Collins' houseman, were a lovely creamy white.

"What a delightful room, Charlotte," Lizzy cried, grinning widely. "Such a cheery space."

"Thank you," her friend said. "Lady Catherine gifted us with the paint I used on the shutters, but I chose the blue. We sent to London for it."

Candlelight reflected off silver and crystal stemware. Charlotte had been collecting crystal since her sixteenth birthday. Lizzy's heart softened. At long last, her friend could use the glasses she had so carefully collected.

"Please, everyone sit. My husband will be down at any moment," Charlotte said. "We do not have a footman to serve, but Hibben, our houseman, will do nicely."

"Thank you, ma'am," the middle-age houseman said, holding his mistress's chair for her while she sat. He had gray hair and dark eyes, with a lean, wiry form. Hibben moved swiftly to assist Lizzy and then Mary. Sir William held Maria's chair back.

"I've been a footman in a large household," Hibben explained. "However, when me dear mother became poorly, I returned to Hunsford to help her."

"That was kind of you," Sir William said, sitting himself. "How is she getting on?"

"As well as could be, sir. As well as could be." He bowed to his mistress. "I'll just pop down to the kitchen to see how Cook's doing."

Lizzy waited until he had left, closing the door behind him, before she opened her eyes wide at Charlotte. "How…loquacious he is."

Her friend laughed. "Mr. Collins wishes he could break Hibben of his habit of free intercourse with his employers, but it is to no avail. I must say I prefer it to the stony silence of servants in large establishments, like Rosings. They are a formidable lot."

"Are they?" Sir William asked, appearing daunted for a moment. He made a recovery and said in a knowing fashion, "Well, well, that is how the Great like their servants. Seen and not heard."

"Hibben seems jolly," Maria said, then clamped her mouth shut when her brother-in-law entered the room.

"Ah, you are all seated," Mr. Collins said, beaming. He took his own chair and looked around the room. "Dear heart, has Hibben gone down to the kitchen?"

"Yes," Charlotte said. "I hear him returning." She picked up a small hand bell and shook it.

The door to the back regions of the house opened and Hibben entered. He bowed to his master and then his mistress. "Cook is ready, ma'am."

"We are ready also. Kindly serve the soup," Charlotte ordered.

"At once," Hibben said, turning on his heel and leaving them.

"Lady Catherine found us our cook," Mr. Collins explained, beaming again. "So you may be certain that we will have an excellent repast. Nothing to what we would have at Rosings for our dinner, I need not say. But excellent even so." He raised his eyebrows at his wife. "What is the soup, dear heart?"

"Hare," Charlotte explained. "And you need not worry. I told Cook to leave out the turnips and replace them with parsnips."

Her husband sighed. "Thank you. I really cannot bear to eat turnips." To his father-in-law, he said, "Lady Catherine had her gamekeeper bring the hares over for our first meal here together with our guests."

"That was excessively considerate of her," Sir William said.

"She is the kindest of patronesses," Mr. Collins said reverently.

Mary chose to add her mite to the conversation with a quote. "William Penn said, '*I expect to pass through life but once. If, therefore, there be any kindness I can show, or any good thing I can do to any fellow-being, let me do it now, and not defer or neglect it, as I shall not pass this way again.*'"

"Who is William Penn?" Maria asked the table, looking first at her father, who shrugged, and finally at Mary.

"He was a member of the Religious Society of Friends," Mary

explained, clearly pleased to be the center of attention. "He founded the colony of Pennsylvania and died in 1718."

"It was an apt quote, Cousin Mary," Mr. Collins said, nodding benevolently at her.

"Thank you," she said, blushing.

The service door opened and Hibben backed into the dining room, carrying a tray of steaming soup bowls.

After their meal, Mr. Collins led Sir William to his study. The ladies repaired to Charlotte's sitting room where they chatted about the news from Hertfordshire. Mary and Maria, yawning over their cups of chamomile tisane, went to bed after half an hour, leaving Lizzy alone with Charlotte at last.

"Will we be disturbed here?" Lizzy asked, picking up her cup of tisane and taking a sip.

Charlotte shook her head. "No. This is my particular domain. Now, Lizzy, what did you mean when you said it was busy here? If you did not mean…*them*."

Chuckling, Lizzy explained, "I meant that there are many energy lines in this area. There are three going through your garden, one along the road in front of the parsonage, and five others going through the church or the churchyard."

Frowning, Charlotte set down her cup. "Why?"

"Why are there so many?" Lizzy asked. Her friend nodded. "I cannot say for I know nothing of this region."

"There is a holy well over near the old church ruins," Charlotte explained. "Cook told me about it."

"Standing stones?" Lizzy asked.

"There are several on the Rosings' estate," Charlotte said. "One is part of the rose garden—its center. The other two are at the edge of the home wood. There is a track leading into the woods that goes between them."

Lizzy's eyebrows shot up. Tracks around and between standing stones were common enough, but she wished human beings were not so careless about these powerful monoliths.

"You have not been in this area long, but have you learned if there are any local regions that seem unnatural?" she asked. "Places where no one likes to walk, or sit, or linger."

Charlotte shuddered a little. "I only know of one. Cook said it was between Cranley Hill and the ancient bridge crossing the creek in the midst of the Rosings home wood."

"And you said there is a path that runs between the standing stones?"

"Yes."

"And people use that path?" Lizzy asked, incredulous.

Shaking her head, Charlotte said, "Not often. The game keeper, of course, and the charcoal burner. Almost no one else. Yet, the path remains clear and is not overgrown."

Lizzy drank more of her tepid tisane. There must be more reasons for the energy lines to be so thick in this area. They crisscrossed every which way. From her childhood, she had been able to see the lines like a faint tracery overlaying the landscape. They had become so familiar to her that she had learned to ignore them. She had never before seen so many in one place.

"Well, my friend, this is an interesting puzzle," Lizzy said, putting down her cup. She played absently with her charm bracelet, frowning a little. "However, I did not come into Kent merely to examine energy lines. Tell me, what is causing you concern?"

"Concern?" Charlotte asked. "What do you mean?"

"Your letter."

"What did I say in my letter?"

Lizzy took her hands. "Nothing specific. I read a feeling of general…unease…between your words."

"Did you?" Charlotte asked, seemingly surprised. "I cannot think why."

Astonished, Lizzy leaned a little away from her, but did not release her hands. "Can you not?"

Charlotte made no attempt to remove her hands from Lizzy's grip. "No. I swear it, Lizzy. I can think of nothing to arouse such suspicions in you."

"The feeling was particularly strong, I promise you."

Charlotte looked away from her, staring off into the middle distance. "I am struggling to remember the day I wrote the letter," she explained. "Miss Anne de Bourgh and her maid had been over to take tea with me. We had a nice visit. Miss de Bourgh is sickly, as I mentioned in other letters, but she always seems a mite better when she comes here."

Lizzy snorted lightly. "She has an autocratic mother. I am not surprised Miss de Bourgh's spirits revive when she is away from her."

Charlotte stiffened and fixed her attention back on Lizzy. "I remember now."

"Oh?"

In a whisper too low for anyone to hear beyond their circle, Charlotte revealed her concern. "I remember wondering that day if someone was poisoning Miss de Bourgh."

ဢ

Lady Catherine entered her bedchamber through a tall, ornate door held open by her personal footman. He would stand outside her apartment until she extinguished her lamp and then sit himself in a chair against the wall for another hour before taking himself off to bed. He would be back at his post before she left her rooms in the morning.

"Thank you, Percy," she murmured.

He bowed and closed the door.

"Such goings on, my lady," Winters said, clucking her tongue as she approached her mistress.

Catherine let her harsh, determined expression relax into one of worry. "I do not know what I am to do for my poor girl. I sent for Doctor Stephens."

"Of course, you did, my lady," Winters said, taking the shawl from Lady Catherine's shoulders.

"He is a useless fool," Catherine said sharply. "He has done nothing, *nothing*, for my poor Anne. Instead of gradually improving, she is gradually worsening. The dark circles under her eyes were most pronounced tonight."

"Does he still prescribe sea-bathing, my lady?" Winters asked as she gradually divested her mistress of her evening finery.

"Yes. Sea-bathing? For *my* poor daughter?" Catherine scoffed. "He might as well kill her outright."

Winters clicked her tongue. "Heaven forbid, my lady."

Catherine covered her face with hands that trembled. This fainting spell was a new development. She did not believe for an instant that it had come about because of Darcy's arrival. Her nephews had always been unfailingly polite and kind to Anne. What did her daughter have to fear from Darcy coming to Rosings? Whether she married Darcy or not, the estate belonged to Anne. At twenty-and-five, Anne could not be forced to marry her cousin, no matter how much Catherine wished it.

If only my Anne had some fortitude.

As though reading her mind, Winters observed, "Our Miss Anne is stronger than some people think she is, my lady."

Catherine lowered her hands. "Why do you say that?"

Winters graying eyebrows rose. "She fought so hard to be born, my lady, as you know. Three wee baby boys did not make it, but our Miss Anne was that determined."

Catherine smiled softly and held up her arms so her gown could be slipped easily over her head.

"And, she's not let anything kill her yet," Winters added, carrying the gown over to a chair. She laid the silk dress across the chair and returned to her mistress.

"True," Catherine murmured.

"She might've swooned because of her menses, my lady. I had a niece who used to faint plumb away every month. *Her* doctor told her to eat more red meat. She couldn't afford no red meat, could she? The butcher sold them some nice liver every month the week afore her time. That did the trick."

Winters always had some niece or nephew whom she could draw upon for a homily or example. Catherine was more than used to her stories and advice.

"Before, Winters," she said. "Not 'afore'."

"Of course, my lady. 'Before' her time."

"Unfortunately, Anne cannot bear to eat liver of any type," Catherine reminded her.

"She likes kidneys, though, my lady. Perhaps they would do as well?"

"Perhaps. It cannot hurt. Before you go to bed, kindly leave a note in the kitchens for Cook, asking her to serve braised kidneys this week for Anne's breakfast."

"Yes, my lady," Winters said, approaching with her nightwear.

Catherine lifted her arms again to receive her flannel nightrail. The fire in the corner still crackled merrily, but once it was banked, the coolness of the late February night would seep into the bedchamber.

Catherine sat at her dressing table, a book of sermons in her hand, while Winters undressed her hair, brushed it, and then braided it for the night. The words of the sermon blurred before her eyes as she thought about her daughter and Darcy.

If Darcy does not propose to Anne soon, what will happen to Rosings? Who will Anne leave the estate to?

When Anne turned twenty-and-one, she had sent for the family solicitor and had her will made up. Until that date, her father's will would have prevailed if she had died before reaching her majority. In a rare moment of abject stubbornness, Anne had refused to tell her mother the name of her heir.

"Do not fear, Mother," she had said. "Rosings will stay in the family. You will not be forced out."

"As though anyone would dare," Catherine told her.

"They would be very brave if they did," Anne said, a twinkle in her dove-gray eyes.

Catherine had money of her own and had no fear of being pushed out of her home. The only family Anne had was through her mother's side. There were so many Fitzwilliam cousins that Catherine could not guess at the identity of the heir. She prayed it would not be Georgiana, because then Rosings would become her husband's property once Georgiana married. This was one of the reasons Catherine wished Darcy to marry her Anne. The estate would then stay in the family. Besides, he was her own dear sister's son. After his father's death, her nephew had proven he could run a large estate.

"There we are, my lady," Winters said, standing back after placing a pristine white night cap trimmed in Devon Honiton lace on her head.

Catherine closed the book of sermons on its bookmark and stood. She knelt on the *prie-dieu* beside the bed, clasped her hands on the upholstered armrest in front, and said the same evening prayer she always used from the moment of her Anne's birth. "Dear Lord, I thank thee for not taking Anne today. Please do not take her tomorrow. Amen."

"Amen," Winters murmured.

After standing, Catherine climbed into bed. Her maid took the *prie-dieu* away from her bedside and set it against the wall out of the way. Winters banked the fire, collected the worn clothing, curtsied, and blew out the candles before leaving the bedchamber.

"Good night, my lady," she said while standing in the doorway.

"Good night, Winters."

<Foolish woman. Every night she prays to her Christian God, thinking he can save her precious daughter.>

<Yet we are the ones staying our hands, keeping her alive.>

<She should be worshipping us.>

Chapter Four

Lizzy's eyes widened and she drew in a long, deep breath, held it for a moment, and slowly let it out again.

"What are you saying?" she breathed.

Charlotte tugged her hands free and flapped one in an impotent manner. "I know I am mad to think it. Who would want to poison Miss de Bourgh?" she asked in a tiny, almost frantic voice. "It is lunacy to think it. I do not know why I have done so. There must be another reason for her bouts of malaise."

Lizzy continued to stare at her. Her friend was not a fanciful being. Something must have sparked her concerns.

"I find myself exceedingly interested to meet Miss de Bourgh," she said at last. "Will she be at tea tomorrow?"

"Unless she is unwell—or I should say—unless she is more unwell than usual." Charlotte raised an eyebrow. "No doubt you will find her insipid. Colorless, even. However, you will discover that she can be animated when she is feeling better." She grimaced. "I will admit to you, privately, that she is livelier when her mother is not present."

Lizzy's mouth twitched into a crooked grin. "I expect my cousin would not like to hear that observation."

"You are correct." Charlotte folded her hands in her lap. Frowning delicately, she said, "Mr. Collins requires his patroness' approval. She provides the majority of his income, certainly, but that is not the only reason. Her approbation justifies his perception of himself, and therefore his pride of being. Similar, I think, to how a child seeks his parent's praise in order to feel loved."

Eyebrows raised, Lizzy commented, "You have thought a great deal about this."

"He is my husband," Charlotte said simply, "and is, therefore, my chief concern."

"Just so," Lizzy said, smiling at her.

Wisdom decorated her friend's words and Lizzy felt a little ashamed for not giving Mr. Collins' character enough thought. Even ridiculous people must have reasons for their behavior. Consider her own mother. She smothered a yawn and her friend immediately stood.

"You must be exhausted." She picked up the lamp. "Come, I will show you to your bed chamber."

Lizzy stood and followed her out of the room. "I *am* tired."

"I hope you like where I have put you," Charlotte whispered as she set the lamp down on the front entrance side table and blew it out. A lamp flame on the landing lit their way as they mounted the stairs. "You are opposite our room and beside my father. Maria and Mary are on your other side, down a few steps. You must have a lie-in tomorrow."

"You know I can never lie-in," Lizzy replied. "Not even after a long journey. If I am up before times, I shall take a walk."

"Please leave through the kitchen door if you are up before the household," Charlotte whispered. "The front door is not unlocked until Mr. Collins rises, which is usually at eight."

"Of course."

They reached the landing where a small marble-topped table held two candles in brass chambersticks. Charlotte picked them up and handed one to Lizzy and kept the other for herself. After lighting their candles from the lamp flame, Charlotte turned the flame down low. She preceded Lizzy up the stairs to the next floor and the middle door. She opened it and stood to one side so Lizzy might enter before she followed.

"I know you like to keep a lamp lit in your chamber, so there is one on the dresser, there," her friend said, nodding at a chest of drawers centered on the wall opposite the bed.

Because the lamp had not yet been lit, Lizzy could not clearly see the decoration. She could see that the chamber had pale walls, wood floors covered by a central carpet, a half-tester bed, the chest of drawers, and a dressing table and chair. Beside the bed stood a side table, its top covered with a white cloth. Lizzy approached it so she could look at it better.

Smiling, she set the candle down and looked at her friend. "This is one of your white work pieces, is it not?"

Charlotte turned from where she had lit the lamp and nodded eagerly. "Yes. It is so nice to use all the lovely work I have stored up for years and years."

"It must be," Lizzy acknowledged. She was no true needle woman herself but she appreciated Charlotte's deft hand all the more for her own limitations.

"Earlier, Lady Catherine sent Becky, one of the chamber maids, down to us. You did not see her, of course. While we ate, she unpacked your things. And Maria and Mary's as well."

"That was thoughtful of her ladyship," Lizzy said, meaning it.

"We have a cook and Hibben, as well as a maid-of-all-work. A laundress comes here once a week. We also have a stable lad and groom."

"You are well situated," Lizzy said, grinning now. "Charlotte, you told me all of that in your first letter. Pray do not be uncomfortable with me. We are old friends."

Lizzy could not see it in the dim light, but she could tell her hostess was blushing. Charlotte looked away and down at the floor. Just as alarm began to tickle Lizzy's senses, she saw Charlotte's shoulders shake and soft laughter filled the space between them.

When she had hold of herself again, Charlotte said in a faux-prim voice, "I did not tell you of the stable lad. He is new."

Lizzy chuckled and impulsively embraced her friend.

༄

Awakening before times as she had thought she might, Lizzy climbed out of her comfortable bed and padded across to the windows. She drew back the brocade drapes and stared across to where Rosings Park could be seen in the pre-dawn light. Just over the tree tops, she spied the chimneys of the great house silhouetted against the purple sky.

Determined to have a morning walk, Lizzy turned away and got dressed. When she reached the kitchen, she met Cook.

"Good morning," Lizzy said upon entering the warm kitchen where three lanterns hung above the work table.

Two women of about the same age as Lizzy's mother hastily stood. They had been eating their breakfast before beginning their work day. One wore the all-encompassing apron of the cook and the other wore the apron of the general maid.

"Miss," they both said, bobbing curtsies.

"I'm Cook, miss," said the rail-thin woman with frizzy red hair and a kindly expression in her blue eyes. The other sturdily built woman had smooth blonde hair just turning to gray, brown eyes, and a ruddy complexion. "And this here's Agatha. She's the maid-of-all-work, she is."

"I am Miss Bennet. How do you do?" Lizzy asked. Before they answered her rhetorical question, she said, "I did not mean to disturb you, only Mrs. Collins said that if I wished to take a morning walk then I must leave through the kitchen."

"Does you want a piece of toast or a slice of cake fer yer walk, miss?" Cook asked cheerfully. From the table, she lifted a plate that contained slices of cake and several pieces of dry toast and offered it to Lizzy. "It's date and walnut cake, miss."

Knowing that to refuse the cook's offering would offend the servant, Lizzy smiled with pleasure and took a slice of cake.

"This smells and looks delicious," Lizzy said.

The cook poured out a small amount of milk into a mug and handed it to her.

"A swallow of milk, miss," she said, "t'wet your mouth before the cake."

Lizzy smiled, welcoming the drink, and swallowed it down. Passing the mug back to Cook, Lizzy thanked them and headed for the door, cake slice in hand.

"We normally serve breakfast in a few hours, miss," Cook said, hurrying ahead of her and opening the door. She glanced at a clock on the fireplace mantel. "It's comin' on t'seven, miss."

"Thank you," Lizzy said.

Hibben stood on the doorstep. He smiled and jumped out of the way. "Good morning, Miss Bennet. Goin' fer a walk?"

"Yes, Hibben," Lizzy said, nodding genially. "I thought I would walk around the village and over to the old church."

"A delightful plan, miss."

"How is your mother today? Did she sleep well?"

"Yes, indeed, miss. Ever since I came home, she has done much better."

"No doubt you have eased her mind of worry, Hibben."

"It's kind of you to say so, miss," he said, grinning widely. "Have a nice walk."

"Thank you."

Lizzy nodded to him and began her walk by circling the house to the front, eating the delicious cake. The sun had crested the horizon by now and long shadows stretched across the cobbled lane. Ribbons of color ornamented the dawn. It appeared that the crisp morning would develop into a lovely, spring-like day. She marched down the lane using long strides. Occasionally she met other early risers—housewives sweeping their front stoops, bakers throwing open shutters to cool off their shops and let the wonderful smell of their goods waft through the village, and men heading off to their work.

At the end of the high-street, Lizzy came across a tall, aged man wearing a well-worn frieze coat over his shirt and trousers. A greasy cap of mottled brown adorned his hoary head. He stood in her path, looking down at the Y-shaped twig in his hands. He flexed the arms of the upper two twigs, which he held next to his body, making the base of the Y tip forward and then upward.

Lizzy stopped beside him. When he did not acknowledge her, she said, "Good morning. Yew?"

"No, miss," he said, shaking his head and glancing at her from beneath heavy eyebrows. "I always use hazel. It comes from the tree near the old abbey. I've not seen you afore, miss. Are ye the vicar's company?"

"I am," Lizzy said, smiling. "I am Miss Bennet. Mr. Collins is my cousin and Mrs. Collins is my good friend."

"Aye, miss," he said, touching his forehead with the knuckle of a curled finger.

"I prefer hazel as well," Lizzy said, surprising him.

"You a dowser, miss?

"Yes." She glanced around her, narrowing her eyes to focus on the tracery of energy lines crisscrossing the village. "Finding water in this region must be problematic. So much interference. Is that why you were frowning so?"

"That it is. Excuse me, miss." He heaved a sigh and began walking toward the ruin of a church seen beyond the end of the village.

Lizzy fell into step beside him. "Are you looking for water today?"

"No, miss," he said in a low rumble. "Farmer Clarence's gotta sick milking cow. He's had the animal doctor in, but the animal's still sick.

It's not me habit to use this stick fer animal health, but me other one broke." He appeared pensive, falling silent for a half dozen steps. When she continued to keep pace with him, he finally explained his plans. "I'm goin' to search fer a faerie path crossin' Farmer Clarence's land. Silly animal musta fallin' asleep on the path."

"I understand there is a path running from the old church through to the home wood of Rosings," Lizzy said. "Does Farmer Clarence's farm intersect that path?"

The old man looked at her from the corner of his eye, frowning so heavily that his long eyebrow hairs over-shadowed his wrinkled and age-spot dappled cheeks. His gaze traveled to her wrist where the bracelet with the iron charms jingled as she walked.

"No, miss," he said slowly.

"A different path?" Lizzy asked, her eyes wide. "Are there many paths through this region?"

"Enough," he admitted.

She wondered what he meant by that. *How many paths are enough?*

"May I accompany you to the farm?" Lizzy requested.

He stopped walking and faced her. "As you wish, miss. It's a fair walk, mind."

Lizzy grinned. "I love to walk." She lifted her skirts enough to show her sturdy walking boots.

A smile twitched across his lips. He nodded and began walking again. On the journey to the farm, they discussed their more interesting dowsing experiences. Lizzy told the story of the first time she had tried dowsing.

"I did not learn from one of the men who dowsed in our county," she revealed. "One day, when I was only eleven years old, I was playing near our home wood. I live in Hertfordshire, sir."

"Not sir, miss. Everyone calls me Frank. Not Mister Frank. Jist Frank."

"Then I shall call you Frank, as well."

"Who taught you, then, miss?" he asked, prodding her along with the story.

"A gypsy lady. An *old* gypsy lady."

Frank's eyebrows sunk into a significant frown. "Was she a witch, miss?"

Lizzy cocked her head and considered before she spoke. "I believe so. She had a dark shawl worn over stooped shoulders. Not that that signifies, I suppose. She did not frighten me. I recall that quite clearly. She held a dowsing stick like yours. She knew my name, saying 'Miss Elizabeth, you're special, you are. Come here and I'll teach you something of the art of dowsing.' And then she did. She told me most anyone can dowse, but only a few have the true gift." Lizzy frowned. "I learned that she was right. One of my sisters cannot dowse. She can walk over the same ground that reveals its secrets to me and nothing happens for her."

Frank nodded sagely, leading her down a farm track. "That's right, miss. I've four sons, me. and only two can work the twig."

"Hmm. Well, at the end of our teaching session, she told me to come back again in one year and she would teach me some more. I must confess that I almost forgot the date to return. The night before, however, I had a dream about her leaving her home in the woods and traveling a fair distance to meet me at the appointed time."

Frank held out his hand to assist her over a stile. He climbed into the field after her, saying, "She was a witch fer sure, miss."

"I wonder," Lizzy said softly, thinking back.

"Did you meet her, miss?"

"I did. She taught me some more, and then told me to come back again the next year. That time, I brought Jane with me."

"The sister who can't dowse, miss?"

"No, she is a different sister. Jane is my elder sister and my dearest friend in the family."

"Was the old witch pleased to see her, miss?"

"She did not seem to mind." Lizzy paused beside the hedgerow and stared around. The sun, fully above the horizon now, shone across flat green fields covered in winter stubble and a few wisps of morning mist. Amongst the bramble branches of the hedgerow, dew drops trembled on vast spider webs.

"Not far now, miss."

"I am not tired," she said, smiling. "I was admiring the morning. Let us continue."

"Aye."

They trudged along the firm path next to the hedgerow, heading toward a lone barn squatting in the far corner of the field.

"I returned for three more years and every year she taught me…well…she taught me much," Lizzy admitted. "Then, the last year, she said she would not be coming again. I never discovered anything more about her. I called her Aunty, as she requested."

"You've been touched, miss," Frank said, nodding sagely once more. "You gotta be careful that the wrong sort don't come sniffin' around to take yer measure. Iffen you take me meanin', miss."

Lizzy sighed. "I do, Frank. I do." Worrying that she had been indiscreet, she said, "Pray do not tell my story to others in the village."

"People talks to me, miss, but I don't spread tales. I'll jist mention you in passin', like, to me brother, iffen you don't mind. He won't tell nuffin' to no one."

"Very well," she said, cringing, suspecting that it would be all over the village soon in spite of Frank's assurances. "Thank you."

They reached a grayish-blue ragstone and red brick barn, finding Farmer Clarence standing in the open doorway, leaning on his pitchfork, apparently waiting for them. He was a big, mature man with wide, sloped shoulders and a round ruddy face to match. He pulled off his cap as soon as they approached, revealing his dark-brown hair laced through with gray.

"Clarence," Frank said, nodding. "This here is Miss Bennet. She can dowse too."

"Miss," the farmer mumbled, knuckling his forehead with respect.

"How do you do?" she said, smiling to set him at his ease. "I understand your milk cow is poorly."

"Aye, miss."

"I am sorry for her," Lizzy said. "May we see her?"

Farmer Clarence nodded and led them into the barn. The long, narrow space was lit only by tiny windows. A piteous lowing came from a stall at the far end of the barn. In the dim lighting, Lizzy could barely make out her fawn and white coat.

"When did you start usin' this stall, Clarence?" Frank asked. "Didn't yer pa say never to use this stall?"

"And I didn't until he died last month," Clarence claimed, sounding sullen.

"Every animal yer pa put in this stall sickened and died," Frank explained. "Didn't he tell you so?"

"He did. But I scrubbed it clean and put down fresh straw afore I put her in here."

"You always were a stubborn man, Clarence Heyman," Frank said, shaking his head. "Always thinkin' you knows best with yer modern farmin' practices. Well, sometimes you's right and sometimes you's wrong. We gotta get her outta there."

"I don't think she'll stand, now," Clarence said, his tone indicating his anguish.

Losing a milk cow would be a great hardship to the farmer, Lizzy knew. She touched the farmer's arm. He looked down at her as though he had forgotten her existence.

"I shall help," she said, smiling seriously. "I shall take her head if you gentlemen help her from the rear. We will coax her to stand."

"*You*, miss?"

"Yes, me. Do you think we can get her to stand?" Lizzy asked, reminding him of his superior knowledge of the bovine species.

"We hafta try, Clarence," Frank urged. He stepped around the cow and into the stall. "You take that side."

The big man, galvanized into action, took his place. Lizzy crouched beside the cow's head and lifted its heavy head. She winced when she realized she crouched at the edge of a faerie path.

"What is her name?" she asked.

"Nellie, miss," Clarence said. "Come on, Nellie, girl. Up you goes."

"Yes, Nellie," Lizzy said soothingly. "You cannot lie here anymore. You coax her some more, Mr. Clarence. She knows your voice."

"Up you goes, Nellie, girl," he said, grunting afterward as he pushed on her hindquarters.

They pushed, pulled, heaved, cajoled, and finally managed to get Nellie to her feet. Lizzy scrambled back out of the way, her bonnet askew, the bodice of her pelisse covered in cow slobber. She leapt to her feet and put her arms around the cow's neck.

"Well done, Nellie. We knew you could do it," she said, grinning with relief.

"Lead her down to the stall opposite the doorway, miss," the farmer ordered.

"Yes, sir," she said, walking beside the slow-moving animal while the men continued to support her from behind. "Here we are at last. You have done wonderfully, Nellie."

"We'll back her in, miss," Clarence told her.

Lizzy nodded and did her part in negotiating the sick animal into the stall. Once in place, Nellie collapsed back onto the straw.

Standing in the doorway, Lizzy put her gloved hands on her hips just like the farmer and the dowser. "Should she have some water? The manager of our home farm once told me that cows need lots of water."

"I'll get her all she needs, miss. Thank you fer yer help," Clarence said as though he could not wait for her to leave.

"Right," she said, brushing the hay off the skirts of her coat. "You are welcome."

Lizzy turned and walked away around the corner of the barn and paused near an open window. Narrowing her eyes, she could just spy the two-foot-wide path crossing the field and entering the barn before leaving it again on the other side. While she stood there, she overheard Frank remonstrate with the younger man.

"You aughta be more polite," he said. "And you aughta pull down that corner of the barn so this doesn't happen again when *yer* son don't listen to *you*."

"I'll brick up the stall entrance. I don't want t'mess with me roof. Are ye gonna dowse Nellie or not?" Clarence demanded.

"She won't need it no more," Frank stated. "And you don't need to spend any more money on the animal doctor."

Lizzy heard someone stomp out of the barn and she hastened further down the hedgerow path so he would not think she had been listening to them. It proved to be Frank. The old man joined her and they walked all the way to the stile before either spoke. He helped her over the stone wall once more.

"Don't pay no mind to Farmer Clarence, miss. He's a good sort, but he's missin' his pa."

"I shall not," Lizzy promised, and jumped down off the stile. "Did you think better of dowsing Nellie?"

"Aye."

He did not seem to want to elucidate so Lizzy did not enquire further. They walked back to the village chatting of this and that as though they were old chums. He left her at the gate to the golden-stoned parsonage, pulling on his cap.

"Have a good day, miss."

"Thank you. Good day, Frank," she replied.

Charlotte must have been on the lookout for her because she was standing on the front porch, wringing her hands and watching as Lizzy came through the gate.

"There you are," she said, shaking her head. "Cook said you left almost two hours ago."

"Is it nine already?" Lizzy asked, coming up the walkway toward her.

"Just gone. What have you done to your pelisse?" Charlotte asked, her eyes wide.

"I helped a farmer with his sick cow," Lizzy explained, mounting the steps.

"Come inside and give it to me. Gibbon will have to brush it."

They entered the parsonage and, taking off her outer garment, Lizzy said, "I am sharp set. Is breakfast ready?"

Gibbons hurried out of the dining room door and quickly took her pelisse and bonnet.

"You will need to brush her pelisse before we go to Rosings this afternoon," Charlotte directed.

"Yes, ma'am. I shall do it immediately," the houseman said, whisking her things away.

Lizzy was facing the door as Charlotte closed it. She forced herself not to stiffen in reaction to what she saw as the door swung closed.

She had been followed back to the parsonage.

Chapter Five

Or had she? Was it a coincidence that she saw the visitors? Or had she drawn them here? They had seemed to pause just beyond the iron gate, observing their surroundings. The door had shut just as they glanced through the iron gate toward the parsonage. She could not be certain they had seen her at all.

Their beauty, as always, astounded and terrified her. Three exceedingly lovely visitors. She prayed they would not linger.

She broke her own rule and mentally whispered a plea.

Go away.

<But why?>

Dear Lord.

A shiver galloped down her spine.

Charlotte raised her eyebrows. "What is it? You have gone pale all of a sudden."

Lizzy cleared her expression and gave a slight shake of her head. Now was not the moment to burden her friend. Instead, she made a comment.

"I met Frank and I like him very much. Do you know him?"

"Is he the old man who walked you home?"

"Yes."

"I have seen him at services, but I do not believe we have been introduced."

"I shall introduce him tomorrow after church. He is also a dowser. I went with him to watch him practice his craft. We visited Farmer Clarence and Frank had to give him a good talking to."

"I do not yet know either of these men. How have you met people so quickly?" Charlotte asked, taking her arm. "What am I saying? Of course, you have met some villagers. I have never known a person as sociable as yourself. I would not be surprised to learn that they offered you the comforts of their kitchens this morning and that you have already eaten."

"They did not." Lizzy produced a pout that would have made Lydia envious. "I feel slighted. However, I suppose they ate much earlier so I shall not repine too much upon it."

Charlotte laughed. "Come with me. Breakfast is on the sideboard. Are you hungry?"

"Famished," Lizzy confessed. "Cook gave me a slice of date cake but I instantly ate it."

"You shall have bacon, ham and coddled eggs," her friend promised. "And more cake, if you wish it." They walked together toward the dining room. "Father has just come down. Mary and Maria were almost finished eating before I came outside to watch for you."

"I beg your pardon for taking you from your own meal," Lizzy said, contrite.

"Do not be concerned. I know your ways," Charlotte said, chuckling. They entered into the dining room and she gaily said, "Here is the delinquent."

Mr. Collins and Sir William immediately got to their feet. Charlotte's father bowed his shoulders, giving the example to her cousin who hastily followed suit.

"Good morrow, Miss Bennet," Sir William said in a jovial voice. "Been for a walk? You shame us all with your vitality. Oh, the strength of youth. If only I still had it."

"Good morrow, Sir William," Lizzy said, dropping the hint of a curtsy and gifting him with a radiant smile. "It is a glorious day for a walk." She gave her cousin the same salute. "Mr. Collins. I must praise the beauty of your village. It is quite the tidiest village I have ever seen. Your people are friendly as well."

Her cousin managed a wide, but supercilious smile. "They are but unlearned rustics for the most part, but you are correct. They *are* friendly, and have welcomed me and my dear wife with open arms."

Lizzy moved to the sideboard and picked up a plate before replying. "Is there a school for the children?" She tweaked a slice of ham, some bacon, an egg, and another slice of date cake onto her plate, waiting for her cousin's answer.

When she returned to the table, she saw that he was swallowing. He washed his mouthful down with a gulp of milky tea.

"Yes, indeed, Cousin Lizzy," he said at last. "There is a stone school built by the de Bourgh family. It is down a short lane found between the butcher and the green grocer. The Rosings estate owns the school master's living."

"Another fine example of your patroness' philanthropy," Lizzy observed, picking up her fork. She saw that she had said the right thing, for her cousin nodded approvingly at her.

"Yes, indeed," he said with reverent pleasure.

Lizzy turned her attention to Maria and Mary before he could say more. "Ladies, how did you sleep?"

"Very well," Mary said, nodding. "And you?"

"I also slept well," she said and began to eat.

"My sleep was disturbed," Maria said, frowning a little. "The unfamiliar sounds in the night kept waking me. But it is always so with me. After a few nights, I will sleep as well as at home."

Mary poured herself more tea. "Maria and I thought we would explore the village today. Sir William, would you like to join us?"

Lizzy saw Maria's eyes widen and she gave Mary a 'look'. Maria need not have worried, however, for her father and Mr. Collins had another idea on how to spend the remainder of the morning hours.

"Thank you, Miss Mary," Sir William said. "Mr. Collins has promised to show me over his church today."

Mr. Collins gave everyone an intense look. "We must all be back at the parsonage in good time to make ready for our visit to Rosings Park. Lady Catherine is expecting us at three."

Everyone promised faithfully to heed his reminder.

"What are you going to do today, Lizzy?" Mary asked. "Will you be writing to Father?"

Lizzy regarded her steadily. "I must, of course, but I have not decided what to suggest in regards to Lydia."

"As I said before," Charlotte said, nodding at Mary, "you are most welcome. It is a delight to have you as a guest."

Mary flushed and ducked her head with evident pleasure.

"Lydia may also join us," Charlotte graciously said. She magnificently ignored her husband's pleading look. She focused on Lizzy. "Pray tell your father so."

"Thank you. I will be surprised if he brings her, however," Lizzy confessed. "He hates to travel and it will not do to send her alone." She noticed her cousin's brightened expression.

"I believe he will not wish to leave Mother and Kitty without his support," Mary added.

Lizzy waited for a quote, but nothing was forthcoming. She blinked at her sister in surprise and Mary raised her eyebrows at her.

"Am I wrong?" she asked.

Choosing not to malign her father's character, Lizzy said, "Indeed, he will not. Nevertheless, I will suggest the plan."

Mr. Collins' shoulders slumped. Hastily, he said, "Such a letter should wait for a rainy day. Surely today is too fine a day for letter writing? And you must go over the house with my dear wife."

Privately, Lizzy chuckled at his attempt to defer the time when an unwanted lively cousin might descend on his quiet life. He had never liked either Lydia or Kitty.

Aloud, she answered, "You are correct. Today is lovely. I did not reach the old church this morning on my walk because I met Frank and went off with him to visit Farmer Clarence. After I tour the house, Charlotte and I might walk to the old church. This is delicious bacon."

"F...Farmer Clarence? F...Frank?" Mr. Collins sputtered, completely ignoring her compliment.

Lizzy anticipated a remonstration from him. Charlotte spoke up before he could express his opinion of her easy ways with those beneath her station.

"We shall go directly after we finish our meal. I would dearly love a walk. There are a few items I need to get at the shops as well. We can tour the house later." She glanced at Mary and Maria. "We shall go together as far as the High. Perhaps we shall meet a few young people who will be appropriate for you to know. There is Cara, Doctor Wright's daughter. She is sixteen. And Jennifer Starry. Her father is the solicitor. She is eighteen. There are a number of others, too." Charlotte raised her eyebrows. "You know, I believe we shall have a special early spring tea party and send out invitations. Should you like that?"

The younger women expressed their delight at the opportunity of meeting some of the local young ladies.

"Dear heart, Miss de Bourgh will also enjoy the treat," Mr. Collins reminded his wife.

Charlotte nodded. "Her name shall be the first on my invitation list, husband."

"Excellent." Mr. Collins turned his attention to Sir William. "We will find something else to occupy us that day, sir."

"We must," Sir William agreed.

"My dear," Charlotte said, touching her husband's hand where it rested on the table covering, "This coming week is your turn to visit the almshouses. Father is interested in charitable works, are you not, Father?"

Sir William captured the idea even though Lizzy knew he had no interest in charities. He was, however, an easy-going man, ready to be pleased by any activity.

"I will be delighted to visit them with you," he said to his son-in-law. "What is the purpose of these almshouses?"

"They are for the benefit of destitute infantrymen of the 3rd Regiment of Foot," Mr. Collins explained. "They must be over the age of sixty, have no family living in Kent, and no way to reach family who live elsewhere. They live three men to a cottage, and benefit from a stipend delivered twice a month. Once by myself, and then two weeks later by a solicitor from Sevenoaks."

"There are five row cottages on the Easterlay estate," Charlotte added. "The estate is about an hour away by road. You will enjoy the drive, Father."

"I am certain I will," Sir William said, always amenable.

"*'He who has no charity deserves no mercy'*," Mary quoted.

"Very nice, Mary. That proverb sounds exceedingly apropos," Lizzy praised, smiling at her sister. "We all need more mercy."

Lizzy rested her utensils on her plate, wiped her mouth with her napkin, and set it on the table, signaling that she was finished her meal. Hibben, who had been standing next to the wall, stepped forward and whisked her dishes away.

"Well done, miss," he said brightly.

Mr. Collins slowly closed his eyes, saying, "She is not a child, Hibben. She does not need to be praised for cleaning her plate."

"Of course, sir," Hibben said, just as brightly and clearly unrepentant.

It occurred to Lizzy that Hibben loved having guests in the house. She suspected he would be whistling his pleasure had that not been an indecorous step too far.

ཐ

Darcy and Fitzwilliam entered the stable-side entrance to Rosings after their morning ride and climbed the stairs to the first floor where their bedchambers were found. Fitzwilliam rushed ahead, taking the steps two at a time.

"Why are you in such a hurry?" Darcy asked his cousin.

"I just remembered there will be cobnut cake served for breakfast this morning and I am starving," he said over his shoulder.

Darcy chuckled. He also hastened his steps as though the speed of his tread would quicken the time when Miss Elizabeth Bennet would arrive for tea that afternoon.

He had thought long and often of the consequences of asking for her hand. Though uncertain about how she felt about him, he felt confident that she would accept his proposal. Why should she not? He had a vastly superior situation in society. His wealth was indisputable. All the reservations should be on his side.

Miss Elizabeth captivated him, but her family did not. Unlike his friend, Bingley, Darcy knew he did not have an easy manner, wherein he could accept the foibles and limitations of a person's character. Even Mr. Bennet, a gentleman by birth, seemed to contribute nothing to his village through charities, and permitted his youngest daughters to run wild about the village.

*And Mrs. Bennet…*Darcy shuddered. She had caused him the most agonizing consideration. The sisters would all marry and he might rarely, if ever, see them again. But what of his parents-in-law? When they came for a visit, they might stay for a month. *A month!* How would he bear the company of Mrs. Bennet?

And what of Georgiana? Do I want to expose my impressionable sixteen-year-old sister to Mrs. Bennet's influence?

His family would not obtain any additional wealth, influence, or station through an alliance with the Bennet family, while he would add immeasurably to theirs. He believed all his reasoning bore scrutiny. Anyone would expect him to act with more reserve, to abandon the idea of marrying beneath himself.

But Darcy had not been able to get Miss Elizabeth out of his mind, or his heart. Her arrival in Kent presented the opportunity he needed to discover if he could ignore the longings of his heart, or if having her at his side would be worth going against his measured reasoning. If so, then he could offer for her here, without having to interact with the members of her family at Longbourn. Once Miss

Elizabeth agreed to his proposal, he would travel into Hertfordshire when he left Rosings with his cousin and quietly speak to Mr. Bennet.

If I am very careful, I shall not have to endure a visit with Mrs. Bennet.

Miss Elizabeth might prove unworthy of his intentions, however, forcing Darcy to continue looking for a wife elsewhere. This idea caused his heart to squeeze in protest. Today would be the beginning of his further exploration of a potential alliance between the Darcy family and the Bennet family. The charming Miss Elizabeth would have her chance, for he refused to allow his memories of Mrs. Bennet to intrude on his investigation.

Darcy and Fitzwilliam entered the breakfast room to find both their aunt and Anne still sitting at both ends of a long table made short by the removal of numerous extenders. Anne's companion, Mrs. Jenkinson, sat next to her.

"Good morning, Aunt," Darcy said, bowing to Lady Catherine.

His cousin added his salutation.

Darcy walked over to where Anne sat, pallid and meek. He took her hand in both of his and leaned over, softly saying, "And how are you feeling this morning?"

Anne's cheeks lost their remaining color. "Well, thank you, Cousin Darcy," she murmured in her quiet way.

"I am glad."

"It is my turn, Darcy," Fitzwilliam said in the hearty way he had of speaking to Anne.

He crossed the length of the table to their side. Darcy relinquished Anne's hand to him. Surprisingly, however, Fitzwilliam's voice had gentled, and he bowed over his cousin's hand and said, "Good morning, Anne. You look like you could use some air. Would you care to take me driving in your pony cart after we finish eating? It is a fine day," he added in a coaxing fashion.

"Fitzwilliam!" Aunt Catherine said sharply.

He stood and released Anne's hand before answering. "Yes, Aunt?"

"We are having guests this afternoon for tea. I will not have you tiring Anne."

He bowed his shoulders in acknowledgement, and then addressed Anne. "Will you be exhausted by driving me? If you do, I can always take the reins," he suggested in a coaxing voice. "We shall give your dear Mrs. Jenkinson some time to write letters, or do some other tasks she has longed to have time to do." He bowed to the companion, a nondescript lady of middle years wearing a massive white mobcap. "Good morning, madam."

Mrs. Jenkinson tittered behind her hand. She turned to her charge. "If you wish to take a drive, I shall happily occupy myself with some letter writing. Pray go and enjoy the fresh air."

Anne nodded, looking from her to Fitzwilliam. "I am pleased to take you out. I have a new carriage. A whiskey."

"Is it fast?" Fitzwilliam asked.

"I must put an Irish cob between the shafts," Anne confessed, sighing dramatically. "Mother insists. He is a plodder."

"All the better to enjoy the scenery, the sunshine, and the company," her cousin stated, smiling charmingly.

Darcy narrowed his gaze a fraction, wondering what his officer cousin could be about, flirting with Anne. Fitzwilliam would go off to Canada and Anne would be left behind, possibly pining for him. He shrugged.

I am being foolish. My distraction with love has me seeing the potential among others where none exists. Fitzwilliam is merely being kind.

After loading up his plate from the sideboard, Darcy found his usual place at the table and sat. His usual place was to Anne's right. Fitzwilliam, his plate equally full, sat across the table beside Mrs. Jenkinson.

"You have both had your morning ride," Aunt Catherine observed. "Fitzwilliam is going driving with my daughter. So, Darcy, what do you mean to do today?"

Darcy could not think of a single thing to do. There was no hunting in this season. He knew a few of his aunt's neighbors, however.

"I shall call upon Lord Ansel," he said as soon as he had swallowed. "I heard in town that he has a roan hunter he means to sell. The gelding is used to carrying a lady. If he is suitable, I shall purchase him for Georgiana."

"I should have been a great rider-to-hounds, if I had applied myself," his aunt said.

How does she make statements like that with a straight face? Darcy exchanged a look with Fitzwilliam.

"Why did you not apply yourself, Mother?"

Darcy and Fitzwilliam turned their heads in surprise to stare at Anne. She never challenged her mother in this way. She ignored them, gazing at her mother. They both looked from Anne to their aunt, expecting her to explode in scathing denunciation of her daughter's audacity.

Aunt Catherine's eyebrows had shot up and she looked at Anne with wide eyes. "I beg your pardon?" she demanded in a shocked voice.

Darcy and Fitzwilliam looked back at Anne. She appeared serene, with only a slight frown wrinkling her brow. She continued to ignore their attention and kept her gaze trained on her mother.

"You said, 'I should have been a great rider-to-hounds, if I had applied myself.' I merely wondered, Mother, why you did not apply yourself? Was it because Father did not enjoy hunting?"

Fitzwilliam and Darcy lifted their cups of coffee at the same time, looking down the table at their aunt over their cup rims. Aunt Catherine tilted her head a little and examined her daughter.

"I am surprised you are interested," she said with steely casualness. "You must remember that your father used to hunt. However, he did not like to see ladies hunting. Since I do not like the mud, and the weather that frequently accompanies a hunt, I chose to allow this foible in his character."

"So, it suited you to obey him," Anne responded. "I am surprised you did not attempt to break him of this objectionable habit."

Who is this *Anne?* Darcy set down his coffee cup. *Where has she found the courage to speak like this to Aunt Catherine?*

Darcy's aunt seemed equally surprised at her daughter's behavior. "You are bold with your ideas today, Anne. You must be recovered from your moment of weakness yesterday evening."

The mildness of her response to her daughter's challenges surprised Darcy. Fitzwilliam appeared to feel the same way. To Darcy, the air felt charged with the potential for a storm to erupt.

Fitzwilliam stirred and set his coffee cup down on the table, keeping his hand curled around it. Addressing Anne, he said, "I hunted with your father once. It was with the Quorn." Anne broke eye contact with her mother and focused on him. "In Leicestershire," he explained. "Father has a hunting lodge there. Near Quorn Hall. My grandfather bought the lodge to be near where the pack was kenneled." He picked up a piece of toast and proceeded to butter it while continuing his ramble. "This was, ooh, fourteen years ago. Mr. Hugo Meynell was still Master of the Hunt." He frowned. "It was a shame about his son. I liked him." He took a bite of his toast.

"His son?" Anne prodded, seemingly willing to be diverted from her attack on her mother. "You cannot stop your recounting with such a statement as that and then not explain."

Darcy took pity on her. "Meynell's son died in 1800 from a hunting fall and never had the chance to become the Master. Mr. Meynell sold the pack and Quorn Hall to the Earl of Sefton."

"Oh, that is a shame," Anne said with a *moue* of sympathy.

In a tetchy voice, Aunt Catherine said, "I do not allow sporting talk at my table."

"It is *my* table, Mother," Anne stated quietly. "You will please me by remembering that."

"Oh, dear," Mrs. Jenkinson softly moaned. "Miss Anne, you must not say such things. Did you remember to take your tonic today?"

"I am five and twenty, Mrs. Jenkinson," Anne reminded her, ignoring her question. As was her habit, she waved her hand beside her ear as though swishing away a fly, even though there were no flies in February. "You are my governess no longer. As my companion, you do not have any right to censure my conduct."

Mrs. Jenkinson bowed her head and did not respond.

Feeling as though the foundations of his being had been rocked from its support, Darcy abruptly stood. *I must excuse the servants.* The butler met his gaze and immediately responded to the message in them. He gestured to the two footmen waiting at table and all three servants left the dining room. The butler closed the door behind him.

An almost over-powering urge to shout at his aunt washed over Darcy. Years and years of tolerating her unguarded tongue jabbed at him, spurring him to say things he would regret. Scathing observations on her treatment of her daughter came to mind. Even though Anne should not be speaking to her mother in this manner, Darcy did not want to speak out against his cousin. Instead, he clamped his jaw shut and refused to succumb to the impulse to vilify his aunt. *I am a gentleman. I am a gentleman.*

Catherine did not understand what had happened to her daughter. Anne *never* spoke to her in this way. *Never.*

"What has come over you, Anne?" she demanded. Then, noticing that Darcy still stood, she waved at him. "Sit down, Darcy. I will not have you hovering over the table like a servant."

Darcy hesitated, and only sat after she glared at him. For good measure, she glared at Fitzwilliam too. He raised an eyebrow and looked at her with cautious enquiry.

"I do not know what you mean," Anne said, drawing everyone's focus. "I am merely speaking my thoughts instead of swallowing them time after time, year after year. I wonder if I have not aided you in becoming the Tartar everyone thinks you."

Catherine heard Darcy's whispered reproach, "*Anne.*"

Her daughter's cheeks flamed with color. She did not like her cousin's unspoken rebuke. Her gray eyes snapped in anger, startling Catherine as much as anything Anne had said that morning. She had not thought her only child capable of having *any* passionate emotions. Before today, she had been the epitome of timidity. This behavior had *not* been what she had been praying for night after night.

Fitzwilliam now looked on the point of standing in spite of Catherine's glare.

"Finish your meal," she snapped.

"Yes, madam," he said solemnly, though he did not pick up his fork. "I thought you would prefer to berate Anne in private."

Her nephew's observation so startled her that Catherine could only blink at him. He never spoke back to her. He was always polite and courteous. *Always.* Glancing at Darcy, she saw him frowning at the colonel.

He is also surprised.

"And why should she want that?" Anne demanded. "She never has before."

Her companion released another tiny moan of despair.

To Catherine's annoyance, she discovered that her hands squeezed the arms of her chair as though choking the nonexistent life out of them. She forced herself to release the wood and folded her hands in her lap instead.

"Anne, I thought you much improved this morning," Catherine bit out. "But your discourteous behavior toward me has disabused me of that happy notion. Kindly return to your apartments and rest. A drive with Fitzwilliam is out of the question today. Tomorrow. Perhaps."

Anne leapt to her feet, causing her two male cousins to stand.

"This is *my* house, and I will not be ordered about in it." She looked at Mrs. Jenkinson. "Please fetch my pelisse and driving cloak. Cousin Fitzwilliam, will you go to the stables and order my carriage put to?"

Fitzwilliam bowed first to her and then to his aunt, before stalking from the dining room. Mrs. Jenkinson scurried after him.

"Anne!" Catherine had never felt so furious with her daughter. And so worried. Desperately worried. "I forbid you to go driving. You must rest. You are not well!"

"I feel magnificently well, Mother," Anne claimed.

Catherine could see the signs of exhaustion setting in. Her daughter's cheeks might be pink, but the sight of the remainder of Anne's pale countenance alarmed her.

"If you were well, you would not be talking to me in this way," Catherine insisted.

Anne lifted her chin and marched out of the room, saying nothing in response.

Catherine covered her mouth with fingers that trembled. A sort of odd terror tumbled around in her mind so that she could hardly hold a thought. Darcy put a cup of tea in her hand, and she drank it automatically, finding it hot and sweet. She set the cup on its saucer, releasing a long, jagged sigh.

Darcy sat beside her, self-contained and appearing as strong as ever—someone a wife could depend on. That was the real reason she wanted him for her daughter. Once his character had revealed itself, all the other reasons had become mere additions to the most important one.

She looked him in the eye and waited for him to speak.

"Something is wrong with Anne," he said at last.

Catherine's stiff shoulders slumped. "Yes."

"Do you know what may be causing this behavior?"

Shaking her head, Catherine said, "I do not know."

<That was fun.>

<Yes.>

Chapter Six

The ladies of the parsonage sallied forth together to tour the village and visit the shops. Mary and Maria followed their older sisters, trailing behind a number of steps so they could talk privately together. This preference allowed Lizzy and Charlotte to converse about their own interests.

"Charlotte?" Lizzy said, puzzled. "Why is your home called the Hunsford parsonage when it is in the village of Rosings? The town of Hunsford begins on the other side of the bridge, does it not?"

"Yes, that is correct," her friend said. "The town line is right on the far side. The old church, therefore, sits just within the boundary of Hunsford. Mr. Collins explained that it is tradition, only, that is behind the name of the parsonage, for the new church was built on this side of the bridge."

"I suppose the de Bourgh family donated the land?"

"As you might expect." Charlotte adjusted her net shopping bag on her arm. "Lizzy, I wish you will tell me what you saw outside the door this morning."

"Look," Lizzy said, pointing at the mass of white flowers blooming beneath a jumble of bushes next to a cottage. "Snowdrops."

"Yes, most pretty," Charlotte said, rolling her eyes and tightening her lips. "Lizzy, you will not put me off. There was nothing there. No dog. No villager. Nothing. What did you see?" She lowered her voice to a whisper. "I did not react to anything. Was it *them*?"

"Uh-huh. They must have been too far away for you to feel their presence," Lizzy said, smiling and nodding at a passing woman, who paused and gave them a quick curtsy before hurrying away.

When Lizzy was six-and-ten, not long after becoming friends with Charlotte, the older of the two friends had asked why Lizzy seemed to start at nothing even though most of the time she acted level-headed. Lizzy had felt a great affinity for her new friend and explained to her what three of her own sisters did not know. Even her own father knew nothing of his wife and daughter's affliction. She confided in Charlotte about her mother's distress and the reason for it. They discussed how Lizzy coped with what she could see. Thankfully, Charlotte had believed her, revealing that occasionally the hair at her nape stirred for no apparent reason. Through experimentation, they determined that the reason for this reaction matched Lizzy's sure knowledge.

Charlotte sighed. "It is most disconcerting to know they are around us and we cannot see them."

"You can see them if they choose to show themselves to you," Lizzy reminded her.

"I do not wish them to," her friend said with a shudder. "Did they notice you?"

"I believe the door closed before they focused their attention on us." Lizzy linked her arm through Charlotte's. "If they should ever show themselves to you, remember to be unfailingly polite."

"I remember," her friend said, sighing.

"And, if they should ask you for your name, do not give it. Rather, say, 'My own self.'"

"You have never told me that before. Whyever should I not give my name?"

"There is power in a name," Lizzy explained.

"Power?" Charlotte asked, incredulous.

"Is it so hard to imagine? Look at the power in Lady Catherine's name—particularly in her own neighborhood. Or the power in the king's name." Lizzy held up a fist as though holding a staff. "'Stop in the name of the king!'"

Charlotte laughed, though it sounded forced. "I did not think that is the type of power you meant. I thought you meant a magical power."

"They may be able to do something magical with our names, but I do not know what. The rule I was taught was not to give my name. I have now passed the knowledge on to you."

"Thank you," Charlotte said weakly. "Are they the same ones as you see at Longbourn?"

Lizzy shook her head. "Now, I must ask. Has the hair on your nape stirred since you arrived in Hunsford?"

Charlotte shook her head. "Not so I have noticed. However, you must know that I have been exceedingly busy since I married. I am distracted by my new roles."

"Perhaps my sighting was an aberration. They may have just been passing through."

"I pray you are right," Charlotte said earnestly.

"Sometimes I think I would rather see ghosts."

Charlotte shuddered. "Not me. I could not bear that."

"Do you regret inviting me?" Lizzy asked suddenly, her eyebrows high.

Immediately, Charlotte exclaimed, "I do not!"

Lizzy hugged her arm. "We shall laugh together while I am here. Now that I know they are around, I shall not be surprised and shall forget about them." She spied a large woman coming their way. She appeared to be approximately fifty years in age and wore the tiniest red hat perched atop an elaborately constructed hair style. "Now, tell me, who is that extraordinary woman coming our way?"

Charlotte chuckled and whispered, "She is the butcher's wife. Mrs. Harland considers herself a class above her neighboring shop keepers because her father was a verger. She is exceedingly helpful on our charity committee, and she has taught her children to speak well. The eldest son is a butcher like his father, but the other three are in service at Rosings."

Lizzy and her friend stopped, stepping to one side of the cobbled walkway to wait for Mrs. Harland to reach them. Mary and Maria slipped past them and proceeded to look into shop windows without them, completely ignoring Mrs. Harland.

Besides the red hat, the butcher's wife wore a royal blue pelisse, trimmed in rabbit fur. Lizzy committed her appearance to memory. On the next rainy day, she would write about her in a letter to her father. They shared an appreciation for eccentric individuals.

"Good morning, Mrs. Harland," Charlotte said, nodding pleasantly.

"Mrs. Collins," she said, dipping a small curtsy. Her head tipped to one side and she closely examined Lizzy in a bold manner before looking back at Charlotte. "It is a lovely morning, is it not, ma'am?"

Lizzy could not help but admire her diction, which was a cut above that of other women of her station.

"It is," Charlotte said. "Miss Bennet, may I present Mrs. Harland?"

Lizzy nodded and said, "How do you do, Mrs. Harland?"

"Well, thank you, Miss Bennet," was the reply, accompanied by another slight curtsy.

"I understand from Mrs. Collins," Lizzy said, "that you are a great asset to the charity committee."

"I try, Miss Bennet." Mrs. Harland said, flushing. "We must all do our best."

"Yes, indeed. May I say that your hat is quite remarkable."

Mrs. Harland touched it and preened. "I made it myself."

"You have deft hands," Lizzy praised, smiling. She nodded in such a way that would not encourage familiarities.

The butcher's wife curtsied again. "Thank you, Miss Bennet. Good day, Mrs. Collins," she said, and walked on.

Charlotte looked after her. "I am surprised she did not say something committee related. She usually does. She must have been flustered by the introduction."

"I must say that she does not seem the sort of woman to become easily flustered," Lizzy commented.

"She is not," Charlotte agreed. She shrugged and they continued their ambling walk through the village.

They stopped at the receiving office to see if the lined notebooks Charlotte had ordered had arrived. Unfortunately, they had not. She asked that they be delivered to the parsonage the day they arrived. Once back on the street, Charlotte directed that they head for the chandlers across the way.

"The notebooks are for our charity children whose parents cannot afford to buy them school supplies," Charlotte explained. "The children's charity is a particular concern of Miss Anne de Bourgh. She provides us with a budget and occasionally attends our meetings where we make a report on how the money is being spent. This is a duty I am pleased to take over on behalf of my husband. He does not understand children, and I have so many siblings that my knowledge must be considered superior."

"I can well imagine my cousin's difficulties. But he is young yet. I expect he will grow into his position in time," Lizzy suggested.

"Yes, that is true," Charlotte said, frowning. "I had not thought of that. I suppose I should have."

"Perhaps," Lizzy said, grinning to take the possible sting out of her words. "But you have not known your husband for long. Now, what are we shopping for at the chandlers? Candles?"

"Soap. The chandler's wife makes some lovely, scented soap. She sent word yesterday that a new batch of lavender ones has finished curing and they are ready to be sold."

"Ah. I like lavender. So does my mother and Jane. I believe I shall purchase some for them."

They met Mary and Maria coming out of the shop. Mary held up a brown package tied with string.

"I have bought some lavender soap for our mother," she said. "You could buy some for Jane."

Lizzy laughed. "I had the same notion. As you have not bought some for Jane, I shall do so. We mean to go look at the old church after our shopping. Do you wish to join us there when you are finished?"

The two younger sisters agreed, leaving Lizzy and Charlotte to pass into the large shop where the aroma of beeswax wafted about them. Piles of beeswax candles rested on tables beside even bigger piles of tallow ones. Boxes of sealing wax filled one shelf in a corner, the remaining shelves holding ready-made packets of common wafers. A collection of candlesticks and chambersticks—brass, pewter, silver, and ceramic ones—decorated a long bench behind the counter.

At the opposite end of the shop, a young female attendant stood behind a counter. Soaps, lip balm, mustache wax, beeswax cubes for waxing thread, and a variety of other products designed to appeal to the feminine eye were arranged before her. Lizzy obtained some lavender soap for Jane and herself, and some lily-of-the-valley ones for Kitty and Lydia. Charlotte bought a variety of soaps, and beeswax cubes.

"Mrs. Collins, ma'am," the attendant said, smiling widely. "I've been practicing me needlepoint."

"Have you, Abby?" Charlotte asked, her eyebrows raised, a smile brightening her expression. To Lizzy she said, "Abby joined my needlework class as soon as I offered it."

"Yes, ma'am," Abby said. From a display shelf behind her, she brought a box of white linen handkerchiefs. The edges had been prettily finished with different colored silks. Tiny flowers adorned each corner. "I've been selling them at six-pence apiece."

"How pretty," Lizzy claimed, leaning over the box. "I shall take four. Kindly divide them into two packages."

"Right away, miss," Abby said, grinning. "Does you wants me to put two red-edged ones in one package, miss, and two blue ones in another?"

"Yes, thank you," Lizzy replied.

"Thank *you*, miss."

She turned away to accomplish this task and Lizzy quietly explained her purchase to Charlotte. "I thought I would give them to your cook and maid-of-all-work when I leave."

"That is thoughtful of you," her friend said.

They loaded their purchases into their string shopping bags and left the store. Lizzy could tell that her friend enjoyed being a person of significance in their village. She now lived in a society that expected her to be involved in everyone's life, from the lowliest person to the highest. In Hunsford and Rosings villages, Charlotte was the vicar's wife and her origins prior to that condition did not interest the villagers as much as whether she would be helpful to them. In Longbourn village and Meryton, Charlotte had always been regarded as the eldest daughter of a man of trade, whose rank had been obtained through having been a mayor. This had not created the ideal social cachet for a plain woman of almost no fortune, leaving her a spinster at twenty-and-seven when she met Mr. Collins.

"You enjoy being a vicar's wife," Lizzy observed as they made their way to the ruin of the old church.

Charlotte chuckled in a self-deprecating way. "More than I would have thought." Then she frowned. "It is a great responsibility. The villagers—mostly the women—look up to me and expect me to always know what to do. I find that a daunting proposition. However, Lady Catherine is exceedingly helpful to me in that regard."

"You said in your first letter to me that she was officious," Lizzy reminded her.

Charlotte sighed. "I know, and I am sorry I said that now. But, since then, I have counselled with her on some of the problems the villagers have brought my way and she *always* gives excellent advice and is not stingy with it."

"I look forward to meeting her," Lizzy said, pausing at an open iron gate set between the square wood columns of a roofed arbor.

They had reached the former church yard on the far side of the bridge spanning a shallow stream. "This entrance to the yard is in surprisingly good condition."

"Lord Ansel's great-grandfather set up an annuity for the maintenance of the cemetery, including the stone surrounding wall and the gate. He is a local landowner and his family have been buried in this graveyard for three hundred years."

"Is there a crypt?"

Charlotte nodded. She pointed at a stone building next to the crumbling church. "It is entered through there, but the crypt itself is beneath the stone floor of the church. Also," she said, leading the way through the gate, "there are a dozen or more gravestones with the Ansel name upon them."

"If they are so concerned with the graveyard, I am surprised they let the church fall into ruin," Lizzy observed.

"Oh, it did not fall into disrepair," Charlotte said in a portentous voice.

"But…" Lizzy said, pointing at the tumbled down tower and huge chunks of missing walls. "Clearly no one kept it up."

"No one *rebuilt* it," Charlotte stressed. She pointed at a portion of a wall that looked blackened by soot. "About seventy-five years ago, a man from Faversham entered the church early one Sunday and put a keg of gun powdered inside the tower. Before anyone arrived for service, he blew it up."

Lizzy stopped and faced her, eyes wide in surprise. "Blew it up? Whyever for?"

"He was a papist," Charlotte said simply. "You may stare, but Queen Mary burned seventy Anglicans at the stake here in Kent during her horrible reign."

"But she died in 1558!" Lizzy scowled. "He must have been mad to blow up a church."

Charlotte nodded. "Before the formation of the Church of England, this church was known as St. Mary the Virgin. Then, the priest was run off when he refused to renounce his faith. The building became known as St. Joseph's and an Anglican priest was put in place. The Ansel family used to be Catholic, you see, but they forsook their faith, siding with King Henry."

"So, this madman did not approve of a former Catholic building being used for Anglican worshipers?"

"That is what he said. Fortunately, no one was hurt, and the Ansel crypt and entrance survived."

Lizzy shook her head in amazement and turned to glance at the headstones around her. "Are the de Bourghs buried here as well?"

"No. They have a graveyard on the grounds of Rosings Park. It is lovely, and there is a small praying chapel watching over it. The chapel there was designed like a Grecian temple."

"Oh. Where is the well you mentioned before?" Lizzy asked, searching around them. "No, do not say. I shall find it." She focused on the energy lines in the church yard, searching for where they converged. "There it is," she said, pointing to a circular stone plinth within a tangle of half-tamed briar rose canes. They started for it. "Why is it not as well-tended as the rest of the yard?"

Charlotte pressed her lips together. "The retired gardener who tends the yard will not go near it. He calls the briar rose, Witches Briar. A foolish superstition, if you ask me. Anyone who wishes to collect water from the well can keep the briar cut back themselves, he says."

"The power in a name," Lizzy said dryly.

"Humph." Charlotte waved her hand as though to dismiss the groundskeeper. "As you can see, there is a pump installed in the lid. The baker's son is mechanically inclined and he keeps the pump running." She pointed to a red tile roof beyond the church yard. "The bakery is just there. They need a lot of water, so it makes sense for them to look after the pump. There is a washerwoman who collects from here too. The other village well is near our church yard."

Longbourn House had its own well—as did all the big houses and farms, though many farms made use of streams near their homes. Villagers, though, had to haul their water from the local village well back to their homes—a daily chore.

"A long way to walk," Lizzy acknowledged.

She approached a wooden plank trough that led from the base of the pump across to the end of the church yard. It disappeared into a clump of hawthorn bushes. One of the energy lines followed its path. Or, perhaps the trough-builder had unknowingly followed the energy path.

"Hello. What is this contraption?" Lizzy asked.

Charlotte joined her in examining the apparatus. "Irrigation? I have not visited the well since the first time I came, which was right after I arrived in Kent." She glanced along the trough and spied a young man coming their way. "Here is John, the baker's son."

John proved to be a tall man of Lizzy's own age. He had a shock of brilliant red hair, a face of freckles, and eyes as green as grass. He removed his flat cap when he approached them and knuckled his forehead.

"Good morning, Mrs. Collins, ma'am," he said, smiling politely and then nodding at Lizzy. "Miss."

"Good morning, John. My friend, Miss Bennet, and I were admiring this apparatus. Did you build it?" Charlotte asked.

"Yes, ma'am," he said, flushing. "I asked the vicar's permission first, ma'am, I promise ye."

"I believe you," Charlotte said, smiling in a reassuring fashion. "Does the trough go all the way to the bakery?"

John nodded. "Almost. I dug out t'ground, ma'am, next to bakery, and paid fer t'bricklayer to line it with bricks. Then I built this here trough. Every Monday and Friday, I pump water until tank is full. It holds two hundred gallons, ma'am," he said, grinning. "Me dad says we never had bread that raised better. I don't know how that may be, but I trust he knows his work."

This account did not surprise Lizzy, but she said nothing about the energy lines and their possible effect on the water.

"It is Saturday," Lizzy observed. "Have you run out of water since yesterday?"

John ducked his head. "No, miss. I come most days to check that me trough hasn't been damaged."

"You have done a clever and helpful thing, John," Charlotte said. "Your parents must be exceedingly proud of your inventiveness."

"Yes, ma'am," he said, ducking his head again in embarrassment.

ജ

Darcy climbed the mounting block and swung his leg over the blue roan gelding, settling into the unfamiliar saddle. After fitting his toes into the adjusted stirrups, he looked down at Lord Ansel, a tall and fit gentleman his senior by thirteen years.

"I shall be back in an hour or so," Darcy promised.

"Take as long as you like," Lord Ansel said, smiling broadly. "He is a gentle, but lively mount. Your sister likes to hunt, does she not?"

"Yes, she does."

"She will look magnificent up on Blue Skye here. He loves to jump."

"Blue Skye is a little too tall to be a Connemara pony," Darcy commented. "What else is in his bloodline?"

"A blue roan Andalusian," his host said.

"He is decidedly handsome," Darcy acknowledged. The horse's shoulders quivered in anticipation, but he patiently stood and waited for his rider's directions.

Lord Ansel stepped back. Darcy nodded at the groom, who released his hold on Blue Skye's bridle.

"Follow the path across the fields," his lordship suggested. "You will find several walls to jump, with even ground on both sides, a three-foot hedge that drops about a foot on the far side, then a stream, and you will end at Hunsford village before you circle back here. That should take you about an hour."

"Thank you," Darcy said, nodding his farewell.

Once out of the stable yard and past the paddocks, Darcy gave the signal for Blue Skye to trot, and then to canter. When they entered the fields, Darcy urged the gelding into a gallop. The transition between gaits was smooth and confident, which pleased him.

Blue Skye's ears pricked up at the sight of the first wall and he jumped it neatly. Georgiana was not a nervous horsewoman, but he did not like to see her up on a nervous horse, so Blue Skye's attitude toward jumping also delighted Darcy.

In the next field, he tested the horse's stamina by galloping around the field and then switching to a walk to see how quickly the gelding recovered from his exertions. By the time Darcy and Blue Skye reached the stream lined with willows and rushes, a huge grin adorned Darcy's countenance.

"Well done, boy," Darcy said, patting the horse's shoulder when they paused at the fording point. "Let us wade through this one."

The horse agreed and they splashed through the shallow water to enter the lane beyond that climbed slightly as they moved into the outskirts of Hunsford near the ruins of St. Joseph's. Several villagers doffed their caps or curtsied as he passed, well-used to seeing Lady Catherine's nephews several times a year. He acknowledged their salutes with gratified nods.

Upon approaching the church yard, he glanced into it and wondered who the ladies were who stood beside the well, speaking to a male villager. Then one lady turned her head enough and he saw beyond the brim of her bonnet. His heart lurched.

Miss Bennet.

Chapter Seven

Breath came into Darcy's lungs in short spurts through parted lips. He had not expected to see the woman he loved before this afternoon, and the intensity of his response to the sight of Miss Bennet startled him. He had always prided himself on his well-regulated mind and rigid control, but her presence threw his inner world into chaos.

She has spied me. She is coming this way!

Darcy's jaw clenched.

How is it that she can smile in that provoking way? There is always such a challenge in her fine brown eyes.

"Why, Mr. Darcy," she said, stopping on the other side of the stone wall and producing a polite curtsy.

Darcy bowed his shoulders and lifted his hat. "Miss Bennet."

"I like the look of your horse."

"As do I. Lord Ansel, a local landowner, is selling him. I think my sister will like him."

"As a hack or a hunter?" she asked, one eyebrow lifted.

"A hunter."

She laughed then and Darcy's stomach swooped.

"I confess, Mr. Darcy, that I know almost nothing about horses."

"It is something you could learn, if you wished to."

"Perhaps, if the opportunity to be around more horses presented itself to me," she said, still smiling. "Sir, I did not know you meant to come into Kent."

"How should you?" he asked, then suppressed a wince when her smile stiffened. *My accursed tongue!* Hoping to make a recovery, he made a push to explain himself to her. "My cousin, Colonel Fitzwilliam, and I had planned to come in March. However, he could not make the later date, so we came here together, arriving yesterday."

"I also arrived yesterday," Miss Bennet said. "I came with Mrs. Collins' father. As did my sister, Mary, and Charlotte's next younger sister, Maria."

The vicar's wife had broken off her conversation with the villager and joined her friend. Darcy lifted his hat once more and bowed his shoulders.

"Mrs. Collins."

"Mr. Darcy," she said, curtsying.

Mrs. Collins cast a worried glance at her friend. *Is she afraid of me? Or of how Miss Bennet might respond to me?*

"Welcome to Hunsford," Mrs. Collins added.

"Thank you. Have you been showing Miss Bennet about the village?" Darcy asked.

"I have been, sir."

He addressed his next question to Miss Bennet. "Did Mrs. Collins tell you about the bombing?"

She relaxed her shoulders and mouth. "Yes, indeed. I had thought my friend lived in a quiet, uneventful place."

"The incident *was* seventy-five years ago," Darcy reminded her. She shifted her feet as though she meant to walk away. He floundered around for another thing to say to her before she did. Finally, he settled on the mundane. "May I ask after the health of your parents? I hope you left them well?"

"Tolerably so," Miss Bennet said, that appealing twinkle back in her eyes.

No doubt she knows I cannot abide her mother's company. Has she also intuited that I find I have nothing in common with her father?

He switched his attention to Mrs. Collins. "And your parents, madam?"

"My mother is well, thank you, sir. You shall see how well my father does this afternoon." She frowned a little. "Unless you did not mean to join us for tea?"

"I shall be there," Darcy said. He lifted his hat. "Ladies."

He bowed again and gave the signal to Blue Skye to walk on. The horse blew out, and his ears pricked up, indicating to Darcy that he hoped to enjoy more exciting exercise. Darcy knew another way back to Lord Ansel's stables, where several jumps would enliven the journey.

They passed by Miss Mary Bennet and Miss Maria Lucas on the bridge, walking toward the old church. Miss Mary stared unblinkingly at him in a most disconcerting way, while Miss Maria kept talking to her friend as though she had not even noticed him. He nodded to Miss Mary. She nodded back.

I suppose I do not rate a curtsy.

The spot between his shoulder blades itched and he wondered if Miss Bennet watched him leave. Or, was she merely on the look-out for the younger sisters? Darcy forced himself not to glance back and determine the focus of her attention.

Too undignified. And I would not like to see that she has lost all interest in my comings and goings. How lowering that would be.

Lizzy watched Mr. Darcy ride away. He looked very well up in the saddle. She could not tell if excellent tailoring, or an excellent physique, was the cause.

"Why is he here?" she muttered to herself.

Charlotte heard her and replied, "Visiting his aunt, as he said."

"Did you know he would be in Kent?" Lizzy asked, frowning.

"I knew Lady Catherine expected him next month, but I did not know he would be arriving early."

"What an unlucky chance that he should find us out and about today," Lizzy remarked. "Did you hear him ask after my mother and father?"

From the corner of her eye, Lizzy saw Charlotte's eyebrows shoot up.

"I stood right here beside you when he did so. It was kind of him to ask."

Lizzy's hands clenched into fists. "Mere civility. He does not care for my father's company and positively loathes my mother."

"Loathes?" Charlotte repeated, sounding shocked. "That is a strong observation, Lizzy. And how could anyone dislike your father? He is mildness itself."

"I am not mistaken," Lizzy said tartly. "I observed how Mr. Darcy's jaw tightened when Papa stopped Mary from playing and singing another tune at the Netherfield ball."

Charlotte frowned. "I believe Mr. Darcy could like your father if he knew him better."

"Yet, he did not take the time to do so."

"A different generation, perhaps?"

Lizzy breathed out a shaky breath, struggling to recover the even tone of her mind. She concentrated, instead, on the way the late morning breeze cooled her hot cheeks. After a few more breaths, she managed to say quite calmly, "You may be right."

"I am certain I am. *No one* could dislike your father."

"I do not know why I care so much," Lizzy said, shaking her head. "Ah, here are Mary and Maria."

"Let us call in at Doctor and Mrs. Wright's. We need only stop in for a moment for introductions. I shall sound out Mrs. Wright on the propriety of having a tea party just for the young ladies of the village."

"Surely she will have no objection?"

"Cara is not yet out," Charlotte explained. "Mrs. Wright may not wish her daughter to go to a party where young women who are out are in attendance."

Lizzy waved at her sister and Maria. "That seems rather strict."

"Mrs. Wright is most careful of her daughter. Cara is their only child. She is not a great heiress, but she has a respectable dowry and will come into a comfortable independence upon reaching her majority. They wish her to marry well, of course, and to a gentleman who has no need of her fortune. Or, at least, no dire need."

"I see."

If only I would come into such an independence, Lizzy thought with an inward sigh. *Then, no one would think it odd in me to wait for a love match.*

Mary and Maria entered the church yard, greeting their sisters. Mary stared owlishly at Lizzy.

"Did you know that Mr. Darcy would be in Kent?" she asked in her blunt way.

Lizzy shook her head.

Mary's lips twisted. "What an unfortunate circumstance."

"Yes." Lizzy linked her arm with Mary's. "Lady Catherine is his aunt, so he will be at tea this afternoon."

"I knew of their relationship," Mary remarked. "Mr. Darcy's character is a salutary example for all of us."

"How do you mean?" Charlotte asked, her brows drawn in.

"I have never found him to be kind," Mary explained. "When I marry, it shall be to a kind gentleman, or not at all."

"An excellent pledge," Lizzy commented. "Kindness in gentlemen is too often underrated."

"'*To thine own self be true*'," Mary quoted. When Charlotte and Maria appeared not to recognize the phrase, she added, "Polonius, from Hamlet."

"I thought it must have been him," Lizzy said, squeezing her arm affectionately. "Charlotte wishes to make us known to Doctor and Mrs. Wright, and to their daughter, Cara. Shall we?"

Mary and Maria readily agreed. Presently, they arrived at a pleasant, double-fronted, red brick two-storey home, trimmed with white shutters and window frames. Set back a little from the road, the front garden featured two rows of rose bushes, waiting for warmer weather to release their beauty.

Charlotte knocked on the front door, and they paused in the covered porch until a fresh-faced young maid answered the door. The maid curtsied.

"Good morning, Molly," Charlotte said, nodding. "Is Mrs. Wright at-home to visitors?"

Molly opened the door wider and said, "Please to step in out of the cold, Mrs. Collins, ma'am. I'll check if me mistress is at-home today."

"Thank you."

Charlotte and her guests filed into the wide entrance hall. Once Molly shut the door, she hurried off up the stairs to the first storey. Within moments, a matronly woman with an abundance of graying blonde hair came down the stairs to the landing and smiled at them.

"Mrs. Collins. What a pleasure. Please come up."

The drawing room, done in light-blue and white, faced south. Sunshine brightened the long room, creating a cheerful space where several sofas and half a dozen armchairs had been arranged about the room in groups. Mrs. Wright indicated one such group.

"Kindly sit," she said, waving graciously at the furniture.

They sat and, before Charlotte could make the introductions, a slender young woman entered. Lizzy smiled at her. She had light-brown hair, curled about her pretty face, and soft-gray eyes.

"Ah, Cara, my love," Mrs. Wright said. "Come and be introduced to Mrs. Collins' guests."

"Yes, Mother," Cara said, gifting them with a shy, welcoming smile.

"Hello, Cara," Charlotte said.

Cara curtsied. "Mrs. Collins."

Charlotte made the introductions, and by the time she had completed her delightful task, Molly entered, carrying a tea tray. Soon everyone had a cup of tea and a plate holding a warm-from-the-oven treat. The four guests stared from their buns to their hostess.

"Chelsea buns," Lizzy said in a hushed voice.

Mrs. Wright chuckled. "Cook has worked for years to perfect her Chelsea bun recipe. She tasted the original from the Royal Bun House some years ago when she lived in London, you see. Being a keen baker herself, she set about experimenting. One year, instead of currants, she used raisins. *I* liked them, but I see we are back to currants again."

"I have only ever had these at Easter," Mary said reverently. She set down her tea on the table at her elbow and picked up her fork.

"I have never had one," Maria whispered, her eyes round. "They look scrumptious and sticky."

Lizzy had to agree. The squarely swirling dough, rolled with layers of cinnamon, sugar, butter, and currants, had been glazed with syrup. Lizzy took a bite and closed her eyes in bliss. She swallowed only after she had extracted the last iota of flavor.

"My complements to your cook, Mrs. Wright," she said, opening her eyes. "These are a triumph."

"Thank you. I shall tell her." Mrs. Wright looked at Maria. "Do you like your Chelsea bun?"

Maria nodded vigorously. "I do, indeed, Mrs. Wright."

"Every time Cook thinks she has made a good batch," Cara said, grinning, "she leaves one out as an offering for the faeries."

Her mother pressed her lips together but did not remonstrate with her daughter.

"Does she?" Lizzy asked, intrigued. "Where does she leave it?"

"On the old stump at the bottom of the garden," Cara revealed.

Raising an eyebrow, Charlotte asked, "And is the offering always accepted?"

"Oh, yes," Cara replied. "Once, a strange biscuit replaced the offering."

"Did Cook eat it or accept it?" Lizzy asked, more sharply than she had meant to.

Cara blinked twice and then shook her head. "Oh, no. Cook knows better than to accept food from faeries. She left it behind. I expect the birds ate it."

"I do not like all this talk of faeries," Mrs. Wright said in a firm voice. "It is unchristian."

"Indeed," Charlotte said, flushing. "Let us, instead, talk of the tea party I intend to have so that I may introduce my friends to the young women of our parish. What do you think, Mrs. Wright? Is it a good idea?"

Their hostess appeared gratified at being asked, but frowned and tilted her head to one side. "Do you intend on inviting their mothers as well?"

Charlotte nodded. "Most definitely. It is not the time of year for garden tea parties, but I hope to present a congenial afternoon."

"Perhaps, if Charlotte agrees," Mary said, setting down her empty plate, "all the young ladies could recite a poem or quotation. So as not to leave out any guest who is too shy to stand up and be the center of attention for a lengthy recitation, neither would need to be long."

"Ah," Lizzy said, smiling at her sister. "Turning the tea party into an edifying afternoon? I like the idea. What do you say, Charlotte? Mrs. Wright?"

"Miss Mary," Mrs. Wright said, smiling at her in approval, "what a perfectly unexceptional proposal. I approve. Mrs. Collins?"

Charlotte glanced at Cara and then Maria, who both looked pale. "Uh, yes. As it will be a recitation tea, I shall set the date for this coming Thursday so our young ladies will have time to learn their pieces."

Lizzy caught sight of Maria's gulp and said, "Fear not, my dear Maria, Mary knows as many short quotes and poems as she knows long ones. I am certain she will help you find one suited to your tastes."

Mary smiled in a rather solemn way and patted her friend's hand. "If you can learn no more, there is always John 11:35." Maria looked baffled so Mary elucidated. "*Jesus wept.*"

Everyone chuckled.

Charlotte shook a finger at her sister. "I am afraid that will not do for you, Maria. Other frightened girls may quote it first. You would not like to find yourself with nothing to recite, would you?"

"Oh, no, that would be horrible," Maria readily agreed.

Lizzy suspected she only said what she thought her sister wished her to say.

"Fear not," Mary said, grinning now. "Lizzy is correct, I know many others."

They took their leave of Mrs. Wright and Cara, hurrying back to the parsonage to divest themselves of their packages and to prepare for that afternoon's appointment at Rosings Park.

Hibben met them in the entrance hall and presented a silver salver to his mistress. Charlotte picked up the letter found there, saw it was for Lizzy and handed it to her.

"From Mr. Bennet," she said.

Lizzy had thought she might receive something from him before she wrote. Smiling, she took it. They all retired to their chambers to take off their outer garments and hats. Just as Lizzy opened the letter, her sister knocked once and entered.

"Will you let me read it?" Mary asked, joining her on the side of the bed.

"I shall read it out," Lizzy said, sensing her sister's concern that their father would include her in his anger over the subterfuge. "It reads, *Dear Lizzy, I expect that you are wondering if I will bring that annoying child to Kent and take Mary home with me. What Sir William must think of our harum-scarum household I can only imagine. The answer to your wonderings is that I will* <u>*not*</u> *be bringing Lydia to Kent. She is determined to run wild and there is little I can do about it short of locking her in her room after nailing her window shut. While I have not ruled out that possible solution to my problem, I know your mother would give me no peace if I followed through with my idea. Dear Mary, whom I know was bullied into the ruse, must stay with you. The visit will do her good. If she so chooses, I am certain Sir William will bring her home with them when he and Maria return to Hertfordshire next week. Otherwise, she can return home with you, via London, a month after that. Pray, do not be alarmed if you find yourself a couple of sisters short when you arrive. Kindest Regards, Father.*"

Lizzy set aside the missive and examined her sister's expression. Mary appeared relieved and then pensive.

"What do you think he means by that last line?" she asked.

Smiling, Lizzy patted her arm. "He meant it only as a jest. I believe he will lock himself in his book room until we return."

Mary sighed and stood. "I shall go and change my dress. I confess to feeling reassured by Father's words."

ഌ

Colonel Fitzwilliam met Darcy in the stables when he returned from Lord Ansel's estate. He grinned at his cousin and asked, "Did you like the horse?"

Darcy nodded. "I have purchased him. Georgiana will be most

pleased."

"You will have a hard time of it when she is presented next year."

"I will expect you to do your part," Darcy admonished. They turned their steps toward the stable entrance into Rosings. "As her other guardian, I know you will wish to squire her to various events. Between the two of us, we will keep the fortune hunters at bay."

"You may be married by then," Fitzwilliam said. "If so, your wife will chaperon her."

Darcy looked at him sharply.

What does he know? Or, what does he think he knows?

Instead of questioning him, Darcy asked after their cousin. "How was your drive this morning with Anne? Did you like her whiskey?"

Fitzwilliam grimaced. "The carriage is handsome, but Anne spoke the truth. The Irish cob *is* a plodder."

"The next time you take her out, use one of my carriage horses," Darcy suggested.

"I am not certain that Anne has the gumption to rebel against her mother."

Shaking his head, Darcy asked, "How can you say that after her outburst this morning?"

Fitzwilliam raised an eyebrow but said nothing.

"And Anne will expect your support after your behavior."

"Mine?"

Darcy sharpened his expression again. "Surely you remember?"

"My memory has always been particularly good, as you know. I recall nothing untoward in my conduct this morning."

"You said to Aunt Catherine, that, 'I thought you would prefer to berate Anne in private.'"

Fitzwilliam drew up short. Darcy halted and faced him.

"I never did. I would not say such an insolent thing to her."

"Nevertheless—"

Fitzwilliam sliced a hand through the air, figuratively cutting off Darcy's response. "I also know that you would not jest about something like this, either."

He paused, and Darcy thought he looked a little white around the lips.

Then, his cousin continued, "What did Anne say? I have no recollection of her behavior either."

Darcy recounted the main points of the conversation that

morning at breakfast.

"I must apologize to my aunt," Fitzwilliam said when he finished.

Laying a hand briefly on his cousin's arm, Darcy asked, "What did you speak about on your drive with Anne?"

"Not about any of this, I assure you," Fitzwilliam said, shaking his head in an absent-minded fashion. His eyes lost focus as he thought back. "We talked about the whiskey, as you might expect. Anne was her usual self, though more animated, I thought. But, then, I have always thought she had more life in her when she was out from under our aunt's eye."

"Indeed."

"We agreed another such drive would be pleasant for both of us," his cousin mentioned, resuming their walk toward the house. Darcy fell into step beside him. "After this morning, Aunt Catherine is unlikely to agree to further excursions. What could have come over me? Over us? And why can I not remember?"

"I have no idea. Though, your behavior appeared to be a result of Anne's outburst," Darcy explained. "You were rising to her defense."

"After everything you have recounted, it seems to me that Aunt Catherine was the one under attack," Fitzwilliam said in a dry voice.

"That is so. Anne's behavior and your defection shocked Aunt Catherine so much that she could not muster a significant diatribe."

"So unlike her. She is never at a loss," Fitzwilliam observed. "I have always admired her for that trait."

Darcy produced a little cough of polite disagreement, saying, "Even so, Anne has always been the weaker of the two." He stepped before his cousin and opened the door for them. "Aunt Catherine was mightily shaken."

Fitzwilliam cursed under his breath. "I can well imagine. I shall change into my regimentals before I seek her forgiveness, I think. She always compliments me on how I look in uniform."

"A sound plan."

They had traversed the short corridor where a back stairway was revealed behind a nondescript door. Fitzwilliam wrenched it open and bounded up the steps ahead of Darcy. Imagining the coming scene between his aunt and his cousin caused Darcy to grit his teeth. He would not like to be the one on the receiving end of her tirade. Then, he chuckled.

Fitzwilliam may have just enough address to keep her from raining terror down from above. I do not.

Darcy climbed the stairs in his usual steady fashion. His valet, Thomas, awaited him when he arrived at his bedchamber. Thomas divested him of his riding coat, setting it to one side.

"We have ladies coming for tea," Darcy commented, assisting his valet in the removal of his riding jacket.

"Yes, sir. Mrs. Collins' guests," Thomas said, nodding. His voice dipped when he mentioned the name of one of the guests. "Miss Elizabeth Bennet."

Darcy took a deep breath and let it out slowly. "Yes."

"I've had a basin of hot water brought up, sir," the valet said, indicating the steaming porcelain basin on the washstand. "To remove the aroma of horses."

"Good thinking," his master said, struggling to keep the eager anticipation out of his voice.

"Sir," Thomas said, bowing slightly before continuing to help him disrobe.

Darcy washed and dressed with care. He finished tying his snowy cravat in the cascade style before glancing down at the collection of tie pins Thomas held out in a velvet-lined, divided case.

"The garnet cabochon, I think," Darcy said, plucking the item from the velvet.

"A nice choice, sir," Thomas said, closing the case and carrying it away.

"Colonel Fitzwilliam will be wearing his regimentals."

"This I *will* say, sir," Thomas said, returning with his fresh waistcoat and jacket, "That flibbertigibbet batman of the Colonel's *does* know how to keep his brasses clean."

"You are always complaining that Guildford talks too much," Darcy commented.

He stood still, permitting his valet to fit him into his waistcoat and jacket.

"Oh, sir, he is the same as ever. And Guildford doesn't half-want to be going back to Upper Canada, either."

"Why not? He must have good lodgings, being a colonel's batman."

"It's the cold, sir."

Darcy frowned while tugging his cuffs into place. "They will be there over the summer."

Thomas rolled his gray eyes. "He doesn't like that they are leaving for Canada so early. There will still be ice in the St. Lawrence River, he says."

"The Colonel said they are to stop in Nova Scotia first and wait in Halifax for the gulf and the river to be navigable."

"Guildford is aware, sir, but that colony in April is not warm enough for Guildford," Thomas said.

He produced a clothing brush and began to brush away from his master's coat any impertinent strands of hair and bold pieces of lint.

"Shall I make him a gift of a fur-lined coat?" Darcy asked, jesting.

"An unnecessary kindness, sir. He has a bison-fur coat he bought off a *voyageur* the last time they were sent to Upper Canada."

"Bison-fur?"

"Yes, sir." The dapper little man with the shiny bald pate stepped back to survey their handiwork. He nodded once. "Very good, sir."

Darcy nodded back and approached the door. Thomas hurried ahead of him to open it but Darcy stopped him.

"Sir?"

Quietly, Darcy asked, "Have you had the opportunity to speak with Miss Anne's maid yet?"

"No, sir," Thomas said, just as softly. "Seems Miss Anne stormed out of the breakfast room this morning and kept Danton busy. And last night, Miss Anne wasn't well, so Danton did not come down to the rooms in the evening."

"Hmm," Darcy said.

"She will have a moment to breathe while the guests are here, sir. Mrs. Durling has asked the upper servants to tea in her sitting room after the tea has been laid out in the drawing room."

"Keep an ear open and show compassion to Danton. Draw her out, if you can."

"Sir," Thomas said, bowing. "I'll do my best."

"I know you will," Darcy said. He took a deep breath. "This should prove to be an interesting afternoon."

"Indeed, sir."

Thomas opened the door and Darcy stalked out, eager, but not so eager, to spend an afternoon in Miss Bennet's company.

Chapter Eight

Lizzy followed Charlotte, Mr. Collins, and Sir William into the Chinese drawing room at Rosings. Mary and Maria followed behind her after they had divested themselves of their outer garments and bonnets. She and Mary had put on their best day dresses in honor of the event. Lizzy wore pale-primrose with dark-green piping around the bodice and hem. Mary wore creamy-white with navy-blue rick-rack in three bands around her hem. Maria looked pretty in white, with light-blue riband trim beneath her bodice.

Lizzy's eyes opened wide when she spied the walls of the drawing room, adorned as they were with gold and turquoise silk panels. Matching sofas and chairs in gold and turquoise surrounded a low, black-lacquered table. White cranes and exotic foliage had been painted on the top, surrounded by an inlaid border of mother-of-pearl. Beneath their feet, oriental dragons flew across golden carpets.

"Come in, come in," a querulous voice sounded. "Stop gawking and sit down."

All the ladies curtsied, and the gentlemen bowed, to the grand dame sitting on a high-backed, throne-like black-lacquered chair. It appeared to have no cushioning and Lizzy wondered why anyone would choose to be uncomfortable in their own home.

The lady's domineering manner so startled Lizzy that she did not notice whom else might be in the room. Her cousin had never once intimated in all his conversations about the great lady that she was anything else but agreeable. She should have known better than to trust Mr. Collins' sycophantic opinions as the basis for her own expectations of the lady's demeanor.

Lizzy observed that everyone kept their gaze on Lady Catherine. Indeed, Lizzy did not think she had ever met a more formidable individual. She and Mary sat on the sofa to the left while Charlotte's family took up the entirety of the opposite sofa. Mary discreetly gestured to Maria to join them on their equally long seat but Maria shook her head like a frightened hedgehog and linked arms with Charlotte.

But Miss Anne de Bourgh should be here. Is she ill? Lizzy speculated, inwardly frowning while her expression remained politely inquisitive. She glanced toward the windows.

That must be her.

Miss Anne de Bourgh did not sit alone.

Oh, my…there are three of them.

Lizzy hastily looked back at the imposing woman before them, hoping the additional guests had not noticed that she could see them. Two females stood near the windows, and a male sat on a chair close to them.

Three at once? Why so many? What do they want? Lizzy stifled those thoughts—for what was the use in contemplating the reasoning behind such beings—and concentrated instead on their hostess.

Lady Catherine appeared to be somewhere near Lizzy's father's age. She wore rouge and powder, such as had been popular in her salad days, but she wore no wig. Instead, her graying hair had been piled artfully above a high forehead, a strong nose, and the cheekbones that belonged to a woman who had been handsome in her youth.

Lady Catherine raised an arching eyebrow at her. "Had your fill, miss?" she snapped.

"Have *you*, my lady?" Lizzy asked, wondering at her own audacity. From the corner of her eyes, she noted the horrified expression in Charlotte's gaze.

For Charlotte's sake, I must mind my tongue. I am feeling so quarrelsome!

"Humph. Well, you are no beauty," her hostess stated, "But you will do."

For what?

Thinking again of her friend's unenviable situation, Lizzy bit her tongue and bent her head in mock humility. "Thank you, my lady. You are too kind."

"Nonsense," Lady Catherine replied smartly. "Kindness is a waste of my time." She turned her attention to Mary. "Neither are you."

"Beautiful?" Mary asked, belatedly adding, "My lady."

Lizzy cringed inside for her. This sister was considered the plainest of the five sisters, but she had her own calm presence that Lizzy thought could attract the right type of gentleman. *A studious man, perhaps? Or a doctor.*

This is not proper. Why have we not been introduced to Anne yet? And where is Mr. Darcy? I thought he would be here.

Before she could look for him, Mary responded to her own stark query, keeping Lady Catherine from replying. It was a quote, of course.

"*'Beauty in things exists in the mind which contemplates them.'*"

Both of Lady Catherine's eyebrows shot up. "No doubt. You are permitted to read David Hume?"

"Why should I not?" Mary rejoined in a calm voice. "My father is a well-read man and his library is full of books. Why should I not read them?"

"Because not all books are appropriate for young girls to read," retorted Lady Catherine.

"Surely, my lady," Lizzy interposed, coming to Mary's rescue, "books on philosophy should be read by all inquiring minds. We must learn to think, after all."

"Young women should think like their fathers. And, after they are married, like their husbands," Lady Catherine remonstrated.

Mary stirred, speaking before Lizzy could give her opinion of *those* statements.

"Unfortunately, most gentlemen do not read enough philosophy to hone their ability to think. It is true that I have only the experience of my own neighborhood, but from the gentlemen there, I have learned that, except for my father, horses, hounds, and politics are the preferred topics of the day. *Every* day, my lady," she added dryly.

Charlotte closed her eyes as though praying to be swallowed up by the floor. Mr. Collins' face had turned apoplectic-purple. Maria merely looked confused.

Sir William said, "I say."

Mary looked at him. "Not you, Sir William. You speak often of your children. It is most refreshing."

"You both have decided opinions for such young women," Lady Catherine observed testily.

"Why, thank you, my lady," Lizzy replied, bowing her head in acknowledgment of the compliment that had not been meant as a compliment. "Our reading must, therefore, be considered a successful endeavor."

"Harrumph," Lady Catherine said.

Lizzy decided that their hostess' gray eyes now held a decided twinkle in spite of her lofty scowl.

Lady Catherine waved her hand toward where her daughter sat near to the window, apart from their small group. "My daughter, Anne de Bourgh, and her companion, Mrs. Jenkinson."

Charlotte led by example and stood to face the pale woman dressed in peach silk who appeared to be her junior by a year or so. She waved her hand beside her ear as though shooing away a fly. Lizzy, Mary, and Maria stood. All four curtsied at the same time. Lizzy deliberately kept her gaze on the floor, unwilling to accidentally meet the piercing eyes of any of the unwelcome guests. Sir William and Mr. Collins also rose and bowed respectfully to her.

Miss de Bourgh did not stand, but nodded, saying nothing. They all sat once more.

"So pleased to meet you," Mrs. Jenkinson tittered on behalf of her mistress.

The companion wore all gray as though coming out of mourning. However, her well-cut dress fit her nicely and she wore a short and demure strand of pearls. She flushed a little under Lizzy's candid observation.

"Our dear Mrs. Collins has spoken of you all often and we have so wished to meet you. Have we not, dearest Anne?" Mrs. Jenkinson asked of her employer.

"Indeed," Miss de Bourgh said in a soft, colorless voice.

Lizzy had heard from Mr. Wickham that Anne had been meant for Mr. Darcy since their childhood. The idea of Miss de Bourgh marrying Mr. Darcy did not cheer Lizzy and that puzzled her.

Why does she sit apart from her guests? Surrounded by…them. Does she know they are here? Other than her mother and the old gypsy woman, Lizzy knew of no others who could see the fair folk. Discovering another would be agreable.

Lady Catherine spoke. "I understand from Mr. Collins that you have already met one of my nephews." She indicated a spot near the fireplace opposite the windows where two men stood, one in a scarlet uniform. "Beside Darcy is Colonel John Fitzwilliam."

Lizzy's head snapped around. *How did I not see them when I walked in? Am I being unduly influenced? Are my thoughts being corrupted?*

She heard tinkling laughter of such exquisite beauty that Lizzy had to use all her self-control not to reveal her knowledge of the sound. She spied no reaction in the men's expressions, however.

Both gentlemen bowed and they all acknowledged their bows with nods—except for Sir William and Mr. Collins. They stood and bowed in turn. *Like jack-in-the-boxes.* Lizzy swallowed a giggle.

Colonel Fitzwilliam appeared a little older than Mr. Darcy. He was not nearly so handsome, though he had a pleasing countenance and kindly eyes. The colonel was several inches shorter than his cousin, and his shoulders were narrower, too, though his regimentals hid that flaw. *Mostly.* He immediately left his post by the fireplace, leading Mr. Darcy, who joined their group more closely, standing behind Lizzy's sofa. The colonel, however, crossed to the window, leaned over Miss de Bourgh, and whispered something in her ear. She nodded, rose, and permitted him to lead her away from her position by the window, into the group.

Mr. Darcy brought forward an ornate, upholstered, straight-backed bamboo chair for her and then another of the same design for Mrs. Jenkinson, who brought her charge's cashmere shawl. He placed the chair for Miss de Bourgh next to where Charlotte sat at one end of the sofa, opposite to where Lizzy sat. Mrs. Jenkinson indicated that she wished her chair to be next to her employer, which placed her between Lady Catherine and her daughter. The companion placed the beautiful cream-colored shawl around Miss de Bourgh's shoulders.

The unwanted guests began to prowl about the drawing room. One of the females paused near to Mr. Darcy, so Lizzy kept her gaze averted.

Darcy's insides thrummed in annoyance with Miss Bennet. He wanted her to make a good impression on his family, but she was far from doing so today. Darcy wished to take her to task for it. The extraordinary feeling, similar to the one he had felt earlier at breakfast, could not be fought down this time. She knew better than to be impertinent to his aunt. Yet, here she was, behaving as though she were a duke's daughter, socially superior to his aunt, and not a landed gentleman's daughter, significantly *inferior* to her in rank.

Or, does she know better?

He knew little of her education other than that the five sisters had never had a governess. Her mother did not act as though she had taught them anything of the finer social values. Mrs. Bennet did not come from a station where governesses commonly found employment. So, unless Mr. Bennet had taught her how to behave with high-born ladies, how could Miss Bennet have learned? By example, he supposed.

But whose example has she followed? Miss Jane Bennet's? And who taught her*? Have they learned their deportment from books? From other family members I have yet to meet?*

He crossed around the circle of guests until he stood opposite Miss Bennet. A question popped into his mind and before he had a chance to think about it, he spoke it aloud.

"Miss Bennet, have you no respect for my aunt's position?"

Everyone in the room gasped and stiffened.

Miss Bennet turned her head and looked up at him, fire in her eyes. Without waiting for her response, he asked, "Have you no consideration for your *friend's* position?"

She glowered at him and he felt his countenance slacken. All the air escaped from his lungs.

Oh, my Lord, what did I just say?

He stared at Miss Bennet, unable to look away, waiting for her response to his impertinence. *This is a disaster. What must she think of me?*

She gave no indication, turned from him, and stared at Mrs. Collins, who appeared pale and drawn. *It is like the cut direct,* Darcy thought. He watched Miss Bennet breathe in and out in a slow, measured fashion. Then, she turned her attention on his aunt.

"You have a lovely home," Miss Bennet said in a cheerful, but respectful tone.

Darcy felt the air in the drawing room ease as politeness regained its footing. Everyone would ignore his dreadful questions.

But, will they forget them?

Will she forget them?

She continued, "Mr. Collins has often sung its praise, and I shall say, that though his praise has been effusive, he has not done Rosings justice. You must be rightly proud of it."

"I am, Miss Bennet," his aunt said, turning her awful gaze from Darcy. To all the guests, she explained, "Many of the improvements have been of my own design. In preparation for Anne's birth, my husband commissioned a new nursery to be built. I advised him minutely. I wished to have all the modern conveniences, including a nursery that was not three floors up in the attic of the main wing. Instead, it has merely two floors and is easily accessed from the kitchen. I had a pump installed in the nursery as well, so water did not have to be carried upstairs. Anne's apartments are still in the new wing, though not in the nursery proper, of course. Her rooms are on the ground floor."

His aunt finished her description, waited for the exclamations of admiration from her guests, and then raised a single eyebrow at Darcy. *She will want to have words with me later and justly so.* He bowed his head in apologetic acknowledgment. Glancing Fitzwilliam's way, he caught the colonel watching him, a frown furrowing his brow. *Even my cousin thinks I have run mad.* Thinking back to his conversation with Fitzwilliam that morning, Darcy wondered if he had remembered anything more of his own erratic behavior. Then, Darcy questioned his own memory. Had he said something he had also forgotten?

Bloody hell.

"Did you, my lady?" Sir William was asking, recalling Darcy to the conversation. "I also designed an addition to Lucas Lodge. Did you choose to have the new wing blend in with the old, or to stand out from it?"

His aunt looked approvingly at Sir William. "Blend in. I wished for it to appear as though the wing had always been there."

"An excellent choice," Mr. Collins gushed.

Darcy had watched him throwing dagger glances at Miss Bennet and Miss Mary almost from the moment his cousins had opened their mouths. He suspected that Mr. Collins would give them a tongue-lashing once they left Rosings.

Darcy could hardly tolerate being in the same room with him. *When Miss Bennet accepts my hand, I shall never, ever, permit him to cross the threshold of Pemberley House.*

The doors to the drawing room opened in the midst of another one of the vicar's meaningless and obsequious comments. Billings entered at the head of a line of three footmen who carried silver trays loaded with tea things. The butler directed where they were to set down the repast and then he dismissed them. The footmen retreated and closed the double doors behind them.

"You may leave as well, Billings," Lady Catherine said, waving her hand toward the doors. "Mrs. Durling is waiting for you in her sitting room. Mrs. Jenkinson shall prepare the tea and serve."

"Yes, my lady," the butler said. He left with stately steps.

Mrs. Jenkinson rose and moved toward the tables where the tea had been laid out, taking the key to the caddy out of her reticule as she walked. Mrs. Collins also rose.

"I shall help," Miss Mary stated, rising.

The two women went to Mrs. Jenkinson and accepted the tasks she gave them.

Miss Bennet tilted her head toward the instrument at one end of the long room. "You have a lovely pianoforte, Lady Catherine."

"Thank you. The sound is excellent. I have a different one for every drawing room and one in the ballroom, of course."

"Oh?" Miss Bennet's single word seemed a rebuke for such extravagance.

There are six pianofortes at Pemberley. He mentally frowned. *Will she forgive me for being extravagant? Will she forgive me for rebuking her in public? I must apologize. I must.*

"Yes. Moving a pianoforte will put it out of tune. It seemed simpler to have five rather than to keep having one re-tuned after each relocation." His aunt fixed Miss Bennet with a direct stare. "Do you play, Miss Bennet?"

"Only a little," she replied with indifference. "At Longbourn, we depend on my sister Mary for our entertainment. She is an earnest player of the pianoforte."

Darcy inwardly winced. The description was apt. Miss Mary had no feeling for the music and seemed more intent that everyone should notice her playing rather than in taking enjoyment from it.

"Mary plays for us and we sing together," Miss Bennet explained. "As a family."

In a falsely gracious way, his aunt said, "If she wishes to play, or if you both wish to practice, you may use the pianoforte in Mrs. Jenkinson's room. I have told Mrs. Collins often that she may also practice there. You will not disturb anyone in the nursery wing."

Anne stirred but said nothing. Darcy caught her eye and she swiftly looked away. *Except for Anne.* Fitzwilliam touched her shoulder and she glanced up at him.

"Shall I make up a plate for you?" he asked, smiling pleasantly. "It seems like a long time from breakfast and you only take toast and chocolate for your morning meal."

"I am a little hungry, thank you," Anne said. "You know what I like."

Darcy watched this interlude, a slight frown upon his brow. Before he could consider what seemed to be happening before his eyes, Aunt Catherine spoke his name with imperious inquiry.

"Darcy?"

"Aunt?" he asked, dragging his gaze reluctantly to her. He knew what she wanted. She had wanted him to be the one to prepare a plate for his cousin. "I shall make up a plate for you, shall I? What would you care for?"

Her eyelids tightened, but she merely said, "One of whatever Cook has sent up."

He bowed his shoulders and faced Miss Bennet. "And you, Miss Bennet? Shall I make up a plate for you?"

"Thank you," she said in a solemnly polite voice.

Darcy proceeded slowly toward the offerings, thinking, *all she said was thank you.*

Lizzy inwardly fumed at her own behavior. *Poor Charlotte.* She had never meant to create possible difficulties for her friend due to her own accursed tongue. Lizzy looked at Charlotte, silent apology in her eyes. Charlotte replied with a faint forgiving smile.

I will be so good from now on.

But…to be reprimanded by Mr. Darcy! Angry humiliation made her look away from her friend, seeking the impossible man so she could slay him with her gaze. When she had his back in her sights, Lizzy saw him hesitate for half a step, shake his head once, and then continue toward the table. He had walked right through the male, who had shimmered and laughed, sharing the jest, whatever it might be, with his companions.

Lizzy smoothed the fabric of her dress over her lap, glancing downward in a hopefully natural fashion. In the tiniest mental voice she could manage, she thought, *Remember, we are not alone. Think of something else.*

Looking up at the ceiling, she examined the turquois dragons flying across a golden painted sky in seemingly wild abandon. The Eastern dragons, long and slim like giant snakes, had no wings, which made her wonder how they could fly at all. *It must be by magic.*

"Mr. Collins," she said, deliberately injecting enthusiasm into her tone, and tearing her gaze away to look at him. He wore a pinched expression and his eyes darted about, his agitation plain to see.

With apparent reluctance, he met her gaze. "Yes, cousin?"

"This ceiling is as beautiful as you described it," she praised without any mockery in her voice. "I declare, the dragons frolicking above us do so with great abandon. So life-like."

He opened his mouth to answer her, but before he could do so, Lady Catherine spoke. Her cousin immediately turned his slavish attention on her.

"The man who painted the ceilings in the drawing rooms took three years to do so," she explained.

"Goodness," Sir William said, looking up for the first time. "Marvelous. Simply marvelous. The ceilings at Lucas Lodge are quite simply done."

Lizzy hoped he was not formulating a plan to have his drawing room ceiling painted. She doubted that he had the money to waste on such a project. Fortunately, Lady Lucas would have something to say about such an extravagance when he had six other children to provide for.

Mr. Darcy and Colonel Fitzwilliam returned to the group with the first cups of tea and plates of refreshment. Mary brought a cup and plate for herself.

"The great man himself is bringing yours," she whispered, accompanying her words with raised eyebrows.

Lizzy gave a single shake of her head, watching Charlotte carry a plate and cup to her father and then to her husband. The colonel came back a second time with a cup and plate for Maria. Mr. Darcy brought Lizzy her tea and some delightful looking cakes, tiny savory pies, and biscuits adorned with small dabs of cheese topped with walnut pieces. She felt an unnatural desire to throw the food back at him. Resisting the outside pressure, she set the plate on the lacquered table with a hand that shook. It was at that moment Lizzy realized she had forgotten something.

Oh, why did I leave my charm bracelet on the dressing table?

"I noticed you like cheese," Mr. Darcy said quietly. "This is a soft and salty cheese made at the Rosings Park dairy. There is ground black pepper in it as well."

This proof that Mr. Darcy had thought her tastes important enough to remember startled Lizzy so much that she stared up at him in surprise. Their gazes met, and what she saw in them—mute apology—caused her to hastily look down at her tea.

"Thank you, sir," she murmured. "I shall certainly enjoy the cheese."

Drat. Now he has been thoughtful.

"My dairyman's wife at the Pemberley home farm also makes a superior cheese. It is much firmer than this one, however," Mr. Darcy mentioned. He bowed and turned back to the tea table to collect his own refreshment.

Lizzy thoughtfully stared after him while picking up one of the biscuits. *That had almost been a conversation.* She tasted the cheese and crispy biscuit, finding both agreeable.

"Tell me how you like this tea," Lady Catherine ordered.

Everyone obediently took a sip and murmurs of appreciation came from the group.

"Most excellent, my lady," Mr. Collins praised.

"Yes," said Charlotte. "So kind of you to invite us to taste it."

Lizzy felt the weight of Lady Catherine's gaze upon her, so she took another sip before offering an opinion. With a smile and a twinkle in her eye to show that she considered her supposed superior knowledge a jest, Lizzy said, "Twinings, of course, as any connoisseur of the beverage could tell after a single sip. Indeed, after a single sniff. What a great aroma."

Both of Lady Catherine's eyebrows shot up. "They are the best purveyors of tea in the country."

"Indubitably," Lizzy responded. She took another bite of the cheese and biscuit.

"Do you enjoy green tea as well, my lady?" Mary asked. "I quite like it."

"I prefer black tea," Lady Catherine stated unequivocally.

Their cousin glared at Mary, seemingly disapproving of any thought expressed that was not solicited from his patroness. Mary stared wide-eyed back at him, which disconcerted him enough for him to turn his censorious stare upon Lizzy. She chose to return his look with a puzzled one of her own. She truly did not know what she or Mary had done to make him angry with her again.

One of the uninvited guests leaned over Mr. Collins and stroked his shoulder. Lizzy hastily shifted her gaze to her plate of treats and gulped down some tea.

His feelings are being manipulated. Mr. Darcy's must have been as well—else he would not have spoken in such a way to me in company. Who else's? Mine. Everyone's? Lizzy drew a shuddering breath. *Oh, Lord, the sooner this appointment is over the better.*

"Are you unwell, Miss Bennet?" Mr. Darcy asked softly.

Lizzy started a little for she had not realized he stood so near to her. And had she spoken that last thought aloud?

"I am quite well, thank you, Mr. Darcy," Lizzy said, nodding once to him and offering a small smile.

He glanced at her empty cup. "Perhaps some more tea?"

"Thank you," she said, broadening her smile.

ஐ

Mr. Collins moved with angry swift steps across the gravel drive toward the damp grass path that led across the park, through a meadow, to the parsonage. He walked too quickly to be considered polite. The ladies trailed behind him with only Sir William as their escort. Maria held onto one of his arms and Charlotte the other. Once they reached the path, however, Mr. Collins stepped to one side and waved his wife and in-laws ahead of him. Charlotte looked over her shoulder at them, revealing a troubled expression.

The overcast sky carried only a hint of the dying sun to light their path. Though Lizzy did not relish walking the rest of the way in twilight because of this delay, she touched Mary's arm and they paused beside their cousin.

"Mr. Collins?"

Spluttering, he said, "I…I have never…never, I say, seen such impolite behavior to one who is my patroness. Y…you know, you *know*, how important Lady Catherine is to my sweet wife and me. We depend on her continuing g…good will! You know this, and yet…and yet…"

Overcome with ire, he could not go on. He tore off his black parson hat and slapped the side of his leg with it, turning partially away from them. This gave Lizzy the opportunity to hastily glance around. She sighed inwardly and relaxed her shoulders. They were quite alone. None of the guests had followed them.

Mary stirred as though she meant to speak. Lizzy squeezed her arm and Mary turned her head and met Lizzy's eyes. She followed her elder sister's example and when Mr. Collins faced them again both women hung their heads, meekly accepting the rebuke.

"We are dreadfully sorry, sir," Lizzy said quietly. "I do not know what came over us. All I can offer as a reason is that the grandeur and…and…sheer magnificence of Rosings Park and Lady Catherine overpowered our senses. We could not manage our natures in the midst of such unaccustomed splendor."

"Indeed," Mary said, her manner humble, "we have never experienced anything like Lady Catherine or her daughter. They are beyond anything we have encountered. So gracious. So much condescension."

Breathing heavily, he eyed their submission with lips tightly pressed together into a thin, disapproving line. Lizzy held her tongue and waited, praying Mary would do the same.

"I shall be surprised if you receive another invitation to Rosings during your visit," he finally said. "Which is all you deserve after your behavior today. I was never more ashamed of my family."

Both ladies nodded as though chastened. He turned on his heel and stalked off after his father-in-law. His wife disengaged her arm from her father's, touched her husband's arm, and walked back to them.

"Charlotte," Lizzy said, holding out both hands to her friend. "I am extremely sorry. Pray forgive me."

Charlotte took her hands and squeezed them. "You are both forgiven," she said, including Mary in her tender glance. "But, Lizzy," she whispered, leaning close. Mary leaned in as well. "I felt it. An air of chaos pervaded that drawing room. I have experienced it before. Was it *them*?"

"Them?" Mary repeated in an intimate whisper.

Lizzy drew in a breath and decided that the time had come to let her sister in on the family secret.

"Yes," she whispered back. "It was the fae."

Chapter Nine

"The *what*?" Mary asked. She scowled ferociously and whispered. "The *fae?* There are no such beings."

Charlotte ignored her objection, saying in a pained, quiet voice, "I thought you did not want us to use the name. You said it would draw their attention to us." She searched the gathering gloom. "Are there any here now?"

Lizzy joined her searching gaze to her friend's. "I do not see any."

"See?" Mary squeaked. "*See?* Are you both mad? No one can see the fae because they do *not* exist."

Sighing, Lizzy shook her head at her sister. "They do. I can see them, just like I can see energy lines."

This explanation did not appease Mary. "I never believed that nonsense either."

"I know. That is why I have not confided in you about the fair folk."

"Is it *my* fault that you spout insane ideas on occasion?" Mary demanded in a scornful hiss.

Lizzy sighed and took her sister's hand, squeezing it in what she hoped was a reassuring manner. "I am glad you cannot see them, dearest. Charlotte is right, however. I do believe it is best not to name them."

"I cannot see them either, Mary," Charlotte said, her gaze continuing to dash around the field. "I can feel them sometimes, though. Lizzy, I would be more comfortable if we kept moving toward home. There are iron pickets on our fence and horseshoes nailed above the doors."

"An excellent notion." Lizzy linked her arms with Mary's and Charlotte's, and the three walked together toward the parsonage. "I cannot believe I left my iron charm bracelet in my bedchamber. I *always* wear it."

"You wear that ugly bracelet because of this nonsense? Is that why you gave us one as well?" Mary demanded. Without waiting for Lizzy to respond, she asked Charlotte, "Mr. Collins permits you to follow such superstitious practices? I am surprised."

"He is as superstitious as the next person," Charlotte said. "Cook said that when Mr. Collins arrived at the parsonage, he instructed the stable boy to change the horseshoe placement from a 'u' shape to a 'c' shape. More efficacious, he said by way of explanation."

"But what is that supposed to mean?" Mary demanded. "More effective against what?"

Lizzy clicked her tongue. "Against the fair folk. You may not believe us, dearest, but I expect you to use your powerful intellect to absorb the folklore."

Mary turned to look at her in that steady, unblinking stare of hers. "The iron garden," she said at last.

"Yes."

"You and mother sit in there," Mary said. "Often."

"Yes."

Mary averted her gaze and asked her next question. "Does she know you can see these imaginary…individuals?"

"Yes." Lizzy admitted. "Mother can also see them. Her response to their presence is to get more lively, more full of gaiety—all as a guard against their presence. It exhausts her. Lydia's natural high spirits are *not* restful for Mama. They also attract the fair folk. That is the true reason I was so upset about you taking our sister's place. With Lydia here, Mama could have had a break from her unnatural gaiety. Her spirits would calm."

"I see. And now Lydia is not coming. And Jane knows, of course," Mary stated stiffly. "But not Kitty or Lydia. Telling them would be foolish beyond permission." Without waiting for confirmation from Lizzy, she mused in a puzzled voice, "We do not have horseshoes above the doors of Longbourn."

"Father refuses to permit it," Lizzy said. "He does not know anything about…well…about my ability."

"You surprise me," Mary said dryly.

"I do?"

"I thought Father was deep inside your confidences," she said. "You *are* his favorite."

Lizzy heard the thread of bitterness behind Mary's words and squeezed her arm. She did not do her sister the insult of denying her statement. *I* am *my father's favorite. Poor Mary. No one wishes to think they are second best in their parent's eyes.*

"Was there only one of them there?" Charlotte asked, drawing their focus back into line. "At the tea party? It felt to me as though there was more than one. The feeling of chaos *surrounded* us."

Lizzy sighed pensively. "There were three. A male and two females. They enjoy disorder and unharmonious intercourse." Grimly, she said, "They laughed each time they succeeded in influencing us into behaving improperly."

"I experienced no influence," Mary asserted.

Frowning, Lizzy considered her statement. "You felt no inward pressure to behave inappropriately?"

"No. Did I behave in such a manner?" she asked. Looking around Lizzy at Charlotte, she asked again, "Did I?"

"I must admit that Mary behaved much as usual," Charlotte said diplomatically.

"As I said."

Lizzy shook her head at Mary's smug reply. "Some people are resistant by their nature. You, Mary, seem not to have that excuse for your rudeness."

"I was not rude," Mary asserted, appearing affronted. "I merely expressed myself in a straightforward manner."

"That is not what our cousin thinks."

Mary opened her mouth and then closed it with a snap. "I have no influence over what Mr. Collins thinks."

"Ladies, may we return to the subject at hand?" Charlotte asked. "Mr. Collins will recover and no doubt Lady Catherine has already done so. Lizzy, why should there be three of them at Rosings? You saw two others as well, at the bottom of our walk. Were they the same ones as you saw earlier today?"

"One was."

"This means there are at least four of them in the neighborhood. Why?"

"Is that supposed to be significant?" Mary demanded.

"It is never a good thing for a region to draw too much attention from the…*them*," Lizzy explained. "They are mischievous, amoral, and seemingly so bored with their own lives that they take pleasure in making the lives of mortals miserable."

"Oh. I have heard stories, of course," Mary said. "I still do not think that—"

Lizzy interrupted her, saying tartly, "Though I often appreciate your opinion, Mary, this is not one of those times. You asked me only yesterday to let you in on the big secret of our lives. I have done so. Though I wish you believed me, I am not surprised that you do not."

The heavy silence of disappointment fell between them.

"Pray, do not be angry one with the other," Charlotte urged hastily. "Shall we speak of something else? Tell me your opinion, instead, of Miss de Bourgh. Did she not look ill?"

"Yes, indeed," Lizzy said in ready agreement, setting to one side her sorrow at Mary's response to her revelations. "I am amazed at her fortitude. If I felt as ill as she looked I would have lain down upon my bed and sent my regrets."

"As would I. Mary, what did you think?" Charlotte asked.

Mary shook her head. "I have no opinion. She spoke little. Colonel Fitzwilliam was most attentive."

"He was," Charlotte said. "I also noticed that. I have never met him before today. Perhaps he is always so. Mr. Collins has only mentioned him in passing."

"Did you not say Miss de Bourgh is healthier when she comes away from Rosings?" Lizzy asked.

"Yes. When Miss de Bourgh visits me, she does not appear so ill. She is much livelier, too. And did you notice her habit of waving her hand past her ear? That does not occur at the parsonage either."

"I believe that habit may be caused by the fair folk influencing her in some way. There is much iron around your home, Charlotte, keeping them away from Miss de Bourgh." Lizzy raised her eyebrows. "She eats your food and drinks your tea?"

"She does. As does Mrs. Jenkinson," Charlotte assured her.

"Perhaps the air at Rosings does not agree with her," Mary offered. "Also, her apparent health while visiting you may only mean that she awoke that morning feeling better."

"You may be right."

Charlotte sounded dubious to Lizzy, who felt her shiver.

"It is getting dark—almost too dark for us to see the path," her friend observed, looking first at the ground and then up at the sky. "If the moon is up, it is covered by the clouds."

"Lady Catherine should have sent us home in her barouche," Lizzy said, chuckling. "She spoke about it enough. I thought for certain she would have it ready for us to use."

"Highborn ladies like Lady Catherine," Mary said dryly, "are only kind when it suits them."

"I do not believe you have met enough highborn ladies to form such a world-weary opinion, my dear Mary." Charlotte's voice grew a sudden grin. "I am surprised that *Mr. Darcy* did not offer us the use of his carriage."

"Whyever should he do that?" Lizzy demanded, looking at her friend in surprise.

"It would have been the gentlemanly thing to do," Mary pointed out. "But then, he probably expected his aunt to have a conveyance ready for us."

Lizzy laughed. "He must know his aunt better than I and I expected nothing kind from her after being in her company for only a few minutes."

Charlotte looked back at the ground. "I cannot see the path anymore."

"Look, there is a light ahead," Mary said, pointing.

Lizzy stopped and pulled her companions to a stop as well. "Let us wait to see who is carrying the light. We do not want to be pixie-led."

Sighing and shaking her head, Mary faced her sister. "Pixies? You jest."

Sniffing, Lizzy raised an eyebrow at her sister, though she hardly thought Mary could see her face. "If one type of magical creature exists, then why not another?"

Mary said nothing until a young man came into view, carrying a lantern. "There, you see?"

Charlotte gave a nervous laugh. "It is only Jem, our stable boy."

Jem, who the sisters had yet to meet, proved to be a tall young man just on the cusp of adulthood. He tugged on the flat-cap he wore over his dark curly hair, looking at his mistress.

"The master sent me, missus," he explained. "We're not but a step or two from home."

"That was kind of him. Thank you for coming so quickly," Charlotte said, smiling at him. "Kindly lead the way."

"Aye, missus," he said, turning around.

"Have you seen any pixies tonight, Jem?" Mary asked, following close behind him so she would be at the edge of the light circle cast by the lantern.

Lizzy heard the smirk in her sister's voice and groaned under her breath.

"Not tonight, miss."

Lizzy held her tongue with difficulty when Mary fell back a few steps. To Lizzy's observant eye, she appeared taken aback. Mary recovered quickly, however.

Softly, she whispered, "Provincial superstition."

When they arrived at the front door of the parsonage, Lizzy spied Mary eyeing the iron horseshoe hanging sideways above the door. Lights glowed inside and cast dull light onto the porch.

"Thank you, Jem," Charlotte said, dismissing him.

"Missus," he said, tugging on his cap. Jem waited until they climbed the stairs to the porch before he carried the lantern away with him.

Hibben opened the door just as they were about to do so themselves. "Madam, Miss Bennet, Miss Mary," he said, stepping aside so they could enter. "I heard your step."

"Hibben," Charlotte said, smiling. "Is Agatha in the kitchen helping Cook with dinner?"

"Yes, madam," the houseman said. "Shall I send her up to you?"

"If Cook can spare her," Charlotte said. She turned from him and said to her guests, "Shall we go and quickly take off our outer things? There is a fire laid in the drawing room. I did not realize how chilled I was until I stepped in out of that cold breeze."

"Indeed," Lizzy said, grinning.

ꟹ

Darcy watched his cousin escort Anne and Mrs. Jenkinson from the Chinese drawing room. Anne would lie down for a time. Darcy still fumed that his aunt had not provided her guests with a ride home. He had not accompanied them to the front doors, so he had not realized right away that Lizzy had *walked* back to the parsonage. And the other ladies, presumably.

"You are brooding," his aunt stated. "Why?"

Darcy turned to face her. He held out his hand. "Shall we leave this room to the servants? We can sit in the study next to the fire."

Lady Catherine took his hand and permitted him to lift her from the chair. She stifled a groan and smothered a grimace behind a look of hauteur.

"If you are uncomfortable, you have only yourself to blame," Darcy said, recognizing the true cause of her buried distress. "You know that throne of a chair was designed for its looks and not for comfort. I had a thick silk cushion made for you the Christmas after my uncle bought the accursed chair and I have yet to see you use it."

"The color did not go with the room," his aunt explained.

"It was black," he said dryly, leading them toward the open doorway.

"Very well, since you insist on knowing the reason, I would not give your uncle the satisfaction of using it."

Darcy sighed through his nose. "Aunt Catherine, the scoundrel has been dead for years. You use that room and that chair to intimidate your guests, I know, but you could still sit on a cushion."

"I shall have Durling search it out for me, if it will please you," his aunt promised.

"It would," Darcy said, patting her hand. "And kindly use it."

Billings, who had been hovering in the hall with several maids and footmen, stepped forward when they entered it and bowed. "The study, my lady?"

Lady Catherine nodded. "How was your tea, Billings?"

"Excellent, my lady," he said, turning to walk ahead of them to the study, a smaller room that acted like an antechamber to the vast Rosings library.

Behind them, Darcy heard the whisper-soft tread of his aunt's servants as they descended upon the drawing room to clear away any evidence of the tea party so recently completed.

They entered the study to find it occupied by a tall footman closing the shutters and drapes. He finished his work and left unobtrusively. Billings followed directly after he had cast an experienced eye over the room and the coal fire.

As soon as he shut the door, Darcy led his aunt to her favorite chair beside the fire. She sat and he settled opposite her.

"Did you see outside the window before the footman closed the shutters?" he asked her.

She shook her head, looking puzzled.

"It was almost dark."

She raised her eyebrows. "Your point?"

"You sent your guests home without ordering a carriage for them. Your barouche is large enough for all of them."

His aunt shrugged. "What of it? The Collins' frequently walk home."

"I would have ordered my own carriage, but I thought you had arranged one," Darcy said, biting off his words. "What must they think of us?"

Lady Catherine snorted. "They will think nothing of it. What right do they have to think anything of their betters?"

Darcy glared at her and she glared right back.

"It would have been a kindness," Darcy said, gentling his voice. "You must remember how to be kind. My mother, who always spoke fondly of you, would not have cared for you if you had not been kind to her. My uncle could not have squashed all the womanly kindness out of you."

His aunt stiffened. "I do not have the energy to show the outward trappings of kindness. I have other worries on my mind." She swallowed. "Anne…she is not well…"

"She has never been well," Darcy observed.

"This is different."

"How?"

His aunt shook her head absently and looked away from him to stare at the glowing coals. "Something is not right. This morning…"

"Yes," Darcy said, frowning. "When Fitzwilliam returned from driving out with Anne, he claimed not to remember their poor behavior at breakfast."

"That is most disturbing," his aunt said.

"So it seems to me."

Catherine glanced at his expression from the corner of her eye. *He is not going to marry Anne. If he does not, who will look after my girl when I am gone? Jenkinson? What a thought.*

"Could it be Anne's age?" Darcy asked.

"Her age?"

"She is almost as old as I," he reminded her. "Could it be that

Anne is merely exercising some of the authority that comes with maturity?"

Catherine let his words sink in. *Is he right?*

"May I suggest something?"

She met his gaze and waited.

"I thought that, perhaps, if she had a project, something she could be more than just a patroness of, she might feel more in control of her life," Darcy explained. "I know she is a patroness of an orphanage for girls in Canterbury, but she does nothing more than send them money."

"She is also a patroness for a charity here that assists in the education of destitute children."

"Excellent. But, she needs something to do with the estate, I think."

Catherine barely managed to keep herself from objecting vociferously to such an idea. The estate was *her* purview.

"Like what?" she demanded, inwardly wincing at the revelatory tone of her voice. In a quieter, more controlled tone, she repeated her question. "Like what?"

Darcy shook his head. "I cannot know. I do not know her interests."

Glancing back at the fire, she squeezed the arms of her chair, thinking. "I have had her in the office when the estate manager comes for direction and she soon loses interest."

"She will not be interested in something she has no power over," Darcy remarked. He stiffened and said, "Aunt Catherine." His aunt tore her gaze from the fire. Their gazes locked and he said, "You must know that I do not mean to marry Anne. I have told you so before but you have always held out hope."

Catherine almost leapt out of her chair. Her heart pounded against her chest wall in such a painful fashion that she gasped. She *had* known it. But she did not *want* to know it.

"I love another," he admitted. "And even if I did not, I would not have married Anne. We do not suit."

"What did you say?"

"You heard me, madam," Darcy said. He cocked his head to one side. "Anne will need to marry another if she cannot learn to run the estate herself. She is a wealthy woman. Finding her a husband should not be that difficult."

"But I want the estate to remain in the family," she said fiercely. "*Our* side of the family."

Darcy stood. "I am not Anne's only male cousin." He bowed. "Pray excuse me. I have some letters to write."

Catherine watched him leave, her mind in a whirl.

All through their evening meal, Catherine said hardly a word. Instead, she ate first the turtle dove consommé, then slices of roast duck that had been stuffed with dried fruit and wrapped in bacon. She tasted nothing, only eating with automatic efficiency. During her meal, she watched her daughter. Finally, when the sweet course had been delivered, and the footmen had withdrawn, she spoke.

"Anne, my dear, you seem tired."

Her daughter shook her head listlessly. "No, Mother. I am all right."

"I did not say you were sick, Anne," Catherine said, sharpish.

Anne winced and cast a quick glance at her military cousin before she stared down at her bowl of lemon syllabub.

If only she would stop being afraid of me. I have loved her from before her birth. Why can she not see that? Everything I do, I do for her.

Catherine paused to take a breath, continuing once she knew she could speak calmly. "You are tired, merely. And no wonder. You went out driving this morning and then attended our tea party." She bit back a reminder of the words exchanged earlier in the morning. There would be no useful purpose served by canvasing that incident over again, particularly in light of what Darcy had told her. *Least said, soonest mended,* her old nanny used to tell her.

"Perhaps Colonel Fitzwilliam will take you for a gentle stroll down the gallery before you retire," Catherine suggested. "A little exercise always helps you sleep."

A hint of belligerence clouded Anne's countenance. Catherine readied herself for an uncharacteristic hostile retort. Just as her daughter opened her mouth, her nephew touched her hand.

"May I?" he asked, an eyebrow lifted in enquiry. "I have not seen the pictures there in an age and it may be a year or more ere I see them again."

"Oh, no," Anne said breathlessly, turning to him, displaying her anxiety for all to see. "Do not say so. A year? As much as that?"

"There is trouble brewing between our colony and the new United

States. I fear we may soon be at war on another front," he confessed, frowning now.

"But you do not have a regiment," Anne cried softly.

Catherine wisely kept her opinion of the dire possibility of another war to herself. She watched her daughter from beneath her brow while she ate her syllabub without truly tasting it.

"You are correct. I am seconded to Robert Jenkinson, the Secretary of War and the Colonies. He is Lord Liverpool, you know."

Mrs. Jenkinson gave a start.

Darcy raised his eyebrows. "Are you related to Lord Liverpool, madam?"

Her hands fluttered. "Only distantly, sir," she said, shrugging a little.

"I did not know you were so well connected," Colonel Fitzwilliam said, surprise and kindly pleasure on his face.

Catherine knew, of course, but she had not touted it about like a fool. She could not, however, let anyone believe her ignorant about any aspect of the woman's history. Mrs. Jenkinson was, after all, hired to be her only child's companion.

"Very distantly," Catherine said in a repressive voice.

Anne waved such connections aside and demanded of her cousin, the colonel, "You will not be made to fight, will you, John? Because you have no regiment?"

Lady Catherine blinked. *John? She stopped calling him by his first name when he joined the army. Well.*

The focus of Anne's attention frowned and shook his head, not in the negative, but in acknowledgement of the possibility. "Though I have none, I could be assigned a militia regiment. Earlier this month, Sir George Prevost ordered that fencible men are to be recruited from Upper Canada. They will need a leader. If I am on hand…?" He shrugged and fell silent.

Anne covered her pale lips with a trembling white hand.

"Fitzwilliam, you are alarming us," Catherine said, glaring at him.

Her nephew's eyes widened in sudden realization, and he turned to Anne. "I do beg your pardon, Cousin Anne. I am a wretch to be talking of these things at the dinner table. Pray do not regard my speculations, for that is all they are. I shall be back in England in a trice."

Anne took her hand away and smiled tremulously at him. He

smiled back, pointedly picked up his spoon, waited for her to do likewise, and began to eat his syllabub.

"This is exceptional," he praised. "What do you think, Mrs. Jenkinson?"

"Oh, yes," she said with her annoying titter. "Nicely tart."

Lifting a plate of Kentish cobnut shortbread, she offered them to the colonel. He took one and urged one on Anne, who reluctantly took one, giving a shuddering breath of distress seen down the table by her mother.

Catherine felt the force of her other nephew's gaze upon her. She looked away from her daughter and met Darcy's steady, grave regard. Her only response was to raise an eyebrow.

I will not be pushed, she thought. *I must have time to think.*

Chapter Ten

Monday morning, Charlotte and Lizzy ventured out to the smithy, who was also the village farrier. Jem, the stable boy, followed a few steps behind them, carrying several pliable baskets—one empty and one full. Sunday had been spent quietly at church and at home, playing family games. Everyone had gone to bed early.

Once they explained their purpose to Mary in the privacy of Lizzy's room, she had refused on principle to go with them this morning. She was shaking her head at them when Maria had peeped around the door, searching out the ladies.

"Maria and I are going exploring," Mary claimed, much to the evident surprise of her companion, who walked in and closed the door behind her.

Lizzy frowned at them both. "Do not enter the Rosings' home wood through the standing stones."

Mary narrowed her gaze. "Why not?"

Kicking herself, Lizzy merely said, "Because Charlotte told me of a nearer entrance."

"Yes," her friend said, smiling at the two younger women. "If you take the path behind our church, it leads into the woods. Lady Catherine allows the villagers to use that path because then they are not traipsing across her lawn. This is an excellent scheme, Mary, for this will give you a chance to assist Maria in memorizing something for our recitation tea."

Maria groaned, but the fervent light of pedagogy entered Mary's countenance.

Lizzy and Charlotte had led them down to breakfast, and parted from them soon after. On the way to the smith, they stopped at a half a dozen homes, delivering the invitations that Charlotte had written the day before. Once they completed their deliveries, the ladies stopped at the post office to hand over four other invitations. The postmaster promised to have them delivered that very day.

"If all those young ladies and their doting mamas accept, dearest," Lizzy said to her friend, taking her arm, "your drawing room will be stuffed full. And Miss de Bourgh? Have you already sent an invitation to her and Mrs. Jenkinson?"

Charlotte sighed. "And to Lady Catherine. Mr. Collins and my father will deliver the invitations this morning. Lady Catherine will not come, however. To date she has only come to the parsonage to inspect something."

Lizzy leaned toward her. "That is something to be pleased about, at least. What did Cook say when you told her about the party? Is she up to baking the necessary cakes for our refreshment?"

Charlotte nodded. "Oh, yes. She is eager as anything. I dared not suggest that I procure some things from the bakery, however, for Cook and the baker's wife have a long-standing feud between them."

"Indeed?"

"Oh, yes. Every year at the local fête, they each take turns winning the best in show for their baking. On the year that Cook loses, she feels that *she* should have won."

Lizzy chuckled. "And the year she wins, the baker's wife believes *she* should have won."

"Precisely. I have heard the complaints of both women," Charlotte revealed. "They are sisters, you know."

"Oh, ho," Lizzy chortled. "You are learning much about the villagers in the short time you have been their vicar's wife. Well done."

"I try."

Lizzy squeezed her arm tighter. "I am not surprised. You are a kind and practical woman. I am sure they can see that."

"Thank you, Lizzy."

Chuckling, Lizzy said, "They should count themselves fortunate that they did not get me."

"For shame!" Charlotte cried softly. "You are every bit as kind as I. And you are practical. And intelligent. And much livelier of mind than I shall ever be."

Tutting, Lizzy said, "A woman with a lively wit is not what the parishioners need."

Charlotte smiled and shook her head.

Lizzy could tell that her praise pleased her friend. Patting her arm, she asked, "Will Miss de Bourgh attend?"

"I expect so, unless she is too ill." Charlotte indicated the lane beside the butcher's shop and cottage. "This is the way."

Half-way down the lane, the sound of hammer striking iron assaulted their ears. A break came, and then hammering continued. Soon, they entered the smithy yard. A short, burly man, wearing a leather apron, set down his hammer and exited the forge. He knuckled his forehead.

"'Mornin' Mrs. Collins, ma'am," he said, nodding hesitantly at Lizzy. "Miss."

"Good morning, Mr. Smith," Charlotte said, smiling. "This is my friend, Miss Bennet, who is visiting me." She waited until he touched his forehead again before asking, "How are your wife and new baby?"

Mr. Smith grinned. "Excellent, ma'am. He has some lungs on him does that one."

Charlotte chuckled. "We shall step in and see them if they are not sleeping."

"Mrs. Smith will like that, ma'am."

Lizzy cleared her throat. He turned his brilliant blue gaze on her. "First, Mr. Smith, I would like to purchase some old horseshoes."

"Miss?" He looked between Charlotte and Lizzy, a puzzled expression drawing his brows together. "I melt down most of 'em I git."

Lizzy had been afraid of that. "Only most?"

He pointed to a half-barrel under the eaves. "I wait 'til that is full, first. It's almost full now, miss. But I ain't had the time t'melt 'em yet, what with the new baby and all. I have to clean 'em well, miss, 'afore I can melt 'em. I don't like dirty iron."

"Certainly not," Lizzy agreed, smiling widely at him. "But I do not care if they are dirty. Will you sell me twelve?" He seemed hesitant so she added, "I would like them for a project of mine."

"I see," he replied, sounding dubious.

It was not his place to question the affairs of the quality, so he finally settled on a reasonable price. Lizzy paid him, and Jem carried them away in the empty basket to be left in the parsonage tack room.

He passed the full basket he had brought with him to his mistress before he left.

"Thank you, Mr. Smith," Lizzy said.

"Does you want any nails, miss?" he asked, seemingly just thinking of this potential additional sale.

"I do not require any, thank you."

"Very good, miss."

Charlotte took her leave and Lizzy followed behind her along the path to the smith's cottage, which was attached to the smithy by a short corridor. The hammering started up again. Lizzy wondered how mother and child could sleep through the racket.

They visited with the tired-looking mother for a few minutes while her mother-in-law, who lived with them, removed the packages from the basket. Charlotte had knitted some pretty thumbless red mittens and a cap for the baby. Her cook had made them a dried apple and cinnamon cake, some Kentish pasties, as well as a large jar of calf's foot jelly for the recovering mother. Beside the mother on the table, Lizzy spied an iron rattle, hung with tiny bells that dangled from tiny iron loops.

"Did your husband make your darling rattle?" Lizzy asked.

"Aye, miss."

"How charming," Lizzy said, smiling widely. "The faeries cannot carry off a baby who holds that rattle."

Mrs, Smith's eyes widened and she exchanged a look with her mother-in-law. "No, miss," she whispered.

Old Mrs. Smith nodded emphatically. "No, miss. And I'm liking yer bracelet, miss."

Lizzy shook her wrist so the iron charms jingled against themselves. "Thank you."

Well, they at least know to take precautions.

Walking back to the parsonage together, Lizzy continued to glance around to see if any of their 'friends' lurked about the village. She saw none, though she had been warned by the gypsy witch that not seeing a member of the fae meant little.

"Do you still have your iron bangle?" Lizzy asked Charlotte suddenly. Her friend nodded. "I have not seen you wear it since I arrived."

"I have not worn it since I married. There has been so much to do…I have not given a thought to…" Her voice trailed away. "I shall put it on when we get home."

"Perhaps we should have bought some nails," Lizzy mused.

"I saw a container of them in the stables. If we need some, we can use those. When shall we take the horseshoes to Rosings?" Charlotte asked softly.

Lizzy swiveled her head around to stare at her friend. "You shall not be coming with me."

"What?" Charlotte demanded, her eyes widening. "You cannot be thinking of going alone."

"I must. If I am caught, you will be in disgrace," Lizzy explained quietly. "Think of what Mr. Collins would say."

"You cannot go alone. At least take Mary with you."

"Mary? She will argue against my actions from the house to Rosings and back again," Lizzy claimed in affectionate disgust.

"Quite likely. Take Jem, then. You cannot take a lantern. Someone will see you."

"I will wait for the moon to rise. It is nearing full tonight, I believe. I cannot take Jem. If I should be seen or caught, you must be able to blame it all on me and you cannot do so if Jem comes with me. I can manage the basket."

Charlotte glanced about to see who might overhear them, and then spoke even more quietly, "Surely, it would be better for us to convince Lady Catherine to place iron around her home instead of sneaking about in the dead of night?"

"Do you honestly believe she would agree?"

Charlotte had no reply.

"Do not repine too much upon my adventures," Lizzy told her. "We shall distract ourselves this afternoon by planning your party and choosing a piece to recite. We wish to present a good showing, do we not?"

"Yes, indeed," Charlotte said weakly.

ℵ

The moon rose before it grew dark. All through the evening, Mary and Charlotte gave her significant looks Lizzy blithely ignored. After dinner, they arranged themselves to play whist and had just chosen a dealer when a knock sounded at the front door.

"Now, who could that be?" Sir William asked, swiveling in his chair until he half-faced the door to the parlor. "One of your parishioners, Mr. Collins?"

Mr. Collins lips tightened. He did not like parishioners to call in the evening. He was available all day long, he had told the Bennets at Longbourn, but he kept his evenings as his own. Only the dying had a claim on his attentions after his evening meal.

Charlotte rose, which prompted her husband to join her. They could hear men's voices in the corridor, then footsteps, and finally Hibben opened the door, stood to one side, and said, "Mr. Darcy and Colonel Fitzwilliam."

Everyone else stood in polite anticipation. The ladies curtsied and the gentlemen bowed. Lizzy's gaze met that of Mr. Darcy. The intensity of his expression caused her heart to flip. She closed her hands into fists and raised an eyebrow, challenging him for some mysterious reason she could not fathom.

Why does he look at me this way? What have I done to draw his attention?

"Come in, come in," Mr. Collins cried, his countenance adorned with smiling welcome. He waved at his own place at the card table. "What an unexpected pleasure. How pleased I am that you found us at home. Will you not join us?"

Mr. Darcy opened his mouth to respond but his cousin spoke first.

Colonel Fitzwilliam grinned and clapped his hands once so he could rub them together. "What are we playing, eh? Could it be silver loo? Or perhaps whist?"

"It was to be whist," Charlotte explained. "But now that you two are here, would you care for a round or two of loo?"

"Button loo," Maria said, grinning. "Charlotte has a whole jar of buttons we use instead of money."

The colonel sat down in Mr. Collins' place, tucking his chair forward, eager to begin. "Do we get to keep the buttons?"

"No," Maria said, laughing. "They all go back into the jar when we are finished."

She shifted her chair to one side so another seat could be fitted between her and Lizzy. Mr. Darcy took a chair from the wall and placed it in the new spot.

"We are playing for the satisfaction of winning, then?" Mr. Darcy asked in a quiet voice, sitting after being urged to do so by his hostess.

"Yes," Lizzy said tartly. "And for the enjoyment of the game."

"Naturally," Mr. Darcy said. "Are you a proficient card player?"

"I know the rules, but I am not always lucky."

Mary, who sat on Lizzy's other side delivered a polite snort. "Do not listen to her, Mr. Darcy. She *always* wins."

"I do not!" Lizzy cried, ruining the effect of her affected outrage by grinning widely.

Darcy's gaze met her darling, provoking, laughing eyes, and his stomach tightened. He suspected his expression also tightened in reaction for she stopped grinning and raised a quizzical eyebrow at him. No other woman in his life affected him the way Miss Bennet did. He was more aware of her sitting beside him than of Miss Lucas who sat on his other side.

The game began and Miss Bennet played button-loo with as much vivacity as if they played for gold sovereigns. She seemed to glow from within and more than once he could not seem to catch his breath. As a result of his distraction, he played rather poorly. Darcy dropped three buttons into the pot just as Miss Bennet passed him the cards so he could deal.

"Do not be dismayed by the meagre number of buttons sitting in front of you, Mr. Darcy," she said with a false moue of sympathy. "I have designs on those red ones and mean to relieve you of their burden."

Darcy placed a protective hand over his ludicrously small pile of buttons. "Do not concern yourself, Miss Bennet. They are no burden, I assure you."

She laughed.

His cousin spoke up. "Darcy, I have never known you to play so poorly. Miss Bennet will begin to think you a dullard if you cannot win back some of the buttons from her mammoth pile."

"I warned you all that Lizzy always wins," Mary said, shaking her head in apparent resignation. "*'A foole and his money be soone at debate: which after with sorow repents him too late.'*"

"I do not know that one," Miss Lucas complained, placing three buttons in the pot because she had taken no tricks.

"I believe it is the origin of 'A fool and his money are soon parted.' Or buttons, in our case," the colonel explained. "Do not despair, Miss Mary, your sister may covet Darcy's red buttons, but I mean to have those blue ones of hers."

Everyone chuckled, except for Darcy. However, he could not stop himself from smiling at his cousin's sally.

Loo was a game that lasted until the players tired of it, or the tokens belonged to only a few of the players. The game, therefore, continued until Hibben brought tea in at ten o'clock. Miss Bennet had saved her blue buttons from the colonel and had not managed to take Darcy's red ones. The amused, playful gaze she cast his way more than compensated him for his distraction from the game and the loss of most of his stash.

"You are fortunate, sir, that loo is not played with partners," she said, collecting her buttons to return to the jar. "Else you would have had him staring daggers at you throughout the evening."

"No doubt," Darcy acknowledged, the corners of his mouth lifting.

The buttons dropped home, tinkling or rattling as they fell. Darcy secretly separated his red ones, held them in his closed fist, and when he and his cousin took their leave, he surreptitiously slipped them into Miss Bennet's hand as he bowed over it. Her startled gaze leapt to his. He inclined his head to the side in acknowledgement of her look.

Following the colonel down the parsonage steps, he felt even more hopeful that the woman whom he intended to marry showed some interest in him. While there was no Godly reason why she should refuse his offer of marriage, he did not want a wife who only married him for his £10,000 a year.

ꕥ

Lizzy climbed the stairs to her bedchamber, her fingers curled around the three buttons, wondering what Mr. Darcy had meant by the gift. The red glass trinkets were not really his to give, yet she felt peculiarly reluctant to return them to Charlotte's collection.

He is a strange man…yet, oddly compelling…why do I think that? He has hardly spoken to me in the months that I have known him. If I wrote down every word he has said, I doubt I could create a single printed page. And most of those words have been indifferent to the point of rudeness. Frequently, all he does is look at me.

Lizzy confessed to herself that Mr. Wickham's charming, easy manner pleased her far more than Mr. Darcy's stiff one. On the surface, at least. But she had recently discovered that she could not love the militia officer. She did not understand why, however. Was it that he had no money? *Am I so shallow?* No, she realized, it was not shallowness that held her back. If she had loved him, Lizzy would not have cared about his money or his prospects—even though her practical side urged her not to be foolish about it.

I do not love the penniless Mr. Wickham any more than I love the fabulously wealthy Mr. Darcy.

Now where has that thought come from?

Of course, I do not love Mr. Darcy. How could I?

An hour later, Lizzy rose from her seat by the window, picked up her dark-green cloak, and put it around her shoulders. She would not wait any longer. The clock in the entrance hall had chimed midnight and everyone should be asleep. Tugging on her gloves, she crept softly across the bedchamber carpet, turned the door handle, and nearly screamed when she spied someone in the corridor.

Mary.

In her nightdress and robe.

The light of the lamp on the stair landing threw her sister in shadowed relief. Mary put a finger to her lips and pushed past Lizzy into her bedchamber. She sat on the edge of Lizzy's bed and swept her hand in a signal that her sister should close her door. Lizzy did so and frowned at her.

"What are you doing here?" Lizzy whispered, approaching. "Why are you not asleep?"

Mary rolled her eyes. "Someone must be awake to await your return from this foolish bit of unasked for service." She sniffed and glanced away. "Besides, I could not sleep a wink knowing you are going out into the cold, dark, and undoubtedly dank night. Alone. Do no worry. I waited until Maria fell asleep. She is a deep sleeper."

Still whispering, Lizzy said, "There is no reason for anyone to come with me. Or stay awake for me. I am perfectly capable of—"

Mary waved her words aside. "Yes, yes, you told me so already. I am aware that you think you do not need anyone."

Lizzy frowned. "Whatever can you mean?"

"I believe my remark was perfectly understandable."

Perching beside her, Lizzy softly refuted her sister's statement. "I assure you, I need all my family and friends. *No man is an island,*" she quoted. "One of Sir William's favorites."

"*Entire of itself,*" Mary said, adding her mite to the quotation. "Perhaps I shall use John Donne's poem for my recitation. Unless you mean to?"

"Do you know it all?" Lizzy asked, an eyebrow cocked.

Mary raised her eyebrows and gave her a "look".

"Of course, you do," Lizzy praised with a lopsided grin.

"However, I do not mean to recite John Donne," Mary said, shaking her head. "You are free to use it."

"Truly? Because, I think I already know half of it."

"Truly."

"If you will teach me the rest, then I shall recite it at the party. You know so many and can choose from hundreds, I daresay. Will you be my instructress?" Lizzy asked, praying that her sister would accept this olive branch. "I thought you might quote from Walter Scott."

Shaking her head, Mary sighed. "I expect some of the other young women will quote from his romantic poems. I wish to avoid the humiliation of being considered a dreadful copier. I have chosen something else. I shall write out 'No Man is an Island' for you if you do not arrive home in disgrace from this night's folly."

Lizzy gave her an impulsive hug, awkward in her cloak. "I shall return safely, I promise you."

"There is no way for you to promise such a thing," Mary whispered harshly. "The most you can say is that you will do your best to return safely." She pressed her lips together as though attempting to hold back her opinions. She failed. "Your best would be not to go at all. Are you planning on wearing that ridiculous bracelet on such a furtive enterprise? It makes enough noise to alert the devil to your movements."

Lizzy pressed her right hand around the bracelet, silencing it. "I must wear it. The charms are iron."

Mary rolled her eyes. "I shall wait in here. No one will think it odd, for you always have a lamp on. I have brought a book."

From within her tied robe, she brought out a thin blue volume, opened it to a bookmarked page, and stared down at it, seemingly ignoring her sister. Sighing, Lizzy touched her shoulder.

"I shall be back as quickly as possible."

"No doubt," Mary expressed in a tight whisper.

Lizzy let herself out the back door, locking it after her, and dropping the key into the reticule that dangled from her wrist. She was not so lost to what was due her cousin and her friend that she would leave them vulnerable to thieves.

The almost full moon lit the yard most satisfactorily. A cold nip sharpened the air, but she believed exercise would mitigate its influence. Besides, she wore her wool pelisse beneath her cloak.

A night lantern hung outside the stable. By its light she found the basket holding the iron horseshoes. Her cousin's Welsh cob nickered a greeting. The black and white cob lifted his head over the door and watched her heave the basket into her arms.

Lizzy took a few steps and knew at once that she could not carry the heavy basket all the way to Rosings across the park. Spying an empty wheelbarrow propped up against the side of the shed, she determined that she would simply have to borrow it, and hope that pushing it along the path across the park would not prove too arduous.

Oh, dear, I hope its wheel does not squeak.

The wooden device had low sides and an iron strapped wheel. Lizzy quietly deposited the basket on the bed of the wheelbarrow, picked up the handles and gave an experimental push. She sighed with relief—the wheel did not squeak. The horseshoes rattled, however. Lizzy folded the soft basket over the iron and hoped for the best.

I could use a trowel, she thought, looking around the silvery, lighted yard. The shadows seeped darkness as though attempting to steal back everything revealed by the moon. Seeing no hand tools left out of the locked shed, she set her chin and proceeded to make her way out into the park. The path they had used to take tea with Lady Catherine could easily be seen now that Lizzy's eyes had fully adjusted to the dark.

Concentrating, she brought the dim energy threads always hovering in the background into brilliant focus. Three crossed the park in straight lines. They came in varying degrees of intensity, with the brightest of these leading directly to Rosings. This did not surprise her. Lizzy expected a well could be found in the bowels of the house. Perhaps because water was a life-giving element, lines formed between sources of the liquid—ponds, wells, rivers, creeks, lakes, and so forth.

The lines did not light her way, however, because they did not shine on other objects the way a candle or lantern did. She relaxed her concentration and the lines faded to golden filaments lying in the background of her attention.

Lizzy saw no members of the fair folk on her journey, which did not surprise her. Her bracelet, the iron horseshoes and the iron wheel of the cart kept them away. She took several rest breaks, shaking the discomfort out of her arms before picking up the handles of the wheelbarrow again and continuing. When she reached the edge of the gravel drive where it swept through a brick fence encompassing the close-in garden, she found the ornate black iron gates shut.

"Oh, bother," she said beneath her breath. "I should not be surprised to discover that these hinges squeak."

However, they did not squeak because they were locked.

Lizzy clamped her mouth shut against an unladylike expletive burning her tongue. Having no wish to push this confounded wheelbarrow another inch, Lizzy opened the basket and thrust the horseshoes through the bars of the gate two at a time. Folding the basket in half, she shoved it through the gate as well. She looked up from her completed task only to see a large dog staring at her from within the garden. He sat on his haunches, his head tilted to one side.

Lizzy pressed a flat hand to her chest. "How long have you been there, boy?" she asked softly. "You gave me quite a turn."

The dog chuffed in reply. Charlotte had told her that the Rosings Park dogs seemed very approachable. Her friend, however, had never attempted a middle-of-the-night visit when the dogs were on duty. He rose to his feet and padded across the gravel toward her. Instead of stopping in front of her, he went to the side and slipped through the gap between the brick pilaster and the gate frame. Pleased with his trick, he stood before her with tail wagging and mouth open in a canine grin.

Lizzy held out her hand to be sniffed. He obligingly sniffed and waited for his pat. She petted him and pulled gently on his ears.

"Do you think I am small enough to get through the same way you did?" she asked. "You are quite a big dog. I shall try. Do you want to go first?"

The erstwhile guard dog turned away from her and slipped back into the garden as though he spoke perfectly good english. Lizzy tucked her hood and cloak around her and followed the dog. Turning sideways, she stepped over the lower hinge and under the middle hinge. Fortunately, the tall gate had hinges set far apart. Once on the other side, she straightened and brushed herself down, looking around for the dog. He was greeting two other dogs.

"Does your mistress know you receive strangers to your garden like long-lost friends?" she asked them softly.

The other two dogs chuffed at her, approached for a sniff, and gamboled off together. *Perhaps,* she thought, *they are used to women and do not consider them potential enemies.*

Hurrying over to the horseshoes, Lizzy piled them into the basket and lugged them down the drive to the front door. The sound of her feet on the gravel made her wince. When she could, she stepped off the drive and onto the grass verge. Resting often, she finally left her basket near the corner of the big house, and carried just two horseshoes to the front door.

Crouching, she pushed the leg ends of one of the horseshoes into the damp dirt of the flower bed next to the shallow steps leading into the house. Lizzy had to lean on the iron with all her weight to get it buried up to the top arch of the shoe. Only the apex of the arch stuck above the cold ground. She stood, panting, and scurried around to the other side of the door to repeat the action.

This is more difficult than I thought it would be.

Lizzy shrugged with resignation. It had to be done. A slight sound behind her made her think one of the dogs had returned to see what she was doing. Perhaps they hoped to help her dig.

"Are these yours?"

It was not a dog.

Chapter Eleven

Startled once more, Lizzy fell back from her crouch onto her bottom, her hands behind her splayed in the grass. Her heart pounded the type of beat a drummer would have been proud to create.

"Heavens!" she cried softly. "You frightened me half to death!"

One of the dogs began licking her face.

"Stop that," she ordered, sitting up and pushing him away.

"They're not much good at guardin' against ladies, miss."

The man crouched a little, seemingly to make himself less of a threat. The moon hung behind the house, leaving them both in shadow.

"I trained 'em t' come an' git me if they find an intruder, miss," he continued. "That's why they didn't bark at ye. Her ladyship don't like 'em barkin' at night."

Ah, he is one of Lady Catherine's servants.

"I do not blame her," Lizzy repeated, relaxing. She held out a hand. "Kindly assist me in rising, if you please."

"Aye, miss," he said, taking her gloved hand. He pulled and stood in one movement, then he released it the moment she found her feet.

"Are you one of the gardeners?" she asked quietly.

"I am, miss. Harold's me name. I'm Frank's brother, who y'met t'other day."

"Did he tell you we met?"

"He did."

"Come with me, please. Now, how did you recognize me, and do you know what I am doing?" Lizzy asked quietly, leading him along the front of the house toward the right side. According to Charlotte, there was an entrance at the end of each wing.

"Frank was that impressed w'ye, miss that he told me all about ye. Who else might be brave enough t'bury iron at either side of the big house's doors?" he asked, holding up the basket of horseshoes for emphasis. "To protect against *them*? No one 'round 'ere."

"Not even Frank?"

"Nooo, miss. Not Frank," he said, chuckling. "He's afraid of Lady Catherine, he is."

"She is a formidable lady," Lizzy acknowledged, chuckling and glancing up at him. Now that they had turned the corner, moonlight fell full upon his grizzled countenance and she blinked, slowing her step. "Goodness."

"I'm Frank's twin, miss," he said, grinning.

"So you are," she replied. One of the dogs brought her a long stick. She took it and threw it behind them. The dogs took off. "Do you mean to help me with the shoes, Harold? I would be grateful."

"Well, miss," he began hesitantly. "Her ladyship—"

Interrupting him, Lizzy said, "If one of the other gardeners finds a shoe, you can tell him *I* buried it. I have no desire for you to get into trouble because of *my* precautions."

From within the shadows of the doorway, a male voice asked, "What precautions are those, Miss Bennet?"

"Goodness," Lizzy said, jumping, and then glaring at Mr. Darcy's dark shape. "We were speaking quietly, were we not, Harold?"

"Aye, miss," the gardener said. He touched his hand to his cap. "Mr. Darcy, sir."

Lizzy faced the newcomer. "Therefore, we could not have woken you, Mr. Darcy. Then I must suppose, sir, that you have come outside for a breath of fresh air? In the middle of the night?"

"Indeed. Imagine my surprise at finding you here…er…fraternizing with Harold, my aunt's head gardener."

Lizzy scowled, not liking his tone. "I have a perfectly good reason for being here."

The dogs came tearing back before she could explain further, and dropped the stick in front of Lizzy. Then they noticed the new presence in the shadows and one of them growled.

"That is enough," Mr. Darcy said to them, stepping out of the shadows and into the moonlight.

Recognizing his voice, the dog abased herself, whining in a bid for forgiveness from her friend.

"They like you," Lizzy commented.

"You need not sound surprised," Mr. Darcy replied dryly. He held out a hand to the gardener for the basket. Harold immediately surrendered it. Apparently, Mr. Darcy did not expect the weight of the iron within, for the basket dropped out of his hand and fell to the cold ground with a distinct clunk. "What the devil?"

Lizzy stiffened. "I beg your pardon. Is it the darkness that leads you to believe that such language is acceptable in my presence?"

Darcy cursed silently and bowed to her. "Forgive me. I forgot myself."

She delivered a most provoking sniff.

"What, may I ask, is in this basket?"

He leaned over to pick it up. He waved away Harold's offer of assistance. He would have dismissed the gardener, but he did not wish to damage Miss Bennet's reputation even further. *It is the middle of the night, for God's sake—as she pointed out herself. Whatever her reason for being on the grounds of Rosings at this hour must not bring about her social ruin.*

"Horseshoes," she stated in a soft, bald voice.

"And what are you doing with them?" he asked, hoping he sounded merely curious and not accusatory.

"I am burying them."

Darcy could only stare at her shadowed features.

"Yes, yes. It may seem foolish to you," she said, quiet exasperation in her voice. "But you asked."

Glancing at the patient gardener, he enquired, "And you meant to assist Miss Bennet in this odd behavior?"

"Aye," Harold said, touching the brim of his cap. "Iffen you've no objection, sir."

"May I have two of those?" Miss Bennet asked rather impatiently, reaching for the basket. "It is freezing out here and I mean to get some sleep tonight. *And*," she stressed, "Mary is waiting up for me, too. Why would that be, you might ask? In order to give the alarm if I do not return in a timely fashion. I do not mean to give her cause to be alarmed."

After that speech, Darcy automatically opened the handles so she could fumble inside until she withdrew two shoes. Then, to his utter astonishment, she knelt beside the door and pushed one of them into the ground. She had to lean her entire weight upon the shoe to push it most of the way in.

"Pray, do not be offended if I offer you some advice, Miss Bennet. But, once it is partly in, why do you not simply step on it?" he asked, unable to help himself from giving this piece of advice. "Your leg muscles are much stronger than those of your arms."

Miss Bennet stood and shook her head at him. "I am surprised at you."

Harold interrupted their exchange. He hurried over and took the second shoe from her. "Beggin' yer pardon, miss, I'll do that. I shoulda done the first."

"Thank you," Miss Bennet said, stepping aside.

Darcy stirred. "Why are you surprised at me?"

She huffed out a cloud of breath. "I expected you to demand to know why I am out in the middle of the night, wandering around Rosings Park, putting horseshoes beside the doors."

Darcy frowned. This unexpected opportunity to be alone—almost alone—with Miss Bennet had gone to his head. She was right, of course.

"What *are* you doing out here?" he asked, and then looked down at the basket. "Hold on…iron." A growl of annoyance laced his next words. "Is this some superstitious nonsense?"

Miss Bennet nodded. "Pray, what other reason could there be?" She put her hands on her hips and cocked her head at him. In a teasing voice, she asked, "Really, Mr. Darcy, are you that unfamiliar with the folklore of our great nation?"

Through gritted teeth, he said, "I am not unfamiliar with folk tales and stories told to little children to keep them in their beds at night. But I am surprised that a modern woman of your intelligence acts on something so ludicrous that it begs to be stared at."

"Are you? Ignorance of the reality of 'others' does you no credit, Mr. Darcy."

Her tart comment made him stiffen. In a voice dripping with hauteur, he said, "Natural mysteries are just that. Mysteries. Superstition merely attempts to explain the unexplainable."

"There are explanations for the natural mysteries of our world, Mr. Darcy, even if you do not wish to know them," she said quietly. "If you mean to accompany me, let us move along to the next door.

Harold is done."

Darcy ground his teeth at her implied insult to his intelligence, and walked with her to the next door. It led to the kitchens. Two iron boot scrapers adorned the entrance, one on each side of the door.

"We do not need to bury any here," Miss Bennet whispered. "The door knocker is iron, as well. It is a shame the knocker on the front door is brass. Come along."

"Are you attempting to ward off evil, Miss Bennet?" Darcy asked, stalking along beside her hurried footsteps. "Surely we have left the dark ages behind us."

"Open your mind, Mr. Darcy. Warding off evil is not precisely my intent."

Slowing her steps, she peered around them in a suspicious way, her eyes narrowed and searching.

"Who are you looking for?" he asked, following her gaze. "The dogs?"

Shaking her head, she began walking again. "Not the dogs. I was looking for *them*."

"Them? Whom do you mean?"

"The fair folk," she whispered.

Darcy stopped in his tracks. *I was concerned about my future wife's family. Now I must wonder if she is mad.* Yet, he had seen no evidence of madness in her when he stayed at Netherfield. *The fair folk? I must not jump to conclusions. Perhaps I did not hear her correctly.*

He trailed after her, since she had not waited for him even though he carried the basket. Harold, who was walking just behind Miss Bennet, took the carrier from his unresisting fingers.

"I'll jist take that, sir," he murmured. "Makes no sense fer you t'carry it when I'm here. It's an addle-headed thing t'do and I ain't addle-headed."

Darcy did not reply. Instead, to Miss Bennet, he said, "Faeries? *Faeries?* Miss Bennet, I—"

"—know nothing about them," she said, interrupting the beginning of his rant by finishing his sentence. "Most individuals of our class know little to nothing about them, so do not berate yourself for your ignorance. Simply acknowledge it. Harold, here, knew instantly what I was about."

Smarting, Darcy replied pompously. "The superstitious thinking of the lower orders is well known."

"They, at least, have the commonsense that we have abandoned in favor of book-learning. Ah, here is another door," she said, standing to one side so the gardener could 'plant' the horseshoes. "I understand there is a door at the end of every wing. I brought twelve shoes. We have used six so far and there is only one other door."

Harold rose from the ground to move to the other side of the entrance. He paused and said, touching his cap, "There's three double doors in the outside wall of t'ballroom, miss. There's not been a ball here fer ever so long. Mayhap missus didna know about them."

"Do they open out onto a terrace?" Miss Bennet asked.

"Aye, miss. A stone 'un."

"Oh, dear."

Against his reason, Darcy sought to reassure her. "There are iron drapery rails in that room. Drapes hang over every door and window."

"That will do nicely," Miss Bennet said, looking up at him. "Thank you for sharing that information."

The moonlight fell upon her countenance, and he saw that she was beaming. His heart, usually a reliable muscle, flipped and he could hardly breathe. He smiled back, but she turned away as though she had not seen it. Swallowing his disappointment, he offered her his arm.

"One more door," he said, "and then I shall escort you to the parsonage."

Miss Bennet took his arm. "You are kind to offer to accompany me. It is unnecessary, however. The moon is full, and I can clearly see my way."

"I insist," Darcy said quietly.

"Very well."

"Miss Bennet, surely you realize there is an excellent chance that one of the other gardeners will see the horseshoes and remove them, thereby negating all your efforts tonight?"

She waved that concern aside. "Harold will keep an eye on them. Will you not, Harold?"

"Aye," the old man said from behind them. "Iffen it pleases ye, miss, I'll keep the extra shoes. Some of these we've planted might go missin' and I can replace 'em."

"An excellent notion," Miss Bennet praised.

Lizzy stood watch with Mr. Darcy while Harold planted two iron shoes on either side of the final doorway. He needed to wiggle the shoes into the soil beneath a carpet of winter grass. The gardener climbed to his feet and pressed the final one partially into the ground with his foot.

"That should hold 'em off, miss," Harold said, turning to face her.

"The old ways are often the best ways," Lizzy said, nodding. "Thank you, kindly, for all your assistance."

The gardener knuckled his forehead. "Does y'need this here basket back, miss?"

"I do."

Harold fished the last of the horseshoes out of the basket and handed it back to her. Mr. Darcy took the carrier before she could.

"I shall carry it," he said. "You may go now, Harold."

"Sir," Harold said, touching his brow once more. "I'll jist unlock the stable gate fer ye, Mr. Darcy, sir. You won't fit through the gap at the front like miss did. And I'll wait fer yer return. I don't like t'go t'bed with the gate unlocked."

"Thank you," Mr. Darcy said.

Once they left the stable yard, Lizzy paused and thanked Harold again for his help and bade him goodnight. She saw Mr. Darcy slip a coin into the older man's hand.

"Well done," Mr. Darcy said quietly.

"Good night, Harold," Lizzy said.

"Thank ye, sir. Miss."

He watched them until they had reached the path that encircled the walls of the inner park. Lizzy directed Mr. Darcy in the direction of the front gate.

"Since you deem it necessary to accompany me, I will ask you to kindly push the wheelbarrow back to the parsonage for me," Lizzy said, relief coloring her voice. "I was not looking forward to the return trip. Pushing it along the grass path through the park proved decidedly difficult."

Mr. Darcy chuckled. "I imagine it did. Why did you bring it?"

"The basket was too heavy for me to carry very far," Lizzy confessed. "I believe, in the end, that I struggled just as much with the wheelbarrow as I would have simply carrying the basket. I am not as strong as I thought I was. It is a lowering thought."

"You will have sore muscles tomorrow," Mr. Darcy predicted.

"I suppose you think that will serve me right?"

"Not at all."

She heard the amusement behind his reply and fell silent.

"Are you enjoying your visit with Mrs. Collins?"

"Yes. She is my closest friend, besides my dear sister, Jane."

"I know."

Lizzy's gaze flew to his shadowed features. "You do?"

"Are you surprised to learn that I know?"

"I do not scruple to tell you that I am," Lizzy admitted. "I did not think you paid me much mind when you were in Hertfordshire."

"I see." He cleared his throat. "The, uh, society is limited, so discovering something so obvious to all did not prove difficult."

Lizzy frowned.

What an odd thing to say. I cannot tell if he is being dismissive, or is offering me a compliment. Hmm.

Hesitantly, she asked, "Did you make an effort to discover who my friends were?"

After a pause long enough for her to think he had either not heard her question or did not mean to reply, he admitted that he had.

"Oh." Lizzy licked her cold lips. "Why?"

Instead of answering her simple question, he said, "I saw your eldest sister in London."

Lizzy gasped. "Did you? And did you speak to her?"

"I did not. Miss Bennet had a number of children about her. We exchanged nods."

"Those are our cousins." Sighing, Lizzy said, "I am awaiting a letter from her. Did she look well?"

"I thought so. You miss her very much, do you not?"

"Excessively," she readily admitted. "Was…was Mr. Bingley with you?"

"No."

She waited in vain for him to elucidate.

"May I ask," Mr. Darcy said, "when you began to believe in the existence of faeries?"

Why should I tell him anything?

"When did you *stop* believing in them?" she asked.

"I promise you, I have *never* believed in them," he swore. "Nanny did not fill my head with imagined creatures. Instead, she told me about elephants and hippopotami."

The idea of the stiff and arrogant and haughty Mr. Darcy as a little boy in his nursery, softened Lizzy's heart. Gently, she added, "Lions and tigers, too, I suppose?"

"Yes. I remember I had a fine set of wood blocks with a different animal on each side."

"Where are the blocks now?"

"I expect they are still in the nursery. I always looked after my toys."

The unexpected scent of hyacinths filled Lizzy's nose. She stopped walking and sniffed experimentally.

"What is it?" Mr. Darcy asked, pausing to glance back at her. He moved toward her. "Miss Bennet?"

"One moment, please."

Grasping Mr. Darcy's arm, she tilted her head to one side, narrowed her eyes, and the image of a wide silvery pathway, shimmering in the moonlight, appeared before her gaze. This magical path bisected their route. If she had not slipped through the side of the front gate, she would have seen it earlier and known to avoid it on the way back to the wheelbarrow.

"Oh, dear," she whispered, looking along the path toward the village and then in the other direction where the enchanted path disappeared beneath the park wall.

"What is it?" he asked again.

Lizzy released his arm and turned to face him. "There is a faerie path, here," she explained, pointing to a spot to her left. She traced its direction with the sweep of her arm. "Can you help me over it? You can hold my hand and elbow, and then we can leap together. I shall have a better chance at getting clearly over if you help me," she explained. "The path is three feet wide, or near enough to make no difference. I do not know why it is so wide here. Most paths I have seen were only two feet wide. Perhaps there is more traffic here?"

"What is this?" Mr. Darcy demanded in a loud whisper, fisting his gloved hands. "This…this nonsense? Really, Miss Bennet, you are so frustrating at times."

"Am I?" she asked sweetly. Her voice hardened a little as she continued her observation. "I am not so provoking as you are, sir, at this very moment. I asked you a simple question. Pray, answer it. Can you, or rather, *will* you, help me over the faerie path?"

He bit out his reply. "I see no other path than the one beneath our feet."

Lizzy applied a tart sting to her soft reply. "I am *not* surprised."

She released his arm and backed away from him along their own path, blinking away unexpected, disappointed tears. Clearing the tightness out of her throat first, she said, "It is best to take it at a run, I think."

"What are you doing now, Miss Bennet?" he demanded quietly.

"I am going to leap over the faerie path. Kindly step to one side," she directed him. "I advise you to follow my directions. If you choose to step on it, you will likely have nightmares tonight, or wake with the headache. Some unlikely souls become enchanted and discover they must follow the path. They are unable to step off it."

"I cannot credit that you believe such nonsense," Mr. Darcy muttered, turning to step aside.

"No!" she cried softly. "Not that way. Come toward me, instead."

He obeyed her—out of politeness, she did not doubt—continuing to mutter.

"A modern, educated woman does not believe in the…uh…the fair folk."

"I suppose that is written down somewhere?" she asked, indicating that he should stand behind her. Without waiting for an answer, she continued, "At least we do not have the worry of how to get the wheelbarrow over the path for it is already on the other side. Now, I shall go first. Take note of where I step."

"I think you must be mad, Miss Bennet."

Lizzy chuckled, gathering her skirts in both her hands. "I have done my duty by warning you. It is your choice to follow my admonition."

She had not backed up far enough to be in a full run as she approached the path. Even so, she leapt and landed safely on the other side. She came to a halt, and turned to watch Mr. Darcy. Shaking his head first, he followed her example. For a fearful second, she thought he would wait too long to begin his leap. However, he took off without touching the dreadful path and landed beside her with a thump and a huff of expelled air.

"There you go," Lizzy said. "You are game as a pebble. Come along, Mr. Darcy, if you please." She thought she heard him grind his teeth.

He held out his arm for her. Once they were on their way again, he posed a question. "Tell me, Miss Bennet, do your faeries know that you can see them?"

Lizzy bit her lip and thought before responding.

Should I explain even more of my secret to him? Can I trust him not to spread word of my strange ways to others?

He is not exactly loquacious. Foolishly, perhaps, I want him to know. Sharing secrets is a form of intimacy, I suppose. Hmm, I shall blame this madness of revelation on the darkness.

"Miss Bennet?" Mr. Darcy whispered.

His words felt like a nudge to reveal more.

"No, they do not know."

"Are you certain they do not?" he asked.

"I should have said that I do not believe they know. I go to great pains to conceal my ability from them. I never look at them directly, and I act as though they are not present."

"If there were faeries out for a moonlight stroll," he said, seemingly choking on his words, "and they saw you jump over their path, surely they would become suspicious?"

Lizzy swallowed hard. "Good Lord, you are correct," she said quietly, taking a surreptitious glance around them. "We appear to be alone," she whispered. "I forgot to look first. What a fool I am."

"Someone is."

Looking sharply up at him and scowling, she said, "You, Mr. Darcy, have a bad habit of muttering."

"Only around you, Miss Bennet," he shot back.

"Indeed?"

He sighed. "I beg your pardon. I am unused to these sorts of midnight activities."

In spite of his jab about being out in the night, his quiet tone of regret touched her. The cloaking aspect of the dark stripped away some of their drawing room restraint. Lizzy patted his arm.

"The magical world is strange and awe inspiring, particularly to one who has not encountered it before. You are doing exceedingly well."

"I must confess, Miss Bennet, that I do not believe I have encountered it yet."

"Oh, that is not true," she replied without thinking. *What is wrong with me? How can I let Mr. Darcy, of all men, distract me so much?* Rather than elucidate on her statement, she pointed ahead. "Look. The wheelbarrow. There, in the shadows beside the gate. Do you see it?"

"I do."

Darcy moved away from her and Miss Bennet released his arm. He took hold of the wheelbarrow handles and manipulated the cart until they walked together along the path leading across the park in the direction of the parsonage.

"What did you mean," he asked, "when you said that I had encountered the magical world before?"

"In the Chinese drawing room," Miss Bennet stated.

Darcy frowned. "I do not understand."

"Three of the fair folk attended your aunt's tea," she said calmly. "One male and two females."

My mind is in a whirl…how can she believe in…

"No one else can see them," he said with a low growl of annoyance. "How do you expect me to believe your stories?"

"It is true that few have my gift. However, many can 'feel' the creature's presence."

Darcy straightened and released the wheelbarrow handles so that it fell to the ground with a thunk. Turning to face her, and with all the loftiness of his nature, he demanded, "Indeed?"

Miss Bennet faced him, glanced furtively around, and softly asked him, "Do you think it possible that your cousin is being poisoned?"

His mind in a whirl because of this change of subject, he stupidly asked, "The colonel?"

She solemnly shook her head.

"Anne?" he demanded just as softly. "Are you mad? What makes you ask such an absurd question?"

"I understand she has been sickly since her birth. That is rather unusual, is it not?"

"No." Darcy tightened his jaw and repeated his question. "What makes you ask such a question? Who could possibly want her to die?"

"Oh, no," Miss Bennet said. The moonlight fell full upon her face and she grimaced. "Not *die*. There are other reasons to poison someone."

"I know of no other. Kindly explain."

"There used to be a widow woman of independent means living in Meryton. She had two children. One was healthy—the boy. The other was sickly—the girl. When the boy turned eighteen, he joined the navy and left home. He came back to England every few years for a week or two and then left on another voyage. The daughter—twelve when her brother went away for the first time—became sickly after he left. Her mother claimed that the girl pined and that her sadness made her ill."

"What did their doctor say?" Darcy asked. The unreality of this conversation kept his mind reeling.

"Their doctor was old. He did not know what to think, and agreed with the mother that the daughter had no specific malady. He retired when the girl reached her twenty-third year, never having cured her. A single, younger man took his place. He made it his business to attempt to find a remedy for the girl, whom he rapidly came to love."

"And did he?"

"Yes. For, you see, he discovered that the home remedy the mother had been using for years contained a poisonous substance. As long as only a quarter of a teaspoon of the elixir was diluted by a cup of water, the poison only made the daughter ill."

"Why would she poison her own daughter?" Darcy demanded in a low growl.

"She made her ill so the girl would never marry and leave her," Miss Bennet explained. Frowning, she added, "I think she also enjoyed having a sickly daughter because it made the mother more interesting to her friends. They had compassion on her trials, you see."

Darcy picked up the wheelbarrow handles, saying, "I do see. My aunt does not need Anne's illness to make her more *interesting*."

"We should not take the story too literally, sir. The poisoner need not be Lady Catherine."

"No one is making my cousin ill, Miss Bennet."

"I pray you are right."

He did not like how dubious she sounded. His next words grated off his tongue. "You have only met her once. Do not presume to know Anne."

A long silence fell between them. Finally, Miss Bennet sighed.

"I assume I have spoken out of turn, sir. You must know your cousin's health better than I do. I apologize for discomposing you."

He gritted his teeth. "I am not discomposed. How can you suggest that anyone in my aunt's household could possibly wish to keep Anne ill? Your audacity knows no bounds."

"Quite possibly. Pray consider my words."

"No one wou—"

"Mr. Darcy," Mis Bennet said in a colorless voice, "I am exceedingly tired. Must we continue this discussion tonight? If you deem it necessary, kindly let us proceed to the parsonage while we speak."

Put in his place, Darcy resumed his progress, choosing not to make further enquiry. *I thought I loved Miss Bennet. Now, I am not certain I know her well enough to love her. Perhaps I was merely fascinated by her?* The cool night air stirred into a breeze that sent shivers down his spine. *Confound it! Well, one thing remains sure, I am still fascinated by her. Faeries! Poison! Madness!*

"Have you lost your interest, Mr. Darcy?"

He glanced her way, and for a moment he wondered if she had read his mind. Then he realized what she meant.

"You are tired," he gave as an excuse. Gently, he added, "*Exceedingly* tired."

"Thank you," she said in a softened voice. "We shall speak of less contentious things, I think." She paused and brushed some tendrils of hair away from her mouth. "I hope to receive that letter from Jane tomorrow. Does your sister write you often?"

"Georgiana writes once a week, at the very least," Darcy replied, a smile coaxed out of him at the memory. "Her letters are chattier than my estate manager's reports. I learn all the common news from around the estate from her. My manager mostly writes facts and makes requests."

"News is always good to have," she remarked while trying to stifle a yawn. "Even unhappy news."

<Kiss her…kiss her…kiss her…>

Chapter Twelve

"Did you hear that?" Darcy asked, dropping the wheelbarrow again and looking at his companion. Miss Bennet now had her hood pulled up over her head and stood gazing at the ground. The meekness of the pose startled him.

"Hear what, Mr. Darcy? I heard nothing." She pointed at the wheelbarrow. "Pray pick up the handles and let us be on our way."

<KISS HER…KISS HER…KISS HER…>

"That!" he demanded. "It was so loud. How could you not have heard it?"

"I heard nothing," Miss Bennet repeated. "Perhaps it was simply a thought. *Your* thought."

Darcy scowled. He realized that if Miss Bennet could not hear it, then the imperative must be internal. *What sort of thoughts are so loud I imagine the sound can be heard by others?*

Miss Bennet clasped his arm and squeezed it using significant force. With all her strength, he suspected. The action caused the folds of her cloak to fall away from her arms, revealing her strange iron charm bracelet. He thought he heard a mental gasp.

Is madness contagious?

"We are almost there," she said urgently. "Come along, Mr. Darcy. Do not fail me now."

Darcy shook his strange thoughts away and picked up the wheelbarrow handles. He strangled an exasperated groan and returned to pushing it along the path. Up ahead, he could see the dark outline of the parsonage and the square tower of the church beyond.

They did not speak, leaving him to think. It was not that Darcy did not wish to kiss Miss Bennet—he did, most desperately—but this urgent silent command disconcerted him. He would kiss her when the time was right—not when some odd impulse attempted to overtake his reason. This was not the time for kissing. If he followed the odd impulse, he would be taking advantage of a lady in a most despicable way. Whatever he felt for her at the moment, he had too much respect for Miss Bennet to impose on her in the middle of the night, away from those who might defend her from unwanted advances.

Darcy glanced down at her while she continued to latch onto his arm as though the devils of Hades surrounded them.

"Let us hasten our steps," she begged. "Mary is waiting for me."

Darcy was not loath. Obediently, he put more effort into his pushing. Miss Bennet had to skip once or twice to keep up with him, leaving hold of his arm in order to lift up her skirts. She seemed frightened in a way that she had not been during this entire adventure.

<DON'T BE A FOOL…KISS HER…KI—>

BE STILL! Darcy shouted to his mind.

<But why should I?>

Darcy stumbled and almost dropped the wheelbarrow again. His grip convulsed around the handles. He refused to engage the voice. He stiffened his mental resolve, imagining iron walls around his thoughts.

"Are we running now?" Miss Bennet asked him breathlessly, grabbing hold of his arm once more.

Darcy marginally slowed. "It is getting colder. We will be warmer if we move quicker."

"No doubt," she replied, keeping up with him. Then she muttered, "These blasted skirts…"

"Miss Bennet!" he exclaimed softly, diverted. A chuckle escaped with his next words. "What would your governess say about your language?"

"No governess, remember?"

"Ah, yes. I forgot for the moment."

"Perhaps, as we are approaching the house, we should slow down?" she asked in a hushed voice. "Be stealthier?"

"Indeed," Darcy whispered. "To the rear yard?"

"Yes, please."

They entered the rear yard as quietly as possible. The wheelbarrow squeaked once and they stopped moving, standing like a pair of wax figures, waiting to see if the sound had wakened anyone. The only response to the squeak came from a horse in the stable, who stamped his foot and snorted.

Darcy breathed out a long sigh of held-in air. Miss Bennet released his arm and pointed to the shed, miming that he should put the wheelbarrow there. Deciding not to risk making another sound, he picked up the heavy cart and quickly carried it to its place.

When he returned to Miss Bennet, he found her standing at the corner of the parsonage, out of sight of the house windows, holding a large iron key in her left hand, pressed to her chest. She lifted her right and he took it in both of his. She pulled on his hand and leaned forward. He leaned in as well.

Her warm breath fanned his cheek when she whispered, "Thank you so much for your help, sir. I hope Rosings has no more unwelcome visitors."

"As you say," he muttered, unwilling to succumb to a belief in folklore.

"Yes. You still doubt me?" she breathed against his cheek. "There was a male fae on the path just now."

Heart skipping beats, he tried not to sound excessively skeptical when he said, "Was there? Has he gone?"

She nodded, causing her cold soft cheek to rub against his. Darcy longed to pull her into his arms and kiss her cool lips just as the imperative had commanded him to.

"Oh," she said, drawing back a little. Pressing one gloved hand against her cheek, she murmured, "I beg your pardon."

"Do not apologize," he ordered gently. Darcy wondered that she did not hear the loud beating of his heart. It seemed to roar through his own ears.

"Did he try to influence your mind?" she asked breathlessly. "They can, you know. You must be vigilant."

Darcy thought back on the unusual behavior of his family and wondered at this odd explanation for their conduct. *Those urgings just now…*

"Miss Bennet, I…" His voice trailed away for he could not tell her what the *possibly* unnatural urgings had been.

She cleared her throat and swallowed. "Uh…perhaps you can suggest to your aunt that she put more iron drapery rods above the entrances? Other than the ones in the ballroom, I mean. I noticed she had none above the front door. A gift of fine brocade or velvet for the draperies might induce her to follow your advice. The horseshoes will do for now, but the rods will be infinitely more effective. Particularly if someone should remove the horseshoes."

Darcy injected some dry humor into his muttered reply. "*Your* advice you mean?"

"I do *not* think you should tell her that," she said, chuckling a little. She glanced around the corner at the back door. "I should go in."

Daringly, Darcy lifted her hand to his lips and kissed her knuckles. "Good night, Miss Bennet. This time together has been revelatory."

"Th…thank you…I think," she said, withdrawing her hand. "Remember to go the long way around the wall so you can avoid the faerie path."

"The path…yes." *Not bloody likely. It is too cold to extend my return because of a mythical path.*

"Good night." She started to turn away and then she paused and said, "Think about what I said before. Who would gain the most if Miss de Bourgh remains sickly?" She tapped her temple. "And be vigilant."

Before he could respond, she slipped away. Darcy watched over Miss Bennet until she unlocked the door and entered the house, her charm bracelet clinking lightly in the silent night. He listened for the click of the lock before he began his walk back to Rosings. Recalling that Harold would be waiting for him, Darcy lengthened his stride, following the exact path taken earlier.

Lizzy put the empty basket on the kitchen table and quietly scurried upstairs to her bedchamber, muffling her bracelet in the folds of her cloak. She struggled to believe that Mr. Darcy would obey her warning. He would stalk back across the park, taking no care at all. Perhaps luck would dog his steps. She suspected he had too much education to easily believe in the magical world. He needed more faith.

She eased open the door to her room, expecting that Mary would have fallen asleep in spite of her determination to wait up. Mary, however, stared back at her, one eyebrow raised. She closed her book and waited for Lizzy to enter, shutting the door behind her.

"Well?" Mary asked softly.

Lizzy untied her cloak, nodding. "They are all in place. The head gardener, Harold, helped me, as it happens."

Mary sighed. She stood and shook out her robe so it settled appropriately around her slipper adorned feet. Dryly, she commented, "Only you would find a helper in the middle of the night."

"He is Frank's twin brother," Lizzy explained. She hung her cloak on the wall hook next to the door and then removed her pelisse.

"Of course, he is," Mary whispered in pithy disgust. "Turn around and I will help you undress."

"Thank you."

"You are welcome," Mary said automatically. "Tell me, please, what you think I should learn about these mythical creatures?"

"Have you decided to believe in them?"

Mary delivered a soft snort. "You said that I should use my powerful intellect to learn about the fae whether I believe in them or not. I do not have to believe to learn."

Lizzy sighed and stepped out of her dress. "That is what I said."

"I know about the iron, but what else should I know? Do they really make milk curdle?"

"They can if they wish." Lizzy picked up her dress and laid it over a chair.

"What else?"

"They cannot lie, but they can prevaricate," Lizzy instructed, continuing to undress. "If they should ever show themselves to you, never lie to them. Never thank them for anything and never ask them for anything. You must not put yourself in a position where you owe them a favor."

"How does thanking them do that?" Mary asked, frowning.

"Thanking them implies that you owe them a debt. You *never* want to owe them a debt."

Mary's jaw tightened. "Never owe them a debt. Next?"

"Never eat any food they give you. Do not accept a gift—that would incur a debt. Do not give them your real name. Make something up, like, 'You may call me…Susan,' say."

"That sounds like a lie."

Lizzy shook her head. "It does not count as a lie. You do not say 'My name is Susan'. That would be a lie."

Mary scowled but said nothing.

"Do not be nosy about them. The best thing to do is ignore their existence. Oh, and do not dance with them, no matter how handsome the fae gentleman is."

Her sister's eyebrows shot up. "Are they handsome?"

"Incredibly so. They glow with beauty. They look like they could be wingless angels, but do not be fooled. They are not."

"They are evil, then?"

Lizzy shrugged into her nightdress. In a muffled voice she said, "That depends on your definition of evil." Her head poked out of her neckline. "Let us say, rather, that they are amoral."

Mary shook her head and held up a hand. "I have heard enough for now. I do not expect to ever see one, so I am going to bed."

Lizzy worried at her lip and said, "I wish you had brought your bracelet."

"I would not have worn it," Mary stated.

"If I bought you something from the smith, would you wear that?"

"Wear what?" Mary asked, suspicion etched across her features.

"I cannot say until I see his wares," Lizzy replied. "He does some fine work."

"I see. Well, perhaps. It would be better if you did not waste your money." She gestured toward the dressing table. "I have written out the entire 'No Man is an Island' poem for you."

"You are a darling," Lizzy said, grinning. "How kind of you."

Shrugging, Mary said, "It is a short poem."

"But full of philosophic intent," Lizzy observed. "Do you think John Donne would turn over in his grave if I changed the wording in favor of women? '*No* woman *is an island / entire of itself; every* woman *is a piece of the continent'*, for example."

Mary's eyes widened and then narrowed. "You are making a May-game of me."

Lizzy held up her hand and pinched her thumb and forefinger together until only a sliver-sized gap existed between them.

"Only a little." She impulsively hugged her outraged younger sister. "I would not dream of changing the wording. Go to bed now. I pray we are not hollow-eyed tomorrow."

Mary withdrew from the embrace, muttering, "It would serve us right if we are."

"Possibly," Lizzy admitted.

Shaking her head morosely, Mary let herself out of the bedchamber, closing the door softly behind her.

ꕥ

<Annoying.>
<Indeed. Have you tried every entrance?>
<I have.>
<The roof?>
<Ah…>

ꝏ

Darcy strode across the moonlit parkland. The night had grown cold enough that a touch of frost tipped the grass, silvering the ground. The cry of a fox startled him and made him jump. He paused to take several deep breaths while he looked around him. No animal crossed his line of sight.

No person.

No *faerie.*

The bright night seemed more eerie than it had when Miss Bennet and he had traversed the park only a few minutes before. The hair on the back of his neck stirred. He rubbed his nape with one hand.

This is madness.

Darcy pressed his lips together and tightened his jaw, setting off again. When he reached the approximate spot where they had leapt over *naught*, Darcy gritted his teeth and determinedly marched across it. Nothing happened.

Humph. Just as I thought.

Darcy reached the stable gate. It groaned softly when he opened it. Harold came out of the nearby cottage, the dogs at his heels. He lifted his cap and closed the gate after Darcy, locking it against intruders.

"Sleep well, sir," he said.

"Thank you. You, too. Thank you for staying up for my return. I am sorry we disturbed your night."

"'Twas no trouble, sir. Don't sleep so much as I used t'," Harold confessed. "I wasna asleep afore, neither, when t'young lady came."

"Miss Bennet will be comforted to know that," Darcy said, nodding his dismissal.

Harold tugged on his cap brim. Darcy strode toward the entrance where he had earlier seen Miss Bennet.

What an unaccountable woman. I do not know what to make of her. She attracts me as much as ever. Yet, I never thought of Miss Bennet as…odd. There is much I still do not know about her.

Darcy let himself into the house and locked the door behind him by the light of the lamp he had set on a small table inside the entrance. He picked up the lamp and climbed the back stairs to his bedchamber.

If tomorrow is fine, I shall ask her to drive with me in the afternoon. Perhaps Anne will lend me her whiskey so we shall not need a groom and Miss Bennet will be able to talk freely. He scowled, thinking of his own taciturn nature. *Curse it, I must force myself to converse more.*

He reached his door. Once inside the bedchamber, he discovered his valet slumped in a chair beside the banked fire, snoring. The additional light coming from the lamp in Darcy's hand reflected off his servant's prematurely balding pate.

"Thomas, you devil. Why did you stay up for me?" Darcy demanded, causing the valet's chin to fall off his propped hand.

"What? What?" Thomas sputtered, scrambling to his feet. He swayed once before catching himself. Tugging on his waistcoat, he advanced on his master. "I'll take that coat from ye, sir."

Darcy turned around and did as much as Thomas permitted him to do to divest Darcy of his outer coat.

"I told you to go to bed," Darcy reminded him.

"I know ye did, sir, but I wanted to take yer damp boots away and tend to them straightaway."

Thomas steered his master to a chair, knelt down, donned gloves, and lovingly removed Darcy's boots and then his stockings. "And yer boots *are* wet, as I thought."

"You are always right," Darcy observed, standing again.

Thomas raised his eyebrows but did not object to the observation. He set the boots to one side and assisted Darcy in removing the remainder of his garments.

"Will you be able to sleep, now, sir?" he asked, holding up the nightshirt.

Darcy put his arms in the sleeves, his head in the open neck, and shrugged the garment over his form. Thomas straightened it over his shoulders.

"The fresh air has done me good, I think," Darcy said, climbing into bed. "Tomorrow morning, I will give you a note for a footman, who is to deliver it to the parsonage. Miss Bennet is the recipient. He is to wait for a reply."

"Aye, sir."

The manner of his response brought Darcy's eyebrows together. "Thomas? You were born in Scotland, were you not?"

"On the Outer Hebrides, sir," Thomas said, gathering the boots and discarded garments in his arm. "North Uist. Lochmaddy. My father is a herring fisherman."

Darcy leveraged himself onto his elbow and watched his valet. "I see. This is an unusual question, but do you believe in faeries?"

Thomas shivered dramatically and whispered, his accent more pronounced, "Oh, aye. The *Sithichean*, they're called. When me nan lay dyin', I heard the wailin' of the *Bean Shith.* I was only six, and I hid under her bed. I was still there when she died."

"Good Lord," Darcy said softly.

Thomas sighed. "Aye. I knew of a woman who claimed she saw a *cù-sithe* while walking home from a *ceilidh.* There'd been a wedding, sir," he explained. Shaking his head, he added, "A *cù-sithe* is a faerie hound. The woman said it didn't hurt her, but…noo…I'd soon as not see one, or hear one, e'er again, sir."

As was his habit, the valet dug his hand into Darcy's overcoat pockets before he took it away. His fist withdrew and he opened his hand flat to see what he had found.

"Where did y'find this, sir?" he asked, holding out his hand to Darcy. "It looks to be an iron charm."

"A horseshoe," Darcy murmured, picking it up from his valet's palm.

She must have slipped it into my pocket when we were standing so close in the yard.

"Do you want it in with y'rr fobs, sir?"

"No, put it on the mantel," Darcy ordered.

He watched Thomas place it beneath the mirror. He felt oddly touched that Miss Bennet had cared enough about his safety that she had given him one of the charms off her bracelet. He also felt peculiarly ungrateful for ignoring her admonition about the faerie path.

"Beggin' yer pardon, sir," Thomas said, frowning a little, "Why did you ask me about the *Sithichean?*"

Darcy lifted one shoulder. "No reason. Good night,"

Forced to be satisfied with his master's answer, Thomas replied, "Good night, sir."

The valet blew out all the candles except the one beside the bed, and carried off the lamp when he left the bedchamber. Darcy listened to him walk away down the corridor. He blew out the final candle, rolled over, punched his pillow into the shape he preferred, and settled down to sleep. He had one last conscious thought.

I will not have nightmares.

Darcy woke with a start for the fifth time that night. Sweat drenched his body and gasps forced their way out of his mouth in explosive bursts.

"Not another one," he muttered, rubbing his nightshirt sleeve across his damp forehead.

"Another what, sir?"

Darcy's eyes widened and he looked around the bedchamber. He spied Thomas at the windows, drawing back the drapes. Morning had arrived at last. Gray, predawn light seeped inside, sparking relief in Darcy's chest.

"Finally," he muttered, swinging his legs out from under the covers. They felt shaky and useless, so he sat there, waiting for the feeling to pass.

Thomas took one look at him, tutted, and brought him a warm, damp cloth. Darcy swiped it over his face and neck. He felt immeasurably better.

"Nightmare, sir?" the valet asked, exchanging the cloth for a towel.

In a long, drawn-out sigh, Darcy said, "Yes."

Thomas peered at him closely. "Y'look done in, sir. Mayhap y'should stay in bed."

Darcy shuddered and stood. "No. I have had enough of my pillow." He handed back the towel. Without waiting for assistance, he stripped off his damp nightshirt and threw it onto the bed. Beneath his breath, he acknowledged his error to himself. "I should have listened to Miss Bennet and stayed off that damned faerie path."

He walked across the chamber to the steaming washbasin next to the fireplace, grabbing the wet cloth from Thomas as he passed, and had a good wash. When he held out his hand behind him for a towel, Thomas did not have it ready for him. Darcy turned and discovered him standing like a statue in the middle of the bedchamber, the towel in his limp hand.

"What is it?" Darcy asked, snapping his fingers for the cloth. "What the devil has got into you? I am wet and cold."

Thomas blinked rapidly, coming out of his daze. He hurried across the room to Darcy.

"I beg y'pardon, sir," he said. "I couldn't have heard correctly. Did you say *faerie* path? Did y'walk on it, sir?" He gulped and added, "Y'must be more careful."

"You have the ears of an elephant," Darcy claimed, scowling and ignoring his questions.

"Thank you, sir."

Darcy's lips twitched. "I am fairly certain I did not mean it as a compliment, Thomas."

"Aye, sir."

Once dried and dressed, Darcy commented, "I feel more the thing, now."

"Very good, sir," Thomas said. He stared at the mantel.

Darcy glanced at it, frowning. His valet seemed fascinated by the tiny iron horseshoe. Darcy's expression tightened. "Wait a moment while I write that note for Miss Bennet."

"Sir."

The note, soon written, was passed to the valet, who bowed to his master and quickly left the chamber. Darcy took the charm from the mantel and slipped it into his waistcoat pocket.

"It never hurts to be cautious," he muttered.

ꟹ

Lizzy entered the dining room in the midst of the morning meal. She had risen at her usual time—she rarely slept in. Consequently, she felt wooly-headed and hoped eating would make her feel more herself.

"Good morning," she said to the other diners. Mr. Collins and Sir William stood. She nodded at the curtesy and they sat again. "Is Mary not yet down?"

Maria swallowed and said, "She only groaned when I tried to wake her."

"Oh, dear," Lizzy said, pasting a crooked grin on her lips. She picked up a plate from the sideboard and began loading it with her favorites. "We stayed up late together. I am afraid her tardiness is my fault. I asked for her assistance with my reading for our recitation tea on Thursday."

"What have you chosen to recite, cousin?" Mr. Collins asked.

Lizzy found her place and sat down, saying, "'No Man is an Island', by John Donne."

Her cousin nodded. He focused his attention on Maria. "What have you chosen, sister?"

"'A Hymn to the Moon' by Lady Mary Wortley Montagu," Maria said, grimacing.

Mr. Collins almost spewed his morning coffee across the table. "That…that is *not* appropriate," he sputtered.

"N...n...no?" Maria asked, taken aback. "I have not yet read it. Mary suggested it."

Mr. Collins, somewhat mollified, looked to his wife. "Dear heart, pray review the readings of our guests before your little party. We must remember my calling, must we not?"

Charlotte flushed. "Yes, husband."

Lizzy wondered if her friend reddened from embarrassment or from anger at her husband for his mild rebuke. Mary entered the room a little later and all eyes turned to her. She paused to look at each in turn.

"I beg your pardon for my tardiness," she said at last into a silence poignant with meaning. "Is all the bacon gone?"

"No, miss," Hibbon said, lifting the silver lid off the chafing dish, revealing four remaining rashers.

Mary smiled, picked up a plate, and tweaked the bacon onto her plate. She added a boiled egg, a slice of pound cake, and a dish of stewed apples. Lizzy picked up her fork and began eating again, signaling the others to stop gaping and resume their breakfast. Her sister sat beside Maria.

"We must pick another poem for me," Maria said softly. "Mr. Collins does not think 'A Hymn to the Moon' appropriate for the recitation tea."

Mary stared owlishly at Maria for a second and then transferred her fixed stare to her cousin. "Perhaps you would prefer Maria to learn a passage from the scriptures?"

Mr. Collins beamed. "I felt sure you would understand."

Anticipating Mary's reaction to being censured, Lizzy held her breath and opened her eyes wide at her sister, who ignored her warning look.

"Song of Solomon 7:1-3, perhaps? 'How beautiful are thy feet with shoes, O prince's daughter! the joints of thy—'"

"Mary!" Lizzy cried softly. She cleared her throat and forced a chuckle. "You must not tease our cousin so early in the morning."

Mr. Collins stared, white-faced at Mary.

Mary's eyes met Lizzy's. Two spots of color marked Mary's

cheeks. Her sister's jaw worked as she got her ire under control. She lowered her gaze to her plate.

"I beg your pardon, cousin," Mary said meekly. "I shall pick something unexceptional for Maria to learn. Lizzy and Charlotte shall approve my selection first, of course. Pray forgive me. I am not my best after a restless night."

Charlotte touched her husband's arm. "I am sorry you did not sleep well, Mary. Were you cold?"

Mary shrugged and sighed. "That may have been the problem."

Focusing on their houseman, Charlotte said, "Hibben, see that Agatha provides Miss Mary with another blanket. And one for Miss Maria's bed too."

"At once, madam," Hibben said, nodding respectfully before leaving the dining room.

"I was not cold," Maria mentioned.

"Regardless, you may find it useful to have," Charlotte said. She looked at her husband, who continued to sit in rigid outrage, and prompted, "Husband, dearest, pray say something kind to Mary, who has apologized most prettily."

With tight lips, he said, "You are forgiven."

"Thank you," Mary murmured. To the table at large, she said, "After I finish my meal, I shall go for a walk and consider the best possibilities for Maria."

"And for your own recitation, I hope?" Mr. Collins asked, his eyebrows high.

"I have chosen 'The First Swallow' by Charlotte Smith," Mary replied.

"Ah, I know that one," Lizzy hurriedly assured her cousin. "Perfectly unexceptional. Very pretty, too."

Mr. Collins nodded once.

Hibben returned, then, carrying a silver salver. He held it out to Lizzy. She picked up the folded and sealed note. Aware of the attention of the others, she opened the note and read the few lines written there.

"It is from Mr. Darcy," she explained. "He has invited me to drive with him this afternoon if weather permits." She rose. Sir William and Mr. Collins also rose. "Please excuse me while I write a reply. I do not wish to keep a Rosings' footman waiting." To Hibben, she said, "I have finished my meal. Thank you."

Charlotte said, "There is writing material and wafers on the desk in my sitting room."

"I hope you mean to accept?" Mr. Collins asked.

"That is for her to decided, dearest," his wife said.

"Of course, dear heart," he replied. To Lizzy, however, he said, "You might consider my position, cousin."

Lizzy smiled reassuringly at him. "Mr. Collins, I am certain your position is secure whether I choose to drive out with Mr. Darcy or not." She watched his expression turn pensive, and added, "However, I will accept his invitation." Her gaze twinkled. "I shall have him help me with my memorizing. It will do him some good, I expect."

She left the dining room without waiting for a comment from her cousin. In the sitting room, she found the note paper, wafers, and writing implements.

Charlotte joined her just as she closed the folded note with a wafer. Hibben entered at her heels, carrying the salver. Lizzy set the note on it and he left them to deliver it to the waiting footman.

"Come, join me on the sofa," Charlotte said, waving at the two-seater next to the windows. The spring sun bathed the room with gentle warmth and light. "You must tell me of your adventure."

"I shall be delighted," Lizzy said, standing and moving across the room. "Did you leave Mary to endure my cousin's disapproval?"

Charlotte shook her head. "Mr. Collins and my father left soon after you did."

"Oh?"

"They are driving to Sevenoaks to visit the parish church of St. Nicholas. Your talk of John Donne reminded my husband that Donne was the rector of that church for fifteen years."

"That is a happy coincidence, indeed," Lizzy said, grinning.

"The drive is about an hour there and back, so they shall find something to eat in Sevenoaks if they are hungry, and be back before dark for the evening meal."

"So, we are quite alone to chat."

"Yes, for Maria went with Mary. Tell me all, if you please," Charlotte ordered.

"And so I shall," Lizzy promised, composing herself to tell the tale. "Mary came to my bedchamber before I left and tried to convince me to abandon the scheme." Charlotte's eyes widened. "Once she saw that it was a hopeless endeavor, she swore to stay up and wait for my return."

"And did she?"

"Oh, yes."

"That must be her excuse for her behavior this morning," Charlotte acknowledged. "I thought Mr. Collins would have an apoplectic fit. Do you think Mary would have completed her recitation of those verses?"

"Not all of them. The remainder of that line would have been sufficient, I think," Lizzy said, chuckling. "*'How beautiful are thy feet with shoes, O prince's daughter! The joints of thy thighs are like jewels,'*. If she had finished that part of the song, I think Mr. Collins would have sent her to her room."

"*Lizzy!*" Charlotte cried softly, coloring. She looked around as though suspecting her husband of hiding behind the furniture. "I do not know what the compilers of the bible thought they were about by including that song."

Lizzy fell back against the cushions, convulsed in giggles. Charlotte held out for a few seconds, and then joined her in merry laughter. They laughed until tears streamed from their eyes.

Chapter Thirteen

Mr. Darcy arrived at the parsonage in the middle of the afternoon, driving his cousin's new whiskey. Though the day was fine and sunny, a breeze enlivened the air, so he had caused the whiskey hood to be unfolded to shield them. The stable boy must have been on the lookout for he hurried from behind the house and went to the horse's head.

"Jem, is it not?" Darcy asked, climbing down.

"Aye, sir," Jem said, tugging on the bill of his cap.

"I shall be back in only a few minutes. There is no need to tether him. Just hold him."

"Right you are, sir," Jem said, nodding.

Darcy started down the walk toward the front door. He glanced up at the horseshoe mounted sideways above the entrance and cursed beneath his breath. If it had occurred to him to think about Mr. Collins at all, he would not have thought of him as a superstitious man.

A man of the cloth, too.

The door opened before he could knock.

"Good afternoon, Hibben," Darcy said, taking off his hat.

"Good afternoon, sir," the houseman said, bowing and opening the door wide. "Miss Bennet is awaitin' yer arrival in the drawin' room."

"Thank you," Darcy said, keeping hold of his hat and following the houseman to the drawing room door.

"Mr. Darcy," Hibben intoned to his mistress.

When he entered the drawing room, he found Mrs. Collins and

Miss Bennet waiting for him. She was ready, wearing an unbuttoned wool pelisse, navy, with a generous skirt, full-length. A black velvet bonnet, ornamented with a swirling black feather adorned her head. Instead of a muff, she had tan gloves in hand. She appeared exceedingly fetching and he smiled automatically in response.

"Good afternoon, ladies," he said, bowing his shoulders.

"Good afternoon, Mr. Darcy," Mrs. Collins said, curtsying along with her friend. "How is dear Lady Catherine?"

"My aunt is well, thank you."

Miss Bennet did up her pelisse and pulled on her gloves. "And Miss de Bourgh? How is she today?"

"She passed a troubled night," he said. "My cousin is taking her for a gentle airing in the gardens this afternoon."

Miss Bennet nodded. Mrs. Collins picked up a reticule from the table behind her and passed it to her friend. Miss Bennet thanked her.

To Darcy, she said, "That should do her good."

"It usually does," he said. "Shall we?"

"I am ready."

Mrs. Collins saw them out. "Pray have her home before dusk, Mr. Darcy."

"I shall."

Darcy assisted Miss Bennet into the whiskey, placed a rug around her legs, hurried to the other side, and climbed up into the seat. He took the reins in hand and released the brake. "Stand aside, Jem."

The stable boy stepped back to the fence.

"Walk on," he said to the horse. To Miss Bennet, he asked, "Are you comfortable? Warm enough?"

"Yes, on both accounts. My, this is a light vehicle. Is it lighter than a gig?"

"Lighter than any of *my* gigs or curricles," Darcy replied. "Even though it limits our peripheral view, I put the hood up to protect us from the cool breeze."

"That was considerate of you," Miss Bennet said. She peered closely up at him. "You know, Mr. Darcy, now that more light is falling on your countenance, I perceive that Miss de Bourgh was not the only person who passed a troubled night. Nightmares, sir?"

Darcy's lips lifted in a crooked smile. "Indeed."

"You did not heed my warning," she stated, shaking her head and twinkling up at him. "I thought as much. It would have hurt you not one jot to go the long way around. Instead, you have suffered. Headaches?"

"No."

His clipped reply did not seem to cause her the least distress. It did, however, irritate Darcy. *Less taciturn, remember?*

"I found the iron horseshoe charm you placed in my pocket," he said, tooling the horse into a quiet country lane. "It did not protect me as I assume you meant it to."

Glancing at her, he caught her grimace.

"It is very small," she admitted. She shook her wrist, revealing her array of charms. "I wear many. And, it was *inside* your coat pocket, so it had limited effect."

"I cannot wear a bracelet," he reminded her. "What a quiz I would look."

Her tart reply came quickly. "I thought you could attach it to the end of your watch fob. Indeed, you could commission an iron bar for your fob with loops to hold charms and a seal."

"I can imagine what my valet would say to that," Darcy quipped. "I do not like to jingle when I walk." He decided not to tell her that Thomas also believed in faeries. Or that the charm even now rested in his waistcoat pocket.

"Iron is so much more effective on the outside of your clothes," Miss Bennet replied.

Enchanted by her small frown of worry, he said, "I wonder that you gave it to me, then."

She blushed and looked out at the countryside. "Spring is coming. I saw snowdrops earlier this week."

Darcy suppressed a smile, though his lips twitched. "I also saw evidence of spring. Crocuses. A de Bourgh ancestor bought a few corms from the Netherlands in the mid-1700s. There are entire beds of them now in the Rosings gardens."

"How pretty they must be. I did not notice any last night," Miss Bennet admitted.

"You had other things on your mind," Darcy said, hoping he sounded generous of spirit. "By-the-by, did you receive the hoped-for letter from Jane?"

"I did not, more is the pity," she replied. "I did, however, receive one from my father. He is livid at Lydia for the trick she played on us all."

"Trick?"

Lizzy brought her gaze back to his, expecting to see scorn in his eyes. Instead, she read only interest. She wrinkled her nose.

"Lydia and Kitty convinced Mary to let them dress her up in widow's weeds, including a veil, in order to impersonate Lydia." Shaking her head, she explained further. "Lydia was to accompany me on this visit. *Not* Mary."

"Good Lord," Mr. Darcy said, appearing taken aback. "She would have cut up your peace, would she not?"

Lizzy shrugged the idea away as unimportant. "I wanted her away from all the militia officers. She is only fifteen and *much* too young to be flirting with them."

Mr. Darcy's expression hardened. "Has she encouraged Wickham?"

"She has not focused her attention on any one officer," Lizzy replied. "Wickham is much too old for her in any case."

"Do you consider him too old for you?"

Mr. Darcy's biting question caused Lizzy to draw back a little—a very little since the whiskey seat did not allow distance between the driver and his passenger.

"I beg your pardon," he said stiffly. "I suppose no one has told you that George Wickham is not a fit person for any young lady to know?"

Lizzy cleared her throat a little, swallowed, and admitted her ignorance. "No, for he is new to our county. There is no one to warn us. Are you doing so now?"

"I am," he replied, directing the horse to halt where the lane widened into a field access point.

"Oh, dear. I must say that his manners are quite pleasing," Lizzy commented. "He is charming. You must admit that, surely."

"Hah!"

Mr. Darcy's exclamation of derision startled her.

She peeked up at him. "Um…I suppose you must know him very well?"

"I do," he said in a low growl. "From childhood. Pray, trust me to know of what I speak."

Slowly, she said, "He revealed his relationship with you and your family…to me…and what he claims you took from him."

"Did he?" Mr. Darcy asked tersely. He stared across the field as though looking into the past. When next he spoke, it was with a hollow voice laced with pain. "I suppose he told you that I cheated him out of his inheritance? *Me?* A living my father wished him to have when, or if, Wickham took holy orders? From jealousy and spite, I suppose?"

"Yes, that was the tale he told me."

"My father was, in every important way, an estimable gentleman. However, his blindness to Wickham's character flaws frequently baffled me."

Lizzy looked down at her hands. "I am somewhat ashamed of how I believed him at the time. After further thought, I came to the conclusion that he had spoken with a regrettable lack of reserve, on a subject that any gentleman should wish to keep private."

"He is no gentleman," Mr. Darcy stated baldly, drawing Lizzy's gaze. His jaw muscles worked. "I do not speak of his birth, for his father was a gentlemanly man from a respectable family."

"I gather it is Mr. Wickham's behavior that has put him beneath reproach?"

He met her gaze with eyes that blazed. Lizzy had not thought him capable of such strong emotions, and it pleased her, somehow, to see it now.

"He is a scoundrel, madam," he growled. "He cannot be trusted with any young woman of fortune."

Lizzy's eyebrows shot up. She brushed a stray lock of hair out of her face and back under her bonnet while she considered the implications of his words and how she would reply to them.

Finally, she said, "I am pleased to say that we may consider both my younger sisters safe from his attentions, sir, for their portion is only fifty pounds a year upon their marriage, or my father's death. Indeed, it is the same for all of us. Such a sum is not sufficient to tempt a man of Wickham's tastes."

Mr. Darcy's expression turned grave and the light in his eyes calmed. "I agree with your assessment."

"I should warn my mother, but, uh, I am not certain that would do much good," Lizzy admitted. "She is mad for officers. I wish, now, that the militia would move out of Meryton. There is talk that they will go to Brighton for the summer."

"It would be best for every young woman if Wickham transferred into the Regulars. To a line regiment. A northern regiment, I think."

"The Regulars? He might be sent to the continent—into battle," Lizzy said, a little shocked at the ferocity of her companion's views.

"If he means to make his living serving his king, then he may as well know what war is like," Mr. Darcy said. He flicked the reins and said to the horse, "Walk on."

"You make a good point."

In a voice just loud enough to be heard over the noise of the horse's hooves and the wheels, he said, "The militia is charged with protecting us at home. I would not trust that man to protect a block of wood."

The carriage wheel on her side dipped into a rut and Lizzy grabbed onto the frame of her seat. In a matter-of-fact voice she said, "Our choler is up, so to cool it, I think we should change the subject."

Mr. Darcy nodded, letting out a breath. "What is your choice of subject?"

She dug around in her reticule and brought out a piece of paper. "On Thursday, we are holding a recitation tea. I have chosen 'No Man is an Island'. I expect you know it?" He nodded. "Mary wrote out the entire poem. I know only the first few lines. Will you assist me in learning the rest? As a favor?"

Mr. Darcy smiled. "Yes. As a favor."

She held out the paper and he shook his head.

"I do not need it. I had a tutor obsessed with the writings of Donne. I had to memorize it."

"Ah, excellent." Lizzy beamed at him, having thought she would have to work harder for his assistance. *That was a foolish belief. Of course, he will assist me. He is a gentleman.*

His smile softened. Lizzy frowned a little at what she thought she saw in his expression. *It cannot be…no…I am imagining it.*

"To begin, then," Lizzy said. She shifted the paper so she could not see it and recited the poem as far as she could manage before she faltered.

"*'If a clod…*'" Mr. Darcy prompted.

"Yes, I remember," she said, and quoted the rest of that line. "*'if a clod be washed away by the sea,'…*"

"Say it again from the beginning," he directed, "adding this new line."

Lizzy obeyed, automatically adding the next few lines she could remember. They continued in this manner until they came to the base of a slight rise where three yew trees grew on the summit. Mr. Darcy stopped the whiskey.

"Shall we step down for a moment?" he asked.

"Hmm?" Lizzy asked, glancing around. "Certainly. I would not mind stretching my legs before we return."

Mr. Darcy engaged the brake and tied off the reins. He moved around the whiskey and assisted Lizzy to the ground, holding on to her hand longer than was strictly proper.

Lizzy looked up into his warm gaze and felt herself flush. Glancing hurriedly away, she asked, "What is this place called? Does it have a name?"

"It is known locally as Cranely Hill," he explained. "Shall we climb to the top? I know how much you like to walk, and it is only a gentle rise."

"I shall enjoy the climb," she assured him.

Lizzy stared up the hill at the three trees and frowned. Concentrating on her second sight, she immediately spied the silvery, straight trail of a faerie path. It ran east-west. The one on the Rosings' estate had run north-south. Two local paths. *No wonder I have seen so many faeries.* Fortunately, she and Mr. Darcy could use a normal path without stepping foot on the new dangerous one.

"Heavens," she whispered.

"What is it?" Mr. Darcy asked, holding out the crook of his arm for her to grasp.

"Uh...do you think we can see Rosings from the top?"

"We can. Just the roofline, mind. There is a wood in between that obscures part of the park."

As they approached the trees, a flock of gray and mottled brown birds flew from the branches, chackling in annoyance as they abandoned their afternoon meal.

"Fieldfares," Mr. Darcy said, gesturing to the birds. "The birds are migrants from Scandinavia and Russia."

"I do not believe I have seen them before," Lizzy confessed, watching them fly away.

"They cannot be seen after April until the autumn."

They did not speak again until they stood beneath the ancient trees, staring out at the landscape beyond.

"It is a lovely view," Lizzy said, turning her back to the breeze. She focused her attention and noted the path of both the east-west and the north-south faerie path. The north-south one traced a route in the direction of Rosings Park. *The one we leapt over last night.* To Darcy, she said, "It is a lovely view even in early spring. Thank you for bringing me here."

"My pleasure, Miss Bennet." He shifted his weight and observed, "There are many beautiful vistas to be seen in Derbyshire."

"I imagine so," she murmured. "My aunt and uncle are planning a summer vacation and they have invited me to go with them. We are traveling north, so perhaps I will have the chance to see some of your country."

"If you come into Derbyshire, I will be delighted to show you Pemberley—the house and its gardens. I would also like to introduce you to my sister, Georgiana."

This confession startled Lizzy so much that her gaze met his. She swiftly looked away from the earnest warmth she saw there.

This is madness. Why am I seeing interest in his eyes?

In defense of these odd new feelings, she suddenly challenged him. "Mr. Darcy, did you influence Mr. Bingley against my sister, Jane?"

ᘓ

Lady Catherine stood at one of her bedchamber windows, staring down at the garden where Anne and Fitzwilliam strolled amongst the long beds of purple and gold crocuses. Both had dressed warmly against the cool breeze.

Winters approached another window and glanced down. "It's nice to see Miss Anne outside, my lady. The sun and exercise will do her good."

"You always prescribe sun and exercise for any ailment," Catherine said absently.

"And so I should," Winters said, tutting and turning to pick up a thick Aran shawl. "And now it's time for your nap, my lady. You lay down on the chaise longue in front of the fire today."

Pulling her dressing gown closer about her, Catherine said, "I shall wait until Anne returns to the house."

"My lady—"

"When Anne returns," Catherine repeated.

In an unhappy tone, her maid replied, "Yes, my lady. I'll put the shawl on the chaise."

"Hmm. Do go away, Winters."

Catherine heard the door close behind her. She and Winters had come to Rosings together upon Catherine's marriage. They had grown old together, though Winters had five years on her. She hoped Winters outlived her, because Catherine could not imagine finding a new maid. Winters still seemed hearty, but at their age, any illness could have a significant deleterious effect.

Who will be on my side if Winters dies before me? Will Anne? If she marries Darcy, where will she live?

Catherine's lips tightened.

Pemberley. Where else? And when will I see her then?

Pressing a fist against suddenly constricting stomach muscles, Catherine steadied herself against the window frame.

I cannot lose her to a husband.

She stiffened her spine and released the window frame.

But what am I thinking? Anne is too ill to marry. She will live with me for some time yet.

Her daughter and nephew had turned a corner and faced the house as they strolled. Fitzwilliam threw back his head and laughed heartily. Anne covered her mouth with her gloved hand.

What humorous conversation makes them so happy? Look at the pleasure in my daughter's countenance. And in Fitzwilliam's.

Catherine turned away, unable to watch them anymore.

When did I ever look so? When I was courted by Sir Lewis? Possibly. Certainly, not after I lost my first little one. Not even when I was expecting Anne.

She drew nearer the fire and reclined on the chaise longue, covering herself with the deep-blue Aran shawl. She stared into the glow of the coal fire.

Such dread I felt during all those long months. Like all men, Sir Lewis wanted a boy, but his money and property could be given to a girl, so I did not care. I only needed a healthy baby. Well, Anne was not healthy, but she lived. She lived. Thank you, Lord.

ഇ

Darcy stared owlishly at Miss Bennet. She repeated her question.

"Mr. Darcy, did you influence Mr. Bingley against my sister, Jane?"

He gathered his wits about him and said, "Did you know that Bingley has only twenty-and-two years? His next birthday is in four weeks."

Miss Bennet narrowed her eyes. "And what has that to say to

anything?"

Darcy shifted his feet and took a deep breath. "I only mention his age to support my opinion that he is young, yet, to know his own mind."

Miss Bennet opened her mouth and he held up his hand. She closed it again.

"Thank you. Miss Bennet is also only twenty-and-two years of age. For a lady, that is considered by society as an excellent age to marry. Possibly even older than some may prefer. Would you not agree?"

Miss Elizabeth nodded once, remaining silent.

She is glaring at me, now.

"Thank you for permitting me to continue," Darcy said, bowing his shoulders.

"I am biding my time," she expressed through gritted teeth.

"Of course," he said, and then continued. "Bingley, however, is considered by most of society to be too young to marry. Too young to be sure of his own heart. Too young to know his own mind." Pressing his lips together, he shook his head. "Miss Caroline Bingley and her sister certainly think in that fashion. *I* am of the opinion that Bingley needs to learn to stand up to his sisters' influence. I am hoping that he will use this time away from Miss Bennet to examine his feelings and be certain of them. *If* he is convinced of his affection for her, then he will resist his sisters' warnings."

"And that is why you did not use your *own* influence to keep him at Netherfield?" Miss Bennet demanded, her expression flushed.

"I am convinced that if his fondness for your sister's company proved strong enough, *no one* could have made him leave," Darcy retorted. He turned and took several steps away from her, turned around and faced her. "When we managed to convince him to return to London, I took it as a sign that he had not developed strong enough feelings for your sister to resist the discouragement of *his* sisters."

"Your discouragement, you mean," Miss Bennet snapped.

"Or *anyone's* discouragement," he stated forcefully. "I did not observe any partiality in your sister's conduct to warrant the possible heartbreak of my friend."

"You did not permit Jane and Mr. Bingley the time they needed to fix their love for each other," Miss Bennet complained. "Jane is a shy, retiring woman. She cannot be rushed into revealing her feelings. Ooh, you are arrogance itself!"

She stomped away from him, leaped inexplicably over a portion of the ground, before she stomped back, leaping again over the same spot. Darcy refused to question her about her odd behavior. *Faeries, no doubt.*

Drawing herself up in a regal manner, Miss Bennet said, "Kindly take me back to the parsonage."

He had no answer other than the gentlemanly one. "Of course."

She held up her hand. "No. I have changed my mind. I shall walk."

"Miss Bennet, pray be reasonable. It is too far for you to walk in those shoes."

She glared at him again. "It is not." Then she marched off down the gentle hillside, her iron bracelet tinkling.

Darcy hastened after her. "Miss Bennet, you have not yet memorized your poem."

"I shall learn it on my own," she asserted without looking at him.

Desperate, he asked, "Are you not afraid of meeting some of the fae?"

"Do not pretend to believe in them," she snapped, increasing her pace.

Darcy hurried back to the carriage. By the time he had the whiskey turned around, she had managed to cover a fair distance. He leapt up into the seat, grabbed the reins, and set off in pursuit. When he caught up to her, he slowed the horse to match the speed of her walking.

"Miss Bennet, pray do not be childish."

Her gasp caused her to slow her step.

"Childish?" she repeated with withering scorn. "Childish? Good day to you, sir."

To Darcy's vexation, she spied a stile, climbed over it, and continued her journey across a farmer's field, taking long strides and completely ignoring him.

"Confound it," he said to the horse. "Do you suppose she was influenced by the blasted faeries?"

The animal shook his head.

"I suppose you think I was?" he muttered.

The horse nodded.

"I must have been," he moaned. "Why else would I tell the lady I love that she was being childish? I would not call *Georgiana* childish."

Shaking his head at his own stupidity, he flicked the reins and the whiskey began to roll. At the bottom of the lane, they turned in the direction Miss Bennet had been heading. Darcy looked out over the hedgerows, searching for her. He finally spied her in a different field, making her way toward the woods on the outskirts of the village of Rosings.

If she loses her way, Mrs. Collins will be most unhappy.

ꟾ

Lizzy entered the shadow of the trees, her heart pounding with exertion and furious frustration. Exquisite snowdrops blanketed the ground and the sight of them eased her heart. A little. She picked her way through them, stepping on bare patches whenever possible. She searched for a path, found one, and commenced to stomp along it.

How dare the pompous and arrogant Mr. Darcy interfere with my sister's happiness?

"One of these days…" she muttered, leaving the thought open-ended.

Arriving at a fork in the path, she paused, looked both ways, and chose the most heavily trodden trail.

"When next I meet him," she murmured beneath her breath, "I shall…"

Lizzy could not think of a suitable lady-like way to censure Mr. Darcy and so her threat petered away.

"Dear Jane," she whispered, making another path choice, "how I wish you were here with me."

The track she chose ended in a mass of cobweb-studded brambles, naked of leaves and sporting dried bunches of fruit.

"Oh," she said, pausing for a moment to stare numbly at the obstruction.

Lizzy surmised that this track must have been formed over the years by the berry pickers. She turned around and returned to the fork in the path.

Maybe I should go back out the way I came in.

Shaking her head, she chose to continue onward. The village could not be that far away. She listened for the sound of water, recalling that she had crossed a stream on the morning she spent with Frank. She followed a gurgling sound until she reached a shallow stream and leapt over it, stepping on two large, dry rocks to do so.

"There you go," she said, grinning to herself as she climbed the bank.

Lizzy continued to follow the path, certain that the village would be just around another bend. However, the sky began to darken and worry took the place of assurance. She found a fallen log nudged up against an alder tree trunk. Continuing to roam around the unfamiliar woods seemed like a foolish thing to do, so she sat on the log to rest and take stock.

"I wish I had a muff," she stated in quiet resignation, staring at her gloved hands. "My fingers are cold."

I was a fool to rush off. I should have stayed on the lane. Why did I not follow an energy line? Surely the right one would have taken me to the well in the old churchyard?

But which energy line was the right one?

Without thinking through her actions, Lizzy squirmed to get herself more comfortable, covered her legs with the skirt of her pelisse, and laid her head back against the trunk.

I am so tired. I shall just rest my eyes for a moment. Not enough to sleep, though. I am…so tired. So tir…ed.

<I think she sleeps.>

<Does she? I am not certain.>

"I am not asleep," the human woman mumbled. "I am only resting my eyes."

<She heard me.>

<Did you mean her to?>

<No.>

<Ah. Perhaps she is talking in her sleep. Some humans do.>

"But I do not."

The woman stirred and almost fell off the log.

"Whoops," she said, blinking rapidly and flailing her arms. "That's better," she said, chuckling as she steadied herself.

Looking around, she gazed past them as though they were not standing on either side of her, leaning over, staring at her. She seemed to absently search for something up her sleeve while she examined her surroundings. After a little hunting, a hideous object came into their view.

<Iron!>

<I feel it. How horrid it feels. Where is it?>

<On the female's wrist. An ornament.>

<Does she know about us?>

<Look out, she is stretching!>

Lizzy cautiously watched the two faeries glide away at an astonishing speed. She had nearly revealed herself. Only training had kept her from crying out at the sound of their voices so close by, the sight of their faces so near her own. Even so, responding to their comments could have been disastrous. In the gray world between waking and sleeping, magic things walked and talked.

"I might have been caught," she whispered, shivering. "So foolish of me."

Just as she was about to stand and continue her search for a way out of the woods, Lizzy heard her name being called.

"Miss Bennet!"

A male voice?

Too far away to recognize.

Should I answer it? I must not allow my pride to leave me almost lost in the woods. Very well, definitely *lost in the woods.*

Chapter Fourteen

"Miss Bennet!"

"Mr. Darcy," Lizzy whispered in wonder as she recognized his welcome voice. She leapt to her feet. "I am here."

She scowled. Her dry mouth betrayed her efforts. Her response could not have been heard more than a few feet away.

"Miss Bennet!"

Lizzy scrambled to the shallow stream, stripped off a glove, and scooped some freezing water into one palm. She sipped it up, cleared her throat, and called out again.

"I am here!"

She took another drink, shook the water drops from her fingers, dried off with her handkerchief, and tugged her glove back on. Unwilling to stay here while she could still see a path, she hurried back the way she had come until she reached a crossroads of three trails.

Cupping her hands around her mouth, Lizzy called, "Mr. Darcy! I am here!" She repeated the call in the other two directions.

Pausing to listen, she heard someone running along a path to her right. *What if it is not Mr. Darcy? What if it is a faerie trying to trick me?* Caution struck aside her anticipation and Lizzy stepped off the path to hide behind a tree.

She peered through the evergreen bows and spied a man approaching the intersection. It *was* Mr. Darcy. *Drat. Now I feel like an idiot hiding here.*

"Miss Bennet!" he called, spinning around, searching. "Where is she?" he muttered to himself.

Lizzy heard and had to smile. She came around the tree, wading through golden winter grass, and said, "Here I am."

Darcy whirled to face the voice and spied Miss Bennet coming toward him. He wanted to grab her and shake her.

Skirting a low bush, Miss Bennet asked with a nonchalance that infuriated him, "Were you searching long? I am sorry."

He reeled in his angry fear and replied with tolerable sangfroid, "Not too long, no."

"Good," she said, reaching him. Taking his arm, she raised an eyebrow and asked, "Which way?"

Darcy pointed to the path behind him, to his right, "That way."

Her eyebrows shot up. "I meant to choose that direction next."

"I see you were not so lost as you thought," Darcy said, a trifle grim. "Come along, Miss Bennet. Mrs. Collins is awaiting your return."

"Yes, indeed. She will worry."

"And your sister? Will Miss Mary be worried?"

Miss Bennet chuckled wryly. "Not she. It is not so easy to fluster Mary. When I returned the other night to the vicarage, she was calmly reading in my bedchamber. Uh, where is the whiskey?"

"At the end of this path," he supplied, beginning to walk with her in that direction. "Fortunately, it is not as dark in the lane as it seems in the woods."

"Good," she said, her voice solemn.

Darcy waited for her to apologize. When she did not, he stopped walking.

"What is it?" she asked.

And still she did not offer an apology. *Incredible.*

"Miss Bennet, I am beside myself with…with frustration," Darcy stated in a low voice. "How could you traipse off into an unknown wood? You might have been lost for hours."

"Your gentlemanly composure has disserted you," she claimed. "Do not concern yourself with my safety, sir."

Miss Bennet attempted to draw her hand away from the crook of his elbow. He would not permit her to do so. Darcy took her hand and held it tightly between his two.

"When you are in my company, I am responsible for you." He stared down at her. Two spots of color adorned her cheeks. "Surely you realize that?"

"You should not have made me angry."

"It was not my intention to create animosity between us with my explanation." Darcy managed a wry chuckle. "Only today I reminded myself that I must talk more. And this is the result of my ineptitude. I have no turn for polite conversation. Pray forgive me."

Miss Bennet's color receded and she gave a short nod. "Very well."

"Thank you. I merely meant to help my friend," he added, relieved. Her eyes flashed at him and he hastily said, "But, no more on that head."

Darcy put her hand back in the crook of his elbow and he gestured toward the path. "Shall we continue?"

"Yes," Miss Bennet said, falling into step beside him. "Sir, our…argument…has resulted in a potentially delicate situation. I suggest that the moment I know my direction, you should put me down so I can walk back to the vicarage. You can drive ahead and meet me there."

"I would not do anything so ungentlemanly," Darcy replied sharply.

"You have not considered properly," Miss Bennet chided. "All you must say is that we argued—no one would be surprised by that, I assure you—and that I insisted on walking home in a high dudgeon."

Darcy gritted his teeth. "Which would have the advantage of being true." He swallowed his exasperation, saying, "And why did I not drive beside you, or behind you, to be certain you arrived home safely?"

"Because I struck off across the field," she explained. "More truth. There is no difficulty in explaining why you did not follow me on foot—you could not leave the horse. You could not leave the carriage." She looked up at him. "Really, sir, must I think of everything? Or, do you wish this day to result in our being affianced?"

Yes, I do.

Darcy clenched his fists.

But not this way.

He supposed Miss Bennet took his silence to mean he disagreed with her plan for she continued to press her reasons upon him.

"Driving about in the dark? Home much later than we promised to be?"

"Miss Bennet," he said, exasperated. "I am not ignorant of the dangers of our situation. I am also considered quick-witted so you need not cut at me in this manner."

Silence rose between them.

"I beg your pardon," Miss Bennet finally said quietly. "I know we are in this predicament because of my reaction to your honesty. I did not mean to offend you."

Now she apologizes?

Nevertheless, Darcy experienced a pang of remorse for his hasty words.

"I must also apologize," he said quietly, covering her hand on his arm with his other hand. "Pray, forgive me. I have thought of a better program, Miss Bennet. When we get to my carriage, you shall drive—if you can—and I shall walk back to the vicarage."

"I have only driven a cart," Miss Bennet said doubtfully. "I think it would be better if I continue to walk and you drive beside me. I am not at all tired. Or, at least, I am not too tired to finish this trek. I had a rest right before I heard you call for me."

"This search for solutions reminds me of the Greek fable of the old man, a young boy, and a donkey," Darcy said, projecting a hint of humor into his voice. "In the fable, a man and his young son set off to market. At first, no one rode and fellow travelers jeered at him for not riding. The man put his son on the donkey's back. They proceeded until he was ridiculed again for having a lazy son. So, he and his son switched places. More ridicule followed because he made his young son walk while he rode. In the end, they tied a wood rod to the donkey's feet and carried *him*."

Miss Bennet chuckled. "They would never have been able to lift a donkey."

"It is a fable."

"Even fables should make sense," she argued. "I think I remember it now. Did the donkey fall in the river and drown?"

"Yes, I am afraid so."

"Are you standing in for the man or for the boy?"

"I am relieved you think of me as human," he said. "I was sure you would cast me in the role of the donkey."

She laughed and his shoulders relaxed.

"I do not think of you as so lowly," she said, grinning. "The moral of the fable, I believe, is that it is impossible to please everyone."

"Indeed."

Such a rush of pleasure in her company swept through him that it took him a moment to produce another idea.

"I have an alternate suggestion. You sit in the carriage and I shall lead the horse." Darcy looked down at her. She opened her mouth and he held up his free hand. "No, pray do not argue. This is the best option. Everyone on the street will see that we are not seated together and your virtue shall remain intact and my honor shall be satisfied."

"We will look rather odd," Miss Bennet said doubtfully.

"Does that matter so much?"

"Not to me, no. But you are so proud."

A muscle in Darcy's jaw twitched. "I do not think of myself as proud. I simply prefer not to be the subject of gossipmongers. Surely you do not enjoy it?"

His companion sighed. "I do not. It seems we are forever at each other's throats. Will we ever deal companionably together?"

Darcy did not know what to say in response to what seemed to him to be a rhetorical question.

Finally, he softly said, "I would like us to deal more kindly with each other. You have a lively mind, Miss Bennet. I admire that trait in you."

She looked up at him but said nothing.

After a few steps he tried once more to engage her in conversation. "Did you see any of the fair folk amongst the trees? Wood nymphs, perhaps?"

Miss Bennet searched around her, turning her head this way and that, leaning around him to see on his side of the path. Seemingly satisfied that they were alone, she focused on him.

"I have never seen a wood nymph. But I saw two fae," she whispered. "A male and a female. They came upon me while I rested. I almost gave myself away."

Sigh.

"Indeed? How?"

"They spoke to me while I dozed, and I answered them."

Darcy felt her shudder. Her hand convulsed on his arm. Before he responded to her comment, he took a moment to remind himself that he had just finished saying he wanted them to deal more kindly with each other. He would not dispute with her about the existence of faeries.

"It seems to me that you completely gave yourself away," he said, frowning. "Why did you say that you *almost* gave yourself away?"

"Because when I fully awoke, I acted as though they were not there. They assumed that my reaction to their words had been caused by my being mostly asleep. They left when I casually shook my bracelet out of my sleeve. I dearly *hope* it seemed casual to them."

"Oh. I am surprised you allowed yourself to fall asleep. You are forever speaking of their danger to us."

"I had no intention of dozing off," she retorted. "I may be able to see them, but that does not mean I see them all the time. There was an excellent chance that none would have come along. I had no reason to believe I was not safe from them at that moment."

He had to force himself not to look over his shoulder. "Of course. Do you usually see so many of them? I did not think they could be so numerous."

"You did not think of them at all," she said with sudden wry humor. "It is odd, though. Sometimes I will not see one for months. But here…something is bothering them, I think."

"What could that be, pray?"

She shook her head. "Fathoming their thinking is impossible."

"Indeed."

"Uh, Mr. Darcy? Did you consider my concerns from last night?"

He frowned. "Which were those?"

"About your cousin, Miss de Bourgh?"

Darcy ground his teeth and shook his head.

"I see." She released a distinct sigh. "Well, it was only a thought. I expect the possible poisoning of your cousin is nothing to be concerned with."

In spite of her words, he could tell that she continued to be troubled.

The trees grew farther apart and they could see the whiskey. The horse turned his head in their direction and nickered.

"It is only us," he told the horse, who snorted in response.

"You were correct. It is not quite as dark as I thought," Miss Bennet commented. "The shadow of the forest canopy was deceiving."

Someone stood at the other side of the horse's head. He stepped around the animal and faced them. Darcy's eyebrows shot up. It was the Rosings head gardener. Miss Bennet spoke and he realized his mistake.

"Frank? Is that you?" she asked pleasantly. "Good evening."

Frank, the gardener's twin brother, touched his cap. "There ye be, miss. Sir," he added, nodding to Darcy and tugging at his cap brim. "I looked 'round an' 'round and didna see a driver."

"Miss Bennet took it into her head to explore the woods," Darcy explained. "I thought she might get lost and went looking for her."

"You'd know the way, sure enough," Frank said, nodding.

"Frank, will you ride up behind?" Darcy asked, seeing a way to rescue them from their propriety predicament. "Are you able? As a sort of chaperone? We are later than we meant to be, you see. I believe there is a stand for a groom."

Lizzy's eyebrows shot up. "You *are* clever, Mr. Darcy," she praised, beaming up at him before she turned back to the old man. "Will you, Frank?"

"I'll do it, sir. Miss," Frank said, touching his cap again.

"There you are, Miss Bennet, our solution," Mr. Darcy said, waving her toward the carriage.

In a whisper, she asked, "Do you truly think he can hold on? He is awfully old to be standing on the back of a carriage."

"I shall check to see if there are straps for him," he whispered back.

Lizzy accepted his assistance in climbing up into her seat. She settled herself while he went around to the back of the whiskey. The vehicle swayed. It irked Lizzy that the hood kept her from seeing if Frank was safe.

Mr. Darcy joined her, covering her lap with the rug. "He is well situated. My aunt installed straps when she ordered that a small platform be fashioned for a groom."

"If he falls off on our journey, I shall never forgive myself," Lizzy swore quietly.

"I will be careful," Mr. Darcy promised. "It is good of him to do this service for us."

Lizzy bit her lip and nodded. "How far must we travel?"

Mr. Darcy pointed to a stone marker at the side of the lane. "Only a half mile."

"Good. The villagers will be surprised to see Frank as a groom." She clenched her fists. "I do not believe we will escape being gossiped about, sir."

"It is inevitable. However, my honor and your virtue have been salvaged."

"I hope you are correct."

"I believe my word is enough to convince anyone of consequence that we experienced an innocent adventure," he expressed with a degree of hauteur she had not heard since the Lucas' ball.

"You will freeze them in their place with your uncompromising stare," Lizzy remarked. She sighed and relaxed her fists, struggling to regain the even timber of her mind. "At this moment, I am thankful for that talent."

Mr. Darcy expertly maneuvered the whiskey around a deep rut, and then said, "Do I have such a stare?"

"You must know that you do," she said, honestly surprised at his question. He had sounded startled as though no one had ever remarked upon it before.

"Like any gentleman, or lady, I know how to put down pretension," he admitted.

"No doubt," she said and fell into a glum silence. Calmness of mind seemed out of reach.

He turned his head and looked down at her. "I believe I must also beg your forgiveness for my behavior at the ball at Meryton. I am sorry."

Lizzy nodded. "I suppose it is difficult to be amongst so many strangers. Everyone stared at you so. I forgive you."

"Thank you," he said, turning his attention back to the road. "I often wish I had Bingley's easy knack for interacting with his fellow creatures. I have no charm of manner. My mother, who died during my twelfth year, despaired of me ever acquiring some. Any, in fact."

Chuckling, Lizzy asked, "Do boys of twelve have charm?"

"Wickham had it," he replied grimly. "More than his share, in my opinion."

"He has it still," Lizzy admitted. "If you have no charm—I am forced to agree with your mother in that regard—then you must learn to be kind."

He straightened and she felt his glare.

"I *am* kind."

She looked away and then back up at him. Lizzy doubted he could make out her features in the shadows of the whiskey hood now that the sun had gone down, so she hoped he could hear the regret in her voice.

"I beg your pardon. I should not have said that. I have a cursedly forthright tongue myself at times—as you have noticed, I am sure." Lizzy laid her hand on his arm and squeezed. His muscles felt taught beneath her grip. "What I should have said, is more *obviously* kind."

In a tight voice, he said, "I do not know what you mean by that."

Lizzy swallowed and decided to back away from this conversation. Instead, she said, "Thank you for searching for me. It was *kind*ly done."

Mr. Darcy barked a short laugh. "You wretched girl. It would have served you right if I had left you to the faeries."

She retrieved her hand and touched a finger to her lips. "Shhh, you *wretched* man. Do you wish to draw their attention?"

"Could I?" he asked. "Wait, say no more about faeries, for here is the bridge."

In the distance she heard the sound of a clock bell. "I think that is the stable clock at Rosings."

"It is," he said simply. "And I think Frank has managed to stay on."

"Oh," Lizzy said, round-eyed. "I almost forgot him."

Mr. Darcy snorted lightly and she shook her head at him. He ignored her, focusing on the pedestrians and carts still on the village road. Lanterns had been lit outside several establishments and in the village square. In their light, she saw several people pause and curtsy, or touched their cap brims, as they went by.

"Do you think they noticed Frank?" she asked.

"I expect they did."

"I think so too."

Mr. Darcy chuckled grimly. "It will be better for us if they did."

"So it will," Lizzy conceded.

The vicarage door opened in such haste when they drew up before the house that she easily concluded Charlotte had been on the look out for her. Both her friend and Mary rushed down the walk to the gate, wool shawls about their shoulders.

"Where have you been?" her sister demanded, her annoyed expression clear in the light of the two lanterns mounted on either side of the gate.

Charlotte gave Mary an exasperated look. "Angry words serve no purpose."

"They permit me to vent my spleen," Mary retorted. "Well, Lizzy?"

By this time, Mr. Darcy stood waiting to assist her to alight. The whiskey swayed and Frank joined him.

"I'll be off, then, sir. Miss," he said, touching his hand to the brim of his cap.

Lizzy stepped down and nodded to him. "Thank you, Frank. Do you have a long walk?"

He nodded. "A fair piece."

She touched Mr. Darcy's arm. "*Kind* Mr. Darcy will take you up and drive you where you meant to go. It is only fair."

Frank appeared doubtful, searching her expression.

"Nay, miss. I don't mean t'be any trouble."

Lizzy gazed up into Mr. Darcy's face, expecting to see hauteur there, a result of her presumption on his time. He merely looked a little amused.

"Frank can sit up beside you with his arms folded like a groom," she suggested.

"Indeed. He has stood long enough," Mr. Darcy said. "Up you go, Frank. I shall turn the horse by hand."

"Sir," the old diviner said, touching his cap again. "I'll do that fer ye."

Mr. Darcy nodded and took Lizzy's hand. "Thank you for a fascinating drive, Miss Bennet. I pray you will suffer no ill effects from your encounter in the wild wood."

"As do I," she said, grinning up at him.

He turned to Charlotte. "I beg your pardon for returning your friend so late. She got lost in the woods."

"Lizzy?" Mary asked, her eyebrows shooting up.

"You are forgiven, sir. Thank you for bringing her home safely," Charlotte said, dropping a slight curtsy.

Mr. Darcy raised a hand in farewell, climbed up into the carriage, and took up the reins to assist Frank, who stood at the horse's head, in turning the horse and whiskey.

Charlotte opened the iron gate and drew Lizzy inside. "It is too cold out here to wait for Mr. Darcy to leave. Lizzy, you must be frozen to death."

"I am not so cold," Lizzy said. "Though, I must confess that I longed for a muff. I never thought to bring one. My gloves are insufficient to their purpose and so my hands are cold."

"I think you deserve to be cold," Mary said, following behind them. "Mr. Collins is hopping angry. Though, since you were out with Mr. Darcy, he could hardly express it."

"Hush, Mary," Charlotte said, frowning.

"I expect you feared for me," Lizzy said, turning and tucking her arm through her sister's.

"Hmm," Mary hummed, looking away from her. "I am surprised, however, to hear that you got lost in the woods."

"I am confident I would have found my way out," Lizzy said. She made them pause at the bottom of the steps. Whispering, she revealed, "I sat down to rest and while I dozed, two of *them* came and spoke to me."

"What?" Charlotte gasped.

Mary merely sighed.

ꟃ

Darcy arrived back at Rosings with barely enough time to change for dinner. His valet awaited him in his bedchamber, a stony expression on his face.

"Her ladyship dines at half six, sir," Thomas reminded him.

"I have not forgotten," Darcy said testily, turning his back so Thomas could help him with his coat and jacket. "I have no interest in incurring my aunt's displeasure. The delay could not be helped."

Thomas sniffed, setting aside the two garments. He automatically checked the pockets. When his hand came out of one it held a tiny black object.

"Another charm, sir," he said, presenting it to Darcy. "A fox's head."

Darcy took it and set it in the middle of his palm. He poked at the bit of iron, turning it this way and that. *She gave me a charm even though we quarreled.* Darcy could not help a swirl of excitement as he closed his fist around the tiny object.

"It's already six, sir," Thomas reminded him, coming forward to undo the waistcoat buttons.

Darcy evaded him and strode across the bedchamber to place the fox charm next to the horseshoe one.

"Before you retire tonight, kindly sew these charms onto my key fob so that they are visible when I wear the fob," Darcy directed, turning around so he faced his impatient valet.

"Aye, sir," Thomas said grimly. "A little iron ne'er hurt nobody."

"Anybody," Darcy murmured automatically.

"Anybody, sir," Thomas repeated. "A little iron ne'er hurt *anybody*."

Darcy and his valet hurried him into his evening rig. His aunt preferred gentlemen to wear silk breeches and white stockings when they came down to dinner. Once he was ready to leave the tender hands of his valet, Darcy contrived a quizzical look and faced him.

"Thomas, you seem to know a fair bit about the fae," he said, noting Thomas' infinitesimal step backward. "Do you know of a reason why they might congregate in a particular neighborhood?"

"Sir?" Thomas asked, a bid for time to think. He licked his lips. In a whisper he asked, "Are there many *Sithichean* in *this* neighborhood?" Deepening his voice even further, he asked, "Have ye seen any near *here*?"

"I have *never* seen any," Darcy replied. He glanced around the chamber. He saw no one, but a growing sense of awareness made him keep Miss Bennet's claims to himself. "Do some people have the ability to *always* see them?"

Thomas made a slow, almost imperceptible nod. "Aye. They ken make *anyone* see them, sir, but only a few ken *always* see them." He glanced into the four corners of the bedchamber, and then added in a whisper, looking into his master's face, "No one ken understand the workings of their minds, sir, but something must be afoot if they're busy nearby." He shuddered. "As God is m'witness, I hope I *ne'er* see them."

"I am not convinced they exist," Darcy muttered. To Thomas, he said, "We have been at Rosings many times. Why are they active now?"

"Perhaps they were active afore, sir, an' we didna know it," Thomas said in a quietly dismayed voice. "I want t'go back t'bein' ignorant."

His faithful and steadfast valet's fear touched Darcy more than he liked. At no time had he ever seen Thomas afraid.

"As do I," Darcy admitted.

He turned and left the bedchamber. The spot between his shoulder blades itched and he rolled his shoulders, determined not to admit to anyone that he heard soft laughter all the way to the top of the stairs.

I am imagining it.

<Are you?>

Darcy had learned enough from Miss Bennet to ignore the

random thought. He grasped hold of the railing and hurried down the stairs, feeling unaccountably glad when he caught up to Fitzwilliam on the second landing.

Chapter Fifteen

Wednesday morning brought rain, a steady mizzle that made spider webs glisten and seemed just a single step away from being mist. After they finished their breakfast, Lizzy settled with Charlotte, Mary, and Maria in the ladies' sitting room. A fire burned in the grate, and cups of tea soon littered the small tables. They were all determined to learn their readings for the recitation tea the following afternoon. Not Mary, of course. She already knew her piece by heart. Instead, she sat opposite Maria in one corner and helped her.

Hibben entered, carrying a silver salver. "Mail, madam," he said, bending over and presenting the salver to Charlotte.

"Thank you, Hibben," she said, collecting several letters and cards.

He nodded and left the room.

"Here is one from Jane, Lizzy," Charlotte said, handing one to her. "And one from Jane for you, Mary. Maria, mother has written," she said, rising and crossing the room to offer the letters to Mary and her sister. "One for you, and one for me."

All the ladies pried open their missives and spread them out upon their knees. They started by reading silently, and then they shared those tidbits that were of interest to the others.

"Finally," Lizzy said, beaming around the room.

"What, pray?" Mary asked, glancing up from her letter. "Mr. Bingley?"

"Yes," Lizzy said. "Did she tell you?"

Mary nodded.

"She did not write to me, though," Charlotte said, smiling from the settee across from Lizzy. "Will you not share this bit of news? Are they engaged?"

Both Lizzy and Mary shook their heads.

"At least, she did not tell me so," Mary amended, her eyebrows climbing.

"Nor I," Lizzy swore. "Jane wrote that she met Mr. Bingley in the park one day. He turned his steps aside so he could walk with her and our cousins."

"Were his sisters with him?" Charlotte asked.

"She did not say," Mary said. She frowned slightly. "Jane is an excellent, and thorough, correspondent. If Caroline Bingley had been with him, Jane would have said. Do you not agree, Lizzy?"

"I do," Lizzy said, folding away her letter.

"Will they meet again?" Maria asked, setting her letter aside. "I do hope so. I liked Mr. Bingley enormously. He is so affable. It would be nice if he stayed at Netherfield much of the year."

"Yes, indeed," Lizzy replied. "She said Mr. Bingley means to call at our aunt and uncle's house this Saturday afternoon."

Mary scowled. "If his sisters do not talk him out of attending, you mean? Do they know that Aunt and Uncle Gardiner live on Gracechurch Street? It is not a fashionable district, even if fashionable people shop there."

"I do not believe that will count with Mr. Bingley," Charlotte said. "He does not rate himself so high as to be above his company."

Mary shrugged. "True, but his sisters do."

Lizzy remembered Mr. Darcy's comments about Mr. Bingley's lack of resistance to outside pressure. At least one of those influences currently resided at Rosings Park. She prayed Mr. Bingley felt strongly enough about her dear Jane to overcome his sisters' averseness to the match.

Mary and Maria returned to their practice. Charlotte eyed them and crossed to the other settee so she could sit beside Lizzy.

Recognizing in her the desire for a private word, Lizzy softly asked her friend, "What is it?"

Charlotte turned her head away from Mary and Maria to lessen even further the possibility that their sisters could overhear her, and whispered, "Now that you have met Miss de Bourgh, what do you think of the possibility that she is being poisoned?"

"I have only met her once," Lizzy said, temporizing.

Charlotte nodded reluctantly. "Yes. True."

"I also thought you had decided that the idea was fanciful."

Her friend bit her lip. "I did, but…I cannot shake the feeling that there is more wrong here than we know. Do you remember that lady in Meryton who kept her daughter sickly by poisoning her?"

"I do, and I have thought about that likelihood, but I have no way of determining if that is happening here," Lizzy said. "I admit to being quite distracted when I met Miss de Bourgh. Besides Mr. Darcy being there, three of *them* hovered around Miss de Bourgh," she reminded Charlotte. "I did not know where to look. I am certain Lady Catherine thought me most odd and more forthright than can be considered seemly." She paused and took a deep breath, letting it out slowly. "Three in one room. I do not see that every day…or even every month."

Wringing her hands in her lap, Charlotte asked, "Could it be *their* fault that Miss de Bourgh is always ill?"

"I believe it is possible."

Charlotte moaned softly.

Lizzy covered her hands with one of her own. Frowning, she said, "You mentioned that Miss de Bourgh has been sickly all her life. If you are correct, they may have been pestering her from the moment of her birth."

Charlotte gasped a little. "Surely not."

"They have been known to take babies," Lizzy reminded her in a hushed whisper. "Mayhap she is a changeling?"

Charlotte paled and leaned away, a hand covering her mouth.

Lizzy shook her head. "Forgive me for frightening you, dearest. I was thinking aloud. This possibility is highly unlikely. A changeling, once in a human family, is not visited by his or her people after the switch. It grows up as a human and never returns to the faerie realm."

"Thank the good Lord," Charlotte breathed.

"Have you received a reply to your invitation from Miss de Bourgh?"

"Yes. It was amongst the letters I received today. She is coming."

"Good," Lizzy said, patting her arm. "Tomorrow, I will observe her more closely. The fae will not come into the vicarage. There is too much iron here."

"Perhaps that is why dear Miss de Bourgh seems better when she visits."

"That may be."

Charlotte reached over to the small table where she had put her correspondence. "I would like your opinion on another matter."

"Oh?"

Her friend put a card in Lizzy's hand. The front read, *Colonel John Fitzwilliam.* She turned it over and silently read the neat hand on the back.

"He wishes to escort Miss de Bourgh to your tea? He *and* Mr. Darcy?" Lizzy asked, incredulous. Her gaze met Charlotte's. "They mean to stay for the tea, as well. It is rather an audacious request, is it not?"

"I can hardly refuse," Charlotte said, her brow furrowed. "Our patroness' own nephews."

"I can see that," Lizzy mused. "But when you talked to the mothers of your young friends, you told them only women would be attending. They may be offended if gentlemen are present when their daughters are not yet out."

"That is my dilemma."

Lizzy tapped the card against her lips as she thought. Charlotte watched her minutely.

"Do you think," her friend asked slowly, "it would be appropriate to excuse their presence by explaining that they are there to be ready to take Miss de Bourgh home if she becomes fatigued?"

"The tea is to be held in the drawing room," Lizzy reminded her. "Will the mothers not think you could have set them up with a pack of cards in here, or in Mr. Collins' study? They do not need to wait with us."

Charlotte appeared momentarily stymied, then brightened. "I know. I shall say that Miss de Bourgh specifically wished them to attend."

"If you whisper it in confidence to the right guest, the others will soon know," Lizzy said, smiling shrewdly.

"I know just the lady."

"I do not think you should permit them to attend if they are unwilling to recite something, however," Lizzy advised, grinning. "It will not be a hardship. I know nothing of Colonel Fitzwilliam's accomplishments, but Mr. Darcy told me his own tutor made him memorize many worthy pieces."

Charlotte smiled back. "I shall send them an invitation,

underlining the requirement so they are not surprised when we ask them to perform."

"Remind them that the passage must be appropriate for young ears," Lizzy advised.

Charlotte rose and headed for her escritoire positioned next to a window. Over her shoulder she asked, "Are you ready for your turn to recite? Was Mr. Darcy helpful yesterday?"

Lizzy gave a half nod and quiet smile. "He was. And I believe I am."

"After I have sent this invitation, you shall recite your reading to me. I also need more practice."

ꟃ

His cousin ran Darcy down in the library, sitting in front of a warm fire, reading. Fitzwilliam plopped into the chair opposite him and held up a letter.

"We have been invited to accompany Anne to the recitation tea tomorrow," he said. "It is at two."

Darcy raised an eyebrow and closed his book around a finger to hold his place. "I thought the tea was for ladies."

Fitzwilliam grinned. "It was. I asked if we might come and Mrs. Collins agreed as long as we recited something. Something *appropriate*, she writes."

"You have put Mrs. Collins in an awkward position," Darcy remarked, shaking his head. "You know she could not have refused."

His cousin nodded, still grinning. "I want to spend more time with Anne away from Rosings. There are few opportunities. An attentive gentleman must be willing to grasp whatever one chance presents to him." He frowned suddenly. "It was odd, Darcy. When I drove out with her, Anne did not appear sickly at all. A little pale, but otherwise quite animated." Scowling, he added, "It is our aunt's doing, of course. She dampens Anne's natural liveliness."

"Aunt Catherine loves Anne," Darcy stated. "Surely you do not doubt that?"

"Of course, of course," the older man said. He suddenly stood and paced around the vast space, his hands behind his back. When he came nearer, he said, "We shall have to find something to memorize. Do you have any thoughts?"

A great many.

"Miss Bennet is reciting 'No Man is an Island'. Perhaps I shall choose something else by Donne."

"Hmm," Fitzwilliam hummed, pinching his lower lip as he paced and thought. He held up a finger, turning. "Ah. Psalms 23. 'The Lord Is My Shepherd'."

"It may be a popular choice," Darcy commented. "Someone else may have chosen it."

His cousin stroked his chin. "Perhaps you are right. Very well, let it be Psalms 121, 'The Song of Ascents'. It was popular amongst the junior officers when I joined. We would recite the last verse after every evening meal before we were dismissed. *The Lord shall preserve thy going out and thy coming in from this time forth, and even for evermore.*"

"Mr. Collins could not find fault with those verses. I wonder what he will think of mine. I think I shall recite 'The Sun Rising'. I know it by heart."

"If Mrs. Collins planned to catch us out, she will discover her mistake," Fitzwilliam said, grinning again. Then he lost his smile and glanced around the library. "I must refresh my memory. Where is a bible? There must be one in here somewhere."

Darcy pointed to a wood lectern sitting on one of the desks where a large open bible resided.

"Ah, yes," his cousin said, taking rapid steps toward it.

℘

Anne and her mother were already seated at breakfast the next morning when Darcy came down. Mrs. Jenkinson sat beside Cousin Anne and smiled nervously at him.

"Good morning," she tittered and then craned her neck. "Are you there, too, Colonel? Good morning."

Darcy stepped to the side of the dining room door, permitting his other cousin to hurry past him with quick steps. Near the table, he paused, bowed to his aunt, and then hastened to Anne's side.

"How are you this morning, Anne?" Fitzwilliam asked, taking her hand.

Darcy bowed to the ladies at the table and exchanged a meaningful look with his aunt. She tightened her lips but said nothing.

"Fine," Anne replied in her soft voice.

"I am so pleased," her swain said, grinning. "I am looking forward to the tea party at the vicarage this afternoon. Have you finished learning the piece you are to recite?" he asked, releasing her hand. "If not, we can go over it after we eat. I shall appreciate your help with mine."

"I hoped you would offer," Anne said. "We can practice in my sitting room. There is a fire in there."

Darcy's eyebrow rose. Again, his aunt said nothing. Mrs. Jenkinson would be with Anne, no doubt, but even so, he thought his aunt might have objected. Perhaps she was seeing the wisdom of having a different son-in-law.

I suppose they think I might not need to practice, Darcy thought, silently chuckling at being ignored. *Miss Bennet would twinkle her eyes at me, believing I have been put in my place.*

Having collected his meal, he sat at his usual place. He spied the brown bottle next to his cousin's place.

"Anne?" he asked, reaching for the tiny dish of pepper before him.

Turning to him, Anne lifted her eyebrows. "Yes, Fitz?"

"Who makes your tonic?"

"My tonic?" she asked, glancing down at the bottle.

Mrs. Jenkinson simpered. "Why, Mr. Darcy, you must know that it is an old family recipe of mine."

Darcy stilled for a second and then smiled at her. "How long have you been making it for Anne?"

"From the moment I arrived when dearest Anne turned six years of age," Mrs. Jenkinson said, smiling dotingly on her employer. "I noticed immediately that she looked peaked."

"How kind of you to make her some," Darcy praised, concentrating on cutting his slices of beef.

"I already had a bottle prepared," Mrs. Jenkinson explained. "I always take it myself. Every morning."

Darcy took a bite and nodded at her.

"What is this interest in Anne's tonic?" his aunt demanded, frowning heavily.

Swallowing first, he said, "I wonder if a different tonic might work better for Anne. Perhaps her humors are used to it after so many years?"

"Do you have a recipe?" his aunt asked.

Darcy shook his head, carefully watching Mrs. Jenkinson for a reaction. She would not like it so much if Anne's health improved and she married. Her usefulness might be over.

The companion leaned fully back in her chair as though she had been slapped. She pressed her fingers onto her pale cheeks.

Remembering Miss Bennet's charge to be more obviously kind, he gently asked, "Have I offended you, Mrs. Jenkinson? I did not mean to."

The colonel frowned at Darcy and hurriedly said to Mrs. Jenkinson, "We are all concerned about our dear cousin's health, ma'am. Perhaps you and the apothecary could consult together and develop a more effective tonic for Anne."

"The a...apothecary?" Mrs. Jenkinson stuttered. "He would steal my family recipe and sell it as his own. I…I…cannot trust him."

"He will not," his aunt stated, a militant light in her eye. "But I have a better notion. I do not know why I have not thought of this before." She lifted a finger and Billings hastened to her side. "Send for Harold. Have him meet me and Mrs. Jenkinson in the distillery in an hour and tell him to bring the 'book'."

"Yes, my lady." The butler bowed and started to leave the room.

"Billings?" she called.

He stopped and turned around. "My lady?"

"What are you wearing around your neck?" She waited until he touched his black cravat before she asked, "Is that an iron nail?"

His hand fell. "It is, my lady."

"Are the servants all feeling superstitious today? Winters had a nail hanging around her throat this morning."

"They are, my lady. Mrs. Durling and I thought there could be no harm in permitting it."

"Or joining in, I see," Lady Catherine observed dryly. "I have no objection while our guests are family, but I will not be made to look a fool whenever non-familial guests are present in the house."

"No, my lady."

She waved him away. "Continue."

"Harold, Aunt Catherine?" Colonel Fitzwilliam asked impatiently. "Is he not the head gardener?"

Darcy could tell he cared not a whit about servants and their superstitions.

Looking entirely self-satisfied, his aunt smugly said. "He is. His wife was the best herbalist in the district before she died, and I know she had a scrapbook of recipes. They had no daughter to pass it to and so he has it still."

The companion's hands fluttered. "But—"

Four pairs of eyes stared at Mrs. Jenkinson, who appeared to be unable to continue with her protest.

"Do you have an objection, ma'am?" Darcy asked, spearing her with his gaze. "Surely there is no danger to Anne."

"Unknown formulae," she explained in a rush, "can be dangerous."

Anne flicked her finger at the bottle near her. "I am not afraid. And I am tired of this one. Let us attempt another." Her brows drew together. "Something that tastes better."

"Taste is not the most important thing," her mother told her.

"It is if I cannot make myself swallow it," Anne retorted gently. To her companion, she said, "Pray try, Jenky."

Mrs. Jenkinson's expression softened at the use of Anne's childhood name for her. "I will, dearest Anne."

Darcy did not know if his intervention would make any difference to Anne's health, but he hoped it would be counted in his favor by Miss Bennet. In fact, he did not think a new tonic would make any difference at all if Anne was not being poisoned.

When he joined the recitation tea party that afternoon, he whispered his success in changing his cousin's tonic as soon as he managed to find a moment with Miss Bennet. She had been smiling the pleasant sort of smile adopted when guests milled about. This froze at his news. She maneuvered herself so no one could see her speak or hear her whispered words.

"Are you saying, sir, that you put the two ladies who would gain the most by Miss de Bourgh's continuing illness in charge of making the next tonic?"

He stiffened and his features hardened. "Harold, the gardener, is assisting them."

"Good. All the same, I expect you had no say in the matter," she offered, shaking her head once. "Your aunt has a forceful personality, and you are a gentleman."

Darcy could not tell if he preferred to be thought stupid or ineffectual. Perhaps she considered him both. *What a lowering possibility.*

"You are wearing the charms," she observed. "Excellent."

His fingers brushed across his key fob, feeling the tiny charms. "Uh…yes. I thought I may as well. When my valet woke me this morning, he had a nail pushed through the knot of his cravat. His influence below stairs could be readily seen when I went down for breakfast."

"How is that?" she asked, twinkling up at him now.

"All the servants have taken to wearing iron nails. The maids are wearing them around their necks on lengths of ribands, and all the male servants are wearing them like my valet."

Miss Bennet chuckled. "I can just see it. What of the men who do not wear cravats?"

"Inside servants have shoved them into their vest buttonholes. The outside ones have put them through their caps." Darcy mimed his meaning, pretending to shove a long nail first into an imaginary cap and then out of it, like a needle. "Harold wore one that way."

"Hmm, I am not surprised by his precautions," she murmured as she turned to face the front of the drawing room where Mrs. Collins stood, calling them all to order.

Darcy indicated two straight-back chairs in the rear and they hastily sat behind sixteen other guests.

"Welcome, ladies. Gentlemen," Mrs. Collins added, nodding her head at Darcy and his cousin. "Thank you for gathering with me to enjoy each other's company. I have our list of presenters here," their hostess said, holding a piece of paper up where all her guests could see. "We shall have the pleasure of hearing the reciters' selections and then we shall have tea and conversation. I see that no one has chosen identical pieces." Charlotte waited for a moment while the stragglers settled into seats, and then gracefully indicated her most important guest. "Miss de Bourgh has graciously agreed to give her presentation first."

Lizzy closely watched Miss de Bourgh when Colonel Fitzwilliam stood and held out his hand to her. She accepted it and rose. Her cheeks had a rosy tint that Lizzy had not noted the one and only time she had seen her in the Chinese drawing room at Rosings. This could be caused by her pleasure at being away from her mother, perhaps. Miss de Bourgh shyly smiled at her attending cousin and Lizzy folded her lips to keep an answering smile from blooming.

Peeking up at her seating companion, she saw that Mr. Darcy seemed unconcerned by this obvious fondness between the lady meant for himself and his military cousin. He glanced at her and caught her observing him. He raised an eyebrow. Lizzy looked at his cousins and then back at Mr. Darcy. His eyebrow lowered and he leaned over to whisper softly in her ear.

"My cousin appears to have finally realized Anne's true feelings."

Lizzy opened her eyes wide. "So you know?"

"For years."

"Does your aunt—"

A dragon of a dowager who sat in front of them, looked over her shoulder, frowning. They fell silent, focusing on the first performer.

"For my recitation today," Miss de Bourgh began, "I shall perform the first two stanzas of a poem by Miss Carter. It is called 'Ode to Melancholy'. I shall not recite the remaining stanzas because I find them too…melancholic."

Light laughter sounded, which she accepted with a chuckle of her own.

"Ode to Melancholy," she said, and everyone fell silent.

"Come, Melancholy! Silent power,
Companion of my lonely hour,
To sober thought confin'd;
Thou sweetly sad ideal guest,
In all thy soothing charms confest,
Indulge my pensive mind.

No longer wildly hurried thro'
The tides of mirth, that ebb and flow
In folly's noisy stream:
I from the busy crowd retire,
To court the objects that inspire
Thy philosophic dream."

Lizzy thought she had done the poem justice. She clapped along with the other guests when Miss de Bourgh bowed slightly.

"Thank you," she said, flushing with the success of her performance.

Colonel Fitzwilliam stepped forward, returned her to her spot, waited for her to be ready, and composed himself for his own performance. He explained why he had made his choice, and then recited Psalm 121, the Song of Ascents.

Lizzy spied Miss de Bourgh touching her fine handkerchief to the corner of her eyes.

"Why is she upset, Mr. Darcy?" Lizzy whispered.

"Fitzwilliam is to leave for Upper Canada in a few weeks."

"Ah."

"Mr. Darcy?" Charlotte called. "It is your turn."

He stood, drawing a puzzled Lizzy to her feet. "Pray, Mrs. Collins, permit Miss Bennet to take my place. She is anxious to perform. I shall take my turn after hers."

"You wretch," Lizzy whispered, blushing. "You should be ashamed of uttering such a tarradiddle."

He squeezed her elbow.

"Certainly, Mr. Darcy," Charlotte said, raising her eyebrows at her friend. "Are you ready, my dear?"

Lizzy nodded.

"I see that she is. May I present Miss Elizabeth Bennet?"

Mr. Darcy escorted her to the front of the group and returned to stand near the far wall. Lizzy ignored his presence while she recited her lines until she hesitated before a forgotten phrase. When she glanced his way, he mouthed the next line and she gratefully accepted his social salvation.

His turn soon arrived and he also recited from John Donne, his choice being "The Sun Rising". She hardly breathed from the moment he began to when he finished the last two lines.

"…Shine here to us, and thou art everywhere;
This bed thy center is, these walls, thy sphere."

Lizzy never would have thought that quiet, serious Mr. Darcy had the ability to emote like an accomplished actor. His…passion…for the words intrigued her. Enthusiastic applause came after a moment of silence while his audience drew breath. He bowed and made his way around the outskirts of the room to her place. As soon as he settled, she leaned close.

"You put us all to shame, Mr. Darcy," Lizzy whispered. "What a talent you have. You should stand for parliament."

He shook his head, controlling a tiny lopsided grin. "I have no interest there."

After his performance, the young ladies shyly fumbled over their recitations until Mary stood up for her turn, which would be the last.

Composing herself, she began, "I saw snowdrops beneath the hedgerows just a few days ago. Surely a sign that spring is coming. In anticipation of that happy event, I have chosen 'The First Swallow' by Charlotte Smith."

Lizzy listened, and caught her breath at the sisterly pride swelling within. So often, Mary's deliverance of her quotes sounded wooden and sanctimonious to her sisters' critical ears. However, this time, whether through thorough practice, or through attentiveness to the impression of the piece, Mary managed to convey the feeling of joyful spring found in Charlotte Smith's lines.

"Miss Mary did exceptionally well," Mr. Darcy said, clapping quietly along with the group.

"I thought so, too."

Lizzy looked up at him, a wide grin marking her expression. He met her gaze and what she saw in his eyes startled her into realizing she had been mistaken to believe he had no interest in her. *But is it only friendship he seeks? Surely, it must be that. It cannot be anything more. Yes, I relieve the tedium of this visit to Rosings. That is all there is to that softening—*

"What is it?" he asked, an eyebrow lifting.

Blinking rapidly, Lizzy searched for something to say. Nothing came to mind, her quick wit disserting her. Fortunately, the door to the drawing room opened and Hibben entered the room, carrying the tea things. A liveried servant followed behind him.

"One of Lady Catherine's footmen," Lizzy commented. "An exceptional kindness by your aunt."

"I believe Mrs. Durling deserves the credit," Mr. Darcy said dryly. "My man told me that when she heard Anne would be attending, she suggested to my aunt that it would be appropriate to send along a footman to see to my cousin's needs."

"Hmm. Even so, your aunt did not have to agree."

"True," he said, bowing his head to her. "Though, I heard Anne tell him that he must assist Hibben in any way needed."

Lizzy patted his arm. "You insist on giving no credit to your aunt for altruism."

Mr. Darcy appeared to choke.

"I beg your pardon?" she asked. "Are you quite all right?"

"Perfectly, thank you," he responded.

She narrowed her eyes at him. "Could your aunt have prevented the footman from coming?"

Reluctantly, he nodded.

"There you are then," she said, rising. "We should circulate and politely congratulate the young ladies on their performances."

"*Kindly,* you mean?"

Lizzy laughed softly and moved away.

Chapter Sixteen

Darcy found the tea party insipid except when he managed to find himself next to Miss Bennet. The local ladies and their young daughters held no interest for him. They either simpered—both the mamas and the daughters—or the mamas stiffened while their frightened young daughters stood pale and shivering.

Do they think I will bite them?

Having just arrived at his side, Miss Bennet said, "Power is of little value if you do not use it sensibly." She nodded at the doctor's wife and her daughter who had curtsied and left him to join more comfortable company. "A kind word to Cara and—"

"Who is Cara?" he asked, frowning.

Miss Bennet shook her head at him. "Mrs. Wright's daughter. You must know Dr. Wright. Charlotte told me he is Miss de Bourgh's doctor."

"Yes, of course. A kind word to Cara and…?"

"You could have stepped away from their company without them thinking you haughty and unpleasant."

Darcy shifted his stance so he faced her. "Does it trouble you that they may have this opinion of my character?"

Both her eyebrows lifted. In a disturbed voice, she replied softly, "Surprisingly so."

Miss Bennet left his side, moving after Mrs. Wright.

She is going to smooth their ruffled feathers. Darcy realized he did not like the idea of her making excuses for his poor behavior. *I must do better. Why would she want to spend the remainder of her life with a husband she must always apologize for?*

Darcy glanced around, searching for someone he had not congratulated on their performance or frightened away. He discovered Miss Mary standing beside Miss Starry, a solicitor's daughter. He approached them and bowed his shoulders. Both young ladies curtsied.

"Well done, Miss Mary. And Miss Starry. I enjoyed your choice exceedingly," he managed to say with a straight face. Miss Mary raised an eyebrow and nodded her head in polite acknowledgement. Miss Starry, a slender young lady, blessed with masses of blonde curls, giggled.

"Thank you, Mr. Darcy," Miss Starry said. "Mama wished me to quote something from the bible, but I prefer the romantic poets."

"Indeed," Darcy said, smiling a little. He bowed and moved away before the young ladies took the opportunity to draw him into further conversation.

Miss Maria stood with her sister, acting shy. When Darcy approached them, the girl scurried away. He watched her join Miss Mary and Miss Starry. Turning back to Mrs. Collins, he bowed slightly.

"Congratulations on a successful recitation tea, madam," Darcy said.

"Thank you, Mr. Darcy."

Quietly, he added, "I hope having two gentlemen intrude did not throw your arrangements into disarray?"

She smiled. "Not at all, sir. I am certain all my guests enjoyed the colonel's and your presentations extremely."

"You are kind," he replied. "Where did you sequester your husband and father today?"

"My father accompanied my husband on his rounds of the alms houses."

"A fortuitous choice of date for your party," he praised.

"Yes. They would have been quite in the way," she admitted. Then she flushed with apparent embarrassment.

Chuckling, Darcy observed, "As my cousin and I are, no doubt."

"Oh, no," Mrs. Collins said, her eyes widening.

"Do not be concerned, madam, else Miss Bennet will slay me for upsetting you."

"I am certain she would not." Mrs. Collins fidgeted with her handkerchief.

"Are you? I am not." Darcy bowed again. "Thank you for a

diverting afternoon."

He moved away, making for his cousins. Fitzwilliam had his hand under Anne's elbow.

"We have made our excuses," the colonel said. "Are you ready to leave?"

"I mean to walk," Darcy said. He took Anne's hand. "You both did very well."

"Thank you, Darcy," Anne said shyly.

"You had nice color in your cheeks, too," Fitzwilliam praised.

This mild compliment caused Anne's cheeks to redden. "I feel healthier when I am out and about, instead of sitting at home alone. I notice the difference at once when I come to the vicarage."

Her illness cannot be the result of the tonic. If it was, being out in company would not make the least difference.

They left the drawing room without Darcy speaking to Miss Bennet again. However, when their eyes had met across the intervening space, she nodded once and then returned to her conversation. In the front hall, the cousins donned their outer garments. At the bottom of the front walk, he waited with them until their carriage drew up.

"I shall see you back at Rosings," Darcy said, and struck off across the park.

As he walked in the cool, early evening, feeling the dampness of gathering fog against his cheeks, he thought about Anne. He chafed against Miss Bennet's suggestion that his cousin was being poisoned. Yet, he could not set aside entirely the idea that *something* appeared to influence Anne's health.

What is the difference between the vicarage and Rosings? Anne's health cannot be significantly better simply because she is away from my aunt. Or can it?

Remembering the result of his walk across the invisible faerie path, Darcy deliberately avoided what he could not see by following the drive through the front gates of the big house. This reminded him of the iron charms and he checked the pockets of his overcoat. He found nothing.

Pausing in his walk, he tugged off his gloves and searched again. The sensitive fingertips of his left hand touched the tiny object. He brought it forth and settled it in his palm. A flat iron disk sat there. A moment of disappointment rustled through him. He had childishly hoped for another interesting shape.

Is Miss Bennet upset with me?

Disgusted with himself for imagining more into the choice of charm than his love likely meant to express, Darcy closed his hand around the disk, making a fist. A smile slowly blossomed.

She still wants to protect me.

ꟈ

Lady Catherine sent for her nephew as soon as the three cousins returned from the parsonage. The colonel smiled at her the moment he stepped through the doors of her private office, situated next to her bedchamber. He still wore his red uniform and looked rather splendid.

"Fitzwilliam," she said, gesturing him forward.

He closed the door and advanced toward the desk with quick, light steps. She lifted her head to accept his salute upon her cheek.

"Aunt," he said warmly. "How well you look today."

"You mentioned that at the breakfast table," she replied testily. "In my day, a gentleman knew how to give an abundance of charming compliments to the ladies in his life. He did not repeat himself."

"My grandmother calls me a dull dog," Fitzwilliam admitted, his broad grin slipping into a rueful one. "I do not think I can manufacture another tribute with you staring balefully at me. I am all a-flutter."

Catherine allowed herself a tiny smile. "You should make a study of little compliments like Mr. Collins does."

The colonel barked a laugh, moving to draw a chair near to the desk. "I shall ask his advice, shall I?"

"You could do worse," Catherine said dryly. "It is not the words, precisely. It is the delivery. You have address. He will never have it."

Chuckling, her nephew said, "Sadly, I must agree."

She frowned at him and he sobered.

"What is it, Aunt?"

"Are you the only person Liverpool is sending to Upper Canada?"

He shook his head, appearing puzzled. "No. I will have a small staff."

"There is trouble brewing there, according to Major General Brock. He is the administrator of Upper Canada, is he not?"

The colonel nodded.

Lady Catherine fixed him with a fierce stare. "War? With our former colonies?"

"Brock thinks so. I am to confer with him when I arrive."

She pressed her lips together and noticed that her hands gripped the arms of her chair. She forced them to relax, folding them in her lap.

"He is not supported in his thinking, however," her nephew mentioned.

"Which is why Lord Liverpool is sending you to Upper Canada."

"Indeed."

"Is there someone else Liverpool could send?"

Fitzwilliam rubbed his chin in thought. Finally, he gave a half nod. "Possibly."

"I want you to sell out," Catherine stated.

His eyebrows shot up.

"You cannot be surprised," she scoffed. "Did you think I would permit my daughter's husband to remain in military service?"

Fitzwilliam stood so abruptly his chair toppled backwards. "Aunt," he gasped.

To gather his thoughts, she surmised, he smoothed the front of his uniform and then picked up his chair, setting it to rights. He sat on its edge before he spoke again.

In a hesitant, quiet voice, he said, "I thought you wanted Darcy for Anne."

Her body twitched. His eyes widened at this sign of her angry frustration.

"I have waited long enough for Darcy to come up to scratch," she said with blighting accents. "As he pointed out to me recently, he would be an inconvenient husband for Anne, and an absentee landlord of Rosings. I could continue handling the estate, of course, but he has a managing disposition and would be tiresomely interfering for me. You have no other estate to take up your time. You would live here, for the most part, and I would teach my methods to you. When I am gone, the estate will go on with you at the helm."

Fitzwilliam shifted even more forward on his chair until he barely sat at all.

"Has Anne confided in you, Aunt?" he asked.

He sounded eager, and that encouraged her.

"She has not," she admitted. "However, I can see that she favors you over Darcy."

Now he looked vastly pleased with himself. He sat there with a lovesick grin on his lips. This also pleased her. Catherine longed for Anne's happiness. Her daughter needed someone like Fitzwilliam—attentive and kind.

"Are your feelings for Anne true?" Catherine demanded, drawing his focus back to her. He opened his mouth but she held up a beringed hand. "Claim nothing you do not feel. There is no sinecure in love. Faithfulness, honorable behavior, and gentleness mean far more."

"I have always cared for Anne," he stated. "But I knew she was meant for Darcy. When he told me he did not mean to offer for her, I dared to hope."

Catherine leaned forward and fixed him with a steely gaze. "Have you asked her to marry you? Before you asked my permission to pay your addresses?"

Fitzwilliam swiftly shook his head. "Not yet. I meant to speak with you first, Aunt. You know my situation. I can bring no advantage to the match except for a most sincere desire for Anne's happiness. All the worldly advantage is on my side." He stood, his posture straight, and added, "I promise to always care for Anne. I promise to learn from you how to manage the estate. I expect we will quarrel now and now but I believe debate can be useful." He paused when Catherine raised an eyebrow. She said nothing so he continued. "I will be faithful and cautious with Anne's inheritance. Pray, will you give me permission to pay my addresses to your daughter?"

Catherine watched him and made him wait to hear her reply. Rising, she stepped around the desk to face him. Lifting her hand for him to kiss, he took it and bowed, kissing the air above the back of her hand.

"You have my permission, Fitzwilliam." He released her hand and she folded both of hers in front of her. "If she agrees, you must sell out."

He grinned. "I will, I will."

"Very well then. Off with you," she said, waving him away.

Catherine watched him go, permitting her shoulders to relax a little when the door shut behind him.

That is settled at last.

A singularly disturbing thought entered her mind.

<Is it?>

In response to the odd thought, her hands formed fists at her side.

I am determined on this course, she told herself. *They will live in Anne's apartments in the new wing.*

A thrust of such intense rage struck her brain that Catherine stumbled against her desk. Pain lanced through her, forcing her to cling to the desk edge to keep from falling, gasping in reaction.

Am I having a stroke?

The rage dissipated.

Then the pain left her.

<Not yet!>

Catherine shuddered.

She made her way to her chair, continuing to grasp onto the desk. She slumped into her seat. Holding her head in both hands, she struggled to make sense of what had happened.

"What was that?" she asked aloud just so she could prove she still had use of her voice. "I do not speak as though I had a stroke."

Catherine released her head and wriggled her arms. She stood and walked to the fireplace, turned around, and trod back to the desk where she picked up the hand bell and shook it.

I move well.

The door to her office opened and her personal footman entered.

"M'lady?" Percy asked.

"Bring me a glass of sherry, please."

"Yes, m'lady."

He left, and when he returned a few minutes later, she realized he also wore an iron nail like the other servants.

"Are you afraid of faeries, too?" she asked.

"Me mother taught me to be cautious, m'lady." Percy nodded at the silver salver in his hand. "I brought one for you."

Catherine prepared herself to deliver a blistering denunciation of the superstitious nonsense, but her thoughts paused.

I wonder…those thoughts…the pain…the rage…

"Place it on my desk," she said quietly. "There is no harm in being cautious."

&c

After an eventful day, the parsonage household retired early to bed. Lizzy stood in front of the mirror, brushing her long hair. She was not paying much attention to her automatic actions and her eyes remained unfocused as she mused over the day. The recitation tea had been a thorough success. Charlotte's expression had glowed when she said goodbye to her guests as they departed.

Miss de Bourgh had stayed right through the recitations and then partook of tea before she left, taking her cousins along with her. She had kindly insisted that the Rosings' footman remain to help Hibben.

Lizzy examined her jingling bracelet. She had slipped one of the iron disks into Mr. Darcy's pocket. She hoped that the next time she saw him, the charm would be dangling from his watch fob with the other charms. She had more iron disks than she had figure charms so she had sensibly given him one of those. Besides, when she had chosen the charm she had been feeling a trifle annoyed with him. He had given the two ladies who would benefit the most from Miss de Bourgh remaining ill the opportunity to make another, possibly poison-tainted, tonic.

What had he been thinking?

Putting down her brush on the dressing table, Lizzy blew out the candles in the sconces on either side of the mirror. The night lamp on the small desk lit the room in a soft, golden glow. She turned it down a little and then, sighing, climbed under the covers.

I should not be annoyed with Mr. Darcy. My theory may be wrong. There may be another reason for Miss de Bourgh's ill health. I am not a doctor. Or an herbalist. The fae…

She composed herself for sleep, pondering the mystery as she snuggled under the covers. *I wish I could speak to…*

Lizzy pulled her favorite olive-green shawl around her shoulders and examined her surroundings. She stood in the middle of the largest clearing in the home wood of Longbourn house. The odd light gave no indication of the time of day, though it seemed to be daytime. The trees swayed in the breeze and the rustling of the leaves almost drowned out the sound of wagon wheels and jingling harnesses. A piebald Irish cob, pulling a painted gypsy caravan, emerged from the gap in the trees.

"It is Aunty," she whispered, hurrying forward.

The stout old woman sat on the floor of the front porch, her feet propped on the shafts, her black bombazine dress decorated by an apron embroidered with red roses and green leaves. She had the tanned, wizened face of an apple-headed kitchen witch. She pulled on the reins.

"Stand," she said in a deep, authoritative voice. The cob obediently stopped pulling. Aunty wrapped the reins around the brake handle.

Lizzy reached her side. Grinning up at her, she said, "Aunty! I missed you."

Aunty scowled. "What did you get yourself into, gal? Why am I here?"

"I…I cannot say," Lizzy said, frowning now.

"I didn't mean to come here, Elizabeth." Aunty stood and carefully swung herself down from the front porch of the caravan. "You drew me here."

Lizzy offered her arm. "Truly, I do not know why you have come."

"Something must be troubling you," the old woman insisted, taking her arm.

"Walk with me."

"There is," Lizzy admitted. "I did not mean to send for you, though." She glanced around the clearing. "I am not even at Longbourn. I am away in Kent."

"I am not at Longbourn either. This is a between place," Aunty explained.

They walked half a dozen steps without Lizzy speaking.

Finally, Aunty spoke, "Is it the fae? I have the feeling it's the fae."

Lizzy nodded, grimacing. "It is the fae."

"Well, spit it out, gal. I'm on my way somewhere else."

"Sorry, Aunty." They paused beside a stream. "I am at Charlotte's new home. I have been there almost a week and I have seen numerous members of the fair folk." She explained about the faerie paths and the energy lines crisscrossing the area.

"What have you done to protect your friends?" Aunty asked.

"I planted iron horseshoes," Lizzy said. She tucked a few stray hairs back beneath her bonnet. "I have reminded people about the value of iron. But, while the number of fae seems excessive, they are not my only concern."

"The sickly woman," Aunty said, her eyes closed.

Her knowledge of Miss de Bourgh did not surprise Lizzy. "Yes. Are the two worries related?"

"I taught you to trust your instinct, gal. What does it tell you?"

Lizzy rubbed her own cheek as she "felt", searching for the nebulous sparks that hinted of the metaphysical world.

"I…I feel…I feel that they are." Lizzy sighed. "But how?"

Aunty turned them back toward the caravan. "You must investigate. Carefully."

"Yes," Lizzy whispered.

At the side of the horse, Aunty put her hand up and rested it on the horse's flank. The muscles quivered under her touch. "The paths…there's more than one."

"There are."

"Hmm. There's something there," the old woman said. Suddenly, she hurried to the step and climbed onto the front porch. "I have to go. I need to feed Jeffry."

"Jeffry? A new apprentice?" Lizzy asked, stepping back to be clear of the caravan.

Aunty laughed. "No, gal. Guinea pig."

"A guinea pig?" Lizzy chuckled at the idea of owning such a quaint pet. Not for Aunty a simple cat or dog.

She respectfully walked alongside the caravan until they reached the gap in the trees on the opposite side of the clearing. The horse stopped, and Aunty leaned over, giving her a fierce stare.

"The fae are getting impatient!"
"Oh?" Lizzy asked, her eyes widening.
"Gal, they attacked!"

"Attacked what?" Lizzy cried out, sitting up in bed, her heart battling rampant fear. She covered her mouth. Behind her fingers she whispered, "Attacked who?"

Chapter Seventeen

Lizzy and Mary joined the others at the breakfast table the next morning. Charlotte looked up from her place at the table when she entered. Her smile drooped into a questioning frown. Lizzy gave a tiny shake of her head before her friend questioned her about how pale she looked. Mary had given her opinion of Lizzy's appearance when they met in the corridor outside the bedchambers.

"You are excessively pale this morning, Lizzy," Mary had commented.

"I dreamed."

Mary took her arm. "I detest nightmares."

A mistaken assumption, but Lizzy did not clarify. "As do I," she said, giving an exaggerated shudder.

Once they had both sat down, Mr. Collins beamed around his board.

"What are you charming ladies doing today? Cousin Elizabeth?"

Lizzy swallowed her mouthful of sausage. "If no one needs me, I will go to Rosings and practice on the pianoforte in Mrs. Jenkinson's room. Charlotte, can you spare me?"

Her friend nodded. "Willingly. I mean to visit the smithy's wife and baby this morning." She grinned at Lizzy. "You will be very much in the way for I mean to have a comfortable coze with her, and I saw how timid she was around you."

"You are an excellent clergyman's wife," Lizzy praised, grinning back. She turned to Mary. "Would you care to come with me?"

Mary shook her head. "Jennifer Starry told Maria that their kitchen cat had kittens just after Christmas. She invited us to visit today and see them."

"Charming, charming," Sir William said, smiling at the young ladies. "Mr. Collins and I are off to call on Lord Ansel."

Lizzy's cousin hurriedly set down his coffee cup, dabbed at his wet lips with a napkin and said, "I need to discuss the annuity his great-grandfather set up for the maintenance of the old graveyard. It looks as though a section of the crumbling church wall is in danger of falling on some of his family graves. I mean to ask him if he is willing to have the wall pulled down before it falls, or if he would rather have that section repaired."

"Will the annuity pay for rectifying the situation?" Charlotte asked.

Her husband pursed his lips and waggled his head a little. "Perhaps. We shall discuss it."

Hibben entered through the door leading toward the back of the house. He carried a silver salver. Leaning over slightly, he presented the salver to Mr. Collins.

"Ah," his master said, taking the missive. "I sent around my card, requesting the honor of an appointment with Lord Ansel. This must be his reply." He tore open the letter, scanned the few lines, and abruptly stood. "Make haste, sir," he said to Sir William. "Lord Ansel said he can see us at ten-of-the-clock if we can but make it there in good time."

Sir William climbed to his feet. "Shall we take my carriage?" He turned to the ladies. "Unless any of you need it?"

Everyone shook their heads and the gentlemen rushed out.

"Well," Maria said, her eyes round. "How abrupt they were. Is Lord Ansel an important gentleman?"

"He is the local magistrate," Charlotte explained. "I have only met him once. After I arrived at the parsonage for the first time, Lord Ansel invited us for a quiet dinner. He is a bachelor and does not entertain often for he has no female relative nearby to act as a hostess for him."

"Is he handsome?" Maria asked, grinning.

Her sister frowned at her. "He is too old for you, dearest. He must be almost forty. And you are only eighteen."

"I will be nineteen in two months," Maria reminded her. "I might fancy an older husband. Particularly a titled one. *Lady* Maria," she said pompously. "How grand it sounds." She ruined the effect of her assumed manner by giggling behind her hand.

The other ladies laughed.

"I think you should marry a country squire's son," Mary said. "If you can find one. The war…"

"It will be over soon," Lizzy said, attempting to sound confident and reassuring. "Then, the young gentlemen will return and we will have our pick of husbands."

"We will if Mama has her way," Mary retorted.

"So true," Lizzy murmured. She held out her hand. "Will you pass me the butter, please, Mary?"

ꟗ

Charlotte threw on a shawl and walked to the gate with her friend. There had not been a private moment for them until Mary and Maria left for the Starry's home. Lizzy linked her arm through her friend's, and they stood at the gate, enjoying the early spring sunshine.

"Why did you look so odd this morning?" Charlotte asked. "Did you have a nightmare?"

Lizzy took in a deep breath, held it for a heartbeat, and let it out slowly. "I dreamed, but it was not a nightmare." She met Charlotte's concerned gaze. "Aunty visited me in my dream."

"Ohhh," Charlotte breathed. "It has been years, has it not?"

Nodding, Lizzy replied, "Indeed. She warned me that the—you know—are getting impatient. I laid awake for hours worrying at her warning. *And*, she said that *they* have attacked someone."

Charlotte gasped. "Who?"

"I cannot say."

"What form of attack?"

Lizzy shook her head and shrugged.

"Miss de Bourgh?" Charlotte asked, her hand going to cover her mouth.

Lizzy gave her a one-armed hug. "I am going to Rosings this morning in the hope of doing some investigating."

"I shall come with you."

"No, dear one, you will not," Lizzy said, smiling gently. "You have your own business to conduct this morning. I will go to the kitchen door and tell the servants I have been given permission to use the pianoforte in Mrs. Jenkinson's sitting room. I will explain that I did not come to the front door because I do not want to disturb Lady Catherine. They may be hesitant, but I am certain the housekeeper or the butler will support my claim that I have permission."

"They will think it very odd in you," Charlotte said, frowning. "Mrs. Jenkinson will vouch for you…and talk your ear off."

"She will not, for today she and Miss de Bourgh are going to visit an old friend. Colonel Fitzwilliam is to accompany them. I overheard her say so yesterday."

Quite reasonably, Charlotte offered another objection. "Then, if they will not be there, Mrs. Jenkinson will not be able to assure the staff that Lady Catherine invited you."

"An excellent point. I suppose the kitchen staff will send for Billings or Mrs. Durling, and if they are reluctant, I will ask Billings to approach Mr. Darcy for verification."

Charlotte appeared taken aback. "Mr. Darcy? Will he support your claim?"

Lizzy's eyebrow shot up. "And why not? He is too much a gentleman to lie and say his aunt said nothing of the kind to me about practicing the pianoforte." She grinned. "I suspect the butler will not even ask Mr. Darcy."

Charlotte wrung her hands. "He is more likely to ask Lady Catherine. You must not antagonize her, Lizzy, Promise me."

"Fear not, Charlotte. I shall be careful."

"Careful? You?"

Lizzy decided not to mention her plan of sneaking around Rosings. If Charlotte knew nothing of it, she could not be blamed.

"I meant that I will be careful not to say anything untoward to Lady Catherine—you know my tongue. However, I do not believe Lady Catherine will *deign* to request my presence."

Charlotte narrowed her gaze. "You said you would do some investigating, remember?"

"I will learn what I can learn," Lizzy temporized without further explanation. "I shall be back in a few hours."

"Cook is making fresh scones for us this afternoon," Charlotte said, opening the iron gate for her. "She told me she has some blackberry preserves to serve with them."

Lizzy grinned. "I cannot wait."

Crossing the park, Lizzy decided to enter the grounds through the front gate in order to avoid the faerie path. The ornate gate stood fully open. She walked up the wide drive to where it branched off to go around the house. Spying Frank near the entrance to a walled garden, she nodded and he touched his hand to his cap.

At the kitchen door, she knocked and waited. After a few moments, the door was opened by a tweeny. The young maid of about fifteen bobbed a curtsy.

"Yes, miss?"

"I am Miss Bennet. I am visiting Mrs. Collins," Lizzy said, smiling kindly at the homely young woman who would likely never rise to be a parlor maid because of her poor looks. Instead, she might spend her entire working life waiting on the upper staff, being pulled this way and that by the cook, the housekeeper, and the butler. "When we visited Rosings to take tea with Lady Catherine, she said I might practice playing on the pianoforte in Mrs. Jenkinson's room. May I come in through the kitchens? I do not wish to disturb Lady Catherine."

The girl hesitated. "Me neither, miss. But, beggin' yer pardon, I think I should get Mrs. Durling."

"Of course. She is the housekeeper, is she not? Perhaps you could take me to her sitting room to wait while you fetch her?"

"Yes, miss." She stepped back, pulling the door open wide enough for Lizzy to step through. "I'm Molly, miss."

"I have always liked that name," Lizzy said.

"Thank you, miss," Molly said, blushing.

Lizzy followed her down a flagstone passageway to a smaller corridor leading to the right. A kitchen boy and a scullery maid popped their heads around the corner further along the main passage to see who had come to the back door. Their eyes widened at the sight of her.

"This way, miss," Molly said, indicating the side corridor. To the other young servants, she sharply said, "Git back t'work, you. Ain't you never seen a fine lady afore?"

The two heads disappeared.

"I'm sorry about that, miss. They're jist gawkers," Molly said. "Lookin' fer a bit of excitement, they are."

"I am not offended," Lizzy replied, smiling gravely. "I see you are wearing an iron nail about your neck."

"That I am," Molly said, pausing beside a door. She clasped her hand about the nail. "It don't hurt to be careful, now does it, miss?"

"No, indeed," Lizzy said, shaking her wrist so her bracelet came fully into view.

"Coo, miss, that's nice."

"Thank you."

Molly tore her gaze away from the iron charms and rapped sharply on the door. When no answer came, she opened the door and stood to one side for Lizzy to enter.

Lizzy stepped confidently over the threshold into a largish room that contained a desk and chair, a small fireplace, and several comfortable chairs placed around a table. An old-fashioned red and gold carpet covered most of the limestone flagstones—one of the perks of being the housekeeper in such a prestigious and wealthy house.

"I'll go and fetch Mrs. Durling fer you, miss."

"Thank you, Molly."

The girl bobbed a curtsy, closing the door after herself. Lizzy approached a chair and started to sit in it when the door opened again. Straightening, she faced the plump, middle-aged woman who entered. She wore a severely-styled black dress with white cuffs and collar, and a crisp white apron tied beneath her bosom in the Empire fashion. A key chatelaine hung from her waistband. A mobcap of generous proportions adorned her head and tied beneath her chin.

"Miss?" she said, dropping a slight curtsy.

"Good morning, Mrs. Durling," Lizzy said, smiling. "Will you conduct me to Mrs. Jenkinson's sitting room so I may practice on her pianoforte? Lady Catherine said I will be in no one's way there."

"Yes, miss," the housekeeper said, turning around and leading her from the room. "Would you like some refreshment while you practice? Some lemonade, perhaps? And cobnut shortbread?"

"That sounds delightful," Lizzy praised. She allowed a moment or two to pass and then asked, "How is Miss de Bourgh today? Is she recovered from her afternoon at the parsonage?"

"Yes, miss. She was well enough to go out this morning. Thank you for asking."

Hmm. It seems there has been no attack on Miss de Bourgh. Surely she would not have been well enough to go visiting, elsewise.

"And Lady Catherine? Is she well?"

"Yes, miss."

Not her, either? But, would the great lady speak of her ills to her housekeeper? No, I expect not. To her maid? Yes. Does the maid tell tales below stairs? I wonder.

Mrs. Durling led them through green baize double-hung doors into the family part of the great house. A long corridor stretched to the right and left. Thick crimson, pale-blue, and gold Axminster carpet runners extended in both directions, set end to end. Lizzy only knew that the carpets were Axminster because her cousin had taken great delight in telling her so. He apparently had not recognized, or valued, the extensive Turkish carpets brought back to England from her father's Grand Tour, and laid liberally upon Longbourn floors.

Enormous windows graced one side of the corridor and ornate doors dotted the opposite side. Paintings and tapestries decorated the blue silk-covered walls. A parlor maid stood to one side so they could pass, dipping a small curtsy for Lizzy.

Mrs. Durling stopped them in front of a door, opened it, and stood to one side. "This is Mrs. Jenkinson's sitting room, miss." She nodded to the corner. "And there's the pianoforte."

"It is a lovely instrument," Lizzy praised, walking across the carpet to it. "I did not bring any music sheets, so I suppose I will practice my scales and fingering."

The housekeeper, who had moved to apply fresh coal to the fire, turned and indicated the walnut cabinet next to the wall behind the pianoforte.

"Mrs. Jenkinson keeps her music sheets in there, miss. I am certain she won't mind if you make use of them."

Lizzy approached the cabinet and touched the polished top. "If you are certain?"

"I am, miss," the housekeeper said with firm assurance. "After I add some coal to the fire, I'll go and send out some refreshments for you. Whenever you are ready to leave, kindly pull the bell."

"Thank you," Lizzy said, nodding her dismissal.

After removing her shawl, spencer and bonnet, then setting down her reticule, she sat on the pianoforte bench and lifted the cover over the keys. Lizzy began by practicing her scales. She must appear to be doing exactly as she had said she would do for a while before she could leave the room and explore. There should be no fae in Rosings since the iron horseshoes had been placed by the thresholds. If the attack had taken place inside the house, then how had the fae come in?

By the time a maid arrived—the same one who had been in the corridor earlier—with a small pitcher of lemonade, a glass, and a plate of cobnut shortbread, Lizzy had progressed to a familiar piece she had found in the music cabinet. The maid set the small tray on top of the same cabinet and left again after bobbing a curtsy.

Lizzy practiced the piece a few more times, set it aside, consumed some shortbread and lemonade, and had just begun on an unknown piece when a knock sounded at the door. It opened before she could call out, revealing Mr. Darcy. Her hands lifted from the keys.

"Mr. Darcy."

"Miss Bennet."

He entered, leaving the door wide-open for propriety's sake, and bowed his shoulders in greeting.

"Were you looking for Miss de Bourgh?" Lizzy asked, rising. "She and Mrs. Jenkinson have gone out."

"I know. My man heard downstairs that you were here, practicing, and I thought you might enjoy a tour of the house. Excepting the private rooms, of course."

Somewhat taken aback by her good fortune, she smiled brilliantly at him. He blinked twice. Lizzy came out from behind the pianoforte, curtsied, and approached him, saying, "I would enjoy a tour, thank you. My cousin has told me much about the place."

"My aunt is proud of her home," Mr. Darcy said, holding out his elbow.

Lizzy picked up her reticule and took his arm. "Justifiably so."

They left the sitting room and proceeded along the corridor.

"This is the wing built when my aunt was expecting her first child," Darcy explained. "It was completed just before Anne's birth. She was the result of my aunt's fourth attempt to provide my uncle with an heir."

"I see. But…I thought she said the wing had been built particularly for Anne."

"The wing took two years to build," he explained. "In my aunt's chosen memory, the wing was designed and built for Anne, the child who lived."

Lizzy nodded, feeling a surge of compassion for Lady Catherine.

"Miss Bennet?"

"Yes?" she asked, looking up at him.

"Why have you come to Rosings today?" he asked. His eyebrow lifted and he added, "I know you have very little interest in practicing the pianoforte."

"How do you know that?" she asked, her heart tripping at the warm look in his eyes.

"Because I listened when you informed my aunt."

"Did I say that?" Lizzy asked. She thought she sounded a trifle breathless and hoped he had not noticed.

"You did."

Lizzy looked away, gathering her frayed thoughts. "I could have changed my mind."

"But you did not."

She sighed. "No."

"Tell me, please."

Stiffening her spine, she glanced around them to make sure they were alone. They were, so she said, "Last night, in a dream, the woman who taught me about *them* came to me and told me that the—" she mouthed *fae,* "—are getting impatient. Aunty also said that *they* have attacked someone."

"Who?" he demanded in a soft, but exceedingly sharp voice.

"I cannot say because I do not know."

Mr. Darcy made a disgusted sound and paused their walk at the threshold between the new wing and the grand entrance hall. "It was only a dream. A *normal* dream. No one has been attacked in this house."

Lizzy scowled at him and spoke in a ferocious whisper. "Mr. Darcy, I did not claim that someone from *this* house has been attacked. I only thought to start my investigation here because of Miss de Bourgh's ill-health."

"You think *they* are connected to Anne's health?" he demanded.

"I do," she stated. "I have given up on the idea of her being poisoned."

He seemed to realize, then, where they stood. "Come, we will go upstairs to the gallery and speak there. It is not private enough here."

"As you wish."

Darcy guided Miss Bennet to the long gallery on the first floor. Tall windows, draped in heavy velvet curtains of royal blue, overlooked the vast lake where bare weeping willows dipped into the water. On the opposite wall, portraits and landscapes of all sizes, with ornate frames, graced the surface. The ceiling, thirty feet above, had been adorned with raised geometric shapes containing murals of classical scenes. Between the windows, white marble fireplaces stood, lit to keep the damp away, even if no one used the space.

Darcy led Miss Bennet to the middle fireplace, fifty feet away from any entrance. Two royal-blue winged chairs waited against the wall beside the chimney breast. He pulled them out and set one for his guest and one for himself at angles to the heat.

"It is always chilly in here even when the fires are lit," he commented, assisting her to sit. "You do not have a shawl. Are you warm enough?"

Miss Bennet nodded. "Quite warm enough, thank you. I left my shawl beside the piano."

"Shall I send for it?" When she shook her head, he said, "I insist," and pulled a bell cord beside the fireplace. He sat on the other chair. "You asserted that by planting the iron horseshoes Rosings and its inhabitants would be safe from…" His voice trailed away, and he marked his words with raised eyebrows.

She glanced around the gallery in a manner that she no doubt thought was casual. It was not. Not to him, at least.

"And so I thought," she said, returning her gaze to him, frowning.

Apparently, we are alone. Until a maid or footman comes.

"I assure you that when I saw my family at breakfast, no one appeared any different than usual."

"You are certain? No one behaved differently than expected?"

Darcy gave her the curtesy of conscientiously reviewing the occasion. "My aunt seemed a little pale, but the others were quite animated about their anticipated visit this morning. There were no odd outbursts like the other morning."

"What is this? What odd outbursts?"

"My cousin, Anne, spoke against her mother's wishes and then my other cousin, Fitzwilliam, supported her and spoke back to my aunt. He is always polite and affable."

"Was their behavior similar to ours in the Chinese drawing room where we had tea?"

He thought about her question and had to nod.

"Did the morning in question occur before, or after the planting of the horseshoes?"

"Before."

"It was *them.*"

Darcy remained silent, but grave. He watched the butler approach and lifted a finger to let Miss Bennet know that they must pause their discussion.

"Ah, here is Billings," he said. To the servant, Darcy ordered,

"Kindly fetch Miss Bennet's shawl from Mrs. Jenkinson's sitting room, please, Billings."

The butler bowed. "Sir."

By mutual and silent consent, they did not speak until the man was beyond earshot. Darcy picked up the thread of their conversation.

"Why would they interfere with us in that manner? Surely there is nothing to gain by making us bicker and quarrel. What is their purpose?"

Miss Bennet twisted her fingers together in her lap. "I wish I knew what the fair folk want."

"Can you not simply ask them?" he demanded softly. Though he still resisted the idea of a metaphysical presence in the neighborhood, Darcy knew she believed in it whole-heartedly. "Is it so wrong for the fair folk to know you can see them?"

She shuddered, reminding him of his valet's reaction to the mere idea that the fae might be lingering in the region. He instinctively reached out a hand to her. She grasped it and seemed to find comfort in his unexpected touch.

After a moment of silence, during which she stared into the fire, she simply said, "No, I cannot." And then she tugged gently on her hand.

Darcy immediately and reluctantly released it.

"I cannot risk exposing myself or my family to their malicious mischief," Miss Bennet revealed in an apprehensive whisper. "What one of their race knows, the rest soon learns. And they do not travel as we do. They could step from here to Longbourn in mere minutes—perhaps less. The idea of revelation is not to be borne."

Darcy felt the desperation of her words in the pit of his stomach.

Suddenly she sat straighter. Fixing him with a penetrating stare, she demanded. "Is there another way into the house? One we did not protect with iron?"

He started to shake his head and then he remembered. "There are several exits to the roof."

Miss Bennet popped to her feet. "Shall we?"

Darcy rose. "You shall need a cloak."

"I can endure a little cold," she claimed, smiling. "My shawl shall be sufficient for a short time."

"As soon as Billings returns, I shall ask him for keys to the roof," Darcy said, taking her arm and leading her to the gallery entrance where they paused to wait for the butler. "What do you hope to discover by examining the roof entrances? Will you be able to tell if they have been coming in that way?"

"Unfortunately, no." She tucked a stray lock of hair behind her ear.

Darcy followed her motion, wishing that his hand had replaced hers. His stomach muscles clenched.

We are alone.

Chapter Eighteen

I could ask her right now.

I could ask her now…before Billings returns…I could…What would be her answer? What if she says no? What if—

"Here you are, miss," Billings said, approaching them, her dark-green woolen shawl folded neatly over his arm, her York tan gloves resting on top. He held her bonnet in his other hand.

Lost chance…Though time would have run out. How ignoble to have a servant walk in on one in the midst of an offer…On the roof…Maybe…What an odd spot that would be for a proposal. Yes. Not on the roof…and I am not a coward for waiting.

Darcy stepped forward and took the shawl from Billings. He unfolded it and placed it around Miss Bennet's shoulders.

"Thank you," she said. To the butler, she added, "Thank you for bringing me my shawl and my gloves. I should have realized I might have need of it. And for my bonnet."

"You're welcome, miss." The butler looked to Darcy. "Is there anything else, sir?"

"Yes. We would like to go out onto the roofs," Darcy said.

"Sir?"

"To see the view and get some air," he explained. "Are the doors locked?"

"Yes, sir. One key will open both doors. Which roof would you like to go out on first?"

"This one," Darcy said, pointing to the ceiling.

"I'll fetch the key from my office and meet you at the door, sir."

"Very well."

The butler bowed and left them at a brisk walk.

"He walks faster than I thought a butler like him could," Miss Bennet observed, smiling.

Darcy chuckled. "As a young man, he used to be a footman—not a footman like they are today, but a bona fide running footman like they used to be."

"Truly?" she asked, her fine eyes twinkling with apparent appreciation.

"Indeed. He carried messages in a satchel he wore over his livery, and the faster he arrived at his destination, the more likely he would be to garner a gratuity. A quick return would get him a second bit of largesse. Billings was considered the fastest running footman in Kent."

"Do you think he is running down the stairs, to his office, and then back upstairs?"

Darcy grinned. "And will he only slow to a walk after he leaves the servant's stairs? You may be right. He has arrived breathing quickly more than once after I have rung for him."

"I suppose it is a source of pride for him," Miss Bennet observed. "If we do not hurry, he may beat us to the door to the roof."

Darcy took her arm. "I would not be surprised. Come, we must climb two more sets of stairs to reach the door first."

They hastened to the stairs and scrambled up them like a couple of school children, determined to be there before the butler. However, they saw him exit the servant's staircase in time to slow their feet. All three arrived at the foot of the final narrow staircase at the same time, but only the butler appeared not to have hurried.

"Sir," he said, holding out a salver.

Darcy picked up the key. "Thank you. I shall return it when we are finished."

"If you wait but a moment, sir, Thomas is coming with your overcoat."

"Very good," Darcy murmured.

They all turned at the sound of an opening door. The valet exited, carrying a brown garment over his arm.

"Thank you, Thomas," he said, and then turned around to permit his valet to help him on with his finely tailored overcoat.

"You're welcome, sir. Your gloves are in your pockets. I thought, if you'll permit me, to open the doors to the roofs. I could open this one," he said, waving at the stairs, "and then take the key and open the other door in preparation for ye."

Darcy nodded, pulling out his gloves. "An excellent suggestion."

While tying her bonnet ribbands under her left ear, Lizzy watched how her host interacted with the servants and her estimation of his character climbed. Anyone with power over others could be a tyrant, but Mr. Darcy did not act the bully. Instead, he behaved with consideration toward the servants. He thanked them, he praised them. They clearly respected his authority without fearing him.

Have I been blind to his virtues all this time?

Thomas hurried down the stair to their side, bowed to them both, and moved with quick steps away, heading to the other door.

"Is there anything else, sir?" Billings asked.

"We will return to Mrs. Jenkinson's sitting room after we come down from the roof of that wing." Mr. Darcy replied. "I shall ring for tea then."

Billings bowed and left them.

"Shall we?" Mr. Darcy asked her. He held out his hand. "I shall go first. There is no handrail so kindly take my hand."

Lizzy hesitated. She cast a swift glance up at his face and saw the warmth in his gaze. Slowly, she placed her hand in his. Mr. Darcy's strong hand closed around hers.

"Good girl," he said softly. "I will keep you safe."

Her breath caught in her throat so that her reply sounded strangled. "I never doubted it, sir."

And then he grinned…and she was lost to all rational thought. Her heart pounded. Her feet stumbled. She could not force any words out into the air—she could not think of a single thing.

Only after they climbed over the high threshold, and he led her across the stone slab walkway to the parapet, was Lizzy able to think of anything but that smile. The thoughts, however, seemed equally senseless to her.

How handsome he looks. How carefree.

Mr. Darcy placed her hand on the waist-high stone parapet and released it. Lizzy regretted the loss of his strength, but her heart calmed a little. The cool breeze teased hair out from beneath her straw bonnet and whipped the strands across her cheeks. She brushed them away. They immediately returned.

"Can you tell if *they* have been on the roof?" Mr. Darcy asked.

Lizzy looked up at him, flustered and puzzled. "Um?"

Leaning close, he whispered, "The fae."

Memory returned. "Oh…I remember."

His eyebrow lifted and he smiled again.

Drat that smile.

Eyes widening, determined to be sensible, she glanced around her in the most casual way possible. The gentle slope of the roof rose above the walkway to a shallow peak adorned with a lead cap.

"We are alone," Lizzy confirmed. "They leave no trail behind them when they pass. I have often seen them hover above the ground."

"Unfortunate, indeed." He waved down toward the park in front of them. "Are there any on the path?"

Shaking herself internally, Lizzy focused her attention on the view beyond the parapet. The fore park, drive, and gates lay before them. She concentrated her sight on the park beyond the gates. Silvery energy lines crisscrossed the ground, several leading directly into the house.

"I understand there is a well beneath the house?"

Mr. Darcy placed his gloved hands on the parapet. "There is. And another one in the stable yard."

She narrowed her eyes.

"Is the wind too much for you?" Mr. Darcy asked.

"No," Lizzy replied. "I am concentrating on the faerie path. It branches off. The fork is near to where we jumped over it."

"Where does it go?"

She stretched out her arm and pointed. "The main path continues through the standing stones by the woods. The other comes beneath the stone wall, there, and into the fore park."

"And then?"

"May we continue to the far end of the roof?" Lizzy asked, waving in the direction she wished to go. "I cannot see where the path leads from this vantage point."

"Certainly," he said, holding out his elbow for her. She took it and he added, "Is there anyone on the faerie path?"

"Not that I can see."

They reached the new parapet. Lizzy spied the path below. She turned her head and followed it until it disappeared around the corner of the house again. Lizzy straightened, frowning.

"What is it?" Mr. Darcy asked.

"If we are to discover its direction, we shall need to go onto the roof of the nursery wing," she explained. "The house continues to block my sight."

"Certainly," he said.

She took his arm and they turned in the direction of the door. Two fae stood next to the entrance back into the house, seemingly about to enter. They turned to look their way.

"Oh, dear," she whispered, and swiftly glanced down at her feet as though she were minding her way.

"Miss Bennet?"

"We have guests. A male and female. Kindly take your watch out and hold it in your hand so the fob hangs over the edge of your palm," she directed softly. "In a natural way, please."

"As you wish." He complied.

For her part, Lizzy shook her arm so her bracelet fell across the back of her hand.

"Pretend you are showing it to me," she directed, and then said in a normal voice, "That is very fine. I have never seen a man wear charms on his fob. Do you also collect charms? I have collected for many years."

"It has been a recent pastime," he admitted, playing along magnificently. "I particularly like the ones molded into figurines."

Lizzy displayed her bracelet. "Like mine?"

Mr. Darcy held her hand again, lifting it so he could examine her charms more closely. "Very nice," he said. "This mouse is…charming."

They both forced a light chuckle.

"I wonder if the blacksmith here has the skill to make fine charms," Mr. Darcy mused. "I have a few design ideas."

"Animals?" she asked. "A horse head, perhaps?"

"Hm," he hummed. "Yes. Something a little larger than these charms." He lifted her hand to his lips and kissed her knuckles.

Breathlessly, Lizzy replied, "An iron seal shaped like a chess piece? The castle? Or the knight?"

"Delightful." He covered her hand with his, leaned forward, and whispered, "Have they left?"

Lizzy shivered. "Not yet."

Straightening, he said, "You are cold. Come, let us go inside out of this breeze."

"I am a trifle chilled," she acknowledged.

<Iron.>

<Why does she wear so much iron?>

Lizzy pretended she had not heard them talking together. They floated aside so Mr. Darcy did not walk through them.

"Was Mrs. Collins pleased with her recitation tea party?" Mr. Darcy asked her.

"Oh, yes," Lizzy said, studiously looking up into his countenance while she answered him. From the edge of her vision, she could tell that the exceedingly—painfully—beautiful fae appeared frustrated and angry. The male spoke first.

<This duty has become onerous. Why have they been so ignorant of our purpose?>

<How much more obvious can we be?>

Lizzy stumbled against Mr. Darcy. He stopped and she listened keenly, praying the fair folk would continue to complain. They might learn something important from them.

"Are you injured?" he asked, his eyebrows high, his eyes expressing concern.

"Quite all right," she replied, smiling ruefully. "My foot slipped, merely."

The male answered the female's question.

<We are forbidden to show ourselves.>

<Yet our influence is felt. Iron is everywhere.>

<Ignorant, thoughtless humans.>

"I beg your pardon. I must have been hastening our steps without regard to your safety," Mr. Darcy said ruefully.

"Not at all," Lizzy said with automatic politeness. "I was clumsy."

When he would have moved them closer to the door, she pulled back enough to make him stop. He frowned down at her. Lizzy pursed her lips and silently shushed him.

"Pray, let me recover a moment," she said, smiling ruefully. "Falling on a roof is most alarming."

Mr. Darcy patted her arm. "Of course."

Eagerly, Lizzy listened to the male fae.

<Our way has been blocked for decades. The queen assigned me this task and will not release me until I am successful.>

<The impudent humans! What more can we do?>

<I struck at the old woman's mind.>

Lizzy pressed the side of her fist against her lips and smothered a gasp. *Lady Catherine!*

<Why?>

<She had the effrontery to believe we would permit her daughter and future husband to live together in the offending structure. I was very angry.>

<Perhaps it is time to call the Wild Hunt?>

<Perhaps the hunt will carry away the suitor. Lo, the trespasser comes.>

Lizzy blinked, wondering whom they spoke of.

Mr. Darcy gestured to the drive where a carriage rolled through the main gates. "Ah, this must be Cousin Anne and Fitzwilliam returning. Shall we join them for tea?"

Lizzy shuddered and leaned heavily on his arm. Instead of answering his question, she said, "They are gone."

Mr. Darcy looked around the roof even though he could not see the fae. He returned his focus to her.

"What was it? Why did you shush me?"

"I thought you might give me away," Lizzy explained. "I was listening to them talk, you see."

"You can hear them?"

"Sometimes."

"What did they say?"

Lizzy began to walk toward the door. "I shall tell you after we go to the other roof."

"I…uh…yes," Mr. Darcy agreed, hurrying ahead to open the door for her.

Darcy made no attempt to talk to Miss Bennet through the long corridors of Rosings Park back to the nursery wing. In order to avoid meeting his aunt or his cousins, he took her through the lesser used portions of the house, occasionally ducking into, and out of, servant passageways until they arrived at a set of stairs that led them upwards to the top floor of the wing. A final narrow set of stairs approached a short door that they ducked through to get out.

This slate roof sloped downward on both sides of the wide walkway traversing the spine of the roof, surrounded on all four sides by stone balustrades and balusters.

Miss Bennet searched around her, examining the other roof in relation to the one they now stood upon. She drew her shawl closer about her and pointed to the far end of the walkway.

"We shall need to go to the end," she said, nodding at him to lead the way.

Darcy offered his arm. She accepted it and they walked to that parapet. Retrieving her arm, she set both hands on the balustrade and looked down.

"Dear Lord," she whispered.

Darcy hurriedly looked over the edge. All he could see was the stretch of gray roof below him, lead flashing, gutter, and then part of the gardens below where a couple of gardeners worked.

"What is it?" he asked, straightening and facing her. In spite of the brisk breeze that should have turned her cheeks pink, she appeared pale. "I see nothing of note. What do you see?"

She shook her head, and then rushed to the parapet to the right of her. He followed her.

"Miss Bennet, what did you discover?" he asked as he approached her.

She started and swung around to face him. "Mr. Darcy, which rooms are below us?"

"Directly?" he asked. She nodded. He thought about the layout of rooms in this wing. "The attics, of course, and an instruction-playroom on the first floor below. On the main floor, right below, were the nursery rooms which Cousin Anne used as a child. These were made over as her bedchamber when she turned twelve. Is this significant?"

Miss Bennet nodded again. He waited for her explanation. What she said was not what he expected.

Wringing her hands, she said, "It was your aunt, Mr. Darcy."

All at sea, Darcy blinked. "I beg your pardon? My aunt?"

"Yes. Lady Catherine. She is the one who was attacked," Miss Bennet said in an alarmed whisper.

"What are you saying?"

"The male fae said he attacked her."

Darcy stiffened and growled, "How?"

"He must have attacked her *mind*."

Dumbstruck, Darcy merely stared at her. She started to pace, her arms folded now, hugging herself, whether against the cold breeze or from fear, he could not tell.

"I was right. I knew the attack had been against someone in this house. I *knew it*."

Shaking his head as though to start his brain working again, Darcy thought furiously. "But, Miss Bennet, Aunt Catherine never said anything about being attacked."

She threw him a frantic look. "I do not expect she knew what happened to her."

"What form would the attack take?" he demanded.

"I…I think it was like…like a spike of agony," Miss Bennet explained. In a lame voice, she added, "At least…that is how it was described to me by Aunty. I, thank the good Lord, have never experienced it."

A shiver passed over her. He removed his overcoat and put it around her shoulders. Though she hugged it tightly around herself, she did not seem to notice his gentlemanly gesture.

"Who is Aunty?" Darcy asked, exceedingly conscious of her.

"The woman who taught me and trained my abilities," she explained absently.

A little frustrated with the roundaboutation of her information, he demanded a little sharply, "Did they say anything else?"

She nodded. "The male was given a task by his queen many years ago. 'Our way has been blocked for decades,' he said. His goal must be to unblock the way."

"The way?" Darcy asked, his brows furrowed. "What 'way'? Does he mean…does he mean the faerie path?"

Her gaze met his. "I believe so."

Darcy clenched his fists at his side. He started to pace then. "I cannot believe this…this mythical nonsense. How can it be true?"

"I thought…I thought you were beginning to believe," Miss Bennet said.

He glanced at her. At first, she appeared stricken. Then, she put her fists on her hips and glared at him.

"More fool me, I suppose," she said in a harsh whisper.

Oh, Lord, I have done it now.

"Miss Bennet," he said, coming to a stop in front of her. "I—"

She interrupted him. "Regardless of what you believe, I must help your family. The…you know…are done with being subtle." She raised clasped hands before her as though pleading with him to understand. "Mr. Darcy, they spoke of calling the Wild Hunt!"

What is a Wild Hunt?

Darcy's confusion must have shown on his face because she continued without waiting for a verbal response.

"They hope the Wild Hunt will take your cousin, the Colonel, so that he cannot marry Miss de Bourgh," Miss Bennet explained.

Surprised, Darcy asked, "How did you know of Fitzwilliam's interest in Miss de Bourgh?"

"It is obvious," she replied, a touch of exasperation in her voice. "Anyone can see how attentive he is to her. Even the fair folk have noticed."

"The *fae*," Darcy muttered.

Miss Bennet's fine eyes flashed. "The *fae*."

Darcy needed to retrench. He needed to calm her down so that she could recognize how unreasonable she sounded. The nightmares after crossing "the path" had been coincidence. The odd behavior of the members of his family could be chalked up to the natural strain that came from his aunt and cousin living together continuously. Fitzwilliam's ungentlemanly outburst could have been caused by the tender feelings he had for Anne. Everything could be explained away. Yet…a niggling doubt remained.

What if she is telling the truth?

He opened his mouth to describe how difficult it was for him to believe her stories of mythical creatures haunting the region. However, that was not what came out of his mouth.

"You must marry me."

What did I just say?

Miss Bennet stepped backward, her eyes wide. "What did you just say?" she whispered, an echo to his thoughts.

Oh, dear. There is nothing for it…I must plough ahead.

Darcy stepped forward and took her hand. She shook her head, looking even paler now.

"I cannot have heard correctly." Swallowing, she added, "Perhaps you are being influenced."

Miss Bennet looked all around them, even into the air, and down over the side of the barriers.

"I beg your pardon?" Darcy demanded, clasping her hand tighter. "You know that I am not. You would have said if we were not alone. Besides, I confess that I know the feel of being influenced. I assure you, I am in my right mind."

"Kindly release my hand," she requested in a quietly intense voice.

Darcy stared down at their hands and released hers. She stepped back again until the balustrade was directly behind her, pressing against her hips.

"Is my touch so objectionable to you?" he asked, his pride smarting.

She appeared flustered.

"No, no, that is not what I meant by it. I must think clearly." She breathed in deeply several times before she continued. "Mr. Darcy, a man in his right mind—as you phrased it—would not have thought this the perfect moment to propose marriage."

"I am a desperate man, Miss Bennet. Desperate men do not always think straight."

"Clearly not. I know how you feel about my family, my connections, my…my ability. How am I to accept that you have suddenly fallen in love with me?"

"It is not a sudden thing," Darcy admitted. He longed to know if she felt anything for him at all, any tender feeling. "Do you—"

Miss Bennet hastily interrupted him. "This is not the time, sir." She pointed over the side of the roof. "There is too much at stake to be distracted by talk of love and marriage." Her gaze met his. "I…I suppose you are declaring your…your love to me?"

Darcy reached for her hand and she set it in his. Did he imagine that it trembled?

"I am. I do love you."

"Do you? In spite of your reservations? About my abilities in particular?"

Darcy swallowed. "I shall not deny my struggle to believe—even though my struggle may weigh against me."

"I suppose that is an honest admission, and I honor you for it. May I ask you to consider something?"

"Certainly," he said, watching her tenderly. She blushed under his regard and he permitted himself to feel hope.

"Consider what I have to gain by revealing my deepest secret to you."

He lifted an eyebrow.

"I have asked for nothing from you except your trust and belief. I have nothing to gain other than your regard," Miss Bennet said earnestly. "An honest regard, sir. One that reflects who I am, not merely the person I present to the world. Other than yourself, only my mother, Charlotte, Jane, and Mary know of my ability—not my divining ability for everyone knows that, and the skill is unremarkable—my other ability."

"I am honored to be amongst the few," Darcy replied, touched.

"I hope you are speaking truthfully," she said, turning away from him and looking down at the ground. "Because, sir, what must happen next will be no little undertaking."

Dark foreboding trickled over Darcy, causing a tremor down his spine.

"What do you see? Is it the faerie path?"

"It is," she said. "And it is running right through the nursery wing, directly below us. That is the thing the faerie queen wants unblocked."

Darcy's mind stuttered as he felt his way through the consequences. "But…according to your ability…that means that…"

"Yes. The wing must come down." She paused and added, "At least this end of it."

"Good Lord." Darcy could imagine what he would say if someone told him he had to tear down a wing at Pemberley.

"Do you understand now why you must trust that I know of what I speak?"

His mind in a whirl, he stared at her. "Aunt Catherine."

"I shall need your support to convince her. This means, Mr. Darcy, that you must reveal to your family your allegiance to me and my odd beliefs. I confess I can determine no other possible way to make the request."

"They will think me mad," Darcy whispered.

"You? Would they dare?" she asked, gifting him with a half-smile of understanding. Sobering, the smile became a sad one. "That is why you must be sure. Use your reason…and…trust your instinct."

He was not sure and meant to follow her advice.

"Miss Bennet," he said, and kissed her hand, "will you say nothing further about my proposal?"

She shook her head.

"Will you think on it?" he asked, hoping he did not sound like he was begging.

Their gazes met, unblinking, for a long, long moment, during which no sound penetrated, nor temperature intruded.

"I will," she admitted at last.

Darcy grinned. Her expression softened further.

"I will," she repeated. "I promise."

Chapter Nineteen

Lizzy sat in Mrs. Jenkinson's sitting room with Miss de Bourgh, Colonel Fitzwilliam, Mr. Darcy, and Mrs. Jenkinson, herself. Lizzy sipped sweet hot tea and listened to an account of Miss de Bourgh's visit to her old friend—and yet she did not listen to it. She nodded in the right places and smiled when it seemed appropriate, but she did not interrupt the companion's slurry of words with comments.

He asked me to marry him…Mr. Darcy asked for my hand.

My *hand.*

Heavens.

What am I to think of that?

Lizzy turned her gaze to the window, discovering she could see Mr. Darcy's reflection there. Warmth—not the tea—settled in the pit of her stomach.

He is watching me. Standing there, his saucer in one hand, the teacup in the other, watching me. With love on his countenance? For me?

Just about to lower her gaze, Lizzy spied movement behind him. Years of experience kept her from turning to look at the two fae they had seen on the roof. Concentrating, she heard the male speak softly to the female.

<I will make this one so ill she will not be able to leave her bed.>

<Making her ill has not worked in the past.>

Lizzy did not look at them—could *not* look at them.

<I am TIRED of waiting!>

The male's shout made Lizzy wince involuntarily. Only from the edge of her vision did she take in the blade of his hand arched over her hostess' head.

He is going to thrust his hand into her mind!

Lizzy jumped to her feet, set down her cup, and hurried to Miss de Bourgh's side, deliberately jostling the male fae out of her way without looking at him. She did not feel his body, except for a slight tingle on her right side. Even so, he backed away, glaring at her.

"Miss de Bourgh," Lizzy exclaimed in a spritely fashion.

"Yes?" she said, raising her eyebrows.

"Will you," Lizzy began, clasping her hands before her, "kindly show me your bedchamber? I understand your mother designed it herself and her taste is exquisite." She indicated the loveliness of the sitting room. "Please?"

"I…"

"I beg your pardon. You must think me impertinent," Lizzy said, hanging her head.

"Not at all," Miss de Bourgh replied in her soft voice.

She set down her cup and saucer. Colonel Fitzwilliam rose and approached her.

"Miss Bennet will lend me her arm, Cousin," Miss de Bourgh said, blushing a little. "A lady does not display her boudoir to her male friends."

"Of course, my dear," the colonel murmured.

Lizzy held out a hand and Miss de Bourgh took it. She pulled the slighter woman out of the chair, stepping to one side when she stood. Lizzy tucked Miss de Bourgh's arm through the crook of her own. As they passed him, Lizzy let her gaze meet Mr. Darcy's. His eyebrow lifted in enquiry and she opened her own wide to indicate the presence of the fae. Blinking rapidly, he began to instinctively look around him. Alarmed, Lizzy shook her head in tiny movements. Immediately, he covered his mistake by coughing behind his hand.

Once in the corridor, Lizzy kept her peripheral senses on high alert, thinking the fae might follow them. They did not seem to have done so, however.

To continue her deception, Lizzy asked, "Did your mother consult you when she decorated your rooms?"

"Yes, indeed. My favorite color is green," she explained. "Mother and I poured over design plates and silk samples until we discovered which green of the many hues that I liked the best."

"May I guess?" Lizzy asked. Without waiting for an answer, she suggested, "Your favorite green is Pamona."

Miss de Bourgh chuckled. "You may be forgiven for thinking so, but it is not that most fashionable of colors. No, my favorite is much paler than that. I like a light room. You shall see."

A tall, middle-age footman stood against the wall. Lizzy, who had been on the lookout for it, saw that he stood near to the shimmering faerie path. It bisected the hallway and disappeared beneath a wall, beyond a tall set of doors. The footman turned his head to look at them, straightening even more, and Miss de Bourgh signaled to him. He sedately crossed the corridor and opened the door to her bedchamber.

"Thank you, Henry," his mistress said.

"Miss," he murmured, his expression impassive, though his gray eyes twinkled down at his mistress.

Lizzy noticed that he wore an iron disk on a narrow black riband around his neck. This surprised her for she thought all the servants were wearing iron nails. She looked from the disk to his eyes and saw that he was watching her carefully. He glanced down at her bracelet and gave a slight nod. Miss de Bourgh had walked ahead of her into the bedchamber so Lizzy felt safe in whispering a few words to him.

"Can you see?" she asked, glancing significantly down the corridor at the fae path.

"No, miss," he replied softly. "I feel. We all feel it, 'ere in this wing."

"Has it been bad lately?"

He touched the disk hanging just below his cravat. "Yes, miss."

"Miss Bennet?" his mistress called from within.

Lizzy nodded to him and hurried into the beautiful bedchamber. She gasped, pressing her palms to her cheeks as she stared around her. The pale green had been paired with gold brocade in drapes that hung from the ornate bed canopy. Gold and green striped curtains hung at the sides of tall windows, held back by green and gold tasseled cords. A marble fireplace surround dominated one end of the bedchamber where several chairs faced the fire that glowed in the grate. Thick carpet of figured red covered most of the floor and watercolor paintings adorned the walls.

"Is this airy furniture French?" Lizzy asked, hoping she sounded impressively knowledgeable.

"No, it is in the French style, though," Miss de Bourgh explained.

"It is lovely," Lizzy said on a sigh.

Miss de Bourgh began to expound on their choices for the bedchamber but Lizzy listened with only half her attention. The other half of her attention was fixed on the shimmering path that traveled *under* the four-poster bed.

"Have you ever considered using a different room for your bedchamber?" Lizzy asked, turning to look at her hostess.

Miss de Bourgh owlishly stared at her and Lizzy wondered if she had rudely interrupted her descriptions. She blinked several times.

"Perhaps you have considered moving into the main part of the house?" Lizzy pressed.

Sounding rather confused, Miss de Bourgh asked, "Why would I do that?"

"You are so near the kitchens, here," Lizzy noted. "I came through them when I arrived. Perhaps the cooking smells invade this corridor on occasion?"

"I have never noticed them," Miss de Bourgh said, shaking her head. "I am ill so often that the convenience of my bedchamber to the kitchens is worth the possible inconvenience of cooking smells."

"Is it not noisy here because of the kitchens?" Lizzy pressed. "And you are so far from your mother here, as well."

"It is not noisy, and I am not so far from Mother," Miss de Bourgh said, frowning now. "Why are you so concerned, Miss Bennet?"

"Everyone in the neighborhood is concerned with your health," Lizzy said, smiling feebly. If she would not move rooms, then perhaps Lizzy could convince her to move the bed. Lizzy waved a hand toward it. "A traveler witch told me once that, for my health, I should never have the head of my bed on the south wall. That is the south wall, is it not?"

Miss de Bourgh nodded, clearly mystified by her guest's questions. "That is a…fascinating piece of advice. Unfortunately, there is no other wall that will work for the bed."

Lizzy examined the path and the bed size and then indicated the wall beside the door. "You could place the head of your bed here."

"It would be rather cramped there," Miss de Bourgh observed. She passed a hand over her eyes and swayed a little. "Excuse me, will you, if I sit?"

Hurrying forward, Lizzy took her arm. "I do beg your pardon for keeping you standing. How ill-mannered of me."

They sat on the chairs in front of the fire.

"Should I ring for a composer?" Lizzy asked, sitting forward in readiness to stand.

"No, thank you. I am already feeling better," Miss de Bourgh said. She stared into the fire. "Do you often consult with travelers about your health?"

Lizzy shook her head. "On occasion. My mother suffers from headaches and we have received excellent advice about how to help her. Willow bark tea, for instance."

"Yes, it is most efficacious." Miss de Bourgh shifted in her chair, turning to face Lizzy better. "We have tried many, many things to help me. Some of them strange, some of them merely unusual, most of them not sanctioned by my doctor. We were told that the water from the well at the old church had beneficial effects on bodily humors. For a whole year I drank only water from that well. It was used for making our tea, for cooking our food." She sighed. "Alas, I noticed no difference."

Without thinking first, Lizzy said, "Oh, that is because…" She covered her mouth with one hand. Their gazes met.

"Because?"

"Uh…"

Miss de Bourgh lowered her chin. "I understand from Harold that you can divine. His brother told him." Tilting her head, she prodded, "Do you know something about the well water because of your gift?"

Lizzy swallowed and coughed behind her hand. "Uh, yes. That is the reason. You see, Miss de Bourgh—"

"Please call me Anne. I hope we can be friends," Anne said. "I do not have many. All my girlhood friends have married and moved away." Wistfully, she added, "I have always wished I had sisters." Then, she shook herself and said, "Please excuse my interruption. What were you saying about the well?"

"I was saying, *Anne*, that the energy lines crisscrossing the land meet beneath the church well. They are drawn to water, you understand."

"Should not the energy have helped me, then?"

"Yes, it would have, but you see, there is a well beneath Rosings Park too. Just as many energy lines meet here as at the church, so the water is equally affected."

"And I have been drinking my home water all my life," Anne surmised.

"Yes. The benefits are identical, so you could not have noticed the difference."

Anne frowned. "But the other water is in a churchyard."

Lizzy spoke in a sympathetic manner. "It seems not to have mattered. If only we could trust every remedy that comes our way."

"No one would ever remain sickly their entire life," Anne said, a bitter note creeping into her words. She glanced toward the door. "Some people believe having a 'magical' item, or a blessed item—like a sliver of the cross—keeps them healthy and safe from harm. Superstition, really."

"Indeed," Lizzy murmured.

"Mother insisted on buying a sliver of the cross from some traveling charlatan. She placed it on a plaque above my crib." Anne huffed. "Maybe it worked. I am still alive, am I not?"

Lizzy would not argue with that logic. Instead, she said, "I noticed the iron disk about Henry's neck."

"Yes. He has worn it since he was born. When he came to work here as a lad, he refused to wear it on the inside of his shirt. The butler told him he would never be permitted to work at table or in the drawing room as long as he wore it exposed. Henry did not change his mind. He worked below stairs as a tweeny until I was born. Then he became my personal footman. It is odd, but now everyone in the house is wearing an iron nail. Even mother has one on her desk."

Should I tell her about the fae? Do I dare?

"Did Henry ever tell you why he wears it?" Lizzy asked, hoping this could steer their conversation in the right direction.

Anne's lips twitched. "He said his mother put it around his neck as soon as he was born. She died right after, so he feels obligated to honor her wishes." She pointed at Lizzy's wrist. "Have you worn your iron charm bracelet long?"

"Since I was ten. My mother gave me the bracelet part, and the disks were on it already. I have gradually attained the others, either as gifts or as rewards to myself for not strangling one of my younger sisters." Lizzy grinned at Anne. "Having sisters is not always pleasant."

Anne sighed again. Her fingers twisted together in her lap. "Perhaps in the moment, but you must love them in the general sense."

Lizzy chuckled. "I do. My elder sister is my particular friend amongst the lot. I have enjoyed spending more time with Mary on this visit to Charlotte. It is a great pleasure getting to know her better."

"How nice for you both," Anne said. She stood, indicating that their comfortable visit was at an end.

Lizzy wished she could have found the courage to tell Anne about the fae and the danger they represented for the occupants of Rosings. It was her own fault for returning to the topic of sisters, a segue that interrupted their talk of iron and why she and Henry wore it. And now all the servants as well.

Following her new friend to the door, she paused a moment after Anne opened it and passed by Henry. He stood right next to the door, waiting to close it. Lizzy paused once again beside him.

"Your mistress needs iron under her bed," Lizzy whispered swiftly. Her gaze met his. "Plenty of iron. Horseshoes."

He did not reply. Instead, he slowly closed and then reopened his eyes. Lizzy hurried after Anne, confident he had taken her direction to heart.

When she reentered Mrs. Jenkinson's sitting room, the fae had disappeared. Lizzy thanked her hostess for a lovely day, and Anne's companion for the use of the pianoforte. Mr. Darcy insisted on escorting her home. Before long, they were briskly walking across the gardens to the main gate.

"Why did you jump up and ask Cousin Anne to show you her bedchamber? Was it the fae like I thought?" Mr. Darcy asked, furtively glancing around him. "Now you have me doing it!" he exclaimed softly, vexation evident in the tone of his voice. "And I cannot even see them."

"Be thankful you cannot," she replied tartly.

Lizzy paused beside the iron gate, certain she could not be overheard by the fae there. She gazed imploringly up at her suitor.

"The answer, Mr. Darcy, is yes, it was the fae—the same ones as were on the roof. I acted so oddly in order to stop the male from attacking your cousin's mind."

His eyes widened. "I do not understand."

Lizzy explained what had almost happened, ending her narrative by saying, "Anne has been in grave danger for many years."

"How?"

"It is not just that the faerie path runs through the nursery wing. It runs directly beneath her bed," she stated.

He stared at her. She could see him considering the implications of her answer.

Shaking her head, she added, "If you think my behavior in the sitting room peculiar, you are fortunate not to have been in Anne's bedchamber with us. I do not know what she thinks of me now."

Slowly, seeming to ignore her last comment, he said, "Good Lord. She is sleeping directly on the path."

"As close as she can be without lying on the floor."

Mr. Darcy paced to the other gate post, returned, and paced back to it again. Turning to face her, he scowled. She did not like his scowl.

What is he thinking? He says he loves me, but does he believe me?

"We cannot keep standing here in this fashion. People will notice." He approached her and took her arm, putting it through his. "Let us continue on to the parsonage."

"Certainly. Charlotte and Mary will wonder what has become of me. They will also want to know what I have discovered."

"Does everyone know my family's business?"

Lizzy thought she heard a hint of sarcasm in his voice. She looked up at him and discovered he was watching her, a smile playing across his lips. Her stomach clenched.

That smile. Heavens. If I marry him, I will see it often. How will I manage to think clearly?

"Not everyone, no. Just those two," she explained, grimacing a little. "I beg your pardon."

"You are forgiven," he said gently. Chuckling, he said, "That is something to be grateful for, I suppose. Now, back to our problem. Are you saying that Cousin Anne has been ill all her life because of that damned—sorry—faerie path?"

"I am."

Mr. Darcy shook his head. "It is an absurd theory." He held up his other hand, saying, "Please, do not jump down my throat. I am endeavoring to believe. I swear it."

"Did you, or did you not, have nightmares after you stepped on the path?" Lizzy asked, keeping her tone reasonable.

"I did," Mr. Darcy admitted with disgust. "It was the worst night of my life, if you must know. I have had nightmares before, of course, but they pale in comparison." He looked down at her, a confused expression on his face. "Cousin Anne has never complained of nightmares before. Even if she is hiding her nightmares, surely as a child she would have been cursed with them and unable to disguise her terrors."

"Hmm." Lizzy's wrinkled her nose. "Perhaps…I wonder…I suppose it is possible that she has built up an immunity to the effects of the path. I cannot say for certain." She clenched her fist. "Oh, how I wish Aunty were here. I could ask her."

"Does she live nearby? Can we go and see her?"

Lizzy shook her head. "I do not know where she lives. Even in my dreams, she always comes to me."

"Unfortunate, in this case," he bit out. Mr. Darcy made a frustrated gesture with his free hand. "If we can convince my cousin to sleep in a different bedchamber, then we could test your theory."

"I suggested that very option to her—without telling her of the fae, you understand—and she claimed to have no interest in moving into the main part of the house. I even suggested that she relocate her bed to a different wall, but that only confused her more. I believe she thinks I am addled and might prefer to withdraw her offer of friendship."

Mr. Darcy pressed her hand where it rested on his arm. "Cousin Anne has too few friends to baulk at your inexplicable behavior."

"Perhaps." In an urgent voice, Lizzy said, "I cannot conceal from you, dear sir, how frightened I am on behalf of your cousin."

Darcy could hardly breathe. *Dear sir? Does this mean she is considering my suit?*

"Do you believe…" He stopped and whispered, "Are we still alone?"

Miss Bennet glanced all around them, even at the sky and the ground. He inferred from that behavior that she meant to hide her observation from any watching fae. She ended her viewing by looking up at him and smiling. He grinned in response and she blushed prettily.

A good sign, I think.

Darcy was not a practiced flirt like some men. He had never been any lady's *cicisbeo.* Understanding the behavior of women came from observing his friends' wives or sisters. Georgiana had only recently begun to exhibit some of the characteristics of a grown woman so she provided little example. However, he was reasonably certain a blush meant confusion and pleasure in this instance. At least, he hoped so.

He tried to be serious again, though his heart soared with optimism for his future with the charming Miss Bennet.

"What did you mean to say, before you asked me about…company?" Miss Bennet enquired.

"Are we back to euphemisms? Very well, I meant to ask if moving Cousin Anne and Mrs. Jenkinson to the main part of the house will be sufficient to appease *them*—so that the nursery wing will not have to be demolished."

Her brows drew together and she let out a slow breath through pursed lips. "I am not certain. If their queen is determined, then I expect leaving the wing empty will not answer."

"Have you considered telling my cousin about…" Darcy looked at the surrounding region, feeling frustrated by the requirement to worry if they were truly alone. "…*them?*"

She wrinkled her nose. "I did think it. I thought I would try to discover how she felt about metaphysical places. She told me about various spiritual and metaphysical efforts to help her illness."

"Promising."

"So I thought at the time. However, somehow the conversation turned a corner into something else," she said, making a helpless gesture. "Anne brought the private visit to an end and I could say no more. I could have blurted it out, I suppose." They paused before the front gate of the vicarage. "Mr. Darcy, I was not brave enough to reveal my secret to her. I tell you this so you will not be disappointed in my character later. You may as well be disappointed now."

Later? After our marriage?

Darcy kissed her hand. "I could never be that, my dearest one."

She gently retrieved her hand. "Heavens, you are bold. Someone might overhear you and I have not yet agreed to your proposal. We would be in awkward straits then."

"I shall be more careful," he promised, though his heart sang.

Miss Bennet glanced away, appearing delightfully confused.

"Ah, here is Charlotte and Mary to greet us. You will be offered tea."

Darcy chuckled. "I shall politely raise my hat to your friend and sister, like this," he said, suiting action to words, "and I shall bid you *adieu.* At our next meeting, we must discuss how we are to convince my aunt to tear down a piece of her beloved Rosings."

"A monumental task," she acknowledged with a twitch of her lips.

"Good day, Mr. Darcy."

He smiled back. "Good day."

Darcy turned on his heel and strode off, determined not to be put in the position of refusing Mrs. Collins polite invitation.

Miss Bennet called after him. "Oh, Mr. Darcy?"

He immediately turned around, only to find her hurrying after him. "Yes, my dear?" he asked quietly, grinning.

"You promised!" she scolded in a whisper, her eyes twinkling. "Mary and Charlotte are bound to notice."

Darcy folded his lips to control a wayward chuckle. "*Mea culpa.* What is it?"

"I forgot to mention that I instructed Henry, Anne's footman, to place horseshoes under her bed."

Darcy lost his impulse to laugh. His eyes widened. "Is that wise?"

"What do you mean?"

"Will not the iron disrupt the path even more? How will *they* react then?" he demanded in a harsh whisper. Whether he believed fully or not, he had learned the lore.

Miss Bennet paled. She grasped the fabric of his coat sleeve. "What a fool I have been! You are right. The path will be completely blocked by the hated iron. How angry they will be! Stop Henry, Mr. Darcy. Stop him before something terrible happens."

"I shall," Darcy promised. He took her hand and squeezed it. "You may rely on me."

As he walked away, he opened his hand to observe which charm Miss Bennet had passed to him. A horseshoe. *Of course.*

Chapter Twenty

Darcy hurried through the main gates of Rosings Park, avoiding the stable gate because he could not be certain of the location of the faerie path. *No more nightmares.* At the corner of the house, he realized he did not know where the path crossed the inner gardens. By recalling the direction of their nighttime activities, Darcy guessed where it was safe to walk. Shaking his head at the absurdity of worrying where he might step when *invisible* danger lurked—and he *was* wearing iron—he walked as though there was no danger, just as he had been doing since he first visited Rosings as a boy.

The stable clock rung the hour and he realized it would soon be time to change for dinner. He would be joining Lord Ansel tonight and Darcy saw that his carriage had been brought out into the yard. He glanced around, hoping he would see Henry there, collecting horseshoes. There was no sign of him.

It seemed probable that Anne's footman would take the opportunity to put the horseshoes under her bed while their employers sat at table. As the indoor servants commonly ate after the family's evening meal, Henry should still be on duty in the corridor outside of Anne's bedchamber.

"He must mean to come out to the stables then," Darcy muttered beneath his breath.

"Did y' say somethin', Mr. Darcy, sir?"

Darcy spun, startled. It was the head gardener. He had a nail pushed through his cap. "Harold."

"Aye. Did y'need somethin', sir?"

Harold carried a burlap sack in one hand, dangling to the ground, heavy with something.

"Caught some hares, have you?" Darcy asked, nodding at his burden.

Harold shook his head. "No, sir. More horseshoes. My nephew Henry wants 'em."

Darcy's heart raced. "For Miss de Bourgh's bedchamber?"

"Aye."

"I did not know Henry was your nephew."

"Me brother Frank's boy. They named him after me," he said with simple avuncular pride. "His wife died givin' him a son, she did. His eldest daughter was but ten at the time, an' she took charge of him. Frank learned all his little 'uns to know about iron." He held up the bag. "I don't reckon' this will work, sir. I told Henry so, but he said Miss Bennet told him to do it. Told him like she knew things, sir."

"She does know things," Darcy admitted. Harold frowned. "We talked it over just now and she realized she made a mistake in asking Henry to lay iron on the path that runs beneath Miss de Bourgh's bed."

Harold's eyes widened. "So that's what it is. We wondered, Frank and me, when they built that there wing, what would be the result. But what could we say, sir? Miss Anne's father would not have listened to us."

"He would not have," Darcy agreed.

"So, you've come t'stop our Henry, sir?"

"I have."

Harold dropped the bag and it clanged. He pressed two fists flat against his chest above his heart. "I'm that relieved, sir. I even sent a message for Frank t'come an' talk Henry out of it. I was goin' t'hide these horseshoes until Frank comes an' says it's a fine thing t'put the shoes under the bed. If Frank says no, Henry'll listen to him."

"What were you going to say to Miss Bennet?" Darcy asked, curious about how they had meant to avoid her anger over her directions being ignored.

"If Frank says no, I was goin' t'send him t'explain. He took a strong likin' to her. Sir," he added, tugging on his cap.

Darcy pointed at the bag. "You hide the horseshoes and have Frank talk to Henry. That was a good notion of yours. Tell them both that Miss Bennet realizes her mistake and Frank need not approach her about it."

"Aye, sir," Harold said, picking up the bag. "I'll put 'em under me own bed."

"Good." He turned toward the house and then remembered something. Turning back, he leaned closer and whispered, "You might wish to tell your brother that there is a chance of a Wild Hunt."

Harold took a step backward, paling. "A *hunt*, sir?"

"According to Miss Bennet," Darcy said, raising his eyebrows in surprise at the phlegmatic man's reaction.

Harold wiped the back of his shaking hand across his mouth. "It's been a long while since there's been one of those, sir. I'll keep the men inside tonight, I will."

"She does not know when it will be," Darcy warned. "It may not be tonight."

"It's nice t'have warnin' though, sir," Harold said. "I'll tell Frank when he comes an' he'll tell others on the way home."

"Well done," Darcy said, and left him to his preparations.

I need to ask Thomas about the hunt. He chuckled. *I expect he will faint.*

Darcy's valet awaited him in his bedchamber. The pleasant, if noncommittal expression on Thomas' face indicated his pleasure with his master's punctuality. He swiftly whipped away Darcy's outer garments, laid them aside for later use, and assisted Darcy in disrobing entirely.

"Did Miss Bennet enjoy the view from the roof, sir?" Thomas asked, handing him a washing cloth.

"She did," Darcy said. He wrapped a towel around his waist, washed, and then dipped the cloth into another basin of hot water to rinse off. In the mirror above the basin, he watched his valet for a reaction to his next words. "She spied a faerie path."

Thomas did not disappoint. He gasped and dropped the garments he had been gathering onto the floor and swung around to face Darcy, his eyes seemingly starting from his head.

"What did ye say, sir?" he asked.

"I can tell you heard me," Darcy replied, struggling not to smile.

"I knew there was somethin' wrong wi' this house," Thomas claimed, shaking his head.

"You have never said so."

"Not t'ye," Thomas retorted. He shuddered and added a belated, "Sir."

Darcy turned around, drying his chest and neck. "To whom, then?"

"Sir," his valet said, his voice dipping to a mere whisper, "do ye ken the wing where Miss de Bourgh has rooms?"

"Of course."

"We all talk in t'Rooms. None of t'servants likes t'go in it."

"What of Henry?" Darcy asked, throwing his towel over a chair. "He stands there all day."

Thomas clutched the nail hanging around his neck by a black riband. "Iron, sir. Henry has worn iron since afore he came to Rosings."

Darcy nodded to show he understood the significance of that talisman. He waited until he was in the middle of dressing for dinner with Lord Ansel before he broached the subject of the Wild Hunt.

"Tell me, Thomas, if you please, about the Wild Hunt," Darcy asked, flipping a length of his snowy cravat over the other end while standing before a mirror. Thomas stood beside him with fresh lengths of silk on the off-chance his master did not succeed in his first attempt.

The valet started, nearly dropping the precious cloths. "The…the W…Wild Hunt, sir?"

"Do you know anything about it?"

Thomas paled, gulping. "The *Sluagh*?"

"*Sluagh?*" Darcy repeated, frowning. "Is that Scottish, or Irish?"

"Gaelic, sir."

Darcy turned his head and stared at his valet. Thomas did not notice his look, however, for he was tidying the potential cravats once more on his arm.

"Why do ye wish t'know aboot the *Sluagh*, sir?" he asked, patently avoiding Darcy's eyes.

"Stop prevaricating," Darcy ordered. Watching Thomas for the next sign of his distress, wondering if he would truly faint, he added as casually as he could, "Miss Bennet claims the *Sithichean* mean to call out the Wild Hunt."

Thomas swayed. He took a couple of steps backward and slumped into the chair containing the wet towel. He stared down at the silk cravat lengths in his hands. Darcy smothered a grin behind his hand. Thomas' eyes widened suddenly, and he started up out of the chair. He did not apologize for sitting in his master's presence, however.

"Sir, ye canna mean t'go out tonight," he exclaimed, horror on his face. "When the *Sluagh* ride, they carry away any who're out of their homes t'the kingdom of the *Sithichean*. The night hounds, the *cù-sithe,* run with them, bayin' somethin' terrible. Once ye are in their land, time doesna pass the same way. Ye might be there fer two days and return home, findin' twenty years have passed. That's if they let ye return."

Darcy picked up his fob and slipped the watch into his pocket so his iron charms hung down in the open.

"I have iron," he pointed out, and then returned to tying his cravat.

"Sir," Thomas said, shaking his head. "That tiny amount of iron willna protect ye. Not from the *Sluagh*."

"What will?" Darcy asked turning to face him. "My coat, now, please."

"Sorry, sir," Thomas said, reverently setting aside the silk lengths. He picked up Darcy's coat and held it for him. Once Darcy had it on, Thomas automatically began to brush it, continuing to explain. "Nothin' will protect ye. If they ride tonight, you'll be in grave danger if ye're outside." Whispering again, he added, "Some say they can steal men's souls away while they lay asleep in their own beds."

"If they can do that, my being outside will make not the least difference," Darcy responded sharply. "I will take my chances. If I hear them coming, I shall have Simon Coachman race home. And, I just recalled that there is iron on my carriage, as well."

Thomas slowly shook his head. "Ye may hear them, sir, but ye willna see the *Sluagh* unless they want ye to."

"Do not look so glum," Darcy ordered, becoming a little exasperated now. Such superstitions had no place in their modern world. *I am a modern man. I cannot believe in these superstitions…can I?* He heard the merest hint of trepidation in his voice when he said, "They may not even come out tonight."

Even so, once he had his outer garments on, Darcy strode toward the door, determined not to allow fear of the fae to dictate his movements. Thomas held it open for him.

"Be careful, sir," he said, his expression morose as though he did not expect to see his master again.

Deliberately misunderstanding him, Darcy nodded, saying, "It is a clear night and the moon is full. It will be up by the time I leave Lord Ansel's house. The horses will easily find their way. Do not wait up for me."

Walking away, he thought he heard Thomas say, "A full moon, is it? Oh, dear."

ꝺ

Lizzy discovered she had almost returned to the vicarage too late to change for dinner, so it was only when the ladies left the gentleman after their meal that her friend and sister descended on Lizzy for a recounting of her afternoon adventures.

"Where is Maria?" Lizzy asked, taking a seat on the sofa in Charlotte's sitting room. She looked around for her friend's younger sister as though expecting her to be hiding behind the furniture.

"Maria has retired early," Charlotte explained. She sunk onto the cushions beside Lizzy. "She told me she would do so when she came down for dinner."

Mary took the armchair across from the table between them. "She did not sleep soundly last night because of a nightmare." She arranged her apricot skirts in a more comfortable manner, adding, "She should have woken me so I might have comforted her. Maria said she hid under her covers because she thought someone, or *something*, lurked in our bedchamber. *I* slept like a cat."

Charlotte's eyes narrowed at this bit of information and she exchanged glances with Lizzy. "Do you think…"

Shaking her head, Lizzy said, "I do not. It is a coincidence, merely. There is iron around the house and above the doors."

"Are you certain?" Charlotte asked, ignoring Mary's folded arms and tapping toe.

"I have seen no fae in the house, or on the grounds of your home," Lizzy assured her.

Mary's toe stopped tapping. "They can cause nightmares, now?" she demanded in soft outrage.

Her brow drawing together, Lizzy explained, "They have always been able to cause nightmares. But, as I just said, there has been no fae in this house. Not while I have been here."

"You," Mary said, unfolding her arms and pointing her finger at her sister, "were not in the bedchamber last night. You cannot know for certain."

Patiently, Lizzy swallowed a hasty retort. After taking a slow breath, she countered Mary's argument. "I was not. However, they must follow the rules. Iron blocks their way." She considered, one finger held up to pause any response. "If Maria stood on, or even crossed, a faerie path, that may have caused her nightmare. There are two paths in this neighborhood that I have seen."

"*Invisible* paths," Mary said in a scornful manner. "How are we to avoid those?"

"I can show you where they are," Lizzy promised. "But, if you stay to the narrow, single-wide tracks, you will be safe. Those are human-made paths. The locals know that way is harmless and so the grass has worn down."

"Hmm," Mary hummed. She tilted her head and scrutinized Lizzy. "Is this true back home, as well?"

"It is. There is only one faerie path near to Longbourn and it is not in an area we frequent."

Mary's shoulders relaxed. *Perhaps she is beginning to believe me.* Lizzy saw that she had their attention and her eyebrows lifted portentously.

"I have discovered that their location is the key to Miss de Bourgh's illness."

Both Charlotte and Mary recoiled and whispered together, "What?"

To Charlotte, Lizzy said, "Do you remember the cow in the barn that I helped on Saturday? When I went out for a walk on my own?"

Charlotte nodded. "Ooo, I see."

Mary scowled. "I do not, however."

Lizzy tugged on her ear lobe. "I thought I told you. No? Very well. On Saturday morning I went for a walk and met up with a fellow water dowser named Frank."

Mary rolled her eyes. "Of course you did."

Chuckling, Lizzy acknowledged that she did have a habit of meeting odd people. "He was going to visit a farmer with a sick cow. Frank meant to dowse her to help with her health. When we arrived at the barn, we discovered that the farmer had been keeping the cow in a stall that—"

"—had been built over a faerie path," Charlotte breathed. She pressed both her palms to her cheeks. "Oh, Lizzy…Rosings…"

"Yes," Lizzy said, gratified that her friend's quick mind had latched upon the crux of the matter. "The farmer should have pulled down that part of the barn years ago. The faerie path at Rosings runs directly beneath Miss de Bourgh's bed."

Mary narrowed her gaze. "Lady Catherine said she designed that wing herself and oversaw its construction. Are you saying that she needs to pull down the wing?"

"Precisely."

Both Mary and Charlotte shook their heads.

"She will not do it, Lizzy," Charlotte swore. "Not for anything."

Lizzy cocked her head. "Not even to save Miss de Bourgh's life?"

Charlotte appeared dubious. "But will she believe Anne *is* in danger of dying?"

Lizzy opened her hands in a helpless gesture. "I cannot say."

"Could Miss de Bourgh simply move to a different bedchamber?" Mary asked.

"Yes!" Charlotte exclaimed, sitting even straighter. "Surely that would work."

Shrugging, Lizzy slowly shook her head. "That may help Miss de Bourgh's health, but I am reluctant to say if this action will be sufficient for the Queen."

"The Queen?" Mary repeated, drawing back a little. She leaned forward again, saying in a near whisper. "Queen Charlotte? What has she to do with this…this…oddness?"

"Not Queen *Charlotte*," Lizzy explained patiently. "I meant the queen of the faeries."

Mary grimaced. "Oh."

"But…" Lizzy's friend said, clearly unwilling to let go of the easiest answer.

"The male fae said he has been trying for years to clear the path. I believe he would give up the effort but the Queen insists upon it. He is so frustrated that he means to call out the Wild Hunt," Lizzy explained further, shuddering.

"Not the hunt!" Charlotte cried softly.

Lizzy ignored her sister's confused look and sighed. "Yes. I do not know when it will be, though. Tonight? Ten years from now? Time does not pass the same for the fae." She clenched her hands and then relaxed them. "I asked Miss de Bourgh if she had ever considered moving into the main part of the house to be nearer her mother. She said she was happy where she is." Gulping back her own fear, she added, "Also, I managed to stop the male fae from attacking Miss de Bourgh. A mental attack."

Charlotte gasped. "Did you reveal yourself to them?"

Lizzy shook her head. "I cannot be certain, of course, but I believe my secret is still safe."

"I do not know what the Wild Hunt is or why you are so afraid of it, but tell me, are you actually planning to ask Lady Catherine to demolish part of her house?" Mary asked. Her lips twisted into a wry smile. "I have only met her once but I agree with Charlotte. She will not do it."

"I believe Mr. Darcy might stand with me," Lizzy said, ducking her head a little.

"He *believes* you?" Mary demanded. She made a disgusted sound. "Hssk, I would not have thought it. That arrogant, proud man cannot possibly believe in faeries."

Charlotte stared at Lizzy. "Are you blushing?"

Lizzy felt heat blaze across her cheeks. "I do not know what you mean."

Mary ogled her. "You *are* blushing. What has happened? Has he proposed?"

"Goodness," Charlotte said weakly, glancing at her. "What an idea, Mary."

"*I* am not the one whose face is burning," Lizzy's sister retorted. "*And* she is acting guilty. Look at her."

Lizzy waved for her to be silent. Mary, however, would not be silenced. For some unaccountable reason, she seemed particularly testy this evening.

"Well?" Mary demanded. "Did Mr. Darcy propose?"

Reluctantly, Lizzy nodded. Both her friend and her sister slapped their hands to their cheeks in horrified fascination. Charlotte's hands dropped into her lap first.

"You must be jesting," she whispered.

"I am not," Lizzy replied calmly. Then she chuckled. "If you two will not believe me, who will?"

"Did you give him your answer?" Mary demanded, folding her arms again as though to protect herself. "I want you to marry a nice man. Mr. Darcy is not nice."

Lizzy shrugged. "He is shy, merely. You will see. He knows how to be nice."

"So, you have said yes," Charlotte surmised, paling. "Oh, Lizzy. Are you certain?"

Lizzy scowled. "I am certain of one thing—you two are hardly complimentary to me or to Mr. Darcy." They had the grace to look abashed. Tartly, she added, "I have not yet given him my answer."

"Do you love him?" Mary asked baldly.

Lizzy looked down and smoothed out her skirts. "I am not yet sure of how I feel about him. He can be arrogant and prideful, but he is also kind and thoughtful to those he loves and for whom he is responsible."

Charlotte sighed in resignation. "It is an excellent match, Lizzy. You should consider it. Most carefully."

Mary snorted and shook her head.

"You disagree?" Lizzy asked, meeting her eyes.

"I do not disagree with Charlotte's advice," Mary replied. "I simply cannot believe you could possibly love him."

"There is no understanding whom one loves," Lizzy replied in a noncommittal way.

"'Let me not to the marriage of true minds / Admit impediments. Love is not love / Which alters when it alteration finds, / Or bends with the remover to remove.'," Mary quoted. "Sonnet 116. Shakespeare, of course."

"Of course," both Lizzy and Charlotte murmured.

"*'Marriage of true minds'*," Mary repeated. She snorted lightly. "I do not think you are anything alike." She pressed her lips together while she considered her words. "Except for your pride. You are both prideful."

Lizzy drew back, her eyebrows rising. "Prideful? Me?"

Charlotte bit her lip and contributed nothing to the rebuttal.

"Lizzy, do not deny it," Mary urged, her countenance flushed now. "You believe your point of view is the only one of any importance. Society—the *entirety* of society—knows that a woman must do her best to marry well, both for financial advantage and for a good position. Yet you plan to marry only for love. What good is that, pray? In your attempt to find a gentleman whom you love, and who loves you back, will you remain a single woman? Thus, remaining a burden on your family until your death? Or, will you marry someone ineligible because you *love* him?"

Her stomach in knots, Lizzy said with steely calm, "We have had this argument before. I do not know why we canvas it again. Let us, please, retire it from all our future conversations."

Tears started in Mary's eyes, yet she continued hotly, "I use it only as a method to illustrate my assertion that you are full of pride."

Charlotte quietly said, "Mary, you cannot ascribe a person's entire character to one small portion of their beliefs."

"It is not her only instance of prideful behavior," Mary argued, unfolding her arms and clenching her hands into fists and pressing them against her midriff.

"I do not enjoy being attacked, Mary dear," Lizzy said, standing. "I had thought you beyond the age of petty cruelty. I am sorry that you are not. Excuse me while I take a walk."

Charlotte stood, staring from Mary's flushed face to Lizzy's pale one. "But night has fallen. It is not safe. *The Wild Hunt!*"

"I shall remain near the house," Lizzy said, softening a little. "I promise."

"Mary, help me to convince her," Charlotte begged.

Mary shrugged and looked away from them both.

Lizzy left the sitting room with Charlotte on her heels. "I shall fetch my cloak and slip out the back door. Kindly leave it unlocked for me."

Whispering, Charlotte followed her up the stairs. "You have told me stories of the Wild Hunt, Lizzy. You cannot go out tonight. Please."

Sighing, Lizzy entered her bedchamber and took her cloak off the hook on the back of the door. "It is early yet. I have my bracelet."

"I am not so certain that a bundle of charms will protect you from the hunt," Charlotte whispered fiercely.

"To ease your mind," Lizzy said, tying the strings at her throat, "I will collect something of iron from the stables to carry with me. I can hear them coming, remember? And I promise not to go far."

Charlotte had to be satisfied, but she wrung her hands while escorting Lizzy through the kitchen, past the startled servants. Lizzy saw that her promise to be back soon did not quell her friend's fears for her safety.

Chapter Twenty-one

Lizzy made her way through the stable yard to the tack room where she had seen a pair of iron hoof nippers. She lifted the heavy pair off a nail with both hands. She tucked them under one arm where she could retrieve them at a moment's notice.

I shall brandish them like a club, she thought with satisfaction. Walking across the yard, she considered the advantage of having a decorative iron rod made for herself to carry around like a walking stick. Then, her thoughts went to her sister, Mary.

How angry she is. Has she always been this angry with her family? With the world?

With me?

Lizzy released a ragged sigh, realizing once more that amongst such a large family of females, Mary had been lost. A cool breeze danced across her collar, finding bare flesh and making her shiver.

Increasing her pace to stay warm, Lizzy rounded the side of the house and quickly reached the deserted lane in front of the vicarage. She set off in the direction of the village, seeing the flicker of lamps lit in the square. Once she reached the first cottage beyond the church, she turned around and walked back the way she came.

Lizzy meant to keep the promise she had given to Charlotte to never stray far from the safety of the vicarage fence. She glanced around often so she could not be surprised by the appearance of the fae. Concentrating, she increased the glow of the energy lines, discovering a conjunction of lines across the lane on Rosings' land. Six lines crossed closely together, creating a fairly even hexagon shape in the middle, only about a yard and a half wide.

Her spirit still stung from Mary's hard words. *Is she right? Am I prideful?* Lizzy hoped not.

How like my own words about Mr. Darcy's pride. What a lowering thought, to think I am like what I thought he was.

Humbling, indeed.

Lizzy had believed Mr. Darcy an arrogant, proud man. She had told anyone who would listen of her opinion. Now, she felt differently. Though he certainly had those tendencies in his character, she had come to realize he had no improper pride. Mr. Darcy was shy. *Mostly.* He had not been born with the ease of manner that Wickham possessed, but that reticence gave no one the right to despise him.

The idea that anyone could deride his character made Lizzy wish to take up a cudgel in his defense. She chuckled softly, patting the hoof nippers under her arm. He would not thank her for her efforts, she supposed.

If I marry him—what an increasingly pleasant thought—I will encourage him to be more social. Then, with practice, he will relax and be able to set aside his haughty ways.

Lizzy passed from moonlight into shadow and wished she had brought a lamp to carry. She paused and looked around her, searching for evidence of the fae. Though alone, she discovered the lane had dwindled into a track. Realizing she had walked too far, Lizzy immediately made an about face and started back along the track to where the lane began once more.

When she came closer to the house, she spied again the hexagon shape formed by the crisscrossing energy lines. Lizzy frowned, attempting to recall the advice of her mentor. Aunty had said the spaces formed by five or more lines created special opportunities for those who discovered them.

What sort of opportunities? What could she have meant? Have I forgotten, or did she not say? Lizzy tsked. *Why can I not remember?*

She turned aside her steps and walked toward the hexagon space. The glowing full moon shone down, changing every color silvery and gray. The land around her appeared flattish, but actually had furrows, the remains of last year's plowing. The energy lines gleamed among the grain stubble carpeting the field.

Do I love Mr. Darcy? Lizzy crouched, removed one glove, and reached into the hexagon shape. *If only the secret of these spaces would be true knowledge. Then, I would know for certain if I love him, and if happiness would result from marrying him.*

No such knowledge entered her being when her hand passed across the space. Lizzy rested her bare hand on the ground in the center, and again received none of what she longed for.

ꕤ

Darcy pounded on the roof of the carriage.

"Slow down, fool!" he shouted.

The vehicle swayed and he fell back onto the seat. They were returning from his convivial dinner with Lord Ansel. Simon Coachman had whipped up the horses as soon as they rolled over the village bridge. *Sensing the safety of home, no doubt.*

He hauled himself up, grabbed the strap hanging next to the hatch in the carriage roof, and pounded on the wood. The hatch opened and Darcy could see the shoulder capes, muffler, and hat of his coachman silhouetted against the moon-bright night sky.

"Don't worry yerself, guvn'r," the man yelled. "We're almost 'ome."

"If you do not slow down, I shall throttle you!" Darcy shouted back.

"But—"

"I would rather not die in the hopes of avoiding the blasted Wild Hunt!" Darcy felt no slacking of their speed. Fed up with superstition, he growled, "Stop and put me down! I shall walk the rest of the way."

"Walk, sir?" Simon said, pulling back on the reins. "I can't let you do that," he wailed. "Mr. Thomas would thrash me within an inch, he would."

"He *might*, but I certainly *will* if you do not stop," Darcy promised. He glanced out the side windows. Catching sight of a familiar building and then of a lady whom he thought might be Miss Bennet in the field opposite, he said, "Ah, here is the parsonage. I shall be safe there if need be."

Sounding miserable, Simon said, "Aye, sir."

The moment the carriage stopped, Darcy leapt out onto the lane, shaking off the memory of the horrific drive. He slammed the door and indicated the carriage was to go on with an impatient wave of his arm.

"Sir, I—"

"Just go," Darcy ordered. "And I expect you to give special

attention to my horses when you get to the stables. If you have injured them, I shall turn you off."

Simon Coachman, the man who had taught his young master how to handle the ribbons, touched the brim of his hat, looking wretched. He drove on at a reduced speed. Darcy had to believe his driver felt chastened.

Darcy loped across the lane. Miss Bennet rose from a crouch and turned to look his way. He waited until he stood before her and then swept off his hat, bowing.

"Very elegant," Miss Bennet praised, a note of laughter in her voice. "Are you not afraid to be out tonight?"

"I have as much courage as you, my dear Miss Bennet," he claimed. Darcy captured her bare hand and kissed the back of it. Then, he stripped off his gloves, shoved them into his pockets, and encased her cold hand within both of his warm ones. "I did not think you would venture out tonight. Are you not afraid of the Wild Hunt?"

She lifted her face to his and it shone with silvery light. "I am petrified."

"You hide your fear extremely well."

"Often bravery is mere folly," she said, grinning. Tugging her hand free, she pulled something out from under her other arm. "However, I came prepared, you see."

Darcy took it from her, discovering her object to be a heavy pair of iron hoof nippers.

"A formidable weapon, to be sure." Darcy returned it to her. "Well chosen."

"I was thinking that an iron walking stick might come in handy," she admitted, tucking the nippers back under her arm. "You know how I like to walk."

"Indeed. But heavy. Surely iron-tipped might be easier to carry?"

She beamed at him and Darcy's chest clenched.

"Dear sir, an ingenious suggestion."

Darcy took a chance and said, "When we are married, I could train you how to use such a stick as a staff. There are more dangers abroad than the fair folk."

They stood in silence for several breaths before Miss Bennet finally said a single word.

"True."

Deciding not to push further, he changed the subject. "Why are you outside, beyond the safety of house and hearth?"

She sighed and frowned a little when she dropped her glove. Glancing down at the ground, she said, "I needed to walk and work off some anger and frustration. My sister and I had words, you see."

Darcy picked up her glove and handed it to her. She donned it and took his arm when he offered it, and they began to stroll back to the lane across the uneven ground.

"I see," he said. "May I ask what caused you to have words with Miss Mary?"

Miss Bennet stopped moving after a dozen or so steps. "Mr. Darcy, do you consider me a prideful person?"

"I do not," he said readily. "Did your sister accuse you of being so?"

Miss Bennet nodded. "She did."

"Perhaps her rancor is based in something else?" he suggested. Hesitantly, he continued before she answered, "Miss Mary has a sharp mind, I believe, but is often overlooked by others—in her family, among her friends. Is that a fair assessment of her character?"

Nodding, Miss Bennet shrugged in a rather forlorn fashion.

Darcy made a solemn promise. "We shall invite her often to visit Pemberley—without any other family, though, so she will feel wanted and appreciated for her own sake. More conversation amongst those who will listen to her will do her good, too."

Miss Bennet raised her face to his. "Mr. Darcy, you told me on our drive—quite forcefully, I recall—that you *are* a kind man. I teased you a little, then. I was wrong. You *are* a kind man, for I know Mary is not your favorite amongst my sisters."

Darcy touched her cheek with one bare finger. She did not draw away so he flattened his hand against her cheek and she leaned into his touch. *Dear Lord.*

"You are making me blush," he claimed.

At first, she chuckled in a breathless sort of way, as though he had flustered her with his touch, and he feared she would pull away. Darcy prepared to take a tiny step forward, but then he stilled and cocked his head, looking over her shoulder across the field. Before his wondering eyes, he beheld thin, glowing, golden lines, crisscrossing the field. In the distance he could see a wider line—the fae path, he supposed.

Is this what Miss Bennet sees? Does she live in a world where astonishing things exist? How wrong I have been to doubt her. Darcy stopped pondering his error and concentrated his hearing, which had always been excellent.

"What is it?" she asked.

He responded in a harsh whisper. "Did you hear that?"

"What…Ohhhh…" she gasped.

"Is that baying?" he demanded.

Miss Bennet whirled around, disconnecting his touch from her cheek, standing between him and the sound.

"I hear it," she cried softly. Slipping the hoof nippers into her hands, she gripped them before her at the ready.

"The sound is gone," he admitted. "Why?"

"It is the Hunt," she explained, terror in her voice. "Touch my cheek again. Skin to skin. That is how you could hear them."

Darcy reached around her and cupped her chin instead. The baying sounded louder. Hoof beats thundered, vibrating the ground underfoot.

Something was coming.

He had participated in numerous hunts, containing dozens of riders and dozens of hounds, but they had sounded nothing like this otherworldly and terrifying cacophony. Nothing natural could make this combination of sounds and feeling. He imagined a charge of ancient demons, their mounts and their hounds clamoring down a slope, intent on their enemy below.

Or their prey.

"The parsonage!" he shouted, grabbing her elbow and spinning her around to face the building across the field.

Across the lane.

Across the front garden.

Into the house.

The distance seemed further than was possible and he felt the trembling in Miss Bennet's arm.

"There is no time," she shouted back, pulling away. "They are closer than they seem."

"Closer?" Darcy barked. "Can you see them?"

"They mean to take us!" Miss Bennet's breath came fast and hard as though she had already been running for her life. "*You* can see them! They reveal themselves right before they attack."

Darcy searched the land beyond her, across the stubble field. Surely, there they came. Rimed in ghastly silver-gray light, red-eyed riders of red-eyed dark horses, surrounded by crimson-eyed, black-furred *cù-sithe,* the Wild Hunt advanced. Horns sounded, deep and exultant, anticipating success. He felt them vibrating through him.

"We cannot just stand here," Darcy growled. "And we cannot fight them. The iron fence…"

"Too far," she panted.

He took his gaze off the approaching, clamoring hoard when she backed away further. Instead of watching their impossible doom approach, she stared around at the ground.

"What are you searching for?" he demanded.

Miss Bennet approached again and clutched his arm. "Come…safety is closer than the fence…I think…I think…Yes, now I remember what I had forgotten!"

"Remember what?" he shouted, impatient to be somewhere else. *Anywhere* else. "We must try to reach the parsonage. The Hunt might turn aside, giving us time."

"They will not turn aside," she cried, dragging him after her. "Trust me!"

Darcy capitulated to her superior knowledge. They stumbled over the uneven furrows, falling to their knees after a half dozen steps. Miss Bennet dropped the hoof nippers.

"Help me up," she demanded, scrambling to pick up the iron tool.

Darcy leapt to his feet and grabbed her around her ribs, lifting her. In moments she was on her feet and urging him a few steps onward. Then she stopped and turned to face him.

"We are in a *dìonach*," she explained. "It means shield. Put your arms around me and pull me close. Touch my face and look at the ground."

It took all Darcy's fortitude to just stand there, waiting for the Hunt. He followed her direction, gathering her into his arms. Her arms wrapped around him. Through his coat, he felt the long length of the hoof nippers against his back. Both of them heaved great gulps of air in an attempt to calm their racing hearts. His bare palm touched her cheek and he looked down at the golden lines revealed to his anxious scrutiny.

"I see the energy lines. The howling of the hounds…"

"So terrifying…I have to keep reminding myself to trust my knowledge," she admitted. On tiptoes, with her head tilted so she could speak into his ear, Miss Bennet explained, "The sound of the horns and the baying of the hounds are meant to frighten their prey."

"It is working," he responded, his body tense. Returning his hand to the purpose of hugging her tightly, he said, "As delightful as holding you is, how is this going to prevent an attack?"

"A *dìonach* is the center of a conjunction of energy lines. There must be five or more lines that cross closely, but not on a single point. They are rare. This one is a hexagon—only about four feet across the middle." She trembled. "They are so near. Please, Lord, keep us safe."

Darcy pressed her head reassuringly against his shoulder. "So, stay inside the *dìonach*?"

She nodded vigorously. "It acts as a shield, keeping the Hunt out. They cannot take us as long as we remain inside it. Close your eyes. Do not look at them. Do not talk to them, no matter what they say."

Within moments, Darcy felt the hot, fetid breath of the demon mounts on the back of his neck, felt his hair whipped by it, and almost broke. He had to remain strong for the trembling woman in his arms. Though he squeezed his eyes shut, he had no difficulty in picturing slavering hounds pacing the circle.

"Oh, Elizabeth, this is horrifying."

Drawing his head down so it rested in the crook of her shoulder, she whispered, "I know."

Hunting horns sounded again, a violent wail he thought he would remember until he was dead and buried. Now he understood his valet's reaction to even a mention of the Wild Hunt.

"Kiss me," she breathed into his ear. "Like we are lovers."

Darcy turned his head and captured her trembling lips with his. He kissed her like he had never kissed another woman, and yet their kiss did not feel lover-like to him. Darcy could not forget the sound of stamping hoofs and the low growls of the hounds. Under normal circumstances, Miss Bennet's ragged breath against his cheek would have inflamed his senses. Instead, he believed she felt as little as he did. Even so, he hoped she felt as comforted by his touch as he did by hers.

Laughter, grating and lascivious, assaulted their ears. In his mind, he heard the whisper of their promises.

< *Come with us…ride with us…stay with us…and you will have a night of such sport…come with us…ride with us…and you will see wonders beyond your imaginings…come with us…come with us…* >

Darcy stiffened, but immediately relaxed. He hoped they had not noticed his reaction to their menacing litany. Though, perhaps his concern held no danger since the hoard had deliberately revealed themselves. He opened his eyes a slit and shuddered when he spied the stamping horses and the prowling hounds. Darcy dared not look up. Even this little hint of their tormentors caused his fear to slide upward until his eyes started to roll back into his head. He immediately squeezed his eyes shut again and the fear became more manageable. Nonetheless, the urge to race away like a fox before the hunt shot through him. Darcy took firm hold of his panic and kept his lips on Miss Bennet's trembling ones.

Why do they not leave?

Members of the Hunt spoke and for a split second he thought they had read his mind. Darcy could not tell if he heard their words with his mind, or with his ears.

<Lovers and iron.>

<Mad humans!>

<Come, my Lord. The night is passing.>

<To Eire!>

<To Eire!>

And then they were gone.

Or so it felt to Darcy. He lifted his head, breaking their kiss, and listened while Miss Bennet rested her head on his chest, breathing hard. He could hear nothing—not even the sound of the hooves.

Or the baying of the hounds.

Or the wailing of the horns.

"I cannot see them. Are they gone?"

Miss Bennet lifted her head off his chest and nodded.

"How?" he asked. "We did not hear them depart."

"They must have entered one of their *ways.* They travel peculiar pathways. They may be in Ireland by now. Did you hear them speak?"

Darcy nodded.

"If you had not been here, I believe I would have collapsed in terror. I may have fallen out of the *dìonach* and been taken. Thank you."

"My dear Elizabeth, I hope we never experience the same horror again."

She moved out of his arms, adjusting her velvet bonnet back into place.

"May I not call you that?"

"Hmm."

A noncommittal reply. What am I to infer from that?

He took a long breath and released it slowly. "Is it safe to leave the *dìonach* and return you to the parsonage?"

"Yes, I believe so. Though the fae can call the Hunt, they cannot control it. The lure of Ireland drew them away when they saw they could not take us."

"Why Ireland?"

"I cannot say. It is an ancient land, and seems to hold a special place in the hearts of the fae."

They both breathed so hard that more words seemed impossible. She leaned on him heavily as they walked, saying nothing until they reached the lane.

"I was a fool to come out tonight when I knew the Wild Hunt might come into the neighborhood," she admitted bitterly. Elizabeth took a long shuddering breath before continuing. "You, at least, only partially believed. *I* knew better."

"Your self-recriminations are too severe," Darcy protested, leading her across to the iron gate in the parsonage fence.

"Are they? When I first saw the conjunction of the energy lines, I could not remember their importance. I only remembered that they *were* important. *Not* why or how."

"You remembered in time to save us," Darcy reminded her. "Thank you."

Miss Bennet released a ragged laugh. "You are most welcome, dear sir."

"I suggest you write down an account of our adventure tonight so you will remember the truth of the *dìonach*."

"An excellent idea," she said, glancing up at him and then down again. "I suspect this experience is indelibly etched on my being." Lifting the hoof nippers, she stared at them for a moment and then handed the pair to him. "For you to carry home. Would you like to take the cob?"

Darcy took the tool. "No, thank you. I shall walk across the park and be home in a trice. Is the Hunt likely to return?"

"Once a night, only. Mind the path, now."

Miss Bennet opened the gate, went through, and closed the gate after her. Turning back to him, she glanced casually around in the manner he had come to associate with her search for nearby fae.

"There is no one about, but do not dawdle," she ordered, shaking a finger at him so that her bracelet jangled.

"I will not," he promised, frowning. "If my aunt is awake, I mean to broach the subject of the fae path with her."

"Ahh," Miss Bennet breathed. "Are you certain that is wise?"

Darcy cocked his head. "It may not be wise, but something must be done. We cannot continue to let the fair folk escalate their attacks."

"We do not *allow* them to do anything. They require no permission from us. They do as they please," she reminded him.

"Nevertheless, we must do what we can to stop the attacks."

"Good luck," she said softly, and turned toward the house.

"Elizabeth?"

She looked over her shoulder. "Mr. Darcy?"

Softly, he said, "The next time we kiss, I shall do better."

She gasped, and then said, "I have no doubt. Good night, sir."

"Good night, dear heart."

Darcy heard her chuckle but she did not turn around, choosing the path that led to the back of the vicarage. When he could not see her any longer, he strode off toward Rosings.

℘

From one of the windows of the tulip drawing room on the first floor, Lady Catherine watched her nephew stroll across the park toward the house. He carried something she could not make out in one hand. She did not understand why he had sent his carriage ahead. Sighing a little, she turned around and faced her daughter. Anne sat before the fire, a red and blue paisley shawl wrapped around her narrow shoulders. Her gaze remained fixed on the flames. They were alone, for Mrs. Jenkinson had excused herself and Colonel Fitzwilliam had gone to bed early. He had been subdued at dinner, so Catherine thought he had been suffering with the headache. Now she thought differently.

"Anne," she said, making her daughter start.

"Yes, Mama?" she answered, turning her head slightly in her mother's direction.

"Have you and the colonel quarreled?" Catherine asked, moving back toward the fireplace.

The burgundy-veined marble surround had been carved with tulip bouquets. Anne seemed to focus on them when she shrugged, saying nothing.

Catherine bit back a hasty admonition for Anne to look at her mother when she was being spoken to. She chose to sit in a chair across from her daughter so she could watch her expression.

"Did he ask you to marry him?" she asked bluntly.

Anne sighed again, and then nodded, mute.

"And what answer did you give him?" Catherine prodded, having great difficulty in keeping her tone conversational.

"I told him I could not marry him."

Anne's mother observed the tears hovering on Anne's lashes and felt hope. "Why did you refuse him?"

Softly, Anne replied, "You wish me to marry my other cousin."

Catherine's hands squeezed the arms of her chair. Her jaw clenched, Catherine tightly said, "I no longer wish you to marry Darcy."

Anne's gaze flew to hers. "You do not?"

"No. Pemberley is too far from Rosings for him to manage this estate effectively. I have set aside my blinders and realize I do not wish you to live so far from home."

"You want me to keep living here with you?"

"Tsk, gal, you need not sound so dismayed," Catherine said testily. "Is it so surprising that I want my only child to live near me?" She relaxed her hands and smoothed her skirts. "Rosings has no dower house, but we could build one. There is nothing suitable in the neighborhood to purchase."

Anne's eyes opened wide. "*You* would remove to a dower house once I marry?"

Catherine swallowed her dismay, saying, "If you marry your cousin John, you would both naturally live at Rosings. A mother would get in your way."

"John knows nothing of running the estate," Anne pointed out.

"I will teach him."

Anne thought for a moment before slowly speaking. "It would be most inconvenient for you to teach him if you live in a separate house."

Catherine wondered if her daughter was testing her resolve. Girding her loins, she replied, "It will take time for a house to be built. By the time it is finished, I will not need to be as involved in the running of the estate. John is an intelligent man. Weekly meetings should suffice."

Anne nodded, frowning a little. "What would you do if you did not have to look after the estate?"

"Do not concern yourself with that," Catherine said trenchantly.

"Perhaps I shall start a school for girls of the lower orders. A place where they will be taught useful skills like sewing, or spinning, alongside reading and arithmetic. Gardening and animal husbandry, perhaps, and how to manage a shop so they can help their husbands or obtain employment. No woman should feel they are a burden on their family if they do not, or cannot, marry."

"A practical education," Anne said, raising both her eyebrows. "An excellent scheme, Mama."

Lady Catherine nodded at the compliment. "So, you will tell the colonel that you have thought it over some more and have changed your mind."

The blinked away tears, appeared again. Anne shook her head in a disheartened fashion. She returned her gaze to the fireplace.

Patient reasoning deserted Catherine. "What is this nonsense?" she demanded, grasping hold of the chair arms again and leaning forward in a deliberately intimidating fashion. "You have smelled of April and May ever since John arrived."

Anne cringed and a tear overflowed to track down her cheek. Over her shoulder, Catherine noticed the door to the drawing room open softly and observed Darcy slipping into the room. Surprisingly, he still wore his coat, and she saw that the object in his hand was a pair of hoof nippers. She narrowed her eyes at him and he waited quietly at the door, listening. She wished he would go away as she did not need an interruption from him.

Catherine returned her attention to her daughter, played her trump card, and forged on without mercy. "You know that if he does not marry you, he must go to Canada. It is a wild country full of beasts and savages. He might easily be killed. *If* he does not drown at sea. And, if there is a war, then…"

Anne covered her ears. "Do not say such things."

"If you care for him so much, why can you not marry him?" Catherine threw her hands up in disgust. "Anne, I have told you I have no objection." A suspicion entered her mind. Glaring at her, she demanded, "Do you mean to never marry?"

Leaping to her feet, Anne faced her mother, her arms straight at her sides, her hands fisted. "How can I marry *any* man when I am *always* so ill? How can I be a proper wife to him? Will I be strong enough? And if I am, I expect I may never be able to bear a child to term. *You* were healthy, and poor sickly me proved to be the only result of your many efforts to give my father an heir. How should I be able to do any better?" She sobbed once and covered her mouth with her palm, holding back another sob. She pulled her trembling hand away and whispered, "What kind of marriage would that be for poor John?"

Catherine stared at her. Her hard heart ached for the pain she heard in her daughter's voice and the agony displayed on her countenance. Anne slumped down into her chair, beginning to rock slightly, staring at the flames again.

Quietly, Catherine said, "Anne, dear, you cannot make a decision for both you and John. He has known you your whole life. He knows your condition. You cannot deny that he is a kind and gentle man, for you know him very well. There are few ladies who know their prospective husbands so well as you do." She sighed, watching her wretched daughter to gauge whether she was listening. Anne nodded several times so Catherine continued. "John has discussed his intentions with me. I am convinced that he truly cares for you. The financial and positional advantages he gains by marrying you are secondary to his affection for you. As a colonel of modest habits, he does not require your money to support himself so you may be certain of his honest regard. Do you doubt what I am saying?"

Anne shook her head. Dully, she said, "I know he loves me. I love him. That is why I cannot subject him to a life of caring for an invalid."

Catherine gritted her teeth. Before she could muster a further argument, her nephew stepped forward and spoke.

Chapter Twenty-two

"I have a solution to your main concern," he said, startling Anne so much that she cried out, jumped to her feet, and turned to face him, her hands pressed to her chest. "Do not be alarmed. And, kindly forgive me for coming into the drawing room dressed thus," he said, indicating his overcoat. Darcy lifted the horse nippers. "And carrying this, which normally belongs in the stables. I should have given my coat and the nippers to the porter when I came in. However, I raced past him before he could offer to help."

"I care nothing for how you are dressed. What solution? What do you mean?" Anne asked, her eyebrows drawing together. She swayed on her feet.

Darcy rushed forward, set down the nippers on a table next to the tea tray, and grabbed her arm. "You must sit."

"My point is made," she said on a sigh, and followed his order.

"Give me one moment," he said, bowing slightly. "I must send for Miss Bennet. She will help me explain. I have just left her at the parsonage so I certain she is still awake."

"Miss Bennet?" Aunt Catherine demanded. "At this hour? Did you not hear the clock? It is past ten."

Darcy ignored her, wishing he had brought Miss Bennet with him when he came. But, as his aunt had pointed out, the hour was late and so he had left her. He opened the door and discovered both Henry and Percy hovering in the corridor beyond. He focused on the older man.

"Henry, the Hunt has come and gone tonight. I have been assured it will not come a second time. Kindly send your uncle for Miss

Bennet. And tell him to be discreet."

His cousin's footman nodded. "I will, sir."

"Thank you."

Henry hurried off and Darcy turned to the remaining man.

"Percy, go and light a fire in one of the fireplaces in the ballroom."

"The *ballroom*, sir?" his aunt's footman asked, his eyes wide.

"Yes, and have Colonel Fitzwilliam meet us there. Off you go."

"Sir."

Darcy returned to the drawing room to find both his relatives sitting stock still, their expressions indicating shock—and consternation on his aunt's part.

Drawing up another chair, Darcy shrugged out of his overcoat, flung it down on a settee, and sat so the three occupants of the tulip drawing room seemed like the points of an equilateral triangle.

"If your concern is that you are too sickly to marry Fitzwilliam," Darcy said, removing his gloves and taking one of her hands, "then I have a solution. However, we cannot talk about it in here." Darcy casually glanced around the room, imitating Miss Bennet's manner of searching for the presence of the fae. He shook his head, wondering why he bothered, since he could not see them without touching Miss Bennet.

"Why not?" his aunt demanded. "Darcy, if this is some sort of jest, I will—"

Darcy held up his hand, palm forward. "I am not jesting. I swear."

"You must instantly tell us what you are talking about," Aunt Catherine ordered, her color high.

"It is not safe to talk about it here. The ballroom is the place to be," Darcy replied, keeping his temper. Like any grown man, he did not appreciate being treated like a child by his elders. "I hope there is still tea and it is not too cold," he said, getting up.

"Fitzwilliam!" his aunt cried.

He held up his hand again. "We must wait until we go to the ballroom."

"We will freeze in the ballroom," Anne reminded him.

"I have sent Percy there to light a fire," Darcy informed her. In a kind voice, he added while pouring himself some tea, "I have sent for John, too. He must hear what I have to say."

"Oh my," Anne whispered.

Darcy took a sip of tea and made a face. "Tepid. That is unfortunate, but it will do."

"Have you gone mad?" Aunt Catherine asked, her tone a mix of anger and incredulity.

"If you wonder that now, wait until you hear my proposals. But. not in here," Darcy reminded them, sitting again. He focused on Anne's drawn face. "I am extremely pleased that John has finally proposed."

Anne twisted the ends of her shawl between her hands. "I have not accepted him."

"I wish you would."

She made an inarticulate sound of distress and looked away to stare at the fire.

"I am going to be married, too," Darcy announced.

That caught her attention. He suspected it also gave his aunt's thoughts a different direction.

"You are?" Anne asked, her eyebrows high when she looked at him.

"What is this?" his aunt squawked.

Darcy glanced at her but returned his focus to his cousin. "Yes. To Miss Elizabeth Bennet." He laughed softly. "She has not yet accepted my proposal, but I am hopeful."

"Not accepted you? A Darcy of Pemberley?" Aunt Catherine scoffed. She released a disgusted sniff. "She should be thankful you even considered her."

"I have been humbled to discover that I am not such a catch as you seem to think me," Darcy confessed. His relatives appeared dumbfounded by the idea. "No, it is true. I have too much pride, it seems."

"Well…" Anne gently said, eyeing him with a slight grimace in her expression.

He chuckled and pointed a playful finger at her. "You agree with her. No, no, you are right, and so is Miss Bennet. However, she now believes that I am kind."

Anne bristled. "You have *always* been kind."

"Thank you, cousin. Miss Bennet did not think it, you see, but now she does. I am encouraged."

"Insolent, upstart," his aunt hissed.

It was Darcy's turn to bristle. "Madam, I must ask you to restrict your comments about my future wife to common pleasantries."

"I shall say what I like in my own home," his aunt replied tartly.

"But *not* to me," Darcy stressed. "Not about Miss Bennet. She is a lively, quick-minded, kind, generous, and courageous lady whom I mean to marry."

He felt a touch on his arm and looked at Anne, softening his expression.

"You love her?"

"I do," Darcy said simply.

Anne smiled broadly. "I already like her, so loving her will be easy for me as long as you are happy."

Darcy covered her hand with one of his. "Thank you."

"Like her?" his aunt said, dragging his attention back to her. She folded her arms tightly and glared at him, her lips folded shut.

Darcy glared back.

How long they would have stared at each other, he did not know. The door opened and Percy stepped inside, carrying a thick shawl over his arm. Darcy stood and faced him.

"The fire's lit, sir," the footman said. "Sergeant Guildford's gone t'bring the colonel to the ballroom. I've set some chairs round the fire, too, and Danton is bringing a warmer wrap fer Miss de Bourgh to the ballroom." He stepped further into the drawing room and handed over the dark-blue shawl to Darcy. "And this is fer her ladyship. Miss Durling done give it me fer her."

"Thank you."

"Sir," Percy said, bowing to Darcy. He looked at his mistress. "Is there anything else, m'lady?"

His aunt shook her head and waved him away. He bowed again and left them, closing the door behind him.

"Even with a fire, we shall freeze in there at this time of year, at this time of night," his aunt said. "We shall not go. Anne will catch her death."

Anne abruptly stood, scowling at her mother. "Have you forgotten the reason for this strange request? I am on tenterhooks. *I* am going. You may stay here if you wish."

Aunt Catherine pushed herself out of her chair. Through her teeth, she said, "I will come."

Darcy shook out her wrap and held it out for her. She turned around and he placed it around her shoulders.

"I shall bring a light," he said, approaching the tea table where a silver candelabra sat, three lit candles in the holders.

When he opened the door, both Percy and Henry awaited them. A glowing lamp lit the corridor from a plinth opposite the drawing room door. Percy stepped forward and took the candelabra from Darcy.

"We'll light the way, sir," he said, handing off the candelabra to Henry.

Percy then stepped to Lady Catherine's side and held out his arm. She took it as a matter of course. Darcy offered his arm to his cousin, Anne.

"When will you get married?" she asked him as soon as they began strolling down the corridor to the stairs that led to the main floor.

"This summer, I hope," Darcy said. "I must ask her father's permission, first. I think my friend Bingley will want to marry this summer as well. Perhaps we will have a double wedding."

"Bingley? You have spoken of him before. He is a younger man, is he not?"

"Yes. He will marry Miss Jane Bennet, the oldest Bennet sister. I had a letter this morning from him. He asked, and she accepted, pending Mr. Bennet's approval."

"Is Miss Bennet happy about her sister's engagement?"

Darcy frowned. "She did not mention it. Perhaps her sister means to write after Bingley talks to their father. I believe she will be happy, however. Most happy. Bingley is a fine fellow."

"That is excellent," Anne commented in a wistful voice.

"Fear not," he said gently. "You will marry soon. I promise you."

"I pray you are right."

ꟿ

Lizzy stepped through the double doors and into the ballroom. Mary, who had refused to let her go alone, was at her side. She had been contrite when Lizzy returned to the parsonage earlier. They had still been in Charlotte's sitting room when the summons to Rosings Park arrived. Unfortunately, Harold, the gardener, had not been discreet enough, and he woke half the household with his knock on the kitchen door. Mr. Collins, livid, forbade Charlotte to accompany her, even though his wife reminded him of his duty to Lady Catherine. He paused in his rant and lost some of his heightened color.

"I shall accompany you. I might be needed," Mr. Collins said.

"You ain't, sir," Harold bluntly told him. "Sir William neither. Jist

Miss Bennet."

Mr. Collins threw his hands up and said, "She cannot go alone."

"I'll be with her, sir."

"And I shall go, as well," Mary chimed in.

Mr. Collins blustered some more, but in the end, Mary had come. They wrapped up warmly and ventured out into the night, hopping onto the sides, back-to-back, of a dog cart pulled by a gray pony.

And now they were here, in the ballroom, where Lady Catherine glowered at them, Miss Anne de Bourgh watched them hopefully, and Colonel Fitzwilliam stood behind Anne's chair, a set look on his face. Mr. Darcy crossed the room to the door, a welcoming smile on his lips.

"How like you to come when I called," he said, taking her hand. Turning to her sister, he said, "And Miss Mary, as well. Thank you."

Her tone slightly belligerent, Mary said, "Lizzy could not come out alone. Surely you knew that."

"Quite right," he said, closing the doors. "Come closer to the fire. It is deucedly cold in here."

They approached the others and offered polite curtsies. Once they were seated, Mr. Darcy addressed Lizzy.

"I have gathered us here because I thought it the safest place for us to talk. Are we alone?"

Lizzy's eyes widened at him, then at the others. She glanced around the vast room in her casual fashion and then met Mr. Darcy's gaze. "It is a beautiful room. I imagine it must be magnificent when it is not so…empty."

"What are you talking about, Miss Bennet?" Lady Catherine asked sharply. "And you, Darcy? How can you say it is empty when we are all in here? Goodness, I can see my breath."

Lizzy swallowed a chuckle at the *non sequitur*. "Mr. Darcy, why are we here?"

"I mean to discuss…things…with Anne and my aunt. I thought it might be easier if you were here and could explain what I may not be able to."

She licked her lips and nodded. "It is safe to proceed."

Mr. Darcy bowed and faced his cousins.

"We are meeting in here because there is iron above every door and window," Mr. Darcy explained, pointing to the curtain rods. "The fae do not like it in here, so we may speak freely about them. Now, Anne, I shall answer your questions. First, to be healthy, you must move out of the nursery wing. Second, you must tear it down."

Her gaze had followed his pointing finger out across the ballroom, but now her head jerked back to him. "What is this?"

"If you are speaking of vapors that can make one ill, I had the wing tested," his aunt said, her tone annoyed. "There are none."

"We air all the chambers often, too," Anne assured him. "We did not need to gather in this wretchedly cold ballroom for you to tell me to sleep somewhere else." She made a disbelieving face and said, "The *fae*, Cousin?"

"Please bear with me. I know it is not vapors," Mr. Darcy agreed. He seemed to take hold of his courage and he plowed ahead. "A faery path runs through the wing. Directly under your bed."

"A faery path?" Anne asked, her brow furrowed.

"It is a path the fae use to move here and there through the human realm," Mr. Darcy explained.

"That is so," Lizzy said, nodding encouragement at him.

His aunt stirred. She made a slashing movement with her hand. "That is utter superstitious nonsense. Wearing iron is one thing, but to be attributing Anne's illness to mythology is something different altogether."

"Darcy, what are you talking about?" Colonel Fitzwilliam asked, confusion all over his countenance.

"I am talking about the fae and why Anne is always sickly. I *stepped* on a faery path and spent an entire night trapped in horrendous nightmares," Mr. Darcy told them. He looked from his aunt's stormy expression to his cousins' confused ones. "Anne, your nursery is now your current bedchamber. I suspect the only reason you did not die as a child was that your cot was not situated *on* the path. Is that not correct, Miss Bennet?"

"It is," she stated. His family glanced her way and she raised an eyebrow.

Mr. Darcy continued, forestalling whatever query they might have made. "For many years now, you have slept directly on it."

"I have seen no path," Anne said, slowly shaking her head.

"There, you see!" his aunt scoffed.

"Only some people can see them," Mr. Darcy explained. "Your footman knows it is there. The other servants do not like to go in your wing."

"Henry?" Anne asked rhetorically. "Why has no one said anything to me before? Henry has been with me for many years."

"I suspect he feared for his position," Mr. Darcy replied.

Lady Catherine snorted. "I should say so."

"Mama," Anne pleaded, "pray do not say such things. Henry is loyal to me and deserves to be given the benefit of the doubt." She looked at Lizzy. "Is this the reason you asked about moving my bed, or sleeping in the main part of the house?"

Lizzy nodded. "It is." She swallowed and glanced at her sister, who sat silently beside her. Mary raised an eyebrow. Lizzy took that as a sign that she may as well tell them the truth. "I saw the path. I can see the fae." Sudden fear made her add, "Pray tell no one my secret. The fae might discover it and they can be nasty to those who can see them. Say nothing to anyone outside of this room. Beyond this group. I beg of you."

Her audiences closed their dropped jaws and gave no promises.

What have I done?

Mr. Darcy stormed ahead. He appeared, now, to know without a doubt the truth of everything she had told him. As an honorable gentleman, he had to act to save his family. He had to reveal enough to make them believe. Lizzy pressed her fist to her stomach where the warmth of her feelings for him grew. Where the fear for her future resided.

What if they tell people? Their servants? Who will tell other servants. Oh, Lord.

"The fae are angry about the path," Mr. Darcy said. "They are impatient for it to be clear again. That is why they attacked you, Aunt Catherine."

"What?" Anne squeaked. She straightened and shifted around in her chair to face her mother. "Mama?"

"Did you suffer a severe, stabbing headache?" Mr. Darcy asked his aunt.

Lady Catherine started, but she said, "A momentary weakness. It passed."

"Mama?" Anne repeated. "You said nothing."

"Darcy, you are worrying Anne," his aunt charged, glaring at him.

"I mean to," Mr. Darcy retorted. "I mean to make you both understand the danger you are in. You must tear down the wing, freeing the path." Urgently, he said specifically to his aunt, "They called out the Wild Hunt! I saw it tonight! Miss Bennet and I were caught outside when the Hunt thundered through the region. It was a warning."

"A very serious warning," Lizzy said in support. *Perhaps if they understand their danger, they will not speak of my talent.*

"I have heard of the Wild Hunt. There is no such thing." Lady Catherine's anger radiated from her vibrating figure.

"What is this hunt?" Anne asked.

Lizzy explained and she paled even further.

"How did you escape them?" Colonel Fitzwilliam demanded.

"Miss Bennet knew the method," Mr. Darcy explained simply.

His aunt's jaw tightened. "It was she who told you of the path? And its danger?"

"It was."

"I thought as much," she said, curling her lip. "And now she wants me to tear down a wing I designed? You must be mad, Miss Bennet. And you, Darcy, for listening to her."

"Do you, or do you not, wish Anne's health to improve?" Mr. Darcy asked, a low growl in his voice. "Because that is the crux of it, is it not? Do you wish her to remain sickly for the remainder of her life so that she will never leave you? Never marry?"

Lady Catherine gasped. "How *dare* you, sir?"

"Then, consider this, has anything in my character led you to believe that I am the type of person to frighten you unnecessarily? I am not a fanciful person, you know that." Mr. Darcy paused and seemed to rein in his temper. He waited for a response from his family and, when none came, he bowed his shoulders to his aunt.

"I beg your pardon, madam. It was not my intent to make you angry or to make accusations. I merely wish to impart to you the urgency of removing Anne to the main part of the house firstly, and then to remove the wing." To Anne, he said, "Removing the wing will not happen overnight. It must first be emptied of furnishings, and then the process of tearing it down will begin. An architect should be hired to oversee the process so the remainder of Rosings will not be damaged during the demolition. John can take charge of that. He was once involved with the Corps of Royal Engineers."

Anne looked up at the Colonel and lifted her hand, covering his where it rested on her shoulder. He nodded gravely at her.

Lady Catherine stood and said in a regal manner, "There will be *no* demolition of my house."

Anne remained sitting, but fixed her with a stare. "Rosings is not *your* house, Mama. It is *mine*."

Mr. Darcy looked from one to the other. However, he addressed his aunt.

"Madam, of all the cures you have subjected Anne to over the years, I acknowledge that this will certainly be the most expensive one. Even so, it will be the least physically and mentally invasive. Rosings will remain an impressive house."

Lizzy watched his aunt's heavy breathing, and said, "Another nursery wing could easily be built for Anne's children. A small kitchen could be placed on the lower floor. There have been even more advances in plumbing and other systems since you designed Anne's wing. These could be incorporated into the new wing. It is an opportunity to build something even better."

Lady Catherine glared at her and slowly sat. "I do not believe in the fae."

Mr. Darcy responded. "Do you remember the breakfast when Anne and John both spoke intemperately to you? They do not even remember the incident. That was caused by the influence of the fae."

"Is this true?" Colonel Fitzwilliam demanded, stiffening.

Lizzy explained. "They can speak into your mind, sir." She took a deep breath. "It is merely amusement to them. They do not care if we are hurt by their machinations. When this is over, it will be best if you simply forget about their existence. It is safer not to speak of them. But, if you do nothing now, Anne's health may be lost to her forever." Whispering, she added, "Their interference could…kill her."

"I say," Colonel Fitzwilliam objected.

"I am sorry to speak of such alarming things," Lizzy told him. "If you do this small thing, they may never trouble you again, and Anne may regain her health."

"And, Mama," Anne said, smiling across at her, "I could marry John."

"What if this is not the reason for my daughter's poor health?" Lady Catherine asked Lizzy and her nephew in a cold voice. "What then?"

The colonel moved around Anne's chair and took both her hands in his. "Anne, darling. Could you not try and see if Miss Bennet is correct? You could move into a suite of rooms in the main house and see how you feel. We have so much to gain if she is right."

Lady Catherine looked at her daughter and spoke before Anne could respond to her suitor's plea. "Will you promise to marry John no matter what is the result of this folly?"

Anne blinked a few times while she thought. Finally, looking into the colonel's eyes, she said, "I will. I promise."

Lady Catherine beamed. "You shall sleep in the room beside mine from this very night."

"Mr. Darcy," Lizzy said.

"Yes, Miss Bennet," he said, smiling warmly at her.

"Do you think Colonel Fitzwilliam might like to go onto the roof with us? It may be possible that I can show him the path and he will be easier in his mind."

"*May* be possible?" Mr. Darcy asked.

"*May* be," she repeated.

"An excellent scheme," Mr. Darcy said, grinning now. "What do you say, John? Would you like to make the attempt?"

The colonel straightened, keeping hold of only one of Anne's hands. "I would, indeed."

"Could we not see it in the nursery wing?" Anne asked, rising. "Then we can all look. I do not like heights and would dislike being on the roof excessively."

"We shall repair there now, if you wish," Lizzy said, standing. "Come, Mary. I will show you, too."

Mary stood and glared at her. "Do you mean to say that you could have shown me this invisible world any time you wished?"

Lizzy frowned. "No, not any time. We must touch skin to skin. Even with this method, not everyone can see. Charlotte cannot. Jane can." She glanced away from Mary's fuming expression and met the gazes of each of the others. "This is true for all of you, too. Perhaps you will each be able to see, perhaps none of you will. However, I think it is worth the effort. Remember, though, not to speak of any of this to anyone. The house is protected by iron now, if Mr. Darcy remembered to put iron at the doors to the roof?" She watched him nod. "Good, then the fae should not be in the house. We will go to Anne's bedchamber and send the servants away so they will not see our experiment. Is that agreeable to everyone?"

Lady Catherine grumbled and Mary looked stormy, but the others appeared excited. No one spoke on the journey through the long corridors to the nursery wing. They sent the footmen and Anne's maid into the kitchens.

"Are we going to let your companion in on our secret?" Lizzy asked Anne when they stood in a semi-circle in front of the fire in Anne's bedchamber, having been herded by Lizzy so that they crowded to one side to avoid stepping on the path. Lizzy stood before them.

"We will not," Lady Catherine stated categorically. "She is the biggest gossip in the region."

Anne nodded, a smile on her lips. "Mama is correct."

"Very well. Let us try this two at a time," Lizzy suggested, reaching out for Mary and Anne's bare hands. "Can you both see the bed? And the floor behind me?"

"We can," they answered together.

Lizzy squeezed their hands. "Focus on the floor and on your desire to see a path." Both women squinted and screwed up their faces in their attempt to 'see'. "Sometimes, it helps to tilt your head to one side and look out of the corner of your eye. There, do you see it?"

Mary breathed out a long sigh. "I do. Is it supposed to shimmer like that?"

"Like the golden light of the sun reflecting off of a stream?" Anne added. "It is so beautiful."

Lizzy instantly released their hands. "Everything in the fae world is incredibly beautiful. But do not let that deceive you. It is horribly dangerous."

Mary and Anne both looked daunted and backed away so the colonel and Lady Catherine could make the attempt. Lady Catherine took a short look and hurriedly drew back from Lizzy's touch.

"I have seen it," she whispered. "I have no use for taking a longer view." Regarding Lizzy bleakly, she asked, "Tell me, has this been in my home from before Anne's birth?"

"It has," Lizzy replied gently. "You could not have known."

Lady Catherine turned away, hiding her face from the group.

"Colonel?" Lizzy asked. She watched his eyes follow the stretch of path from one wall to the opposite wall. "You can see it?"

"I can," he said, releasing her hand. "I shall need to view it from the roof so that I can see where the path crosses the park and gardens."

"Of course," Lizzy said.

"I would also like to see," Mr. Darcy said, reaching for her hand.

Lizzy grasped it. He looked the longest of all those gathered. When he released her hand, he faced her.

"Thank you for allowing this intimacy. If there had been any other way to make my family understand, I—"

"I am concerned only that my secret remain just that, a secret."

Mr. Darcy fixed a stare on each of those gathered and they all nodded.

"Tonight is not the time for going onto the roof," he said to the colonel. "Tomorrow is soon enough. The day has been long and eventful. Anne must wish to retire, and I shall escort the ladies home to the vicarage before Mrs. Collins comes searching for them."

"Charlotte will not be asleep," Mary mentioned as they filed from the bedchamber.

"You are right," Lizzy said.

Chapter Twenty-three

Lizzy held on to Mr. Darcy's arm as he escorted them to the vicarage. He had offered his other arm to Mary, but her sister preferred to trudge ahead of them, taking aggressive strides, revealing her feelings with every step.

"It seems," Mr. Darcy remarked softly, "that your sister is not pleased. Is she unhappy about discovering metaphysical truths?"

"Mary is eager for all knowledge," Lizzy replied. "I do not think it is new knowledge that irritates her nerves. I am the cause."

He squeezed her hand in apparent sympathy. "I imagine sisters must…challenge their sibling love occasionally. I am so much older than Georgiana that I have been more like a father to her than a brother. You know, my dear, she has always longed for a sister."

Lizzy chuckled, saying, "Is this comment meant to be an inducement for me to accept your suit?"

"I merely sought to reassure you of your welcome at Pemberley."

She lost her smile as one more aspect of her possible future intruded. In a calm voice, she replied, "How kind of you."

How many more of these sorts of references to our marriage can I listen to without Mr. Darcy assuming I acquiesce to his proposal? I must make a decision. Lizzy looked up at the shining moon as though she could find an answer there.

"What is it?" Mr. Darcy asked gently.

Lizzy shook her head. "I am tired. Pray, do not be concerned."

"I hope you know that everything about you must concern me closely."

"You are more gallant than I knew," Lizzy admitted, smiling.

My dithering is not fair to him. Can I love him? Why is my heart so hesitant?

"Thank you," he said, his voice sounding wry. "I think?"

They both laughed together at his mild jest and Lizzy's heart lightened.

"If we do not hasten our steps," she said, "Mary shall beat us."

"We cannot have that," he said, taking longer strides.

When they reached the vicarage, Mary stood at the gate. She fixed him with an interested stare.

"Are you aware, Mr. Darcy, that you jingle when you walk?"

His hand went to where his watch fob hung, covering the charms.

"Do I? I beg your pardon."

Mary scowled. "Lizzy, have you been giving him some of your iron charms?"

"Did you just notice?" Lizzy asked, grinning. "I had to keep him safe."

"Keep *him* safe?"

"You choose not to wear the bracelet I gave you," Lizzy reminded her.

Mary sniffed. "I did not know what it was for, did I?" She opened the gate herself and marched alone to the porch.

"Oh, dear," Lizzy said on a sigh.

Mr. Darcy took her hand out of the crook of his arm and brought it to his lips. He pressed a kiss on its back.

"Good night, my darling Elizabeth," he whispered. "Do not let Miss Mary's crotchets disturb you. I would like you to think on more important matters."

Instead of admonishing him for taking liberties with her first name—as she should have earlier in the night—she merely slipped him another charm and whispered, "Good night, sir."

He waited at the gate for the two ladies to enter the house, tipping his hat when Charlotte opened the door. Unable to resist a final look, Lizzy glanced over her shoulder at him. He bowed to her and she instinctively curtsied. Her next surprised thought was, *I…I…goodness.*

Her burst of realization made her numb to Charlotte's questions, which left Mary to answer them. They sat now in her friend's private sitting room, drinking a chamomile tisane to calm their nerves. Lizzy sipped hers in a sort of daze. Only her sister's annoyance brought Lizzy out of her romantic trance to listen more closely to Mary's words.

"And all these years, Lizzy could have shown me this magical world, and she did not!" Mary exclaimed softly, for no one wished to wake Sir William, Maria, or Mr. Collins.

"You could see the faery path?" Charlotte asked, her eyes wide. Ruefully, she added, "I could not. Jane could. I have often wondered if that was because they are sisters. Or perhaps Lizzy's talent has stronger since we last tried." She set down her cup, shaking her head. "I cannot believe Lady Catherine is willing to pull down the wing. I never thought she would."

"It is not down yet," Lizzy pointed out. She shifted on the settee and focused her attention on her sister. "Mary, I have good reasons for not showing you before today."

"Humph," Mary said, shooting daggers at her. "I suspect you would not have shown me tonight if I had not been there. You expected me to believe you without *seeing*."

"I did, but—"

"Do not *but* me," Mary ordered, bitterly. "You have always treated me as an outsider. Lydia and Kitty are the same. They are only silly girls and I have easily dismissed their taunts. You and Jane, though—"

"Jane has always been kind to you," Lizzy shot back, feeling the sting of Mary's accusations.

Loftily, Mary retorted, "I speak of you as a unit, rather than as individuals."

Lizzy took in a deep breath through her nose, held it a moment, and then let it out slowly. "Mary, there is much truth in your accusations. However, there is no truth in the charge that I deliberately did not tell you of the metaphysical world due to spite. Pray release me from that condemnation. The moment I understood the significance, and the danger, of my ability, I strove to keep it from those I love. Why should you be made frightened by a world you could not see, I asked myself. You know my answer—no one should be made afraid."

"Jane and Charlotte—"

Lizzy shook her head. She set down her cup and clasped her hands tightly in her lap. "It was too late. I had already told them. There was no harm in telling them about the energy lines, or about dousing. Even so, their lives have not been made better by the dangerous knowledge of the fae."

"Now wait," Charlotte said, holding up a finger. "Do not speak for me, please, Lizzy. Though I am occasionally fearful on your behalf, I count myself fortunate to have the *wonder* of knowing there is more to our world than what I see."

"You are kind to say so," Lizzy said, shaking her head.

Charlotte frowned at her. "I am not being kind. I am being truthful."

Lizzy tried to believe her.

"You have not given me the right of choice," Mary said, scowling.

"It is *my* secret," Lizzy stressed. "*I* know the dangers. I could not know how you would react. I could not be certain you would not attempt to contact them—out of intellectual curiosity, of course. They can show themselves to whom they will, and you might have found yourself in grave difficulties." Her sister raised an eyebrow. Hurriedly, Lizzy added, "Besides, Mama would have collapsed immediately—and possibly permanently—if I had told anyone else other than Jane. I did not even tell her that Charlotte knew. Mama cannot be easy with her own ability to see the fae. She has never been easy about it."

Mary's countenance held an arrested expression. "The iron garden…she is like a different person when she sits in there."

"As I have said before, Mama's reaction to them is gaiety, and constant gaiety is exhausting. There is relief in the garden. Lady Catherine's ballroom was a revelation to me. I must convince Mama and Papa to replace all our wood drapery rods with iron ones. Mama should be safe in her own home."

Charlotte looked from one sister to the other and murmured, "An excellent idea."

"You also said that Lydia's lively nature attracts them," Mary recalled, ignoring Lizzy's comment about the iron drapery rods. "It is a shame she is the youngest of the Bennet sisters."

"Indeed," Lizzy said, relaxing a little, recognizing the signs that Mary's angry disappointment was dissipating. "Perhaps she will marry one of the militia officers. *I* have no objection to her marrying before me."

"Why does Mama not wear iron?" Mary asked, her eyebrows high. "She must know its advantages."

Lizzy shrugged. "She does, but she does not wish to appear ridiculous. Iron is not pretty. Even when polished. I am not so nice in my fashion sense."

Mary pressed her lips into a thin line. "Foolish."

"Perhaps. I may feel as worn down as our dear mama when I have had to endure so many years with my ability."

"You," Charlotte said, "do not have the same character as Mrs. Bennet. You have greater resolve and strength. I do not wish to insult her, dear Lizzy, but your mother has more in common with Lydia than you like to think."

Lizzy sighed and passed a hand over her eyes. "Possibly."

Mary stood. "You are exhausted from your experiences tonight, and we are tired. Let us go to our beds. We can discuss this more on the morrow."

Standing, Lizzy said, touching her sister's arm, "Dearest, I have not heard a quote from you today. Have you no words of wisdom for us?"

Mary tipped her head to one side while she considered. "Ah—from Voltaire. *'Life is a shipwreck, but we must not forget to sing in the lifeboats.'*"

Lizzy chuckled softly. "An apt choice."

Fixing her with a direct, uncompromising stare, Mary said, "I must think about everything you have said. Thank you for explaining."

"You are most welcome," Lizzy replied, feeling her stomach muscles relax.

They retired. Mary did not come into her room after they changed for bed as Lizzy thought she might. As exhausted as she was, Lizzy did not sleep for some time, considering her feelings for Mr. Darcy and how they had changed. She admired him for his strength of purpose and for his determination to help his family even though they might have considered him a fool. No man wished to be thought thus. He had not been willfully blind, either, as he might have been.

There is so much to consider before I can accept his proposal. Who can I talk to about this? Jane is not here, and besides, she never thinks ill of anyone. Charlotte will urge me to accept his proposal because she knows the stigma of being an old maid. That leaves Mary. If I talk to her, I will receive only the truth. As she sees it. She will be frank.

Lizzy drifted off to sleep, thinking about what she meant to say to Mary.

ꝏ

Waking the next morning, Lizzy felt a delicious sense of rightness with her world. Mr. Darcy had kissed her, albeit in the midst of a dangerous situation, but it had been her first experience.

She recalled the moment he had embraced her. The strength of his arms and the feel of his lips had surprised her. Even with the Wild Hunt surrounding them, she had felt safer because of Mr. Darcy's courage.

Lizzy touched her lips with trembling fingers, anticipating the next promised kiss. "Mrs. Elizabeth Darcy," she whispered.

She chuckled at her own lovesick thoughts, sitting up and swinging her legs out from under the covers. A knock sounded, and the door opened. Mary slipped into the bedchamber, already dressed.

"Goodness, you are up early," Lizzy said, blinking rapidly in her surprise.

Mary snorted. "It is almost nine. Charlotte insisted you be allowed to sleep your exhaustion out. They have set aside food for you. Unfortunately, they received word that Miss de Bourgh is coming at ten, and you were not to be allowed to lie in after all."

"I have slept quite enough," Lizzy stated firmly. "Will you assist me?"

"I will," Mary assured her. "I mean to dress your hair in a new style. Mr. Darcy is accompanying Miss de Bourgh. As is the colonel, I suppose. You must wish to look your best for your intended."

"I have not given him my answer," Lizzy told her, slipping out of her nightrail. The temperature of the water in the ewer made her gasp a little. "Ooh."

Grinning, Mary said, "It was hot at eight."

"You!" Lizzy cried.

They both laughed and got down to the business of dressing. As soon as Lizzy donned a buttercup-yellow dress trimmed in muted-green, Mary handed her a letter.

"From Jane," she said.

"From Jane!" Lizzy cried, snatching the missive.

Mary walked over to the dressing table. "You may read it while I brush your hair."

"How I have longed to hear from her. I hope she tells us that Bingley has proposed."

"If he has, Mama will become prostrate with happiness," Mary said in her dry way.

Lizzy scanned the letter through once, stopping to exclaim at the part that interested them most nearly. "He has! He has! Two days ago."

"And why did she not write immediately?"

"Um…ah, here it is. *'Dearest sisters, I knew you would not begrudge me the chance of hearing back from our mama before I wrote to you. Charles posted up to Longbourn directly after his proposal so he might speak to our papa. He returned as soon as he had Papa's approval, bringing a letter from Mama. She is in raptures, dearest sisters. I did not think I could be happier than when Charles told me he loved me, but I am. I am.'*"

"Did I not say?" Mary said, beginning to pin up Lizzy's hair. "I pray Mama is calm again by the time we return to Longbourn."

Lizzy slowly closed the letter and set it down on the dressing table to read it over again later.

"Mary?"

"What?" she cried softly, pausing in her efforts. "There was nothing wrong with what I just said."

"No, no," Lizzy hastily said. "I was not chastising you."

"Oh. I beg your pardon."

"Not at all," Lizzy said automatically. She watched her sister's expression in the mirror. "I…I have been pondering Mr. Darcy's proposal."

"I hope you have decided against him," Mary said tartly, fixing a final pin in place. "There. What do you think? Do you like it?"

Lizzy obediently examined her looped and pinned hair. "Very pretty. Thank you." She shifted in the chair so she could see Mary. "I wished to ask your advice."

"*My* advice? Not Jane's? Or Charlotte's?"

Inwardly wincing at the surprise in Mary's voice, Lizzy explained. "You know both Charlotte and Jane would advise me to accept Mr. Darcy. Jane, because she never thinks ill of anyone and believes every situation can be resolved in a positive fashion. Charlotte, because she believes any acceptable offer should be taken since I have no dowry and no way to earn money of my own. You, however, will be honest with me."

"Hmm," Mary hummed, appearing pleased. "Very well, my first objection is that you do not love him."

Lizzy countered with a blush and a simple reply. "I think I may love him."

"Only think?" Mary asked, tilting her head. "I thought you would be more certain before you accepted a proposal."

"There are other considerations."

"He does not like your family," Mary immediately asserted.

Lizzy nodded. "Not all of them, I admit. He likes you, though."

Mary's eyes widened. "Me? I did not think so."

"He admires your intelligence." Lizzy touched her sister on the arm. "And, he told me just last night that when we are married we must invite you often."

"Along with everyone else," Mary said, a touch of bitterness creeping into her voice.

"No, you are wrong there. Alone," Lizzy swore. "He also likes Jane. Kitty and Lydia are still too young for him to think of as adults that he does, or does not like. He has nothing against our papa."

"He does not like Mama," Mary pointed out.

"I will not deny that his feelings for Mama are…ambivalent, shall we say?" Lizzy frowned. "I do not believe there are many who like every one of their in-laws."

"True." Mary sat on the edge of the bed, an arm wrapped around the bedpost. "What are your concerns? Why do you hesitate if it is not because of your feelings for Mr. Darcy?"

Lizzy's brow crinkled. "I am not sure. I know that I am a gentleman's daughter, and Mr. Darcy is a gentleman, but there is a vast difference between his sphere and ours. His income is *twice* that of Mr. Bingley's, *five* times that of Papa's. Pemberley is considered even more grand than Rosings Park. Grander than any house I have ever visited. What will his friends and his family think of me? Will I be a worthy mistress of such a place?" She shook her head in a solemn manner. "I do not enjoy feeling inferior."

"Does anyone?" Mary asked tartly. "Lizzy, I do not mean to discount your concerns, but they are…are ludicrous."

Lizzy's eyebrows shot up. "Ludicrous?"

"Absurd, then," Mary substituted. "You are a gracious, intelligent woman."

"Thank you, but I know nothing of how to look after the needs of Mr. Darcy's tenants," Lizzy pointed out, touched by her sister's praise.

"Do you think yourself unable to learn?" Mary demanded, her tone scoffing. "Lizzy, what you are saying is you are afraid of the unknown."

Lizzy considered her sister's words. *Am I merely afraid?*

In a gentler voice, Mary said, "Everyone is afraid of what they do not know or understand. Your husband will help you. Your sister-in-law must know how to run a grand household, how to help the tenants.

She will teach you."

"She may not like me," Lizzy said, grimacing.

"She will *love* you," Mary asserted.

"How do you know?"

Mary stood and shook out her skirts. "Lizzy, these are not questions for me. These are questions you must ask Mr. Darcy. Only he can allay your fears. My advice—which you asked for specifically—is to *talk* to him about your concerns. Life will be different if you marry him. There is no denying that. But different is not always bad." She waited until Lizzy stood before saying, "Descarte said, '*It is not enough to have a good mind; the main thing is to use it well.*' Lizzy, you have a good mind. Make it work for you. Do not let your fears ruin what could be a brilliant life."

"Did he not also say, '*Doubt everything?*'?"

"Precisely," Mary said, not to be outdone. She slipped her arm through her sister's. "Doubt your fear, but trust your love. And Mr. Darcy's love."

"It boils down to that, does it not? Do I trust Mr. Darcy's avowal that he loves me?"

"Why should he not?"

"Your logic eludes me."

"Never mind. Shall we go down? You do not want to meet him again on an empty stomach."

"So true."

Before they opened the door, Mary squeezed her arm. Lizzy glanced at her, eyebrows raised.

"I may not like it, Lizzy, but I can appreciate your worry for my well-being and I forgive you—albeit grudgingly—for not telling me about the fae."

Lizzy hugged her arm back. "Thank you. I am sorry that you have been hurt by my secrecy. And, I am sorry I spoke with such heat last night. I confess I am glad to have someone else know. It has often been lonely with only Mama, Jane and Charlotte knowing."

"I imagine so. I will help with Mama, too. I shall learn to watch for signs that she needs distracting."

"You are a treasure, dearest," Lizzy praised, resting her head for a moment on her upper arm.

Mary reached for the door handle. "Are you going to Rosings today to show Colonel Fitzwilliam the faerie path?"

"Yes."

"I will find something to do with Maria. Perhaps we can visit some of the young ladies we met at the recitation tea. Or, Charlotte may have an idea about what we can do today."

"You do not wish to be included in the venture?"

Mary shook her head, opening the door for them. "I have seen enough for the moment, thank you."

"Maria and Sir William are leaving on Monday. Do you mean to go with them?"

"Do you wish me to?" Mary asked in a soft voice, closing the door, leaving them in the bedchamber still.

"I do not." Lizzy linked arms with her. "I am enjoying our time together."

"What about Mama?"

Lizzy sighed with vibrating lips. "Pffah. I do not know. And then there is Lydia. However, you are not responsible for her behavior."

"I doubt I could do anything to stop her from behaving badly in any case," Mary admitted. "What did Jane say about remaining in London with our aunt and uncle?"

"Her schedule has not changed. She will wait until we arrive and then we shall return home together," Lizzy said. Her stomach rumbled and they both laughed. "Time to eat."

༻

Mr. Darcy gravitated to her side as soon as the guests arrived at the vicarage. Unfortunately, Mr. Collins and Sir Williams had still been at home when the note had arrived from Rosings so their guests had to carefully speak with circumspection of their experiences the night before. Maria, too, had to be kept ignorant of their odd activities and the cause for them.

"I had the best sleep of my life last night," Anne stated, smiling as soon as she sat in the place of honor in the best drawing room.

Colonel Fitzwilliam rested his hand on her shoulder. "We have something to announce, do we not, Anne dear?"

"Yes," she said, grinning widely now but appearing a little shy. Glancing up at her cousin, she said, "You tell them."

He smiled softly back at her. "As you wish." Encompassing everyone with a look, he said, "Miss de Bourgh has agreed to bestow upon me the great honor of her hand in marriage."

Mr. Collins rushed over to them. He reverently took Miss de Bourgh's hand. "How pleased I am that you will be entering the marriage bonds. It is a sacrament most holy. May Colonel Fitzwilliam strive to be worthy of you."

"Thank you," Anne said, withdrawing her hand. "We wish you to perform the ceremony."

"I shall read out the banns this very Sunday," Mr. Collins vowed, beaming. He looked from her to the colonel. "Once the banns have been read three times, you have ninety days to get married. Have you chosen a date? Before you leave for Upper Canada, I daresay."

"We thought May fifteenth would be nice," the colonel said. "I am selling out immediately, so I will not be going abroad."

"That is a relief, sir," Charlotte said, her expression wreathed in pleasure.

"Indeed," Colonel Fitzwilliam murmured, bowing slightly.

"The wedding will be small," Anne explained. "With few guests. Even so, John and I would like you and Mary to return for it," she said to Lizzy. Then, she smiled at Sir William. "And you and your wife. Maria, too."

"We would be delighted," Sir William said, bowing and beaming. "I love weddings."

"I shall also be delighted to come back. My goodness, it has been settled so quickly," Lizzy marveled, shaking her head. "Who are to be your witnesses?"

"You, if you are willing," Anne asked, a shy note in her soft voice.

Lizzy pressed a hand to her chest. "Me?"

"Yes, please."

"Goodness. Of course I will be your witness," Lizzy said, coming to sit beside her. "But would you not rather have Charlotte?" she asked impulsively, and then regretted her words for Charlotte's sake. "I beg your pardon, but you have known her longer."

Anne frowned and appeared confused. Her gaze swiftly indicated Sir William and Mr. Collins, who were now both heartily congratulating the colonel.

"We owe you so much," she whispered. "If not for you…"

Lizzy, noticing Maria's interested expression, hurriedly spoke, "I am honored."

"Thank you," Anne said. To Charlotte, she anxiously asked, "You are not offended?"

Charlotte smiled in a reassuring way at Anne, at Lizzy, and then back at Anne. "Not at all."

Anne flushed. "Good. Mrs. Jenkinson will need help writing out the invitations for the wedding breakfast. Would you care to assist her?"

"I would, thank you." Turning to Maria and Mary, Charlotte said, "Shall we have Father drive us into Sevenoaks for some shopping later? We could be back in time for our evening meal. This is our last chance before Maria leaves on Monday and we may find some for wedding gifts."

"Oh, yes please," Maria said, clapping her hands together at the proposed treat.

"Lizzy," Anne said, her eyes wide. "I beg your pardon, but Mama is expecting you, especially, to return with us to Rosings. She has some specific matters to discuss with you."

Exchanging a significant look with both Charlotte and Mary, Lizzy returned her focus to Anne. "I am at your disposal."

&

Darcy took Elizabeth's hand and placed it through his arm. He covered her hand with his gloved one. His two cousins strolled ahead of them across the meadow toward Rosings in a leisurely fashion.

"This is the first time I have seen Anne walk anywhere other than the gardens around Rosings," Darcy remarked quietly. "This is your doing."

"And yours. Without your support, I doubt she or your aunt would have listened to me." She frowned up at him. "I may not have had the courage to tell them."

"I disagree. You are a Trojan, my dear Elizabeth," he replied with soft fervor.

Her bright eyes twinkled at him. "I am afraid it is midsummer moon with you, sir."

Darcy chuckled, and then lost his humor. In a deepened voice, he asked, "Have you softened at all toward my proposal?"

She looked away across the meadow and he could not make out her features because of the brim of her bonnet. He felt her arm tense on his and hoped that did not mean she had decided against his suit.

"I cannot see your face." His stomach muscles clenched. "Will you not look at me?"

Elizabeth, for he could not return to calling her Miss Bennet within the privacy of his own mind, obeyed his request. Her delicate brows, furrowed and cautious at first, arched into curious surprise.

"You are easy to look at, sir," she said, smiling slowly. "And I enjoy doing so." Her smile lifted at one corner. "Our discussion of this matter should be left to a more private walk. Do you not agree?"

Darcy's heart clamored so loudly he thought she might be able to hear it. "I do," he managed to say. "Forgive my impatience."

"Of course," she murmured.

"When I escort you home today?" he pressed. "Or, do you need more time? I would rather you be certain of your answer."

"I have a few…questions," she admitted. Chuckling, she added, "What a trial I must be to you, dear sir. No doubt any other lady of your acquaintance would have agreed to your proposal immediately."

Darcy released a dry laugh. "No doubt. I suppose you think me prideful for agreeing?"

Elizabeth smiled. "What does Shakespeare say? So much. Uh...Ah, yes. *'Truth is truth/To the end of reckoning.'* I cannot tell you from which play."

"It is from *Measure for Measure.*"

"Is it?" She pursed her lips in thought. "I have not read that play. I suppose I must have heard the quote from Mary."

"It is an apt one."

"Agreed."

They walked for another half-dozen steps before either spoke again.

"What do you suppose your aunt wishes to talk to me about?" Elizabeth asked. "Did she tell you?"

"She means to go on the roof with us."

"Oh. Well, I have no objection." She made a gesture with her hand. "I suppose there is value in her being certain about the location of the faerie path through the park."

"It would not do for anything else to be built upon it. A summerhouse, for example."

"Indeed."

Chapter Twenty-four

Lady Catherine sat at her desk in the library and signed the letter to her solicitor, folded the thick monogrammed paper, poured melted wax onto the overlapping part, and pressed her signet ring into the red wax. She rang a small bell on her desk to summon her footman, then she addressed the letter. Percy entered, closed the door behind him, and faced her.

"Yes, m'lady?"

She held up the letter. He walked across to the desk. "See that this is posted. Billings will give you money for it."

"At once, m'lady."

"Did you see Miss Anne this morning?" Catherine asked, feeling an unexpected desire to have her observations confirmed.

"I did, m'lady. She looked very well. Very well, indeed."

Catherine nodded. "I thought so too."

"Henry noticed, m'lady. He's ever so glad Miss Anne is sleepin' in the main house."

Catherine raised an eyebrow. "They are speaking of it in the Rooms?"

"They are, m'lady. Everyone's pleased."

"Good. Tell Billings to come in," she ordered.

Percy straightened to attention, eyes forward, and said, "M'lady."

Catherine stared down at her hands folded on the dark-green blotter, thinking about the past twenty-six years. *There has been so many methods, so many remedies, and so many efforts to bring Anne to health—all with no effect. And then, along comes one slip of a girl with the right knowledge and the gumption to reveal it to her nephew. Now Anne appears to be cured. Or at least on the path to a cure.*

Catherine reminded herself to be cautious. Anne had appeared to be recovering in the past and then she had suffered a relapse. *Please, Lord, let this effort be for Anne's good.* Though she did not relish the idea of tearing down the nursery wing of her beloved Rosings, Catherine hardened her heart against her dismay at the idea. *Anything* for Anne. The letter to her solicitor had contained instructions for him to find an architect capable of overseeing the project. He would need to design a dower house for her as well.

Perhaps we should go to Margate for a month in the summer. Sea air had been one remedy she had never dared try for fear it would make Anne worse. Catherine permitted a smile to play about her lips. *Anne will be married by the middle of May. I shall have to consult with John before planning a trip to the seaside.*

Catherine's thoughts strayed to Miss Bennet. She did not know how to feel about her. Darcy had made it clear he meant to marry her. *She will be family and family is everything,* she thought fiercely. Her mind switched back to her most important concern.

I wonder if John has written to his parents yet. They will wish to be here for the wedding ceremony, which will be in the middle of the Season. London is not so far from Rosings. We will have a breakfast, too.

Where is Billings?

As though magically induced, the door opened and her butler entered. He closed the door and advanced toward her.

"Humph," Catherine said. "There you are."

"Yes, my lady."

"I have a few announcements I wish you to make to the staff."

Billings bowed.

"I suspect they already know one of them at least," she said in a dry, ironic voice. "Miss Anne and Colonel Fitzwilliam are to marry"

"That is excellent news, my lady," Billings said, a hint of a smile ruffling his impassive demeanor. "Staff will be pleased."

"The wedding will take place in May. On the fifteenth to be exact. We shall have a wedding breakfast. Mrs. Jenkinson will send out the invitations to the service, and the breakfast. Speak to her about numbers. Tell Mrs. Durling to hire village women to assist her and the maids with preparing the bedchambers for the guests coming some distance. Miss Georgiana will have her usual room."

"Yes, my lady."

"That brings me to my next point. The nursery wing shall be torn down. I am hiring an architect to accomplish the task. Meanwhile, before the work begins, the wing will need to be emptied. You may use the ballroom to store the furniture. Be careful not to ruin the floor."

"Certainly. An immense task, my lady," Billings commented, blinking rapidly.

"Which?"

"Both," he said. "And Mrs. Jenkinson?"

"Give her the Rose suite," Catherine directed.

Billings coughed slightly behind his hand.

"Yes?" Catherine asked.

"Seeing as Miss Anne is marrying, will Mrs. Jenkinson be continuing here at Rosings Park?"

She opened her mouth to say one thing, thought better of it, and said, "That will be between Miss Anne and Mrs. Jenkinson."

"Of course, my lady," he said in the manner of one who thought he should have known the answer before he asked the question.

"There will be extra work for the men in the village when the architect arrives as well." Catherine gritted her teeth and forced out the next words. "The colonel will oversee that project, so the men will report to him, not to me. I expect he will appoint a foreman."

"Yes, my lady."

She made an impatient gesture. "I do not know why I am explaining this all to you. Send in my secretary." The butler bowed. "Also, I am expecting Miss Bennet to return with my nephews and daughter. We will require tea in a half hour after they arrive. Serve it in the Canary sitting room."

"Is that all, my lady?"

"Is that not enough?" she replied tartly.

Billings bowed. "On behalf of the staff, my lady, congratulations on the betrothal of Miss Anne and the colonel. We all like him very much."

Catherine nodded regally. "Thank you."

ꟹ

Lizzy and the others arrived to find Lady Catherine waiting impatiently in the grand entrance hall. She wore a fur-edged green Merino-wool pelisse and velvet hat.

"There you are," she stated unnecessarily, holding out her hands for her maid to assist her into her gloves.

"Why yes, Mama," Anne said, standing still to permit the butler to take her coat and hat.

"You look a trifle tired. I am pleased you do not mean to go up on the roof with us," Lady Catherine said. "I believe we may as well get this over with before the rest of you have removed your outer things."

"An excellent scheme," Mr. Darcy said, tugging his gloves back on.

To her daughter, Lady Catherine said, "I have told Billings to serve tea in the Canary sitting room, if you wish to await us there. Mrs. Jenkinson is waiting for you. This will be an excellent opportunity for you to assure her you do not mean to cast her off."

"Cast her off?" Anne cried. "I have no intention of casting her off."

"Indeed, not," Colonel Fitzwilliam said in his deep, calm voice. "What would Rosings be like without Mrs. Jenkinson?"

"I suggest you change her role from merely your companion, to your companion-secretary," Lady Catherine said, leading the way up the stairs.

"I shall increase her pay," Anne said, a challenging note in her voice. When her mother said nothing, Anne glanced at her fiancé who climbed at her side. "Unless you think that is unnecessary, dearest John?"

"Another…say…twenty pounds a year?" he offered, smiling down at her. "Will that be sufficient, do you think?"

"More than," Lady Catherine muttered.

Lizzy glanced her way and caught an expression of satisfaction crossing the redoubtable lady's countenance.

"Yes, John," Anne replied, a smile in her voice. "She should be pleased with that."

"More than," Lady Catherine muttered again, catching Lizzy's amused gaze on her. "What have you to say for yourself, girl? Are you prepared to show us the path?"

"I am," Lizzy said simply.

They parted from Anne on the first floor and continued to climb up to the level where the stairs to the roof awaited them. On that floor, Lizzy skipped ahead and turned to face the others.

"One moment," she said, holding up her hand. When they stopped, she said, "Once we cross this iron-protected threshold, we will be vulnerable to the…fae," she whispered. "If they are on the roof—and they may not be—they might attempt to influence your mind. They may try to attack us. However, if they are there, it will be an excellent thing."

The colonel's eyebrows popped up. "Why?"

"We need to let them know of our plans," she explained. "We must do this carefully and without reference to the path or to them."

"Will they leave once they see we are pulling down the wing?" Lady Catherine demanded.

"Not immediately. I suspect they will wish to be certain of the outcome," Lizzy replied.

"The complete demolition will take some time," Mr. Darcy warned them.

"What about the finishes—such as the architraves and fireplace surrounds?" Colonel Fitzwilliam asked. "Must all be lost?"

Lizzy shook her head. "No, they do not care about those sorts of things."

"Saving parts will take more time," Mr. Darcy warned.

"I have already sent for an architect," Lady Catherine revealed. She fixed her future son-in-law with a stare. "We shall discuss the particulars with him when he arrives."

The colonel nodded.

Lizzy winced. "Not *all* the particulars, I hope?"

"We are not dunces, Miss Bennet," Lady Catherine retorted. "Shall we proceed?"

Nodding, and praying that her ladyship would keep her word, Lizzy followed Darcy up the stairs. He opened the door, climbed through onto the roof, and assisted her. The colonel helped his aunt. Lizzy casually glanced around. No fae awaited them.

"Well?" Mr. Darcy asked her softly.

Lizzy shook her head. "Come along," she said to everyone, and led them to the parapet from which they could see the gardens surrounding the house. "Bare hands," she said to them, stripping off her gloves. She tucked them into her reticule.

"I have brought an estate map," Lady Catherine said, tugging it out of the front of her pelisse. "I did not think to bring a pencil. Do you have one, Miss Bennet?"

"I do." Lizzy dug down to the bottom of her reticule and found a short pencil she used for leaving notes for people who are not at home when she called.

Lady Catherine took the pencil. "Thank you."

"Shall I draw for you?" Mr. Darcy asked.

"No, I am an excellent draftswoman."

"Give me your left hand, then," Lizzy said. "We must hurry. There are no 'guests' here at the moment. We do not want them to catch us drawing the path."

Mr. Darcy and the colonel held the edges of the paper where it rested on the parapet while Lady Catherine sketched the path crossing Rosings Park.

"What are the other lines I see?" she asked, pointing with the pencil.

"Those are energy lines," Lizzy explained. "The run all over the world, connecting spots, like wells, ancient monuments, groves of trees standing alone on hills. There are many more than usual in this region."

"Are they related to the path?" Mr. Darcy asked.

"Not necessarily, though the paths almost always follow a strong energy line."

"What are they for?" the colonel asked.

Lizzy shrugged. "That, I cannot say. The old gypsy woman who taught me about them said that mysteries exist to stretch our minds and feed our imaginations."

"Can they be found by someone without your ability?" Lady Catherine asked.

"Some dowsers can find them. Frank can, I am sure."

Lady Catherine stopped sketching and looked at Lizzy. "Our head gardener's twin brother?"

"Yes."

"Clever men," she acknowledged, releasing Lizzy's hand. "It is time for John to see."

Colonel Fitzwilliam took her hand next while Mr. Darcy took her other hand.

"Bloody hell," the colonel whispered beneath his breath. He leaned over the parapet and scrutinized the fore garden within the inner park walls. He straightened and looked off into the distance. After dropping her hand, he bowed his shoulders to Lizzy. "I beg your pardon. Thank you for showing me that. I find it fascinating that so much is beyond what humans see."

"You are welcome," she replied. "Perhaps one day, we will

develop a method of seeing these things. Consider how much more has been discovered because of the microscope—things that were invisible to us prior to its invention."

The colonel's eyebrows lifted. "So true."

When her suitor began to release her hand, she squeezed it and opened her eyes wide at him. "Look carefully," she said, making a slight movement with her head.

Lizzy watched him copy her casual way of glancing around. He returned his gaze to hers. He appeared white around his lips, but otherwise projected a calm demeanor.

"Aunt Catherine," he said, pointedly taking the map out of her hands, folding it, and placing it in his coat, "I understand from John that you mean to tear down the nursery wing."

"You know—" Lady de Bourgh paused and looked down at where her nephew held her arm in a strong grip, and continued smoothly, "—I meant to give my daughter a gift for her wedding. I have decided to design a new nursery wing for Anne and John." She pointed down at the gardens below. "The existing wing will be in the way."

The colonel looked from one to the other and played along, saying, "Aunt, what a generous gift."

The two unnaturally handsome fae males moved closer to their group, their heads cocked to the side to listen. Lizzy tried not to stiffen in reaction.

"Lady Catherine," Lizzy said, smiling wide. "I am certain you will design something exciting."

Unexpectedly, the older woman's hand shot out and grasped her hand. She shifted so she could turn a bland gaze back along the length of the flat portion of the roof. Lizzy felt Lady Catherine squeeze her hand tightly and knew she had seen their guests.

"You are kind to say so. I am certain I will." Lady Catherine released her hand and grimaced. "I have never been happy that the wing did not have its own small kitchen," her hostess said. "The new one will. Shall we go inside to discuss it? The wind is sharp."

"In a moment," Lizzy said, placing a detaining hand on her arm. "Can you not show us where you mean to build it? Will you tear down this wing and simply replace it?"

"There is nothing simple about such a project, girl," Lady Catherine snapped, returning to her old self.

"The answer, Aunt?" Mr. Darcy insisted. "I am certain John wishes to know."

"Yes, indeed," the colonel said, gifting her with a winning smile.

Lady Catherine, who could not see the fae anymore, walked perilously close to them, leading the others half-way across the flat portion of the roof in the direction of the door. She waved at the rose garden.

"I shall have the rose garden moved to where the nursery wing now stands, and build the wing there."

"The perfect spot," Colonel Fitzwilliam praised. "There will be shade from those trees during the summer months. A small children's garden could be designed next to it."

"I am excited to begin," Lady Catherine said, continuing on to the door. "I have already sent for an architect."

Lizzy hoped to hear silent comments from the two fae, but they disappeared, revealing nothing. At the base of the stairs, they congregated, the door securely closed and barred with iron above them.

"Lady Catherine!" Lizzy exclaimed softly. "You were brilliant. If I were staging a play for an amateur dramatics society, I would want you for my leading lady."

Her hostess preened. "I have said before that I could have been a great actress if I had not been born into a higher level of society."

"No doubt at all, Aunt," Colonel Fitzwilliam said, lifting her hand and kissing the air above it.

"I bow to your superior skill." Mr. Darcy fitted action to word and bowed deeply to her.

"I saw them. If I did not know better, I would have thought they were angels. Except they had no wings." Lady Catherine turned them toward the main staircase.

"Yes, two males," Lizzy explained to the colonel. "They arrived after we finished marking the map."

Colonel Fitzwilliam began unbuttoning his overcoat as they walked. "I wish I had seen them."

In an acerbic tone of voice, Lady Catherine said, "No, you do not."

"The first time can be unsettling," Lizzy admitted. She frowned, ignoring her hostess's ladylike snort. "I wish they had spoken."

"Why did they not?" Mr. Darcy asked.

Lizzy shrugged. "There is no understanding them. I suspect, however, that they will return to their queen and tell her of their success."

"It will take months," the colonel warned, frowning.

"Time means little to creatures who can live forever," Lizzy said. "You must continue to wear iron until the deed is done."

"I plan to wear iron for the remainder of my life," Lady Catherine stated. "And so shall you and Anne," she ordered, glaring at her soon to be son-in-law.

"Yes, Aunt," the colonel said, smiling. "Basket-weave buttons, I think. What do you say, Darcy?"

"Agreed. We shall establish a new fashion. The smithy here seems to have a deft hand."

Everyone laughed, as much as with relief than because of Mr. Darcy's prediction. On the first floor, they passed their outer things to the footmen and the valets waiting there. At the door to the Canary sitting room, Lady Catherine stopped Mr. Darcy and Lizzy.

"Tea first, and then you two must resolve your situation," she directed.

"With pleasure, Aunt."

"Yes, my lady," Lizzy said, her heart tripping over.

℘

Lizzy tucked her hand through Mr. Darcy's arm and the action felt comfortable—not because she had walked thus with many-a-gentlemen, but because it was Mr. Darcy who walked beside her. This did not mean that she felt no anxiety about the conversation they must have before she could accept his offer. A ragged breath escaped her lips.

"Are you beset with trepidation?" Mr. Darcy asked quietly. "I am not such an ogre, am I?"

"Oh no," Lizzy replied rapidly. "Do not say such a thing about yourself. I…" She swallowed and tried again. "I must discuss some aspects of my possible future life with you. Will you permit it?"

"Of course."

She peeped up at him and discovered his eyes crinkled at the corners when he smiled. A warm flush washed across her cheeks and she hastily looked away.

"My family—"

"Will always be welcome at Pemberley."

He stopped them under an oak tree that stood alongside the meadow, its massive lower branches spreading outward. Lizzy faced him, her back against a fat limb, and he tugged off his glove so he could press his palm against her cheek. She leaned into the warmth of his touch. *It feels glorious. His touch is so welcome.*

"Even my mother and Lydia?" she asked, trying to keep the skepticism out of her voice.

"Even them."

He does not understand. Not fully.

"My mother, dear sir, has the same...ability...as myself," she explained, watching his eyebrows arch. "She has never told my father and begged me to never reveal our secret to him. Mama believes he would not understand. I am uncertain if she is correct, but I have given her my word not to tell him." Lizzy shrugged a little. "She finds the experience quite disconcerting, you see, and acts with excessive vitality to hide her nervous reaction to their presence."

He frowned. "That explains much." His lips dipped at the corners. "I do not feel that I acted as kindly toward her as I could have."

"You did not know her circumstances," Lizzy pointed out.

His frown did not lift. "Nevertheless, I should have behaved more gentlemanly. I hope she does not hold my behavior against me."

"She will learn to love you, for you have charm enough when you wish to use it."

Mr. Darcy portrayed a crooked grin. "Thank you." He lost his momentary humor. "Does this mean that one of our children may also have the ability?"

"Or more than one," she suggested. "Or none."

Nodding, he said in a quiet, calm voice, considering the topic at hand. "That is good to know. Forewarned is forearmed, as the saying goes. I promise to give you complete freedom to make what changes are required to Pemberley House and the estate grounds in order to mitigate the danger. You will not need to resort to secret horseshoes."

"That is well. Will you permit me to make an iron garden?" she asked, placing her hand over his where it still rested on her cheek.

"A garden that grows iron?" he asked, eyes wide at first, and then relaxing into warm regard. "I am teasing. Whatever you desire."

Lizzy explained about the iron garden at Longbourn and the relief it gave both her mother and herself.

"I know just the spot at Pemberley," Mr. Darcy said, nodding.

"There is a lovely lily garden, shaded at the corners with mulberry trees. An iron fence could be installed along the perimeter."

"That sounds lovely," Lizzy murmured. She took a step back, breaking his contact with her cheek. Turning slightly away, she looked up through the bare branches of the oak.

"What is your next concern?" he asked.

Lizzy clenched her hands into fists and then forced herself to be calm. She faced him and closed her eyes as a barrier to the strength of the love she readily saw there.

In a rush, she confessed, "I am concerned that I will not know how to look after your people."

"They will honor you for your kindness and sensible nature," he promised. "I have no doubt of it."

She opened her eyes at that, staring. "I have no training in how to recognize what I may offer your tenants, or in being a hostess at great gatherings, or in managing a large staff."

"Georgiana will introduce you to our tenants and tell you their entire history," Mr. Darcy said, his eyes crinkling a little at the corners. He took one of her hands, removed her glove, and held her bare hand between his own. "You will have your own secretary to help you plan events, if you should wish them. We have an excellent butler, an exceptional cook, and a housekeeper who will take you under her wing. Such an intelligent woman as yourself will learn how to get on quickly." He rubbed her hand. "Any other concerns?"

"My questions may seem as nothing to you," Lizzy offered, a little wary of how easily he dismissed her worries. "Perhaps you think our love will conquer all things. But I dislike disharmony. Marriage is for life, and I do not wish to be unhappy, or to make you unhappy. My own parents…" Lizzy sighed. "This ability of ours has not made their marriage an easy one—particularly since Mama has never told Papa about it. If he knew, then...but that is past praying for."

"Well, I know of your extraordinary ability already, and it does not frighten or alarm me," he replied in a soothing tone. "My dearest girl, I do not discount your cares. They do you credit. I cannot promise that our life together will be perfect, but I can promise to do my best to make you happy." She said nothing and he stiffened, as though bracing himself. "Tell me the worst of your concerns. Is it my pride?"

"No, surprisingly," Lizzy said, managing a short chuckle. "Mr. Darcy, tell me honestly, please, will your sister like me? For you did not at first." His shoulders relaxed and she frowned. "Because, I should dislike it excessively if I upset her life and make her unhappy. She will not enjoy having another woman in her home, rearranging things, ordering things differently."

He kissed her fingertips and said, "My sister will love you, just as I do. Though, not nearly as much." He stroked the back of her hand several times in silence, though her charm bracelet jingled a little. He spoke his next words in a voice that throbbed with emotion."I find, my love, that I cannot bear to think of a life without you in it. Does that seem strange to you?"

Lizzy swallowed and nodded. "It most certainly does."

He turned her hand in his and pressed a tender kiss onto her palm. Lizzy's stomach clenched and her breath hitched in her throat.

"Do you have another concern?" he whispered huskily.

Lizzy released a ragged breath. "You have answered the chief of them," she answered in a soft voice.

"I am glad."

"My dear Mr. Darcy," she said, cocking her head to the side, "if we marry, what shall I call you? I have never liked the custom of calling one's spouse by his title. My mother calls my father Mr. Bennet. That has always seemed extremely impersonal so me. You may continue to call me Elizabeth, if you wish, or Lizzy. What may I call you?"

He hugged her hand protectively against his chest, drawing her even closer to him. "Do you dislike Fitzwilliam? If you do, you may call me darling, or my love, or honey, or dearest, or beloved."

"Oh, you!" she cried softly, swatting his other arm with her free hand.

Darcy laughed, suddenly feeling elated. He lifted her up in his arms and twirled her around. When he stopped, he lowered his head onto her shoulder, placing his face against her neck, and holding her firmly while her legs dangled free of the ground.

"Dearest Elizabeth," he whispered, "pray tell me that you love me in spite of my faults."

Her arms tightened around him. "I do love you, dear one."

Darcy's heart skipped and he squeezed his eyes shut. *Thank you, Lord.*

"Will you marry me, in spite of your concerns?" he asked, holding his breath. Before she could refuse him, he hurriedly added, "Think of marriage to me as an adventure."

She laughed and he felt her laugh throughout his body.

"It could be more of an adventure for you," she warned.

Darcy set her on her feet but did not release her. He tipped her chin up. Her lovely fine eyes sparkled with both merriment and love.

"I welcome it," he murmured, lowering his head for a kiss.

Against his lips, she sighed, "Be careful what you wish for."

Darcy could not help the smile that made his lips twitch over hers. "Stop making me smile. I am trying to kiss you."

"Is that what this is?"

"Yes!"

He stopped talking and tasted her trembling lips. She tasted him back, and he thrilled at her response. Far too soon, he pulled back to examine her beloved countenance.

"What do you say, Elizabeth?" he asked, and held his breath.

"I will," she replied. Then, as though she needed to clarify her simple statement, she elaborated. "I will marry you."

Darcy breathed again.

"My love," he said, and bent to kiss her again.

"Oh, no," Elizabeth said, pushing on his chest. "Release me, please. I do not wish all and sundry to know our business. Anyone could come along and see us."

Chuckling, Darcy did as ordered, glancing around to see if any of the villagers or Rosings staff were about. He saw no one.

"We are alone," he said, "but you are right. Do you wish to make our engagement known?"

Elizabeth shook her head. "Only to our nearest friends and relatives."

"Shall I go to your father immediately?"

"I think...I think it might be best if you visited Bingley at Netherfield after we return to Longbourn at the end of the month."

"There may be a danger that your father will hear of our betrothal before I have the chance to ask him," Darcy pointed out. "However, I shall bow to your request. Do you see how reasonable I can be?"

Elizabeth grinned. "I do." She glanced about them. "Perhaps one more kiss?"

Darcy, never a fool, pulled her back into his arms. "Call me Darcy, then, my darling."

Softly, she whispered, "*Darcy.*"

Chapter Twenty-five

"I said yes."

Lizzy's bald statement caused the three women facing her to stare. They had just returned from their shopping trip to Sevenoaks. Scarcely giving them time to remove their outer things, Lizzy had dragged them out of the entrance hall to hear her news.

"Heavens," Charlotte said, plopping down onto the settee in her private sitting room.

"And you have been waiting all afternoon to tell us," Mary said, swiftly hugging her sister. "Beside yourself with joy, no doubt."

"Are you happy for me, Mary?" Lizzy asked, drawing her down to sit beside her on the settee opposite Charlotte.

"I am," her sister said, the wonder in her voice making the others chuckle.

"Um, excuse me," Maria said, finding a seat beside her own sister. "What did you say yes to?"

"Mr. Darcy's proposal," Lizzy explained, grinning.

Maria's eyes widened. She looked from Lizzy to Charlotte as though to seek confirmation.

"You all knew?" Maria asked, her brows scooting together.

"Pray, do not be angry with me," Charlotte said, taking Maria's hand. "When Lizzy told us he had asked her, you had already gone to bed."

"And the next day?" Maria asked. Then her expression cleared, for she could never be cross for long, and she beamed. "I am sooo happy for you, Lizzy! Imagine all the fine clothes you will have. And the carriages. And the horses. And all the wonderful parties you will go to. I suppose Mr. Darcy goes to London for the Season? How I envy you."

All the ladies laughed.

Once Lizzy stopped laughing, she fixed them all with stern looks. "You must not tell anyone."

"What?" Maria cried.

"No, I mean it," Lizzy said. "Mr. Darcy has agreed to wait until we go home before he speaks to Papa. I do not want my father finding out from anyone before Mr. Darcy gets to Longbourn."

"I am going home the day after tomorrow," Maria said in a soft wail. "I must wait four whole weeks before you get home. How shall I keep my tongue?"

Charlotte shook her head at her sister. "You are perfectly capable of minding your tongue when it suits you. Do not make Lizzy sorry she confided in you."

Maria flushed and looked at Lizzy. "I swear I will tell no one. Not even Mother."

"Thank you," Lizzy said, touched by the sincerity she saw in the younger woman's eyes. "I do not mean to tell Mr. Collins or Sir William, either, so that should make your task easier."

Maria appeared dubious. "So much time in the carriage…"

"Father and you will play games and sleep," Charlotte said, patting her sister's arm.

Sighing, Maria nodded.

"You cannot tell Jane, either," Mary pointed out to Lizzy.

Lizzy's brow wrinkled. "She is no gabster."

"Do you imagine she will be able to keep such news from Mama?" Mary asked, her tone scoffing. "Jane loves to increase the happiness of those she loves."

Lizzy's shoulders slumped a little, and then she straightened them. "Jane will tell no one if I ask her specifically not to tell them. She loves me, too, you know."

"And will Mr. Darcy keep the news to himself?" Charlotte asked. "Will he not tell his aunt and his cousins? And Mr. Bingley, his close friend? And his sister? I think you must face it, Lizzy. Too many people will know of this to keep it a secret from your parents. As much as I would like you to stay, I think you must go home with Father and Maria. Mr. Darcy will ask for your hand and your father will not believe that you love Mr. Darcy. You must go to reassure him. Afterward, perhaps Mr. Darcy could escort you back here to continue your visit."

"Oh," Lizzy said, considering her friend's advice.

"Mary," Charlotte was saying, "I would dearly love for you to stay here and wait for your sister's return."

"Thank you, I would enjoy staying," Mary said, clearly touched by the invitation. "But Lizzy has not agreed to your scheme yet."

Lizzy stood and took a turn about the room. This was not what she and her betrothed had discussed, but there was merit in Charlotte's counsel. Her father might not believe she wished to marry the arrogant and prideful Mr. Darcy, as she used to think of him.

Darcy did not wish to wait—how odd it is to think of him without the mister.

"What do you say, Lizzy?" Charlotte asked. "Is the decision so weighty that you must pace? Surely, the sooner Mr. Darcy asks your father for your hand the better."

Lizzy faced her friends and sister. "I do not wish to…to outshine Jane's news. I can hear Mama now. '*Ten thousand a year! Mr. Bingley's five thousand* will be as nothing to it!'"

Ever sensible, Mary dryly said, "Since Jane will not be at home to hear her say such an immoderate declaration, you need pay it no mind."

"She will write it in a letter for Jane to read repeatedly," Lizzy warned.

Mary snorted. "That also does not signify. Our Jane has such a sweet nature that she will do nothing other than agree with Mama and be overjoyed for your good fortune."

"Mary is right," Charlotte said, shaking her head in fond memories of Jane.

"You know she is," Maria said, grinning.

Lizzy had to agree. She stopped pacing and returned to her spot on the settee. "I shall speak to Mr. Darcy after services tomorrow. If he agrees that this new scheme is for the best, he will not wish to travel on Sunday. If he leaves on Monday, I daresay he will arrive in Longbourn before I do, for his conveyance must be faster than Sir William's carriage."

"I expect it is," Charlotte agreed, grinning.

"Was that rude?" Lizzy asked anxiously. "Do forgive me."

Maria and Charlotte both shook their heads, chuckling. Charlotte said, "You speak nothing but the truth. It is not the carriage, however, but the horses that will be out driven. Father's are sturdy and reliable. I understand Mr. Darcy's are *sweet goers*. That is what our brothers say."

"High praise indeed." Lizzy clenched and unclenched her hands. "I do not know how I will sleep tonight. My stomach is all aflutter."

Charlotte stood, prompting the others to do so. "Come, let us prepare for dinner. Afterward, I believe I can tempt your mind away for a little while with some charades. Before you both arrived in Kent, I had Mrs. Wright, the doctor's wife if you recall, prepare some clues so that I might play along. I swear I have not peeked. We shall draw lots for teams and whoever gets Mr. Collins on their team must be patient. Do you promise? He loves the game, but he does not get enough practice to be good at it."

The others crossed their hearts with mock solemnity. Lizzy linked her arm with her friend's as the other two ladies walked ahead of them.

Softly, she said, "You are very kind to our cousin. He does not deserve you."

Charlotte flushed a little. "Tut, Lizzy. He is very kind to me, also. I am most content with my match. Truly."

"I am pleased for you," Lizzy said, gratified to hear the sincerity in her friend's voice. "I was not certain before I came, but I am now."

"Thank you. I am holding Mary hostage, you must know, to guarantee your return for the remainder of your visit."

Lizzy laughed.

"And, we will have more room once Maria and Father are gone, so you must bring Lydia back with you. Kitty is welcome, too, but I believe you would prefer her to have a rest from Lydia as much as Mrs. Bennet needs a rest from her youngest daughter."

"I never knew you could be so self-sacrificing," Lizzy praised. "I believe the militia needs a rest from Lydia as well. Kitty will have Maria to keep her company, and they will both enter into all of Mama's plans for the weddings of her two eldest."

"I am not so self-sacrificing as you claim," Charlotte said, mounting the steps and dropping Lizzy's arm so they could walk up the stairs, one behind the other. "I have a secret weapon."

"Do you?"

"If Lydia's high-spirits need to be quelled, we shall take her to visit Lady Catherine."

Lizzy covered her bark of laughter with a hand as she pictured her lively sister sitting as quiet as a shivering mouse in the Chinese drawing room.

"And on the return journey, you will have Mr. Darcy to keep Lydia in line," Charlotte added. "You must give him leave to be his most arrogant so she will be quiet on the journey."

"She will pout and pout and pout.

"Possibly, but pouting is *silent*, is it not?"

"It is," Lizzy cried, clamping her hand back over her mouth to stop a giggle from escaping.

"We shall contrive nicely," her friend promised after they reached the landing. "Have no fear. And in the end, Mr. Collins will value me even more for *not* being your sister."

"My sides hurt from holding in my enjoyment of the pictures you paint. I cannot bear it! Poor Lydia."

Charlotte laughed and hugged her.

ꟃ

Hertfordshire...

Darcy dismounted from one of Bingley's horses before the front door of Longbourn House. A groom hurried forward and led the horse away.

He and Elizabeth had set out from Rosings at the same time, but after they stopped for luncheon together he hurried ahead as they had agreed. After stopping at Netherfield, he had washed and changed, borrowed one of his absent friend's horses, and here he was.

Bloody hell.

He stiffened his spine and approached the front door. It opened. Since they had no proper butler, their housekeeper stood before him.

"Mrs. Hill, is it not?"

She curtsied. "It is."

"I am Mr. Darcy," he said, handing her his calling card.

The middle-aged housekeeper took it and said, "Aye, sir."

"May I see Mr. Bennet? Is he at home to visitors?"

"I cannot say, sir, but if you step inside out of the drizzle, I'll go an' ask him."

"Thank you," Darcy said, removing his shallow beaver-skin hat and entering the modest manor house.

She indicated the polished side table next to the door. "If you'd like to put your hat there, sir?"

"Thank you."

Walking off, Mrs. Hill left him cooling his heels in the entrance hall, still wearing his damp riding coat and holding his gloves. Darcy put his gloves on top of his hat, set his riding crop beside it, and shrugged out of his coat. He stood looking around for a place to lay his coat to dry when a male servant entered the hall through the green baize door.

"Shall I take that fer ye, sir?" the man asked, holding out his arms. "I'm Hill. The footman."

"Mrs. Hill's brother?" Darcy asked, passing him the coat.

"I am her husband, sir, though you'd be forgiven fer thinkin' me her brother, 'cause I'm very like."

"Indeed?"

"Aye, sir. I'll be putin' this afore the fire in the kitchen fer you, sir."

"Thank you, Hill."

The man bowed and withdrew, passing his wife as he went. Mrs. Hill curtsied before Darcy.

"Please follow me, sir," she said.

In moments Darcy stood in the midst of a comfortable book room. Every spare inch of the small library held volumes both thick and thin, both tall and short. Newly acquired books sprawled on a round table atop brown wrapping paper and lengths of string. The room smelled delightfully of old books and pipe tobacco.

Mr. Bennet, who waited for him before a warm fire, came forward, hand outstretched.

"Welcome," he said, smiling warily. "Did we have an appointment? I must have forgotten it in the excitement of receiving a new shipment of books." He waved at the table with his other hand to emphasize his words.

Darcy shook his hand. "We did not have an appointment."

"Just a sociable visit, then?"

"I bring you greetings from Miss Elizabeth, who will arrive this afternoon, and from Miss Mary, whom I left in good health at the Hunsford parsonage."

Mr. Bennet's gray and brown eyebrows jumped. "How is this? Lizzy is returning and her sister is staying?"

Darcy glanced around, spotted two chairs, and said, "Shall we sit?"

"Yes, of course," Mr. Bennet said, appearing a trifle flustered. "Draw yours nearer the fire, if you wish, and we shall be snug."

Once Darcy had sat, Mr. Bennet offered him a glass of sherry. "In a moment, perhaps," Darcy said, smiling a little. "Please, be easy. All is well with Miss Elizabeth."

Mr. Bennet sat and rested his hands on his knees, leaning forward a little. "If all is well, why is our Lizzy returning home early?"

Darcy swallowed and wished he had accepted the sherry after all. "Sir, your daughter is returning early to, hopefully, receive your congratulations."

"For what?"

Darcy raised an eyebrow, dearly hoping he did not have to spell out his purpose.

"Oh…oh…" Mr. Bennet said, leaning back and then forward again. "Good Lord," he muttered. "You?"

"Yes, sir." *There is nothing for it. This is so important, why should it be easy?* He licked his lips. "Mr. Bennet, I would like your permission to marry your daughter."

"Are you certain?" her beloved father asked in shocked tones. "My dear boy, I thought you did not like her."

"I love her, sir." Darcy metaphorically girded his loins and charged ahead. "And she loves me."

"Does she now?" Mr. Bennet sat back and pinched his lower lip between his thumb and middle finger. The firelight reflected off the glass in his spectacles. "I hope you will not be offended when I say I am surprised to hear that."

"Miss Elizabeth knew you would be surprised. It is one of the reasons she is coming home for a time—to convince you of the truth of her feelings."

Mr. Bennet let out a long breath.

"Do you need to be reassured that I can support a wife?"

The older man shrugged and shook his head. "Settlements?"

"They shall be generous. Our solicitors shall work out the details."

"I have no doubt you can support a wife," Mr. Bennet said, standing and pacing a little.

Darcy watched him, frowning. "You have concerns?" He almost smiled as he remembered his talk with Elizabeth about hers. "Pray be straight with me."

Mr. Bennet stopped at a window and gazed out it. Darcy suspected he looked more inward than outward. But he was only partially right.

In a slow voice, Elizabeth's father said, "I can see the iron garden from here."

Darcy's mind stilled, then it began churning. "Can you?" He abruptly stood and walked to Mr. Bennet's side. "I would like to see it. I have promised Elizabeth that she may make one at Pemberley."

His host turned and stared him in the eye, his expression arrested. "Did you?"

"Yes, sir. She also said that she admired the iron drapery rods at Rosings Park."

Mr. Bennet's gaze darted to the wooden one above them. Darcy's also looked up. The draperies hung from wooden rings.

"Perhaps iron rings?" Darcy suggested.

Beneath his breath, Mr. Bennet whispered, "That might work."

"I shall be honored if you will accept them as a betrothal gift to you and Mrs. Bennet."

"A generous gift," Mr. Bennet said, staring into his eyes again.

"Your daughter thinks—"

Mr. Bennet held up a hand, stopping him from continuing. "The garden. My wife is off visiting so it will be empty."

The mizzle had stopped, and they stalked across the gravel drive to the iron garden gate. Mr. Bennet opened the gate and gestured for Darcy to enter. He followed and closed the gate after him. They walked side-by-side along a brick path.

"As I suspect you know, we can speak freely in here."

Darcy nodded and waited patiently while Mr. Bennet walked for a time with his hands clasped behind his back, saying nothing. Explaining nothing. Finally, they paused in the center of a wide circle of stone pavers, an iron post marking the middle. Mr. Bennet rested a hand on it, turning only half-way toward his guest.

"When my dear wife learned that our Lizzy had the same curse as herself," he said in a soft, tired voice, "I feared for Mrs. Bennet's sanity. I am reasonably certain that my wife does not remember telling me about them—that is how thoroughly she has buried the idea that anyone other than she and Lizzy know." He clutched at Darcy's arm. "Pray, say nothing to my wife."

"I shall say nothing. Do you wish me to tell Miss Elizabeth that you know? It grieves her to know that she cannot share this part of herself with you. Years ago, Mrs. Bennet made her swear to never reveal anything about her ability to you."

"My poor girl," Mr. Bennet murmured, shaking his head. "You

may tell her, but she cannot tell her mother anything."

Darcy inwardly sighed at the pain all this secrecy caused the Bennet family, but it was not his place to counsel them. "Miss Elizabeth will be comforted to know that when she and all her sisters marry, her mother will have the support of her husband in the trials of her ability."

Mr. Bennet gave a shuddering sigh and let go of Darcy's sleeve. "The iron rings on the draperies will make a great difference. Perhaps, one day, after all our daughters are gone, I will remind my wife that I already know about...the...fair folk."

"Perhaps." Darcy's heart swelled with gratitude that he and Elizabeth would not start out their life together with secrets between them. "We will make Pemberley safe for your visits, too."

They began strolling along the paths again in silence. Darcy found Mr. Bennet comfortable company, but he had still not given his permission for Darcy to marry his daughter.

"Lizzy is a great comfort to her mother."

"I imagine so."

"Sometimes they spend hours in here."

Darcy watched him out of the corner of his eye. He seemed pensive.

"If you will pardon my saying so," Darcy said, waving one arm around the garden, "it wants a summer house of some sort—so visitors to the garden can sit out of the rain. Perhaps it could have its own fireplace. It could be a place you and your wife would enjoy together."

Mr. Bennet's head cocked to one side while he turned slowly around, looking more closely at the garden. "Yes...I can imagine it. Mr. Darcy, you are a clever man." He held out his hand to Darcy, who took it. "I could not have borne it if my Lizzy had wanted to marry a silly, or a foolish man."

"I hope I shall never be that."

"I give my permission." He released Darcy's hand and held up one finger. "Provisionally. I still wish to talk with Lizzy."

Lizzy arrived an hour later to find her betrothed patiently sitting with her mother and two youngest sisters, drinking tea in the morning room. Darcy stood when she entered and went to her side.

"Dearest, your father is waiting for you in his book room," he said softly. "All is well."

"You cannot seem to choose which endearment you mean to use," she teased, smiling tenderly at him.

The corners of his eyes crinkled. "I am trying them all out before I settle on one. Or two."

"Lizzy!" her mother cried, rushing over to them. "Do not keep your father waiting. I am sure he heard the carriage arrive."

"Yes, Mama," Lizzy said. "Are you happy for me, Mama?"

"Happy? Happy?" she cried in response, and this time there were tears glittering in her eyes. "Two daughters betrothed. And both to gentlemen of means. How could I be any happier?"

"Thank you, Mama," Lizzy said, impulsively embracing her.

"Go on," her mother replied gently.

Lizzy went to her father and returned only minutes later with him, her face glowing with happiness. Hill followed behind them, a tray and glasses in one hand and a bottle of champagne in the other.

"Champagne, Mr. Bennet?" her mother exclaimed.

"Yes, champagne."

"Even for us, Papa?" Lydia asked, rushing over with Kitty in tow behind her.

"Even for you," Mr. Bennet said, smiling. "We must toast to the newly engaged couple. But, my dear," he said, handing a glass to his youngest daughter, "we must toast to you, as well."

The glass, half-way to her lips, paused in its path. "Me, Papa?"

"You thought you had missed out on the delight of a trip to Kent," he explained in false sympathy, "but you have not. When Mr. Darcy takes our Lizzy back to Charlotte's, you shall be going with her. What a treat for you."

Lizzy thought Lydia would drop her glass but her father took it away before she could.

"What about me, Papa?" Kitty asked. "Do I get to go?"

"No-o," he said, drawing out the word and shaking his head. "Your treat is in staying behind and keeping your mother company. Maria has promised to visit often. You shall all have a grand time together."

Lizzy took her fiancé's hand and drew him out of the room and into the entrance hall even as both of her sisters began howling in despair.

"Will Miss Lydia be like that the entire drive back to Kent?" Darcy asked in an anxious whisper.

"Oh, no," Lizzy said, grinning. "I shall expect you to stare down your nose at her in your most arrogant, prideful way. That should keep her quiet for most of the journey."

"It is a good thing that I have had so much practice at it."

They clinked glasses and she said, "Yes it is, my darling."

In a husky voice, he asked, "Am I your darling?"

Lizzy's heart swelled. "Yes, you are."

Darcy leaned down and kissed her on the cheek. Pulling back, he whispered portentously, "I have something to tell you. Is it safe to talk?"

Lizzy, disappointed at not receiving a kiss on the lips, frowned up at him, glanced around the hall, saw no *guests*, and nodded.

"Your father has graciously accepted my offer of a betrothal gift of *iron* drapery rings for the entire house."

His eyebrows bounced and he nodded slowly.

"No…" she whispered. "He does not underst—"

"Ye-s. He does."

"When? How long?"

"Many years."

"But—"

"I will explain it all to you later in the iron garden," Darcy promised, raising one of her hands to his lips. "The most important thing, my love, is for you not to worry about your mama anymore, though you must say nothing to her. That is your father's wish."

He gathered her into his arms and pressed her cheek to his chest.

"I do not need to worry?" Lizzy said slowly.

"No."

She sighed. "I am relieved. I love you most desperately."

"Thank you. I love you even more."

"Let us get married in July," Lizzy said.

"I was hoping for June."

"June, then. But near the end, so Anne and the colonel can come."

"An excellent idea, my dearest Elizabeth."

Epilogue

Five years later…

Lizzy and Darcy strolled arm-in-arm, watching their two young boys trying to catch grasshoppers in the long grass beside the path. Decorative iron posts dotted the meadow through which the path wound. She rested one hand on the swell of her stomach.

"Are you happy?" Darcy asked.

Smiling up at him, she replied, "Blissfully."

"Your parents should be here in a few days."

Lizzy nodded, feeling sleepy in the warmth of the summer afternoon. "This will be their last chance to visit before Lydia's baby is due in November. Mother wants to be in Kent for the birthing. I am so glad we took Lydia back with us to Charlotte's that time. Otherwise, she might never have met Lord Ansel's younger brother. George is over the moon about them having a baby so quickly—he told me so in his last letter."

"I suppose Richard will be attending the birth?" Darcy asked.

"Yes. I cannot believe Mary and he have been married for over a year—their anniversary is tomorrow. Time seems to pass quicker as we grow older," Lizzy commented. She felt a kick and stopped. "Goodness, that was a strong one."

Darcy placed his palm over her large abdomen. He smiled when a second kick made his hand move. "Another boy, perhaps?"

Unexpectedly, an elderly voice said from behind them, "Oh, not only a boy. One of them will be a girl."

Though startled, Lizzy recognized the voice and slowly turned around. Darcy joined her in facing the old gypsy witch.

"Aunty," she said, smiling hesitantly. "I have not seen you for years. Are you well? Is anything amiss?"

"Naught. Naught," the old woman said. She nodded at Darcy and bounced her eyebrows at Lizzy. "He's a fine looking one."

Lizzy chuckled. "I beg your pardon. This is Fitzwilliam Darcy. Husband, this is the lady who taught me so much. I call her Aunty."

Darcy bowed. "May I also call you Aunty, madam?"

"You may."

"Aunty?" Lizzy said, glancing around to be certain her boys were still safe. They did not seem to have noticed her old teacher. "Did you say *one* of my babies will be a girl?"

Aunty nodded and smiled, wrinkling up her features so much that her eyes almost disappeared.

"Twins?" Darcy asked, a grin dawning. Aunty shook her head and his smile slumped into wide-eyed amazement. "Triplets?"

"Oh, aye," Aunty said.

"Heavens," Lizzy whispered. "I suspected twins…I am so big this time…but not…heavens. We shall need a second nanny."

"Now, Lizzy, girl," Aunty said, coming close to feel her abdomen, "that brother-in-law of yours can attend you if you wish, but I'll be back to deliver these wee ones myself."

"You will?" Lizzy asked, suddenly alarmed.

"I will. And both of the boys—they'll be identical—will have the gift."

Lizzy clutched her husband's hand and he squeezed it tightly.

"Don't you worry none. I'll be around to teach 'em when the time's right," Aunty said. She stood back, her hands on her ample waist, and took in the field. "You've done a good job here with your warding. I taught you well."

"Thank you," Lizzy said, her voice weak with the wonder of everything she had just been told.

"Oh, and Kitty will marry that nice vicar," Aunty revealed. "Next year. She'll meet him when she comes to help you with the wee ones." She pointed at Darcy. "Your cousin."

Darcy frowned. "My cousin? I have no cousins in the church."

An odd silence bounced between them. Lizzy held her breath, waiting.

"Oops, oops," Aunty said in a rush. "That was another

Kitty…and a different Lizzy."

"Another what?" Lizzy asked, even more startled. She shook her head, struggling to clear it from a zing of power. "Besides, Kitty has been married for two years now—to an old family friend. He is one of our neighbors in Hertfordshire."

"Honey, you must be confused by the news of the triplets," Darcy said, frowning down at her. "Kitty is married to a baronet—you never said your family knew him before—and she lives in Cornwall."

Lizzy stared up at him, feeling the truth in his words. She touched the heel of her hand to her temple. *Why did I think Kitty is married to someone else?*

Aunty waved her age-spotted hands in front of them as though to erase her last confusing statements. "Never you mind. There's been overlap. *Overlap.* Goodness, I've got t' go and fix it before it gets worse."

Lizzy stepped backward and her head cleared a little. "Aunty? I do not understand."

"You don't have to, girl. Look for me at the autumn equinox. That's when those babes will come. Don't you worry none about the overlap, either. I'll look after it."

"Mama! Papa! Look what we found!"

Lizzy and Darcy instantly looked around at their sons. The boys ran toward them, their tiny hands cupped together, exposing the embossed iron bracelets on both their wrists. Lizzy glanced over her shoulder, wanting to know more from Aunty. She tugged on her husband's sleeve.

"She is gone."

Darcy drew her attention back to their sons. "Here they come. With grasshoppers, I suspect. Do not worry about your Aunty. She is old. We must forgive the aged."

A voice surrounded them from every direction, sharp and snappish.

"I'm not that old, boy!"

Darcy blinked.

"Just remember the triplets and forget *about the overlap."*

So they promptly forgot about the overlap, and admired the two grasshoppers in their sons' cupped hands.

The End

Author's Note

I could not resist adding Aunty into this story a little more than we see her in the other P&P variation books. Have you noticed that she is in them? I hope you have. The only book where she is not found is in Kitty's story, *Pemberley Haunted*, which I've hinted at in the epilogue. If *Charming Mr. Darcy* is the first of my variation books you have read, then now you know to look out for Aunty in the other ones.

Aunty is one of my favorite characters. She first appeared in my Christmas cracker romances and she keeps popping up in my P&P books. You can't keep a good witch down, I guess.

My Christmas cracker novellas are time-historical stories. There are two of them so far, though I am working on a third that will be part of a Christmas time-historical novella collection, written by author-friends of mine, planned for a release in time for Christmas 2022.

These stories can be read in any order, so I thought I would give you a taste of the second one in the series, where you will meet Aunty in a little more detail. She is the one who makes the magical Christmas crackers that send people back in time. These are not crackers you eat. These are the crackers you pull. Inside the fancy wrapping is usually found a toy, a motto or a joke, a sweet, perhaps, and a tissue hat. The insides of Aunty's crackers are far more interesting.

A Viking Christmas
Prologue

Aunty scooped her red and black brindle guinea pig off the corner of her worktable and set him on the crook of her arm. She stroked his long hair and shuffled over to the diamond-pane windows. Lacy frost tracings almost obscured the view of her snow-covered back garden. Jeffry purred.

"You're not a cat, you know," Aunty muttered. Her brow furrowed and her thin lips lifted at one side. "It's time, Jeffry. Time for another special Christmas cracker."

Jeffry responded with a chortle.

"No, not a woman this time. A man. Yes. The cracker will be for a man," Aunty replied.

She whipped around and returned to her worktable. Jeffry landed on his spot and whistled.

"Excited, are you?" Aunty asked, carefully gathering up the brightly adorned, but ordinary, crêpe-paper crackers and placing them in a box to one side. "Me too."

Aunty's gnarled fingers hovered over the terracotta pots lined up on the table. Each one held an assortment of decorations for the cracker.

"Gold poinsettias, I think," she whispered, dipping her hand into one pot and emerging with three tiny silk flowers.

From another collection she gathered a golden bead chain. She snipped off a short length and put it with the flowers. A pile of artificial greenery provided the setting for the flowers. She ran her fingers through curly ribbon strands cascading from spools attached to the dark beams overhead. "Gold, I think. Hmm, everything is gold. I hadn't expected that."

Jeffry chirped.

"What?" Aunty cocked her head to one side and observed her companion. "Yes, I've already decided to choose a dark color for the cracker body."

Jeffry switched to wheeking.

"Black?" She turned and faced the dowels holding crêpe paper in many colors. Aunty scratched a spot on her ample waist and considered her options. "Hmm. I think you're right there, Jeffry." She took a sheet of black paper and set it on her worktop. "If it's going to be black, then I'm going to have to choose…" Her hand riffled through a pile of pre-cut decorative sheets of shiny paper. "Yes, this one," she whispered, and chanted beneath her breath as she smoothed it out.

Aunty lifted one hip and rolled her hips back and forth until she'd levered her bulk up onto the wood stool behind her table. She leaned on the surface, lifting her hips, and then settled comfortably back down. During this operation, Jeffry bubbled and purred encouragement.

With each cut, wrap, and glue, she hummed and whispered and sometimes shouted enchantments that went with each element of the Christmas cracker. When the moment came to fill the tube with prizes, she swiveled in her perch and examined the pile she'd collected earlier.

"Yes, he's going to need this for certain," she murmured, picking up the first item. She set it to one side. "And this too. And he better have this one."

Jeffry chirped.

"No, he doesn't need a sword. He already has one." She peered at him over the top of her half-moon glasses. "Besides, how do you expect me to get a sword inside a four-inch tube? Heavens, that would be a trick and a half." Aunty clicked her tongue and went back to collecting, placing an eight-inch bone flute on top of the pile. She shook a finger at the guinea pig. "Now, no noise out of you, Mister Jeffry, sir. I've got to concentrate or else I'm never going to get all this inside the cracker."

Jeffry released a single chirp and then kept his mouth shut when the room darkened and the chanting began again. This time, Aunty sang her charms so that her intonations rose and fell melodically. She finished her spell with a resounding clap of her palms. She sat still, breathing deeply for many long moments. Jeffry chirped again.

"I'm fine. Don't you be worrying about me. Okay. It's time to close this beauty."

Aunty tied the second ruffle around one end, sealing off the black and gold Christmas cracker. She checked that the snap ends remained in place and then she set it before her, admiring her handiwork.

"This will do nicely," she said, smiling. "What do you think, Jeffry?"

The guinea pig commenced to wheeking, adding hopping up and down and twirling in a circle.

Aunty laughed and laughed and when she detected a cackle she stopped and covered her mouth with the back of one hand.

"Oops," she said, grinning.

Made in the USA
Coppell, TX
08 October 2022

84279336R00184